THE REDEEMING

The Redeeming

Age Of Faith: Book Three

Tamara Leigh
USA Today Best-Selling Author

ISBN: 1942326068
ISBN 13: 9781942326069

TAMARA LEIGH NOVELS

CLEAN READ HISTORICAL ROMANCE

The Feud: A Medieval Romance Series

Baron Of Godsmere: **Book One,** 02/15

Baron Of Emberly: **Book Two,** 12/15

Baron of Blackwood: **Book Three,** 2016

Medieval Romance Series

Lady At Arms: **Book One,** 01/14 (1994 Bantam Books bestseller *Warrior Bride* clean read rewrite)

Lady Of Eve: **Book Two,** 06/14 (1994 Bantam Books bestseller *Virgin Bride* clean read rewrite)

Stand-Alone Medieval Romance Novels

Lady Of Fire: 11/14 (1995 Bantam Books best-seller *Pagan Bride* clean read rewrite)

Lady Of Conquest: 06/15 (1996 Bantam Books best-seller *Saxon Bride* clean read rewrite)

Dreamspell: **A Medieval Time Travel Romance,** 03/12

INSPIRATIONAL HISTORICAL ROMANCE

Age of Faith: A Medieval Romance Series

The Unveiling: **Book One,** 08/12

The Yielding: **Book Two,** 12/12

The Redeeming: **Book Three,** 05/13

The Kindling: **Book Four,** 11/13

The Longing: **Book Five,** 05/14

INSPIRATIONAL CONTEMPORARY ROMANCE

Head Over Heels: Stand-Alone Romance Novels

Stealing Adda, 05/12 (ebook), 2006 (print): NavPress

Perfecting Kate, 03/15 (ebook), 2007 (print): RandomHouse/Multnomah

Splitting Harriet, 06/15 (ebook), 2007 (print): RandomHouse/Multnomah

Faking Grace, 2015 (ebook), 2008 (print edition): RandomHouse/Multnomah

Southern Discomfort: A Contemporary Romance Series

Leaving Carolina: **Book One,** 11/15 (ebook), 2009 (print): RandomHouse/Multnomah

Nowhere, Carolina, 2010 (print): RandomHouse/Multnomah

Restless in Carolina, 2011 (print): RandomHouse/Multnomah

OUT-OF-PRINT GENERAL MARKET TITLES

Warrior Bride, 1994: Bantam Books

****Virgin Bride,*** 1994: Bantam Books

Pagan Bride, 1995: Bantam Books

Saxon Bride, 1995: Bantam Books

Misbegotten, 1996: HarperCollins

Unforgotten, 1997: HarperCollins

Blackheart, 2001: Dorchester Leisure

****Virgin Bride*** is the sequel to ***Warrior Bride***

Pagan Pride and ***Saxon Bride*** are stand-alone novels

www.tamaraleigh.com

1

Wulfen Castle, England, June 1157

TO THE DEATH.

Perspiration running into his eyes, the blood of a half dozen wounds seeping through the weave of his tunic, Christian Lavonne reminded himself of what was required to best his opponent.

Think death.

Drawing back his sword, he eyed the knight's neck that glistened with the efforts of the past half hour.

Feel death.

Lunging forward, he shifted his grip on the hilt.

Breathe death.

Smelling his opponent's bloodlust, he arced the blade toward the exposed flesh that would assure victory.

Embrace death.

Putting from him all he had been taught of mercy and forgiveness, he slashed the blade down. And met steel.

"Surely you can do better!" the knight spat.

Christian growled, swept his blade up off the other man's, and swung again—only to yield up the blood of his forearm.

"Ho!" The knight grinned. "Do I unnerve you, Lavonne? Make your heart beat faster? Blood run colder?"

Christian knew it was anger the other man sought. And he would have it. Heart pounding as if upon the stoutest door, he swung again. Missed. *Again!* Missed. *Again!* And finally set his blade to the knight's lower thigh. However, he was allowed but a moment's satisfaction before his opponent leapt at him.

Christian jumped back from the thirsty blade and came up against the fence. If not that the thrust of his weight cracked the wood, the knight would have had what he sought—blood for blood.

With a shout, Christian plummeted backward and landed hard on the splintered rails.

"You are had, Lavonne." His opponent settled the crimson tip of his blade to the great vein in Christian's neck. "Beg for mercy."

Throat raw with exertion, Christian flexed his hand on his sword hilt. "Never!"

Fire leapt in the man's grey-green gaze and the stench of death rose to Christian's nostrils, only to retreat on the knight's great sigh.

"Well, then"—he turned his blade down, set its tip to the ground, and leaned on the hilt—"at least humor me with a recitation of the lesson that applies to the dire situation in which you find yourself."

Grinding his teeth, Christian rolled to the side and gained his feet. "That would be lesson one."

"One?" With a sweep of his forearm, the knight brushed back the damp brown hair that clung to his brow. "Pray, enlighten me as to how that applies to your sound defeat."

Christian glared. "I do not refer to *your* lesson, Sir Abel, but mine—one in which I fear you are in need of instruction."

A suspicious light entered the knight's eyes. "Aye?"

"Address one's better as befits their station."

Sir Abel's gaze narrowed, but just when it seemed the tension might once more see them at swords, he bowed low. "Most esteemed *Baron* Lavonne, pray honor this lowly knight by reciting the appropriate lesson." He straightened. "I humbly await your good grace."

Insufferable! And only a sharp reminder of the reason he was at Wulfen Castle made it possible for Christian to give the knight what he asked. "Lesson three, neglect not one's back."

"Correct. Of course, considering you were already dead, 'tis hardly relevant."

"*I* was dead? You were dead first."

Sir Abel snorted. "You flatter yourself, Lavonne—er, *Baron* Lavonne."

Christian looked from the bloodied and rent fabric behind which the knight's heart beat to the torn fabric centered on his bowels. "Were we not merely practicing at swords, Sir Abel, twice I would have done more than score your flesh. Indeed, your very life would be forfeit."

"Had you a sword arm." The knight raised his blade and pointed at the bloodied tear in Christian's sleeve.

"Which would have been entirely possible with a leg cut out from beneath you." Christian jutted his chin at where the fabric was split above the knight's knee.

And so they might continue until every crimson tear was accounted for, as they had done each day these past three.

Though when they had first faced one another on the training field a month ago and Sir Abel's sword skill had made Christian's appear woefully inadequate, Christian had improved greatly. Despite the knight's disdain for his student, he was an excellent instructor and, given more time, it was possible Christian would attain a level of mastery similar to that enjoyed by his warrior-bred opponent who would soon be his unwilling brother-in-law. And that possibility had to be as surprising to Sir Abel as it was to Christian who had not only been born to the Church but had attained tonsure and monk's robes before gaining an inheritance of which he had only ever dreamed. Unfortunately, the cost of the coveted inheritance had been the death of his older brother, something for which he had yet to forgive himself.

"The lesson is done." Sir Abel thrust his sword into its scabbard and pivoted.

Christian glanced at the sun that had yet to touch the treetops of the distant wood. "Done?"

As if he did not hear the dissension in his student's voice, Sir Abel continued toward the walls of Wulfen Castle.

"Methinks 'tis *I* who unnerves *you*, Sir Abel!"

The knight swung around.

Christian almost smiled. "I who makes your heart beat faster, your blood run colder."

"Flatter yourself if it so pleases you, Lavonne," Sir Abel once more dropped Christian's title. "As for me, I shall be content in knowing that, as long as mastery of the sword eludes you, I am in no danger of forfeiting my life."

"Your blood tells otherwise."

"Ha! Mere scratches."

Why he felt impelled to argue with the insufferable man, Christian did not understand, especially as their mutual animosity had lessened considerably since his arrival at Wulfen. But before he could advance the argument, Sir Abel said, "Do you wish to know the reason you have yet to truly master the sword, Baron?" With half a dozen strides, he retraced his path across the parched grass and halted before Christian. "Regardless of how angered you become when we meet at swords, regardless of how many times I mark your flesh, you cannot wholly commit to the taking of life."

A retort sprang to Christian's lips, but he did not loose it, for what Sir Abel said was true. Though the knight took every opportunity to remind his student of what was required to defeat an opponent—to think, feel, breathe, and embrace death—and several times Christian had nearly succeeded in reaching such a place within himself, he could not fully accept that death should be the end result of all clashes between men. As for attaining that place while at practice, that was the most bewildering of all, for how could one truly seek another's death without actually committing the act?

Sir Abel took another step toward him. "Thus, unless you wish me dead, you will never defeat me, Lavonne."

Suppressing the urge to repay aggression with aggression, Christian said, "Need I remind you that we are not truly at battle?"

The knight shrugged. "Whether that is so or not, a warrior must believe that the only thing that stands between him and death is the taking of his opponent's life. Even when merely at practice."

Christian stared at the man who stood nearly as tall as he. "If what you say is so, it follows that few squires would attain the rank of knight, for all would lie dead."

"Those who train at Wulfen—"

"—learn to control the moment between life and death. Aye, this you have told me many times."

The knight's face, flushed with the exertion of their contest, darkened further. "When you and I are at swords, all I think of is your death."

"And when we are not at swords?"

When Sir Abel finally answered, the anger that had spat words from him was nearly wiped clean. "It is true I am opposed to my sister wedding you, and that your death would resolve the matter, but do I truly wish it? Nay, Baron Lavonne"—titled again—"outside of practice, I do not wish you dead."

Not for the first time amazed at how quickly the knight cooled his emotions, Christian drew a deep breath in an attempt to calm his own roiling. "I shall take comfort in that."

Sir Abel started to turn away, but halted. "Heed me well. Though you have much improved since your arrival, when next you face a true enemy—and you shall—you must wish his death. Can you do that?"

Though Christian had taken lives in battle following the attainment of his title, he had never done so with a desire to see an opponent dead. It was not bloodlust that drove him, but the mere—and potent—need to survive. And survive he had barely done.

"If you cannot, you will make a widow of my sister. Now tell me, can you or can you not do it?"

It was not the first time the knight had issued the challenge, and would not be the first time Christian was unable to offer reassurance.

Sir Abel broke the silence. "Born to the Church you may have been, but it is no longer who you are. Indeed, as evidenced by your refusal to bow your head at prayer or enter the chapel, it is obvious you have given God your back."

His words jolted, not only because they were so near the truth, but that Christian's absence from mass and his inability to show proper respect at the blessing of meals had not gone unnoticed—and by this seemingly ungodly man who told that a knight must seek death to prevail.

"Do not make God your reason for not doing what is required of you, Baron Lavonne. If you cannot protect my sister, your people, and your lands, that title for which you demand respect will be lost." Sir Abel swung away.

Feeling every beaten ridge and furrow of his sword hilt, Christian watched him disappear around the castle's northern wall.

As much as he would have liked to deny it, it was good he had peeled back his pride and accepted the invitation to train at Wulfen Castle. If it was necessary to seek another's death to prevail, he might eventually fail, but with the skills acquired beneath Sir Abel's grudging instruction, there was less chance than before. He *would* protect his people and lands, as well as the woman with whom King Henry had commanded him to speak vows—Gaenor Wulfrith who had fled with her sister nearly five months past to escape marriage to a Lavonne.

Easing his grip on the sword, Christian scanned the walls of Wulfen Castle that had been the Wulfrith sisters' destination all those months ago. Though it was believed that Lady Gaenor had made it here to her family's stronghold, a castle exclusive to men and dedicated to the training of boys into knights, her younger sister had not. While being pursued by the king's and Christian's men, Beatrix Wulfrith had met with ill. Thus, if not for Christian's physician, a man with a powerful reason to hate her, she would be dead. Instead, a fortnight hence she would wed Michael D'Arci, the man who had saved her life. And at that wedding, Christian would finally meet Lady Gaenor who was told to bear little resemblance to her petite and comely sister.

Christian grimaced. Not that he cared what the woman looked like. Rather, he resented being made to wait so long to meet her. Though he had thought he might encounter her during his training here, it seemed she had been removed to one of the family's lesser castles. As for talk of her having been present here, a woman among so many men, there was none—as if she had never come. And perhaps she had not, though it seemed the surest place to secret her.

He eyed the men-at-arms visible between the battlements of the stronghold, then the immense donjon that rose at the center of the enclosure. Ominous. No surprise that King Henry had not brought an army against his vassal to sooner bring about the alliance required of the warring Wulfriths and Lavonnes. Indeed, if not for the bargain Christian had struck with the oldest brother, the Wulfriths might yet defy the king's edict. But Christian had delivered what he had promised and, providing the Wulfriths delivered what they had promised, soon he would wed.

Resolved to meeting his betrothed at her sister's wedding in July, Christian wiped his blade on the hem of his tunic and returned his sword to its scabbard.

Only a fortnight longer, he reminded himself, and the darkness of these past years would begin to recede. Except for that cast by his father, of course—the aged and ailing Aldous Lavonne who vowed he would not seek his grave until the death of his beloved son, Geoffrey, was avenged. Geoffrey, whose passing had made Christian heir to all of Abingdale.

Once more stabbed with guilt, Christian set off toward the castle with a heavy tread intended to grind all thoughts of his brother underfoot. It worked. For a while.

"Accursed cur!"

Everard looked over his shoulder at his younger brother whose arrival on the training field was evident well in advance of his appearance. Noting the numerous rips in Abel's clothing, Everard attempted to suppress the smile begging at his mouth.

Abel ground to a halt. "You think it funny?"

Trying to gain control of the larger smile that sought to crack his face wide, Everard turned back to the squires who had paused in their hand-to-hand combat to await further instruction.

He nodded for them to continue and returned his attention to Abel. "I do think it funny, little brother. Though, in the interest of brotherhood, I would prefer that I not win our wager, it seems I have done so yet again." He tracked his gaze down Abel, tallying the number of times Christian Lavonne had found his mark. "At least a dozen strikes, and your instruction lasted half as long as it should have." He held out a hand. "I have won."

Abel glared at his outstretched palm. "Ill gotten gain," he grumbled, then dug into the purse on his belt and slapped two pieces of silver in his brother's palm.

"'Twas your wager." Everard rubbed the coins together. "I but accepted, and reluctantly, if you recall."

"Reluctant as a groom on his wedding night," Abel scorned.

Though Everard was not one to make free with his emotions, he nearly laughed, for it was true he liked to wager, especially this brother who was determined to best him at every turn. Indeed, any moment now—

"A new wager!" Abel propped his hands on his hips.

"Methinks you ought to sleep off this one ere wagering more coin you can ill afford to lose."

Abel gave his purse a shake. Satisfied with the jangle, he said, "On the morrow, Lavonne will land less than a dozen marks."

"A mere dozen when this day he proved capable of such—and in half the time?" Everard shook his head. "A fool's wager to make against a man who is progressing as well as he."

Abel considered him, considered him some more, then blew a breath up his face that caused the dark hair on his brow to lift. "Aye, a fool's wager. The knave has improved far better than expected. If he but set his mind to the taking of life, he might prove quite dangerous."

Abel and his talk of death! If not that Everard shaved his head, he might drag a handful of hair from his scalp. "You know Garr does not approve of such means, Abel."

"Godly Garr whose knees are surely worn out from the amount of time spent kneeling at prayer." Abel glanced heavenward. "Not that I do not believe in showing the respect due God. It just seems unproductive to expend so much time conferring with the Lord who is more inclined to listen than respond."

Everard narrowed his lids. "You think?"

"No more than you." Abel looked pointedly at the knees of Everard's breeches, the material of which was far from worn. "I suppose I should be grateful you do not seem to mind the manner in which I train those given into my charge—at least, the end result."

Though Everard longed to deny it as he knew Garr would have him do, he could not, for there was a fierceness about the squires trained by Abel—one that made it difficult for other squires to best them. But never would Everard admit it.

Knowing it best to leave the subject be, he returned to the matter of the man whom the king was determined to make their brother-in-law. "What word would you have me send to Garr?" he asked for the dozenth time since Lavonne's acceptance of the invitation to better his sword skill—a self-serving invitation to allow the Wulfriths to more closely observe the baron and determine whether or not to defy the king's order to hand over Gaenor.

"Send word that, with much loathing, I concur that Christian Lavonne does not appear to be the same as his father or brother."

It was as Everard had concluded from his own observations this past month. "You are surprised?"

Abel shrugged. "As you know, I *was* present when Baron Lavonne came to Beatrix's aid."

Mention of the attempt on the life of their youngest sister caused Everard's insides to coil. Though it was true he had not been present, charged as he was with overseeing the training at Wulfen Castle since Garr had wed four years past, he knew what had transpired.

The worst of it was that Christian Lavonne's illegitimate brother, Sir Robert, had done their father's bidding to work revenge on a Wulfrith. If not for the dagger Christian had thrown with surprising skill, Beatrix would be dead. Instead, it was Sir Robert who had fallen. But just as Christian could not seek death now, neither could he then. Thus, the wounded Sir Robert languished in a London prison and would, hopefully, remain there until the end of his days.

The only pity of it was that Christian's father, Aldous Lavonne, was too infirm to suffer the same punishment. For that, Everard and his family feared for Gaenor. The old man might be confined to bed, but when their sister went to live at Broehne Castle as Christian's wife, Aldous would surely take every opportunity to work ill on her. Meaning something would have to be done about the old man. Given a say in the matter, Everard would have him removed to one of the barony's lesser castles.

"It seems Gaenor is to wed," Abel spoke across his brother's thoughts.

Everard slid a hand over his shaved pate. "At least her groom is better able to defend himself at swords."

"Well enough, I suppose. Of course, if there was some way to make him forget all that was poured into that monk's head of his, he might do better than merely defend himself."

Everard clapped a hand on his brother's shoulder. "Then it is good, little brother, that you have a fortnight in which to remedy what ails your student." Providing that Lavonne remained at Wulfen until the journey to Stern Castle to meet Gaenor at Beatrix's wedding.

Lids narrowing, teeth baring, Abel said, "A month I have given him that should have been used for the betterment of my squires. I am done. If he requires further training, it falls to you."

Though Abel surely expected an argument—indeed, was looking for one—Everard had already decided to relieve him of the task. "As you would have it." He strode toward the squires whose hand-to-hand combat had progressed to the far side of the enclosure, his brother's surprised silence following him.

"Everard!" Abel shouted.

Everard looked around.

"You"—Abel jabbed a finger in his direction—"are worse than Garr."

"Aye. Anything else?"

Abel pivoted, causing a cloud of dust to rise in his wake.

Everard allowed himself a grunt of laughter, then glanced at the donjon visible above the castle walls. Wondering if today's contest between Abel and Baron Lavonne had boasted an audience beyond those who patrolled the castle walls, he returned to his squires.

2

HE SHOULD NOT be here—should not have allowed Sir Abel to provoke him to do something for which he was not ready. But he had come and had only to step within to renew a relationship he had allowed to sour upon attaining the title of Baron of Abingdale four years past.

As the priest intoned the morning mass to the gathered knights, squires, pages, and men-at-arms, Christian considered the chapel's threshold and wished he could be like those within who had likely given little thought to crossing it.

He was not like them. He had been nearer God in the long, cool hours of monastery life—grudgingly, it was true, but he had found a measure of fulfillment in serving the Lord despite his resentment and yearning to be a warrior and lord the same as his brother, Geoffrey. However, he did not want to think there, for there lay the sin and shame that had caused him to give God his back as Abel Wulfrith had so coarsely put it on the day past.

Remembrance of their exchange made Christian's pride recoil at giving the man the satisfaction of knowing his words had found their mark, and he nearly turned away. Setting his jaw, he stepped inside.

As the entrance was at the rear of the chapel, only a few of those nearest looked around. Curiosity flashed in the young men's eyes, as it did when Christian appeared at supper, which was usually the only time he came amongst them. Certain they wagered over his identity and the reason one of obvious rank and nobility had come to Wulfen Castle, a stronghold devoted to training boys and young men, Christian eyed the back rows.

Left and right of the aisle, the squires and pages stood shoulder to shoulder, not a gap between them, meaning he would have to traverse the aisle to find a place. And likely draw the attention of the Wulfriths who were at the fore of the chapel. Reasoning that one need not number among the many to join in the mass, he chose the back wall that stood in shadow.

Though, over the next half hour, a few of the priest's words slipped through the cracks of Christian's barricaded soul, most went left and right of him. As tempted as he was to return belowstairs where a simple meal would be set out for breaking fast prior to the commencement of pre-dawn training, he forced himself to remain.

When the priest finally blessed those present and their endeavors, it took all of Christian's will to not be the first to exit the chapel. During that struggle, he acknowledged what was happening—that he was under attack by the enemy who did not wish him here, who was content for him to remain outside of God's will, who preferred the back turned to God over the face Christian sought to lift that he might once more find favor with the Lord. The enemy could not be more displeased with what Abel Wulfrith's taunting had wrought.

Christian watched the others file out of the chapel from front to back and was grateful when neither of the Wulfrith brothers picked him from the shadows.

It did not take long for the chapel to empty, but even when the last of the squires had crossed the threshold, Christian remained unmoving. He watched the priest extinguish half the candles on the altar, then two of the three torches set in wall sconces.

Smoothing pudgy hands down his robes, the priest turned toward the door and, halfway across the chapel, paused. As if sensing Christian's presence, he peered into the shadows, only to chuckle, shrug, and hasten forward. A moment later, he pulled the door closed behind him. The man's lack of regard for his suspicions would have angered Christian if not that he would likely have done the same when his lot had been to pray, rather than fight.

All was different now. As he had learned these past years, if he was to protect his people and lands, he could not ignore such warnings. He must always be prepared for the blade at his back. Or another's back, for which he had been prepared when his illegitimate half brother sought to slay Beatrix Wulfrith—Beatrix, whose death would have imperiled the cessation of hostilities between the Lavonnes and Wulfriths. Despite Christian's intervention, until the Wulfriths entrusted their oldest sister to him, he could not be assured of reconciling with that family whose people had suffered much at the hands of his brothers and father.

"'Twill be done soon," Christian murmured and settled his gaze on the altar. Prominently displayed there, despite the simplicity of the material from which it was fashioned, was a crucifix—a reminder of the one to whom he had turned when he was a man of God. More, a reminder of the one he had forsaken.

Was there a way to cross back to the other side of the divide he had placed between himself and God? Though a part of him longed to return to the relationship that, as a youth, he had forged out of adversity, the other part urged him to stay his course. Or was it the enemy?

Regardless, it *was* less burdensome to rely on one's self rather than wait on the Lord who was not always forthcoming—and when He *was* forthcoming, did not always provide the answer one wished. Of course, had not God cruelly proved that only He knew what was best for those who followed Him? Was Geoffrey's death not evidence enough?

Despite all of Christian's arguments against what he knew must be done to ensure that the life he made with his wife and children would be blessed, he bowed his head. "I yield, Lord. Take me back." And he would have walked the aisle and prostrated himself before the altar had the door not creaked open.

Closing his hand around his sword hilt, he peered out of the shadows at the figure in the doorway.

Seemingly as hesitant as he had been to cross the threshold, the hooded man finally stepped inside and closed the door.

Wondering if he should reveal himself or wait to determine the reason the intruder sought the chapel in the absence of those who had begun their day's training, Christian flexed his hand on his sword.

Something was afoot, he determined as the tall man advanced on the altar. However, he was far from prepared when the hood was lowered to reveal a fall of dark blonde hair. Not a man, but a woman at Wulfen where women were forbidden. All except one who should no longer be here.

Gaenor Wulfrith stared at the cloth-covered altar. As it was always difficult to humble herself before the Lord, she imagined Jesus stretched on the crucifix before her.

Once more wrenched by His sacrifice that was said to forgive her of her sins, she lowered to her knees and bowed her head. Dutifully, she prayed for England, her family, her people, and those in need and hurting. Lastly, and with great apology, she prayed for herself—she whose prayers God seemed loath to answer.

She opened her eyes and considered the hands she clasped so tightly that the knuckles shone white. "I do not know why I even talk to You," she whispered and lifted her gaze to the crucifix.

Months past, when it was believed her sister, Beatrix, had given her life that Gaenor might escape marriage to a Lavonne, Gaenor had refused to attend mass. Not until she learned her sister had survived had she returned to God, and only then to bargain with Him.

Beatrix, accused of murdering a knight, had once more faced death, and Gaenor had promised the Lord that if he delivered her sister free, she would return to Him. He had answered her prayer and, now absolved of the crime, Beatrix would wed the man she loved—unlike Gaenor who was tempted to fall away from the Lord now that she once more faced marriage to her family's enemy. And revelation of her sin.

She shuddered. With each passing day that drew her nearer Beatrix's wedding where she would meet her betrothed, the temptation to abandon God grew stronger, for it did not seem likely He would intervene.

Christian Lavonne had saved her sister—surely by trickery—and gained her family's gratitude. Despite Gaenor's protests, it was doubtful they would make any further attempt to keep her from wedding the baron. The Wulfriths would have their peace and she would suffer her husband's abuses. Abuses he would surely justify once he discovered...

"Answer one more prayer, Lord, this one for me. Deliver me from this marriage. Preserve me for a man of integrity and honor, a man unlike the brother of that beast, Geoffrey Lavonne." Beseechingly, she touched the base of the crucifix. "You know who I would have. You know where my heart lies, though his does not lie with me. Pray, grant me this."

Christian stared at the woman's back. Her softly spoken prayer having reached him in the great silence of the chapel, he curled his hands into fists. He knew she did not want him and might even hate him, but he had not considered that another might have claimed her heart—a man for whom she would yearn when she spoke vows with Christian, when he came to her, when she closed her eyes to imagine it was *he* who touched her.

For some reason, the ache went deep, and he rebuked himself, for he had no cause for jealousy when all he sought from their union was peace between their families.

Gaenor Wulfrith rose and swept around, affording him his first glimpse of a face that was told to be as distant from her sister's as the dark of night was from the light of day. And it was, though not as expected. She did not possess Beatrix's fragile beauty, but neither was she uncomely as he had been told. Dark blonde hair fell in waves about her warmly complected face to frame heavily-lashed eyes, a well-shaped nose, compressed lips that looked as if they knew no tilt or bow, and a firm chin. Severe, but possibly pretty.

As she neared, he looked closer. However, draped as she was in a long mantle, it was impossible to determine if she possessed a pleasing figure. Overly slender, he guessed, likely little to distinguish her from a tall boy. Not that her figure was of import beyond her ability to bear children. Providing she was not narrow-hipped, which would making birthing difficult or even impossible, she ought to bear him many children.

He uncurled the fists he had made of his hands. Peace and children. That was all he required of Gaenor Wulfrith and, regardless of where her heart lay, he would have them.

She gripped the door handle and lowered her chin. Though the fall of her hair denied him her face, he sensed she wept, and a pang went through him that he did not wish to feel. In the next instant, she swung around. The eyes she narrowed on the altar were bright, but her face was dry.

"Regardless of Your answer," she said, "I shall endure." She wrenched open the door, paused, and frowned over her shoulder.

Christian tensed as she delved the shadows in which he stood. He had made no sound, but it was as if she felt him the same as the priest had done. However, also as the priest had done, she ignored her senses.

When the door closed behind her, he considered the altar before which he had thought to prostrate himself prior to Gaenor Wulfrith's appearance. He had asked the Lord to take him back, but now he found he was not ready. One day he would return to his faith, but *this* day he would aspire to seek another's death. And considering the great roiling within, perhaps this time he would succeed.

"What is this?" Christian looked from the heavily-stocked cellar before him to the knight at his side.

"Your new training field," the second-born Wulfrith said.

Struggling toward patience, Christian said, "You will have to explain yourself, Sir Everard."

Candlelight and shadow warring on the canvas of the knight's austere face and shaved head, he said, "As Abel has done all he can do for you, 'tis for me to impart the last of your training."

"In a cellar?"

"There is no better place. Here you shall learn how to engage an opponent without benefit of light and open spaces, how to negotiate unseen obstacles, how to pick sounds from the silence, and how to discern the voice within that will one day save your life."

It seemed a child's game of hiding and seeking, but thus far Christian had not been subjected to any attempt to humiliate him as he had expected upon his arrival at Wulfen.

He inclined his head. "Proceed, Sir Everard."

The knight set the tallow candle atop a barrel alongside the stairs, snuffed the wick, and spoke out of the darkness, "Make ready, Baron Lavonne."

Christian stood unmoving and, when he finally stepped away from the stairs, felt a rush of air as if a sword swept past.

"No hesitation," Sir Everard growled. "Make ready!"

It *had* been a sword. Grateful for the chain mail the knight had insisted he don, though Sir Everard had not done so himself, Christian drew his sword from its scabbard and jumped back to avoid the next swing. Twice more he was forced to retreat before he set his own sword in motion.

"Listen for me!" Sir Everard instructed.

As Christian strained to catch the sound of movement, he heard a footfall. In anticipation of the next blow, he swung his sword up. And steel met steel between them, causing sparks to fly.

"Better!" Sir Everard grunted. "Now again."

Their blades crossed, but this time Sir Everard's found the rim of Christian's ear.

"Hit!" the man declared.

Anger spurting in concert with the blood the knight gained off him, Christian swung again and encountered empty space.

"Seek me, Baron!"

Christian snapped his head to the left whence the voice issued. It *was* hiding and seeking, but no child's game. If not for the chain mail, he might emerge from the cellar mortally wounded. Of course, the mail was also a hindrance, as its shifting links kept the knight apprised of his opponent's whereabouts, an advantage Christian did not share. Though tempted to throw off the mail, he held. And listened.

There—a sound to the right. Either Sir Everard had crossed the cellar, a rodent scuffled amid the barrels of wine and sacks of grain, or the knight had tossed something to cause Christian to turn in the opposite direction.

Disgusted with his inaction, Christian stepped to the left, and the toe of his boot connected with something solid and unmoving. He reached with his free hand and discovered a wall of stacked barrels. Though his ire stirred, he continued to listen as he felt his hand across them in search of a path that would lead him toward Sir Everard. When the wall ended and a sweep of his hand confirmed emptiness, he stepped forward.

Silently berating the iron links that rang softly as he moved, he strained to hear Sir Everard and caught a faint sound. Was it in response to his own movement?

He smiled at the realization he was something of a walking trap. Despite the disadvantage of alerting his opponent to his movements, the mail forced a response from Sir Everard. Whether he was retreating or merely readying for their skirmish, it could not be known.

Again, Christian faced a wall of barrels, but he quickly found a way around it. When the soft scuffling came from the far right, he paused, determined it must be a rodent, and resumed his search to the left. An instant later, the air stirred before his face.

He swept his sword up and was forced back when his blade met Sir Everard's.

"Listen for my breath, Baron!" The knight pushed off and swung again.

Christian knocked aside the blow intended for his shoulder, causing Sir Everard to grunt.

"Smell the sweat of my body!"

Christian did smell it. Or was it his own?

"Look for the lighter shadows amid the darker!"

More sparks as their blades clashed overhead.

"Turn your senses toward me, toward danger, toward death." Sir Everard dragged his blade off Christian's and once more slipped away.

The game went on for what seemed hours, during which Sir Everard drew blood from a half dozen places unprotected by Christian's mail and Christian had the satisfaction of also finding his mark, though only a few times and after much expenditure of effort and frustration.

When Sir Everard finally pounded up the stairs and threw open the door, flooding the darkness with light, Christian wanted nothing more than to seek the cool stream in the wood beyond the castle. Though, physically, the training had not been strenuous, the straining of his mind for things beyond his sight made him feel raw.

"We shall try again on the morrow," Sir Everard said.

Christian squinted up at the knight. "That is it? No lessons you would have me recite?" As Abel would surely have required.

"I but offer advice."

Christian wiped a hand across his moist brow. "That is?"

"When you take my sister to wife, Baron Lavonne, you would do well to proceed as cautiously with her as you did with your sword amid the dark of this cellar."

Christian was surprised, for previous to this day, no word had passed between them regarding Gaenor Wulfrith. Of course, most of his time had been spent with the youngest brother, but Abel had also avoided talk of his sister.

Wondering if either brother knew to whom she had given her heart, Christian asked, "And what other advice would you offer regarding Lady Gaenor?"

The knight arched an eyebrow. "None that comes upon me at the moment."

Disappointed to have gained no further insight into the unwilling woman he was to wed, Christian said, "I thank you."

The knight disappeared down the corridor.

As Christian followed, Sir Everard's advice rolled through him. "Proceed cautiously," he murmured while mounting the stairs.

Though he had told himself that peace and children were all he required of his wife, he knew more was needed if he and Gaenor Wulfrith were to make a life out of the darkness of the past. He must be patient, must not allow her love for another to stand as a wall between them, must find a way to draw her to his side. But how to proceed when all he knew of her was her hatred for his family and her love for another man?

Christian paused in the doorway. Might she return to the chapel on the morrow?

3

SHE WAS NOT alone.

The sensation felt on the day past, which she had convinced herself was mere foolishness, thrummed deeper as she stared at the altar before which she knelt. Who watched? It could not be the priest, for he would not skulk about even though she had made known her aversion to his well-intentioned counsel.

She lowered her gaze past her clasped hands to the scabbard on her girdle. It held her meat dagger, and though only one side of the blade was honed, it was sharp.

Though part of Gaenor urged her to behave as if naught were amiss and directly seek her exit, another part rebelled. If she was right, twice now in as many days, someone had violated her solitude. And would likely do so again when next she returned to keep her word to the Lord.

It was not to be tolerated. For too many months she had sheltered at Wulfen and allowed her brothers to do for her what she could do for herself, but no more. Regardless of what Everard or Abel might say, it was *she* who would out the intruder. And woe to the man who mistook her for a mere woman wielding an eating utensil. She was, after all, a Wulfrith.

She flicked her gaze to the cross. "Amen." She pulled the dagger, rose, and turned to face the dark recesses of the chapel's rear wall. "Reveal yourself."

To her surprise, the man stepped forward, and she saw he was taller than even her brother, Garr, and broad-shouldered like—

Her dagger-wielding hand wavered as the flickering light fell across his fair hair and solemn face. It was *him*.

Though she had only seen him from a distance, it was the one with whom Abel had spent this past month beyond the castle's training field. For lack of other activity, every day she watched the two engage at swords from her chamber in the uppermost floor of the donjon—excepting the day past when they had not appeared. Such a curiosity it was for a nobleman to seek and receive training at Wulfen. So curious that, a sennight after first coming to her notice, she had asked after him when Everard had found her at the window.

A knight who sought betterment of his sword skill, was all he had revealed before warning her to take care that she was not seen at the window. His concern had made her laugh bitterly, for she knew the same as her brothers that King Henry was aware of her presence at Wulfen. The only ones who were yet oblivious were the young men who trained here, and they were of no danger to her.

Halfway across the chapel, the intruder halted. "My lady," he said, as if theirs was an arranged meeting rather than a violation of her privacy.

How did he know she was noble? It was not as if the mantle that concealed the fine raiments beneath were edged in ermine. The simple, woollen outer garment could belong to any common woman. Might she be mistaken in believing those who trained at Wulfen remained ignorant of her presence? If so, why was she still confined abovestairs excepting the rare occasion when Everard or Abel took her riding?

No sooner did the question settle than the answer followed. For the distraction women breed, Everard would say. Regardless if one was a lady or a serving woman, their sex was not allowed at Wulfen. And with good reason, considering the upheaval caused by Lady Annyn Bretanne who had come here four years past in the guise of a squire. Though intent on working revenge against Gaenor's brother, Garr, her attempt on his life was thwarted. Thus, before all, she was revealed to be a woman. Now she was Garr's wife.

"Who are you?" Gaenor continued to brandish her dagger, though he made no move to draw nearer.

"You do not know?"

"I do not, though from afar I have seen you at training with my brother, Sir Abel."

Something turned in his eyes, but she did not think it was surprise that she was Abel's sister. And she had not intended it should be, for if he knew her to be a lady, he surely knew the only woman who would be allowed at Wulfen was the Wulfrith sister who had gone to ground.

As the man before her had yet to answer, Gaenor said, "I still do not know your name, Sir Knight, nor the reason you did not reveal yourself when I entered."

Christian glanced at the dagger, then returned his gaze to the woman who would be his wife. Though he knew he would regret the course he was about to set, he could not tell her the truth, especially as it seemed a truth for which she was unprepared. Not only was it apparent her brothers had told her nothing of her betrothed's training, but despite Christian's prompt, she showed no sign of consideration that the one who had watched from the shadows was the same man whom she believed to be without integrity and honor—a man whom she beseeched God that she not be made to wed.

Silently acknowledging the sin of his deception, making no attempt to justify the means by which he might learn about the woman with whom he would spend his life, he said, "I am called Sir Matthew." He searched out the color of her eyes amid the low light. "And I did not reveal myself lest I disturb your prayers."

Her lids narrowed in a face that was, perhaps, a bit long. "Yesterday as well?"

Gaenor Wulfrith was not to be underestimated, Christian realized as her brother's advice returned to him. Not only had the lady's keen senses picked his presence from the shadows this day, but she knew it was he who had tipped her senses on the day past.

"Yesterday as well," he said. "'Twould seem you and I are similarly inclined to seek the Lord past the dawning of day."

A brittle smile revealing straight teeth, she said, "Nay, Sir Matthew, I am inclined to seek the Lord *without* an audience, and twice now you have denied me that."

"So I have." Though chafed by her refusal to soften, Christian dipped his chin. "Apologies, my lady. I assure you, 'twas not done with ill intent."

"What intent, then?" She appeared unmoved by his show of contrition. But, then, it was not genuine, for he would do again what he had done to better prepare for their marriage.

"'Tis true my presence on the day past was mere happenstance, just as it is true today it was not. I came that I might see you again, Lady Gaenor."

"Me?" Her tone implied it was unthinkable that a man would wish to lay eyes upon her. "For what purpose?"

Christian commanded his features to remain impassive. Was she really such a shrew? Or was his lack of experience with women responsible? Once, before leaving the monastery, he had tasted the fruit forbidden him, but even in the years since eschewing his vows, he had done so only on occasion despite the carnal ache of his body. And only then with women who required no courting or expression of emotion.

Of course, Gaenor Wulfrith was no harlot. Her heart might be given to another, but it was not likely she knew more than the clasp of her beloved's hand.

He took a step toward her. "I am moved by your plight, to which I was privy on the day past."

Her expression slackened as if his admission surprised her, then tightened again. "On the day past when you made free with prayers not intended for your ears."

"Unintentionally."

"Perhaps."

Christian eyed the weapon she continued to point at him. Though it was only a meat dagger, a Wulfrith woman likely knew how to wield a blade. "You do not need that. I intend you no harm."

"Perhaps," she said again.

Beginning to regret having not revealed the truth of his identity, as it did not seem likely his deception would gain him further insight, he asked, "Would you grant me an audience, Lady Gaenor?"

"Why?"

"As told, I am moved by your plight."

Her mouth pinched. "I see no gain in discussing the intimacies of my life with a stranger."

"There may not be, but if you are like me, there is little else upon which to pass the next hour."

Her gaze faltered and something like interest crept into her eyes.

Taking it for assent, Christian strode forward. And was nearly undone when she sprang at him. Torchlight running the silver blade she swept toward him, he felt a rush of air at his jaw that preceded its arrival. He did not know how he did it, she moved so deftly, but he caught her wrist and averted her course before she could draw blood.

As she strained to free herself, he pulled her toward him lest she find advantage in the space between them. She stumbled and her temple struck his jaw, but despite the discomfort she surely suffered, she did not relent.

Beneath the concealing mantle, she was not without form, Christian realized as he felt the press of her chest against his and the womanly curve of her hips. "Lady Gaenor, I vow I mean you no harm."

She whipped her chin up. Anger flushing her cheeks and flying from her eyes, she demanded, "Then loose me!"

Her eyes were brown, large pools of darkness that might warm a man if ever they shone with something other than ire.

"Loose me!"

He looked to the dagger upon which her knuckles were white. Though he considered stipulating that first she relinquish the weapon, it occurred to him this might be the means by which he gained her trust. He released her wrist and took a step back.

From the widening of her eyes, she was surprised. With less than a reach separating them, she searched his face, then slowly lowered the dagger. "You took me unawares, Sir Matthew."

Which was likely as near an apology as he would get. "Will you sit with me, Lady Gaenor?"

She stared, but just when he thought she meant to refuse him, she said, "For a moment."

Christian inclined his head, crossed to the solitary bench positioned against the chapel's left-hand wall, and lowered onto it.

She followed and returned the dagger to its scabbard before seating herself on the far end of the bench.

Christian looked from her face to the pale throat and bit of collarbone revealed by her parted mantle, and when his perusal caused her hands to fly up and snatch the edges of the woolen garment together, he felt like a lecher.

Reminding himself that the audience he had been granted was not without time constraint, he said, "I know of this marriage from which you seek deliverance, Lady Gaenor."

Though she was hardly relaxed, clutching at her mantle and sitting the edge as she did, she stiffened. "As 'tis by the king's command, my marriage to Baron Lavonne is no secret."

"It is not, just as it is no secret that you fled to Wulfen to avoid it."

Gaenor stared at the man before her. He was too bold, and though she knew what he said was true, she was inclined to challenge him. "Is it not?"

He smiled, a tolerant smile that, despite the anger it roused in her, forced her to acknowledge that Sir Matthew was not without attraction. Almost handsome, though not nearly as well-favored as—

"In all of England," he said, "there is no castle more impregnable. Thus, what else is there to conclude than that the Wulfriths hid their beloved sister here?"

Beloved! She, whom her family intended to hand up as a sacrifice? She would laugh if not that the long months of believing Beatrix had given her life that her older sister might escape marriage had made her a stranger to such expression of emotion.

"Why are you opposed to the marriage, my lady?"

"Only a fool or martyr would put their head in such a noose as that which awaits the woman who weds a Lavonne."

The knight looked momentarily away. "You speak from the experience of having met these Lavonnes?"

The man was insufferable! Wondering why she had let him convince her to sit with him, she said, "My family and our people have suffered much at the hands of that family. *That* is experience enough."

He nodded slowly. "Given time, mayhap the Lavonne you are to wed will prove different from the others."

"Ha!" It was as near a laugh as she was capable of producing. "And mayhap one day you, Sir Knight, will surpass my brother at swords."

"'Tis possible—given time."

Gaenor rose and swung away, but the knight was instantly at her back and turning a hand around her upper arm. Before she could retrieve her dagger, he pulled her around to face him.

"What I spoke was not meant to offend, Lady Gaenor, only to encourage."

She opened her mouth to rebuke him, but his words seemed so sincere that she faltered.

Looking up at him—a rarity for a woman as tall as she—something moved in her chest. He was not as handsome as the one who held her heart, but his face was well-formed. Forgetting they stood so near, she considered his defined chin, generous mouth, broad cheekbones, and long, straight nose. Lastly, she settled on his most intriguing feature—brown eyes flecked with gold, unlike her own eyes that could best be described as muddy.

It took Gaenor some moments to realize the knight scrutinized her as intently, but though she knew she ought to be offended, she felt that movement again. And it disturbed her as she could not remember being disturbed the last time she had been so near a man. Why? And why this pang as if she betrayed the man she would choose to take her to wife—a man who did not want her?

She drew a shuddering breath. "Why are you at Wulfen, Sir Matthew?"

"As you have seen, I am training with your brothers."

"I have seen, but 'tis boys and young men who seek training here, not men who have already earned their spurs."

The knight inclined his head. "On the battlefield, I discovered to my near detriment that my previous training was lacking. Thus, that I might not find my legs or life cut out from under me, I came to Wulfen."

"I see." Not entirely, but it was much the same as Everard had told when she had questioned him about Abel's student. "And have you gained what you sought?"

His gaze drifted to her mouth, and the gold in his eyes seemed to shift amid the brown. "Not all, but methinks soon I shall."

Gaenor felt herself sway toward the knight. Horrified, she lurched back and he released her. "I thank you for your concern, Sir Knight, but I must return to my chamber."

He inclined his head. "Good day, my lady."

At the door, she paused. "When do you depart Wulfen, Sir Matthew?"

"Less than a fortnight."

For some reason, the prospect that it was not sooner was not displeasing to her. "Should you be present when next I seek the chapel, I but ask that you not delay in making your presence known."

His eyebrows rose. "I give you my word."

There was that movement again. Wishing it away, she swept the hood over her head and pulled the door open.

Long after her departure, Christian remained unmoving. Though he could not be certain, he had sensed the lady felt something not unlike the attraction that had surprised him when he had touched her and stood so near. Was it possible she had not truly given her heart to another? That it might yet be claimed?

In the next instant, he rejected such thinking. He did not seek nor require Gaenor Wulfrith's heart. He wanted an end to the feuding between his family and the Wulfriths. He wanted children and a wife who neither feared nor loathed him. And now that he had met and spoken with his betrothed, it seemed possible he might gain all he sought—providing his deception did not upset everything. But there was time aplenty to reveal himself and make amends. Time during which he would not only continue to better his sword skill, but meet again with Lady Gaenor.

He looked over his shoulder at the slant of light coming through the eastern window. As it was another hour before he and Sir Everard returned to the darkened cellar, he considered remaining here and seeking God as he knew he must do. He wavered and, in the end, silently vowed he would seek God another day.

She did not understand it—did not know why it was no longer mere monotony and curiosity that drew her to her window to watch for Abel and his student. More, she did not understand the sense of loss when, for the second day, they did not appear.

She should not care, should proceed with her unending day the same as she did every day. But something kept her at the window, and she knew what it was. Despite Sir Matthew's offense of stealing upon her, she was drawn to him.

She recalled his gold-flecked eyes that looked at her as if he truly wished to know who dwelt within; saw those same eyes waver when she flung contempt at him, and in the next instant warm upon her; saw his mouth tighten with impatience, then tuck up as if to smile; heard the ebb and flow of his deep voice that made her skin prick; felt his hand on her that had been firm, yet gentle; felt the pull in the space between them that had made her long to fill it.

She shook her head. She was not attracted to the knight. Could not possibly feel anything for a man she did not know beyond his discomfiting interest in her plight. More, it was another for whom she felt. And though her dream was hopeless, it was surely betrayal to feel anything for another man. Even if only attraction.

Gaenor groaned. She *had* felt something for Sir Matthew—something familiar, yet unfamiliar. Unfamiliar, for it was as if he had also felt it, unlike...

"Durand," she whispered the name of the knight who felt naught for her despite what had gone between them.

Awash in shame, she silently vowed she would not return to the chapel until Sir Matthew left Wulfen a fortnight hence. Though she was surely mistaken in thinking he was attracted to her, if it was true, naught could come of it but more pain.

Less than a fortnight ere he departs, she told herself, only to realize she would also be gone from Wulfen. And that hardly bore thinking on, as it was then she would meet her betrothed on the occasion of Beatrix's wedding.

Resolved to remaining in her chamber and praying for the strength to accept her fate, she pressed her shoulders back, crossed to the bed, and lowered to her knees.

4

Lady Gaenor had not returned. Though three days had passed since they had spoken, she continued to eschew the chapel. Thus, all Christian had to show for these past days were cuts and abrasions delivered by Sir Everard's sword in the darkness of the cellar. Hardly a loss, for he was beginning to sense sounds and movements that had previously eluded him, but neither was it the gain he had expected.

Not for the first time, he wondered if Lady Gaenor had told her brothers of their meeting, but he again rejected the possibility. Had she spoken of it, the Wulfriths would surely have confronted him.

Accepting that his betrothed would not return to the chapel this day, he looked to the altar that beckoned each time he entered. And nearly turned away.

Setting his jaw, he strode from the shadows and knelt before the cross. He confessed his sins, from the private lusting of his body to the godless thoughts that aspired to his tongue. Every sin that came to mind he laid down, excepting the deception worked on Lady Gaenor. *That* he stored up for last. And yet, when he could think of no more sins to list, he hesitated. No sooner did he accede to its confession than he heard footfalls in the corridor.

Though tempted to stand that he would not be found kneeling, he remained with his back to the door. It whispered open and Lady Gaenor—it had to be her—entered.

Whether it was surprise at finding him inside that made her footsteps falter, or the unexpectedness of seeing him before the altar, he could not know, but she resumed her stride and knelt beside him.

"Sir Matthew." She looked at him, the hostility that had previously shone from her eyes no longer in evidence. Still, there was wariness beneath the sweep of her lashes.

"Lady Gaenor."

She averted her gaze and, for a moment, he thought she might smile. "Now 'tis *I* who interrupts *your* solitude."

"A welcome reprieve, my lady."

She clasped her hands and closed her eyes. Unlike when he had watched from the shadows, she did not speak aloud her prayers, the only evidence of her conversation with God a slight movement of her lips.

As it would be unseemly to repent for his deception until he committed to revealing the truth to her, which he was now loath to do, Christian did not bow his head again but used the opportunity to observe her.

He liked the curve of her eyebrows that were darker than her hair, her lashes that threw long shadows across her cheeks, the bow of her upper lip that was not as unyielding as first thought, and the slender column of throat that was surely smooth to the touch.

"If I distract you from your prayers, Sir Matthew," she said, eyes remaining closed, "mayhap I ought to leave."

It seemed her senses were as keen as Sir Everard's.

Christian straightened from the altar. "I had only just finished when you entered."Though he did not wish to withdraw, having waited days to see her again, he said, "'Tis I who ought to leave."

She looked up. "It is not necessary. Indeed, if it would be of little imposition, I would have you wait on me."

This he had not expected. "I shall, my lady." Once again, he settled on the lone bench. It was not long before she joined him, and this time she left only three feet between them.

When Christian smiled, she looked down. Intrigued by the flush that warmed her cheeks, he said, "I had only just accepted I would not see you again when you entered."

"I did not intend to return."

For fear of him. "And yet you came."

After a long moment, her eyes rose to his. "You and my brother, Abel, no longer practice at swords beyond the castle walls."

Dare he believe his absence bothered her? "We do not. It is with Sir Everard I now train. He has set me the task of sharpening my senses to the sounds and movements of the dark."

Her mouth quivered as if tempted to smile. "The cellar."

"Aye."

"That would account for..." She touched her cheek and chin to indicate two corresponding cuts on his face. "...your injuries."

They were not much more than scratches. "Aye, though your brother is not without his own injuries."

She arched an eyebrow. "Far fewer, I wager."

Twinged that his man's pride had caused him to point out that he was not an unworthy opponent, he said, "That wager you win, my lady."

"Then I have but to name my prize, Sir Knight?" Her playful unguardedness surprised not only him, but her, as evidenced by the startle in her eyes.

Captivated, Christian took a risk he knew he should not and moved nearer. He laid a hand over hers. "Name it, my lady."

She stared at his fingers covering hers, then made a small, strangled sound and stood. "'Tis time I return to my chamber."

Silently berating himself for not heeding the voice of caution, Christian stood to watch her go.

Upon reaching the back of the chapel, she looked around, but there was no anger in her eyes. "I should not ask, but I would have you come again on the morrow."

Once more surprised by this woman who seemed less and less a shrew, Christian said, "I shall be here, my lady."

When she had gone, the solitude of the chapel closed around Christian, and once again he felt the weight of his deception and knew that the longer he denied his conscience, the harder it would be to tell Gaenor the truth. He would, but not now when he was just beginning to know her. However, it would have to be done before he left Wulfen, else she would be shaken at her sister's wedding, and that portended ill.

In a sennight, then. Seven days to learn the woman who was to be his wife. Seven days for her to learn the man who was to be her husband.

She should not have gone, should have stayed away as she had vowed she would. But after three days of pacing her chamber, she had ventured to the chapel. And would do so again. Though she had told herself it was the many months of near solitude that had made her seek out Sir Matthew, it was more than that.

On the stairs to her chamber, she halted. What had possessed her to make light with the knight? Despite Beatrix's attempts to influence her older sister to behave less severely, Lady Gaenor Wulfrith was not one disposed to such absurdity as her sister had sought to pull from her. And yet, with little more than a prompt from Sir Matthew, she had teasingly inquired after her prize. One moment she was appalled by her brazen response, the next shocked when he acted upon it. Remembering the warmth of his hand, she shuddered.

Betrayal, a voice warned. *Your woman's heart cannot be two places at once, especially not with a man of whom you know so little.* But neither could it be with a man whose heart lay so distant from hers—at least, it should not be, she reminded herself as she had often done since her arrival at Wulfen.

She remembered her first month here. For those few weeks, there had been hope of deliverance from marriage to Baron Lavonne, even though it would have been by scandalous means, but she could have borne the taint and shame had it meant the baron would reject her—and he surely would have, regardless of the king's decree. However, God had denied her as he denied her almost everything for which she prayed, including relief from the unexpected turmoil that had arisen from her first meeting with Sir Matthew.

What did God want from her? As her marriage to Lavonne was inevitable, why did He place another man in her path? To test her? She, who had been tested more than she cared to acknowledge?

She gripped her forehead. If only He would clear her mind of the knight in the chapel that she might ready herself for her meeting with Christian Lavonne. Instead, He cruelly allowed her a glimpse of yet one more thing forbidden her. And perhaps forbidden in another way as well, for it was possible Sir Matthew was betrothed. Or wed.

"Gaenor?"

She pulled her hand from her face and found Everard four steps above, brow furrowed. Though he could not know with whom she had been minutes earlier, she felt the heat of guilt.

"You are well, Sister?"

She smoothed her hands down her skirts. "I was…thinking." She winced at how feeble her words sounded. "You wish to speak with me?"

He inclined his head. "I did not expect to find you absent from your chamber."

She knew she should not take offense, but her words were chill. "As I am permitted the chapel, one of the few places I am allowed outside of my chamber, I sought prayer there."

Regret replaced the concern on his brow. "Of course."

"Of what do you wish to speak to me?"

When he gestured for her to precede him, she stepped past him into her chamber and turned.

Everard settled in the doorway. "I received word from Garr late last eve. He will arrive three days hence to escort you to Stern Castle for Beatrix's wedding."

Three days. "For what purpose when our sister's vows are not to be spoken for more than a sennight?"

"That you might have time with her and our mother ere—"

"I am sacrificed." How she hated the self-pity that dripped from her voice, but it would not be contained. "That I might celebrate my sister's good fortune in wedding a man of her choice. An honorable man. A man she loves."

Everard stepped forward and laid a hand on her shoulder. "Gaenor, you know what happened at Beatrix's trial, that Christian Lavonne—"

"I know. Thus, I do not need to hear again that the baron is unlike his father or brother. He is honorable. He will make a good husband. All these things I know."

He dropped his hand from her. "You do not know, but if ever you have trusted me, do so again. Upon my word, the match with Baron Lavonne is a good one. Indeed, 'tis fair possible you will come to care for him, mayhap even love him as Beatrix loves Michael D'Arci."

She wanted to believe him. "You say all this, and yet you know him no better than I."

He looked away. To compose an anger to which he was unaccustomed? Had she pushed him so far? "I trust Garr's judgment." He returned his gaze to her. "I but ask that you do so as well."

"If not that there is a motive for this marriage, I might, but one must not forget how highly peace is valued by the Wulfriths. Thus, peace they will have, no matter the price."

A muscle in his jaw worked. "You are wrong. These past months, we did not risk all by defying the king that we might surrender you up to a beast, Gaenor. I tell you, Lavonne has proved himself."

Like Garr, he had set his mind to the union of Wulfrith and Lavonne. He might be the most contemplative of her three brothers, and, on matters of import, his opinion was often sought, but there was no comfort in his assurance.

Gaenor crossed to the window. A glance at the meadow before the wood showed it was empty. Wishing Abel and Sir Matthew practiced at swords amid dewed grass that sparkled in the light of the new day's sun, she sighed.

"Is there anything you require, Gaenor?"

"Apart from the obvious? Nay."

"Then I shall send word to our brother that you will be prepared to depart Wulfen three days hence."

"The messenger has not returned to Stern?"

"Nay, he leaves within the hour."

She turned back to Everard. "There *is* something I require."

As if pleased that he might provide her with some small pleasure, he smiled. "What would you have me deliver you?"

"A sennight. Send word to Garr that you will escort me to Stern Castle a sennight hence."

Gaenor did not think she had ever glimpsed such confusion on his face. An instant later, it was reduced to a frown. "I thought you would be eager to return home."

"Eager if it were yet my home, but 'tis a temporary stay. Will you grant me this, Everard?"

"I shall." His uncharacteristic lack of contemplation surprised her. "Garr will have word this day."

And be displeased, as would be her mother and Beatrix. "I thank you."

Once more left to her solitude, Gaenor sank onto the chest at the foot of her bed. A sennight she had bargained for and been granted. A sennight in which to salve her terrible loneliness in the company of a man who did not look upon her with mere tolerance, who could not compare her to her beautiful sister and find her wanting.

Though naught could come of their short time together, Sir Matthew was hers. And perhaps in the dark days as Christian Lavonne's wife, memories of the knight's attentiveness would be a salve to her discontent.

Within four days, all to which he aspired would be set in motion.

From the woods that bordered Broehne Castle, Sir Robert, the illegitimate issue of Aldous Lavonne and half brother to Christian Lavonne, surveyed the outer walls that stood against him—walls he would scale in his brother's absence.

He almost laughed at his good fortune of finding the castle without its lord. Despite months of plotting during his imprisonment for the attempt on Lady Beatrix's life, what he planned should have been more difficult and carried more risk.

He chuckled. Though he was not a man inclined to prayer, it seemed God favored the wronged son of Aldous Lavonne.

"Sir Robert?" the man at his side queried.

"I am pleased, Sir Timothy," Robert acknowledged the one who had delivered tidings of Baron Lavonne's absence an hour past.

The knight, along with a dozen others who had been released from service by Christian, had thus far proved useful—foremost in securing Robert's escape from his London prison. No easy feat, that, as evidenced by the lives lost. Fortunately, only one of those who fell to the sword was among Robert's men. The other two who bled out their lives had been prison guards. The fools should have taken the coin offered.

"Your father will be pleased to lay eyes upon his eldest son," the knight said.

Would the old man be pleased? After all, he had entrusted Robert to repay the Wulfriths for the death of his second son and heir, and no satisfaction had he been given.

Remembering the trial that had found Lady Beatrix innocent of murder, Robert's mouth turned bitter. As the Wulfrith woman had escaped the noose, a dagger in the back was to have been her fate. Instead, it was Robert who had taken a dagger, and it had been thrown by his own brother, Christian.

As Robert had done every day since, he fed hatred of his younger brother with imaginings of a tortuous death. But regardless of his dark thoughts and past sins, it seemed God yet favored him. For all he had suffered in being born illegitimate—in watching from afar as his younger brothers enjoyed lives of privilege and position, of being given little more than their leavings—his cause was just. And the realization was almost enough to make him gain his knees. Though all of his life he had merely tolerated religion when the situation demanded it, he felt a sudden need to set his hands upon a psalter. Of course, what good when he could not read?

"Something is amiss?" Sir Timothy asked.

"All is well. Soon I shall give my father what he seeks—an eye for an eye." No sooner did the words pass his lips than he was struck by how spiritual he sounded. And found he liked it. Not that he was entirely certain "eye for an eye" was of the Bible, but it was from a priest he had heard it spoken.

"The old baron will finally have his revenge," Sir Timothy mused. "You could not please him more."

Nor suffer more his displeasure if his father learned that the death of his youngest son was nearly as inevitable as the death of a Wulfrith. Unfortunately, despite Christian having proved a bitter disappointment, Aldous Lavonne clung to his one remaining legitimate son. But, eventually, he would have to let Christian go.

"To the grave," Robert muttered.

"Sir Robert?"

Robert smiled so wide his parched lips cracked. "Let us lay our plans."

5

She had not spoken a word upon entering, but he had known she knew he was among the shadows. Now, as she rose from the altar where she had knelt the past quarter hour, he stepped into the light.

"You will sit with me, Sir Matthew?"

He almost winced at the name he had given her. Suppressing the urge to set her right, he nodded.

She crossed to the bench, unclasped her mantle, and drew it from her shoulders. Despite the mass of hair that fell nearly to her hips, there was no concealing her figure in the simple gown cut of dark blue cloth. Though her shape was not much different from a boy's—small breasts, a slight pinch to the waist, and hips that possessed little flare—it was not displeasing, for the lady was well-proportioned and did not slump in an attempt to appear nearer the ideal height for a woman. Indeed, as if to defy any who might counsel otherwise, she stood erect with shoulders square. Because, unlike most men, he stood taller than she?

Struck by the realization there were few men in England who would match well with Lady Gaenor, he frowned. Was this the reason the eldest Wulfrith sister had thrice suffered a broken betrothal? That none of those to whom she was promised could bear to be looked down upon by a wife? Might his own betrothal to the lady, which he had embraced only for the peace and healing it would bring to his people, be the work of God?

Christian saw that she watched him. Though her gaze had been level moments earlier, there was now wariness there. Lest his thoughtless scrutiny cause her to flee, he softened his mouth into a smile.

It did not put her at ease, as evidenced by the white-knuckled hand with which she gripped the mantle.

Christian gestured for her to sit and, when she hesitated, seated himself. When she finally joined him on the bench, she did not perch on the edge as she had done before but sat back and carefully arranged the mantle on her lap.

"I thank you for coming, Sir Matthew." She looked up, and he was relieved to see her wariness had cleared.

"I thank you for asking, though I am curious as to your reason, especially after my unforgivable trespass on that first day."

"It is not unforgivable, Sir Matthew. Were it, I would not have requested that you attend me again."

"I am pleased." He smiled again, this time larger.

From the slight tuck of her lips, she was tempted to respond in kind.

"Is there some way I may be of service, my lady?"

"Simply by meeting with me again, you are of great service." She smoothed a hand over the mantle. "As you surely know, I have been long within these walls and with little companionship excepting that which my brothers are able to spare away from their duties."

"But surely there are others at Wulfen who attend you and would be better company than I?"

"There are a few to whom I have been entrusted, but they are duty bound. You, Sir Matthew, are not, and yet you attend me of your own accord. Why?"

Now was the time to reveal himself, before his deception became further entrenched. But though he could not hope for a better opportunity, he remained loath to do so. "As told, I am moved by your plight."

Her lids narrowed. "The plight of someone you do not know? Why?"

"Few noble marriages are made for other than material gain, my lady. Thus, you are not alone in having others set your course."

Interest brightened her eyes, and she turned to more fully face him. "You also suffer from the prospect of an arranged marriage?"

Suffer...

Carefully choosing words that would not further complicate his deception, he said, "Like you, I am betrothed." Was it disappointment that flickered across her face? "And the choice of whom I wed is denied me, but I would not call it suffering." Indeed, though his initial response to the king's decree was resentment and defiance, after grueling reflection on the benefits of wedding into the Wulfrith family, he had accepted the decision.

"Then you have met the lady you are to wed?"

Yet another opportunity he would let slip by, but at least he could be truthful. "Aye, we have met." Uncomfortable with the turn the conversation had taken, he said, "Tell me, Lady Gaenor, since first you and I were acquainted, have you become better resolved to marrying the baron?"

Bitter laughter escaped her. "Hardly."

Though she knew he had witnessed her prayers that first day, what next met Christian's lips was too bold to speak, but he had to know. "Then you yet pray the Lord will release you from the obligation?"

"Nay. If there is one thing I am resolved to, 'tis acceptance that God shall not grant my request. Thus, as my family has determined I shall wed Baron Lavonne, there is naught for it."

"Unless you steal away again," Christian reminded her of her flight that had nearly cost her sister's life. Then, remembering her heart lay elsewhere, he added, "Or if someone were to steal you away."

Her reaction was delayed, but when it came, it was not as expected. This time, her laughter was playful. "Are you offering, Sir Knight?"

Struck by the sparkle in her eyes and the bow of her lips that not only revealed white teeth but caused comely dimples to groove her cheeks, Christian stared at her transformation from almost plain to pretty.

Her head listed right on her slender neck. "Are you?"

It *was* as implied, though not as intended. "Pardon, my lady, but when I asked, I referred to the man to whom you have given your heart."

Her breath caught and she swept her gaze down.

The minutes stretched, during which Christian chastised himself for mentioning that other one whose absence he preferred. Though not normally prone to speech without forethought, with Lady Gaenor, words stole past his lips before he could check them. Why? Because of this tightness in his chest at the thought or mention of the man who possessed the heart of the woman who would be his wife?

She looked back at him. "He is in my past, and there he shall remain."

There was no mistaking the pain in her voice. Suppressing anger that reeked of jealousy he had no reason to suffer, he said, "That is good, as 'twill make it easier for you when you wed."

She inclined her head. "I do not mean to sound self-pitying, Sir Matthew, but I fear there is little that will make it easier—unless you reconsider stealing me away."

Then perhaps she *would* run, given the chance.

Christian stared at her, one moment offended that she so hated him that she would allow a man of whom she knew little to take her away, in the next flattered at the prospect she would entrust herself to him—rather, Sir Matthew. "Are you truly so desperate to escape marriage, my lady?"

Her brow furrowed. "Do not worry so, Sir Matthew. I would not ask anything of you that would endanger your relationship with the Wulfriths." As if to lighten her words, she smiled. However, the expression wavered, evidencing her forced gaiety.

Had he reacted differently to her suggestion that he steal her away, how would she have responded?

She looked down. "Be assured, I will do my duty to my family, for though I resent being reduced to chattel, I love them well."

Once more, his thoughts birthed words that slipped past his lips before he could consider them. "Then you would not go with me if I did offer to spirit you away?"

Her fingers paused in the midst of smoothing her mantle. "I would not."

Did she speak true? Or did she fear he would alert her family to the possibility she might once more flee?

"I am grateful," he said, hoping to ease the tension, "for I would not like such a temptation set before me."

"Temptation?" She put her head to the side. "I should not tell you this, but I like you, Sir Matthew."

Progress. But was it enough with which to buy forgiveness when she learned he was the man she detested? Relieved that her shoulders had relaxed, he said, "Such a statement begs the question of why you like me."

She shrugged. "You are different."

"From whom?"

"Those who look through me."

He leaned near. "I do not understand."

"I shall enlighten you." She raised a finger. "Though you must promise not to laugh."

"I give you my word."

"Then I shall take the chance, though only because I shall not see you again when you leave Wulfen Castle."

Once more accosted by his deception, Christian clenched his teeth.

She clasped her hands. "When your gaze falls upon me, you look *at* me, and I like that. I like that you see me."

"Who else would I see?"

"'Tis not who else you would see, but who you would not see that would cause such disappointment."

"And that would be?"

"My sister, Beatrix. Had you met her, no explanation would be necessary."

He *had* met her, and though he realized Lady Gaenor likely referred to the differences in their appearances, he still wanted an explanation. "Continue."

Again, she smiled, and he almost wished he had kept count of the number of times she had done so this day, for each turn of her lips was precious.

"Beatrix is not only profoundly lovely," she said with a flicker of resentment that might have been imagined, "but of a height that does not cause men to strain their necks to look upon her. I do not need to tell you I was not so gifted by God. Thus, I have but to be placed alongside her to be reduced to a blemish."

Though Christian did not wish to offend her, he swept his gaze from her darkly blonde hair, to her eyes, nose, and mouth, and down her figure to the slippers peeking from beneath the hem of her gown.

It was true Lady Beatrix was a beautiful woman and that Gaenor presented as plain and, at times, severe, but there was more to her, as evidenced by what he had glimpsed this day. "If that is so, and I doubt it, surely it is because you withhold the smile from your eyes and lips."

She blinked.

"Aye, Lady Gaenor. When you smile, you are most becoming. Methinks you should aspire to do so more often."

She was thoughtful for some moments, then she let her lips turn. "You give me much to smile about, Sir Matthew."

Pretty, indeed. "I consider it an honor, my lady." Attraction pulling at him, he barely caught back the impulse to lay a hand over hers as he had trespassed on the day past. And if she had allowed it this time, it was possible he might have kissed her.

As it was past time for him to join Everard in the cellar, he straightened from the bench. "If you will permit me, I shall come again on the morrow."

She rose beside him. "I would beg it if you did not ask."

He nodded and, shortly, stood in the corridor outside the chapel wondering at all that had transpired between them. And trying not to think on the deception that would soon be revealed if he did not confess it.

"I had begun to believe you incapable of humor, Baron Lavonne."

Christian looked from the squires at a nearby table to Sir Abel who sat to his left. "I am amused when something is worthy of amusement." And the young men's pranks upon one another *had* amused him.

As he had marveled since his arrival at Wulfen, there was much beyond knighthood training that those sons promised to the Church would never see or experience. But then, were they exposed to the exhilaration and camaraderie inherent in a life committed to the defense of one's people, lands, and country, more would surely rebel—as Christian had done until there was nothing left but for him to accept his fate.

Remembering the long, cool, unbroken days at the monastery when he had suppressed his restlessness through prostration and prayer, he silently thanked God for delivering him. Despite all that had transpired since he had left the monastery, he had come to a better place in life.

A place that should never have been yours, his conscience reminded him of the consequence of unholy prayer.

He clenched his hands. Geoffrey was dead, and their father's pain over the loss of his favored heir was greater than the suffering caused by the burns that scarred the old man's body.

"You appear to have sustained fewer cuts than on the day past," Abel said. "I wager that your awareness of the darkness has sharpened considerably beneath my brother's tutelage."

Wondering at the man's rare attempt to engage him in conversation, Christian said, "My time at Wulfen has been of certain benefit."

"Then you are pleased." The knight lifted his goblet and took a long drink.

"I am. Though I do not expect my sword skill will surpass my facility with a dagger, I believe the instruction I have received here will prove more valuable."

Abel raised an eyebrow. "Indeed," he murmured, then frowned. "'Tis a curious thing how adept you are with a dagger considering you were promised to the Church at a young age."

Christian was well aware that he should not be able to easily find his mark, especially at the distances at which he was able to do so, but his relationship with the youngest Wulfrith brother was not such that he felt inclined to explain his skill—that a dagger had been far easier to secrete and practice at without his father's knowledge.

"It *is* a curious thing," he said, then returned the frown. "But tell me, Sir Abel, are *you* pleased with my progress?"

Something flashed in the man's eyes, but then he blinked and it was gone. "As well as I can be." Boredom dragged his words across the space between them. "Certes, you are better prepared to defend your lands and the family you will make with my sister, and *that* pleases me."

The mention of Lady Gaenor nearly made Christian smile. "Be assured, I shall keep your sister safe."

Abel turned his goblet on its stem. "That you shall, lest you know the wrath of the Wulfriths."

It was no idle threat, and one to which Christian tried not to take offense. But he did.

Holding the knight's gaze, he said, "You forget, Sir Abel, that the Lavonnes have already suffered your family's wrath—a wrath that took the life of my brother and for which marriage to your sister is intended to prevent further retaliation."

Though the light in the knight's eyes had not been friendly, at least there had been light. Now there was darkness. "Geoffrey Lavonne murdered and murdered again," Abel said. "For it, he suffered a coward's death—one for which no retaliation is warranted."

It was as the Wulfriths and the king's men told, and as Christian was inclined to believe, but it gave his father no relief. Indeed, it had increased Aldous's pain. And his yearn for revenge.

"See there"—Abel jerked his head to the right and followed with his eyes—"the knight at the end of the table?"

The man was familiar to Christian, and not only because he was among the esteemed warriors who trained Wulfen's squires. "I do."

"He is Sir Rowan."

Christian returned his regard to Abel, the better to enjoy his reaction. "Aye."

"Formerly of the barony of Aillil."

Christian inclined his head. "I am aware he was Lady Annyn's man ere she wed your brother."

Surprise glanced off Abel's face. "Do you also know 'twas he who delivered the blow that killed your brother?"

"I do—and that your eldest brother first disabled Geoffrey."

"Hmm. You are better informed than I believed, Baron Lavonne—and surprisingly adept at holding your knowledge close." He narrowed his gaze on Christian before turning it on Sir Rowan. When he looked around again, his mouth bore the trace of a smile. "Given the chance, you would kill him?"

Christian knew Abel baited him, but the streak of stubborn with which he seemed to have been born was determined to give back in equal measure. "But I have had the chance, Sir Abel, for I have not only recently become acquainted with the man's identity."

Abel's eyebrows drew together. "You are saying you bear him no ill?"

"If 'tis true he killed my brother in defense of Lady Annyn, then I can have no quarrel with him."

"The tale is true," Abel bit and leaned near Christian. "But methinks if he knew whose blood you share, he might kill you, for I do not believe there is anything that would convince him Geoffrey Lavonne's death was not warranted."

Christian stared into Abel's eyes. From the look there and the sweep of his breath, he knew the knight had imbibed beyond good sense—so much that he was of a mind to wield a sword. And Christian was tempted. For that, he withheld his hand from his own hilt.

"If Sir Rowan wishes to meet at swords and test my training," he said, "I shall meet him. But as for the Wulfriths, regardless of whether or not my brother's death was warranted, providing your family delivers as promised, *they* need no longer fear the Lavonnes."

Sir Abel's face flushed, and a movement told that his hand was more tempted to the sword than Christian's.

"Share the joke," a voice came between them at the same moment a hand fell to each of their shoulders.

Sir Abel broke gaze first and looked up at the man who stood at their backs.

Christian followed his gaze to Sir Everard who considered them with warning in his eyes. It seemed little slunk past Everard, the ever-observant.

"I fear you would be as disappointed as I," Sir Abel said, "for 'twas not as comic as our guest led me to believe." He returned his gaze to Christian. "Unless there is more to it?"

Christian stared back. "No more need be told, Sir Abel. Should you meditate on it when your mind is clear of so much wine, methinks what is lacking will come to you."

The knight turned a hand around his hilt, but his brother also saw it and tightened his grip on their shoulders.

"Mayhap another time, then," Sir Everard said with a glance around the hall at the young men who were failing to appear uninterested in what transpired at the high table. "And now we should all seek our beds." He bent near his brother. "Including you, Abel."

The silence between Christian and Abel tensed further, but then the latter smiled. "I can think of naught I would like better than to part present company." He lifted his goblet and drained the last of his wine.

Sir Everard released their shoulders. "Good eve, then."

His brother thrust up from the bench and was less than two strides distant when he came around. "Be assured"—he met Christian's gaze—"I shall meditate upon your good humor, full up in my cups or otherwise." He stalked away amid the murmurings in the hall.

With a sweep of the hand, Sir Everard signaled the end of the meal, in response to which goblets thumped to tables, benches scraped the stone floor, voices pitched higher, and laughter sprang up in the absence of the formality of the supper meal.

Christian stood and stepped away from the bench.

"Normally, my brother is of a more jovial disposition," Sir Everard said with what might have been apology. "I had hoped that, given time, the two of you would cease antagonizing one another."

Christian looked to the man whose shaved pate reflected the light of torches. "Your brother does not like me. As I cannot say I like him any better, conflict is inevitable."

"You know he is opposed to our sister's marriage?"

"I would be blind and deaf if I did not—just as I know you also struggle with the alliance."

Sir Everard inclined his head. "Though 'tis true I was displeased by the king's decree, this past month you have proved worthy and honorable."

Though Christian told himself he neither sought nor required the knight's approval, he was pleased to hear it.

"Thus, I no longer concern myself over your intentions toward my sister. All that remains is a struggle borne of her own reluctance. Unfortunately"—he looked to the young men who had turned their energies to transforming the hall into sleeping quarters—"the same cannot be said of Abel."

Christian waited for the knight to elaborate, and when he did not, said, "Do you intend to keep me in suspense long, Sir Everard?"

"Though 'tis not my place to tell it, I shall do so that you may better understand my brother." He crossed his arms over his chest. "Abel is fond of Gaenor—at least, as fond as he can be of a sister with whom he has only occasional contact—but his greatest objection lies in having himself known the folly of a marriage not of his choosing."

"Your brother is wed?"

"No longer. The woman to whom he was married for ten long months is dead—by her own hand."

"She killed herself?"

"Aye. Though her family attempted to hide the frailty of her mind, Abel knew when they met ere the wedding that something was amiss. But though he asked to be released from their betrothal, the marriage vows were spoken and, for nearly a year, he resolved to make the best of the life dealt him." He looked to the rushes between their feet. "However, the lady, who had seemed of two minds ere their marriage, became of three, then four—one day a sweet and compliant young woman, the next a spiteful shrew, one day a clinging girl, the next a morose old woman who hid in corners and conversed with shadows." He looked up.

"Ere she took her life, voices in those shadows told her Abel was possessed of the devil and that she should kill him."

Sympathy that Christian did not expect to feel for Everard's brother, coiled in his chest.

"That night, when he was abed, his wife took a dagger to him." His throat muscles convulsed with emotions that, heretofore, Christian would not have believed the knight capable of. "He should have died, for though he was able to deflect the blade, it caught his side and he bled out a goodly amount ere he was able to restrain her. The lady was locked away but escaped a few days later. Once more wielding a dagger, she returned to the chamber where my brother recovered—and turned the blade on herself."

Christian imagined the horror of it and could not help but pity the man. "I grieve for your brother and his trials and appreciate the confidence you have shared, for it does aid in better understanding his objection to the marriage. However, I would have you assure him that I am of one mind only and your sister need not fear me. Indeed, I shall endeavor to be a good husband for whom she might come to care." Of course, considering his deception, that might prove difficult. Thus, the sooner he—

"I believe you," Sir Everard said. "Eventually, I am sure Abel will conclude the same."

Which would be welcome, though not necessary. "'Tis time I seek my own bed, Sir Everard. Good eve."

"Baron?"

"Aye?"

"There is one more thing I would tell regarding my sister. She is not Beatrix—in face, figure, or demeanor."

"'Tis as I have heard told."

"I thought you might have." Everard widened his stance. "Still, if you are disappointed when you meet her, I pray you will compose yourself so as not to make your feelings known."

Rancor rising, Christian said, "You make her sound uncomely, Sir Everard—hardly what one expects from a woman's own brother."

The knight's face darkened. "I did not mean to imply my sister is not attractive. My intent was simply to prepare you for one who does not possess the beauty and brightness of Beatrix for which men yearn when they hold Gaenor up against her sister."

Beatrix *was* breathtakingly lovely. Still, Christian had felt little more than concern for her when she had been brought to Broehne Castle barely alive, and grudging admiration when she proved herself innocent of murder. It was different with Gaenor, though he had yet to understand the stirrings felt in her presence that did not seem merely born of desire.

"Of greater hindrance," Sir Everard continued in a slightly more genial voice, "is our oldest sister's ungainly height, which most men find intolerable. Thus, I need not tell you the Godsend it seemed when I met you. Being of a height yourself, Gaenor's size can present no problem."

"A Godsend," Christian murmured, then said, "I thank you for preparing me for our meeting, but you need not worry I will be disappointed, nor that I will allow anything of the sort to reflect upon my face. I am resolved to this marriage, and not grudgingly. Thus, not only will our families have peace, but Lady Gaenor and I are certain to find a fit pleasing to us both."

"I take comfort in that, Baron Lavonne."

Christian looked past the knight and watched as yet another torch was extinguished. Two more and it might prove difficult to negotiate the floor that was fast filling with pages and squires. "Good eve, Sir Everard."

By the light of the single torch set between two men-at-arms posted as sentries, Christian forged a path among the pallets and those sprawled upon them. Shortly, he climbed the stairs and strode the corridor to his chamber. At the door, he paused to consider the chapel that was set in the far bend of the corridor.

She would not be there now, but on the morrow...

6

HE HAD NOT come. He had said he would, but for more than an hour she had sat on the bench waiting for him. Had her eagerness to meet again frightened him away? Like her, he was also betrothed.

With an unutterable sense of loss, Gaenor looked to the altar as she rose to her feet. Though she knew she ought to be grateful the knight had not returned, for it was folly for them to continue to meet when her lot was already cast, resentment welled.

She looked heavenward. "You did this," she whispered, only to squeeze her eyes closed and beg forgiveness. After all, if God was responsible, all He had done was remove temptation—and further heartache. It was for the best. And she must try to be grateful.

In her chamber abovestairs, she closed the door and considered what had become nearly her entire existence these past months. So still. So quiet. So alone. Silence that screamed.

Swallowing to keep emotion from her lips and eyes, she crossed to the bedside table and looked from the embroidered bodice begun too many months past, to the psalter that garnered the least of her attention, to the window that knew her best and from which she watched the days and nights slowly accumulate one atop the other.

She took a step toward the latter, only to turn back and snatch up her psalter. Surely a psalm would offer comfort from this restlessness... this roiling...this terrible yearning for something beyond her reach.

But it was not easy to find relief in the small book, for tucked inside the front cover was a folded piece of parchment that protruded just enough to make it impossible to ignore. She fingered its edges and once more vowed she would burn it. Soon.

"Well done, Baron!"

Perspiration causing his tunic to cling shoulders to hips, Christian stared between met swords into Sir Everard's eyes.

"Well done," the knight said again, then slid his sword off Christian's and sheathed it.

Christian returned his own sword to its scabbard. As he did so, the ruby set in the hilt glinted in the light that slipped through the canopy of leaves. He frowned, only then realizing how much the sky had lightened since he and Sir Everard had entered the wood in the dark of earliest morn. And with that realization came another—Gaenor waited for him, though perhaps no longer.

How many hours had passed since Sir Everard had roused him from his bed and announced they would apply to the wood what had been taught in the darkened cellar? Two? Three? It had to be, and yet it had seemed hardly an hour, so intent had he been on tracking and engaging his opponent. Without the burdensome weight and din of chain mail, the exercise had been exhilarating—a contest of stealth, determination, and will that made him feel young and almost reckless. Unfortunately, it had likely cost him a meeting with Gaenor.

"I am pleased with your progress," Sir Everard said.

"As I am pleased with your instruction. 'Tis far more than I expected."

"Such is the reputation that Wulfen Castle was built upon."

"A well-earned reputation. We are done?"

"For now." Sir Everard wiped a forearm across his brow. "Methinks on the morrow we shall address how well you perform in the saddle." He turned away.

With long strides, Christian drew alongside the knight. "I did not know my horsemanship was in question."

"Only with regards to how well you swing a sword and handle a lance from atop your mount."

"You are proposing I tilt at a quintain?" Were it so, it would be difficult to not take offense, for he had mastered the training device years past.

Sir Everard raised an eyebrow. "If necessary, the quintain, though I had assumed you were skilled at it."

"I am."

"Then we shall tilt at one another."

They did not speak again as they left the wood and strode the meadow toward the castle. Thus, Christian's thoughts turned to whether it was possible Gaenor would wait for him. From the sun's position in the east, it was not likely. Still, upon entering the donjon, he went to the chapel. Though not empty as expected, the one within was not the one he sought.

The priest looked up from where he knelt before the altar and quickly covered his surprise at seeing Christian in the doorway. Starting to rise, he asked, "You seek prayer, my son?"

Christian held up a hand. "Nay, Father. Forgive me for interrupting your time with God." He pulled the door closed. Grudgingly accepting he would have to wait until the morrow, he started toward his chamber. And paused.

He looked over his shoulder down the corridor that ran shorter than the one upon which his own chamber was situated. There were only two doors, but one might belong to Lady Gaenor. And then there was the winding stair at the far end. Might her chamber be in the corner tower?

Remembering when she had told of having watched him at training in the field before the wood, he determined it had to be so, for she would require such a vantage point to see beyond the walls. Too, a tower room would afford her more privacy and make it easier to guard.

That last made him frown, until he reminded himself she'd had no escort when she ventured to the chapel. Though during her first months at Wulfen she must have been kept well under guard, with all that had passed, such measures would no longer be necessary.

Though his belly groaned, there having been no time to break his fast this morn, he moved down the corridor toward the stairs. With each step, he listened for the sound of someone upon them, but it was silent. Twice, the stairs turned upward, and at the first landing was a single door.

Christian looked from it to the next turning of the stairs that led to the tower's roof. Light filtered down from above, evidence that the door overhead had been thrown wide. Was Gaenor up there?

He took the winding stairs two at a time. The light grew brighter and, shortly, he saw sky ahead where the door in the tower roof had been laid back. Hoping he would find Gaenor there, and not another to whom he would have to fabricate a reason for his trespass, he continued upward.

"Do not think I do not appreciate your lack of stealth," Gaenor's voice welcomed him in advance of his appearance.

He stepped up through the hatch, and there she sat with her back against the wall. But she did not see him, her attention turned to the tugging of her skirts down her legs—shapely legs absent hose.

"Had you not taken such pains to alert me," she continued, "I fear you would have found your sister a most wanton sight with her gown down about her shoulders"—she looked up—"and..."

Her eyes widened and smile dissolved.

From where Christian had halted two stairs down from stepping onto the roof, he stared at her. Gaenor *was* pretty. Though most women appeared at their best in dim light that hid their flaws, it did a disservice to the woman before him.

Day's light crowned her bare head, turned through and lightened her dark blonde hair, brushed the tips of her lashes, sparkled in her brown eyes, and fondly touched the bow of her upper lip. Sunlight became her.

"Sir Matthew, I thought you were my brother, Everard."

"My apologies, Lady Gaenor. I did not intend to startle you."

"What are you doing here?"

"Keeping our meeting."

"But our meeting was some hours ago. And you did not come."

"My delay was unavoidable. Could I have sent word, I would have."

Her lids narrowed. "What kept you?"

"Your brother took me to the wood ere dawn that I might demonstrate my ability to detect sound amidst silence."

She lowered her gaze over him. "Only now you are returning?"

"Aye, my lady." He looked down and grimaced at the state of his tunic that bore evidence of his contest in the wood. "When I found you absent from the chapel, I determined to seek you out."

"You should not have."

"And have you, the whole day, believe me incapable of keeping my word?"

A smile crept back onto her lips. "I did think that."

He took the last stairs up to the rooftop but, as he stepped forward, she motioned for him to stay low. "You might be seen!"

It was possible, though only between the notches in the tower wall, as the donjon rose above the outer walls. Still, Christian bent as he crossed to her side. There, he turned his back to the wall and lowered to his haunches.

She looked up at him. "Surely you considered I would be under guard?"

"I did."

"And had I been?"

"My tongue would have had to prove as swift as my sword."

She arched an eyebrow. "You think it possible?"

Christian was surprised by the ease with which laughter rose from him. "I do not. Doubtless, I would find myself dragged before your brothers." Worse, he would be revealed.

Gaenor studied the man whose face was so near, whose unexpected appearance had stolen her breath, whose laughter sent a thrill through her, whose body smelled of salt and steel, who made her fear for a heart already wounded.

Pulling her gaze from his gold-flecked eyes, she looked down. Why did the Lord not deny her this knight's company as she ought to be denied—as she had tried to accept when Sir Matthew had not come to the chapel?

"You have been reading?" he asked.

She glanced at the psalter in her lap and felt a pang at having been caught delving the Lord's word as if in dire need of counsel—which she was. She curled her fingers around the book's thick spine. "Mostly, I have enjoyed the sun."

"I am intrigued, as most ladies eschew the outdoors for fear of freckling. You have no such concern?"

As if freckles would detract from her long face and uneven features...

She looked up and saw he had drawn nearer yet. "Though I would not disappoint you, Sir Matthew, I confess I am not the same as most ladies. I like the sun. Thus, when it deigns to come out from behind the clouds, I seek it—regardless of freckles, regardless of skin that does not gleam like alabaster."

"I am not disappointed, Lady Gaenor. As told, I am intrigued. Indeed, I much prefer the warmth of your skin." He swept fingers across her lower jaw.

I am not breathing. Is he? Drawn to his mouth, Gaenor watched as his smile lowered and lips parted.

"Will you allow it, my lady?"

Do not, a small voice reminded her of the last time she had allowed a man so near. It would be terrible folly to have such pain visited on her again. And it was wrong.

She gripped the psalter tighter. Only a short while ago, she had prayed for the Lord's guidance and now she longed to turn from it. To allow him to kiss her. To sin again.

She met Sir Matthew's gaze and feared she might become lost in those golden flecks. "I cannot, for I am promised to another, as are you. Pray, do not ask me to betray him." *Any more than already I have done.*

"Lady Gaenor"—his fingers curled around her lower arm—"I would—"

She jerked her arm free and sprang to her feet. "Do not ask it of me."

He rose. "My lady, I—"

"Gaenor?" a voice called up the stairs.

She clamped her lips closed against the cry that would have brought Everard bounding to the roof with sword in hand. Desperate to avert disaster, which might have proved mortal had she allowed Sir Matthew to kiss her, she shook her head at the knight, then tucked her psalter against her side and hastened to the hatch. "I am here," she called and stepped onto the first stair.

From half a dozen steps below, her brother peered up at her. "Seeking sun again, eh?" he chided, unaware of the heart that knocked hard upon her breast. "If you are not more mindful, you will turn brown as a nut." He frowned. "You have left your slippers on the roof?"

She had. "Nay," she lied, only then remembering the psalter she held, "my slippers are in my chamber." She took a step down and, as she reached to pull the door closed, glanced over her shoulder at Sir Matthew.

He stood where she had left him, hand on his sword, gaze steady.

Knowing it was likely the last time she would see him, for it was too dangerous to continue to meet, she closed her lids to impress the image of him upon her mind. It was all she would ever have of him.

She looked back around. "You wish to speak to me?"

"I thought you might enjoy a ride."

Though, normally, she would have been flushed with excitement, she felt little more than a dull jolt. Easing the door closed overhead as she began her descent of the stairs, she said, "Most assuredly. Shall we depart anon?" *Pray, let it be now that Sir Matthew might sooner come down.*

"If you are ready." Everard turned and led the way.

Grateful for his back, which allowed her to ease the false smile from her face, she said, "I have but to don my mantle and slippers." As for the latter, it was fortunate she had another pair.

Everard threw open her chamber door and she stepped in ahead of him. Within a quarter hour, they guided their horses toward the wood, and it took all of her will not to look around and search out the tower to see if Sir Matthew watched.

He could have made it right—revealed his identity this day. But Sir Everard had stolen the opportunity, and from Gaenor's response to Christian's desire to kiss her, there would be no more opportunities.

Driven by impulse to do something he should not have attempted, he had frightened her away. But some good had come of it. She had shown herself to be true. Admit it or not, she *had* wanted to kiss him and denied herself so she would not betray her betrothed. That she would not betray *him*.

Hearing the pound of hooves, he stepped into the notch between two embattlements and picked out the riders who headed for the wood—the one on the left undoubtedly Sir Everard, the one on the right, Gaenor, whose hooded mantle hid her woman's figure and hair.

As they entered the wood, Christian looked to the slippers she had left behind and determined he would deliver them to her chamber.

When he stepped into the room where she had spent these past months, he saw it was simply furnished but of good size. Still, it was far from large enough to contain *him* for as long as it had done her. She likely spent a good deal of time on the roof.

He strode across the rush-covered floor and set her slippers on the chest at the foot of the bed. Though it was all he had come to do, he paused and looked closer at the furnishings that might reveal something about Gaenor. However, the only evidence of her occupancy was a side table set with quill, ink pot, parchment, basin, and towel, and a bedside table on which lay a comb, a piece of embroidery, and the psalter she had earlier gripped as if it were life itself.

He stepped toward the latter and drew his fingers across the gilded cover. What had she been reading before his interruption?

He opened to a brightly illuminated page that immediately wafted memories of the monastery where he had bent over parchment to embellish the Lord's word. It was as near as he had come to feeling peace in the Lord's service—an inner calm that assuaged what was too often monotony.

Surprised by a lightening about his heart, he read the first two lines of the psalm, then closed his eyes and drew forth the remainder that was more easily coaxed to mind than expected.

He lifted his lids, flipped forward a dozen pages, and again pulled a psalm from memory. The words were still there. He had but to summon them.

He touched the illumination of King David on his throne, then turned to the front of the psalter. However, it was not a psalm he laid open, but folded parchment spotted where wax had once sealed it against eyes for which it was not intended.

Though Christian knew he should not further trespass, he unfolded it and looked upon bold, black strokes made by a dull quill.

My lady, Gaenor,

I pray one day you will forgive me. ~ Ever your friend, Durand

Christian remembered the knight who had escaped the king's men with Gaenor and delivered her to Wulfen Castle—the same who had later accompanied Baron Wulfrith to Broehne Castle to attend Lady Beatrix's trial. Forgive him? For what?

He had paid the knight little heed other than to be offended by his presence when Baron Wulfrith brought him along to discuss the proposal Christian had put to him—in exchange for the Wulfriths yielding up Lady Gaenor without further defiance of the king's decree, Christian would supply testimony to aid Lady Beatrix at trial.

Remembering the seething Sir Durand who had stood behind the baron, gaze wrathful, face flushed, teeth bared, Christian wondered if he was the one to whom Gaenor had given her heart. The one whose own heart lay elsewhere.

He read again the words that beseeched her forgiveness. Because Sir Durand had not returned her feelings? Because he had rejected her?

It seemed to fit, especially as she had retained the letter and the parchment was worn as if often handled. Indeed, rather than a psalm, perhaps it was this letter over which she had been poring when he had found her on the roof.

Jealousy gripped him. If Sir Durand was the one who held her heart, might he be the reason she refused Christian's kiss, rather than fear of betrayal?

The crackle of parchment brought him back from the unfamiliar edge upon which he found himself, and he saw he had crumpled the edges. With a grunt of disgust, he returned the parchment to the psalter, snapped the book closed, and stalked out of the chamber.

Telling himself it was good that he and Lady Gaenor would not meet again until her sister's wedding and that he did not care how she received him when he was revealed, he shortly found himself tilting at a quintain on the training field.

Time and again, he landed his lance center of the stuffed knight that sought to come about quickly enough to knock him from his mount. But not once did his silent opponent find its mark.

7

It was foolish of her, but as it was three days since last she had seen Sir Matthew on the roof, she had given in to the impulse upon catching sight of him as he struck out across the field. Though only twice before had she stolen from the castle to the wood, she once more risked her brothers' wrath and slipped out the sally port amid the lengthening shadows of day's end.

Guessing it was the stream Sir Matthew sought in order to cleanse away the day's training, she edged around the outer wall, gripped the hood beneath her chin lest it fall, and ran for the trees.

Though she could not be certain, no alarm sounded from the walls as her long legs carried her across the tall grass. Of course, as she knew from her months in the tower, Wulfen's young men sometimes sought the wood the same as Sir Matthew. Providing it was not done under cover of night, they usually went unchallenged.

Reaching the cover of the trees where Sir Matthew had passed a short while ago, she paused to catch her breath. Though it was darker beneath the canopy of leaves, it was not yet so dark she could not see a good distance ahead. Still, she pulled her meat dagger as she ventured forward.

Minutes later, she heard the softly rippling stream. She searched for movement among the trees that she might alert Sir Matthew to her presence should he prove unfit for her company, but all was still.

At the bank of the stream, she looked in both directions. Had he gone farther downstream? Upstream toward the falls? Unfortunately, the dimming sky told that she would be foolish to continue on.

Resigned to returning to the castle, she bent, scooped up a handful of water, and wet her mouth.

"It seems this time 'tis *you* who seeks *me*," a voice sounded from the left.

Nearly choking on the water, she thrust to her feet and swung around to face Sir Matthew where he stood alongside a tree twenty feet downstream. Fair hair clinging to his head, damp tunic evidencing it had been pulled over a wet body, sword in hand telling the fate of any who might attempt to steal upon him with ill intent, he stared at her.

"I neither saw nor heard you."

He smiled tightly. "Then Sir Everard is to be commended for teaching me well." He reached down, retrieved his belt, and strapped it on. After returning his sword to its scabbard, he strode forward.

Senses straining toward this man she *had* sought out, Gaenor returned her dagger to her girdle.

Sir Matthew halted before her. "This is most unexpected, Lady Gaenor."

His tone was different, unlike their previous meetings when he had seemed pleased to see her. Was he angry? These past days, had he awaited her in the chapel she had avoided?

"I thought it best that we not meet again," she said. "Thus, I stayed away from the chapel."

"As did I."

Embarrassment heated her cheeks. "Then we were of the same mind."

"I still am, Lady Gaenor. You should not have followed me."

"This I know, but when I saw you go to the wood, I..." She drew a deep breath. "I wanted to see you one last time ere I depart Wulfen."

"Why?"

The question was so curt, she snapped, "Truly, I do not know."

"Do you not?"

Though she longed to salvage any pride that might be left to her, she did not turn away. What harm to tell him the truth? It was not as if she would see him again once she left Wulfen, and it *would* unburden her. Too, if he had similar feelings and declared them, it would be something for her to hold onto in the dark days ahead. "Aye, I know the reason I sought you out."

He arched an eyebrow.

"I feel something for you that I should not, Sir Matthew, and with a foolish heart, I wished to feel it one last time."

Though she expected her honesty to soften him, his jaw remained hard. "You speak of the same foolish heart given to a man who does not return your feelings?"

Were his words of iron, rather than air, she would have bled. What had she done to incur such wrath from a man who had first offended by listening in on her prayers? Who had first sought her out? And had continued to seek her out? She had but refused his kiss as a lady should, especially one betrothed to another.

She raised her chin. "The same foolish heart that seeks a kiss it refused three days past."

Christian stared at her. Though he had hoped it was her reason for coming to the wood, he had not expected her to admit it. "What of this other man who claims your heart?"

A smile, bordering on winter, touched her lips. "One does not lay claim to what one does not desire, Sir Matthew."

"You play with words, Lady Gaenor."

"So I do."

Holding his arms at his sides, Christian said, "Thus?"

She sighed. "I have determined to take back my heart, and upon my word, I shall."

Warring over relief that the specter between him and his future wife might meet its end, and regret that his deception was becoming increasingly difficult to explain away, he said, "What of your betrothed? Might he then claim your heart?"

Her gaze faltered. "I shall wed the baron as is required of me, just as you shall wed your betrothed as is required of you, Sir Matthew."

"And if I did not—and you did not?" he asked, only to inwardly groan as his deception dug deeper. Now, when he had her to himself and there were no others she could place as a barrier between him and her outrage, he ought to tell her the truth. And he might have had she not dropped her hood to reveal the fall of her hair. Since only a fool would choose her anger over a taste of her mouth, especially as his deception was so dire it surely could get no worse, he drew her near.

"Later we will speak of stealing me away." Her breath fanned his lips. "Now I would have that kiss."

Ignoring the voice that urged him not to postpone the inevitable, he bent his head.

Gaenor's lips were soft and willing, and yet uncertain as if hers was an untried mouth. He was relieved, for though Sir Durand might possess her heart, that was surely all he had gained. Gaenor Wulfrith, soon Gaenor Lavonne, was his. Somewhere in the days remaining before their departure from Wulfen, he would find the right moment to tell her all.

As the kiss deepened, so did the vibration beneath their feet until it was impossible to ignore the riders who rushed across the land toward Wulfen Castle.

Christian lifted his head and glanced at a sky that was fast running toward night. "Riders."

Lips moist, cheeks flushed, Gaenor said, "You know who comes?"

"Nay, though there is urgency to their ride." Liking the feel of her, knowing too soon he must release her, he tightened his hold. "We should return."

"Aye." Still, she did not draw back.

Christian pulled a hand up her side, over her shoulder, and cupped her chin. "On the morrow, will you come to me again—here, in the wood, this same time?"

"I shall be here."

He brushed his mouth across hers. "We will speak then of how I plan to steal you away." And he *would* steal her away if it was required—at least, until she was reconciled to his deception. He released her. "Let us make haste."

Neither spoke as they negotiated the undergrowth, trees, and shadows. At the edge of the wood, Christian motioned her to go ahead of him.

Dusk upon her face, she said, "On the morrow," and dragged the hood over her head and set off across the field.

When she slipped through the sally port, Christian exited the wood and began planning how he would tell her the truth.

On the morrow he would do it, or the day after, or the day after that, but he *would* tell her before either of them left Wulfen Castle.

"We must depart this eve," Sir Hector said.

Girding the tidings like the oppressive weight it was meant it to be, Christian considered the older knight who, above all, had proved loyal to him these past years. "Aye, this eve," he said, the hope he had felt with Gaenor a half hour past strewn in the dirt of his illegitimate brother's escape from prison and the attack upon Broehne Castle—an attack that had left three men-at-arms dead, a half dozen injured, and his infirm father removed.

Of course, he would be a fool to think Aldous had not gone willingly. Not a day passed that the old baron did not curse Christian for throwing the dagger that had injured Robert and seen him imprisoned for his attempt on Lady Beatrix's life. Even he blamed Christian for his eldest heir's death, though he could not know how near the blame truly lay.

"I will have my squire gather your belongings," Sir Everard said.

Christian looked to where his host stood at the center of the solar in which he had received Sir Hector and two other knights. He nearly accepted Wulfrith's offer of his squire but realized it was his only opportunity to seek out Gaenor abovestairs and reveal himself. "I shall collect my belongings myself."

Sir Everard inclined his head. "As you will. I will see that your men are given food and drink while you are about it."

Christian crossed to the curtains that separated the solar from the great hall. As he neared, Sir Abel, who had stood silent throughout the telling of Broehne's misfortune, swept the curtain aside to allow Christian to pass into the hall where the supper meal was being served.

Christian met his gaze as he strode past and guessed the darkness in the knight's eyes was concern for his sister who was to wed into the unrest that had torn through the heart of the barony of Abingdale.

Gaenor will be safe, Christian silently vowed. He would hunt down Robert and the other disaffected knights and men-at-arms ejected from the barony following the attempt on Lady Beatrix's life. And he would not be alone in bringing down the brigands, for the king also sought them. Imprisonment would not be his illegitimate brother's lot this time. Indeed, mortal punishment would more likely be meted out to one who had made a mockery of the king's prison.

Christian passed through the din of the hall and ascended the stairs. On the landing, he paused to subdue his anger and set his mind on the woman to whom he should have already revealed the truth. This, minutes ere his departure, was the penalty for disregarding his God-given conscience.

"Lord," he murmured as he strode past his chamber toward the chapel and the corridor beyond, "let me be well received. Give me the words—"

"Always I marvel at how tragedy and pestilent circumstances so quickly return a man to God," a voice broke upon his back.

Christian halted and stared at the door Sir Abel thought was his destination. Hardly able to believe he had been granted such grace, he turned to the knight who stood on the landing, the darkness in his eyes visible even at a distance.

"Mayhap for this we are made to suffer such tragedy." Christian was surprised at how easily he formed the words. "Darkness ere light."

"As well I know."

He did, as revealed by his brother, Everard. Wondering how far from God Sir Abel had strayed before his unfortunate marriage, and how near his own tragedy had caused him to return to the divine, Christian said, "There is something you wish to discuss?"

Sir Abel strode forward and threw open the door to Christian's chamber. "I would speak of my sister."

Realizing the opportunity to meet with Gaenor was slipping away—indeed, *had* slipped away—Christian's insides churned. There was no time to satisfy Sir Abel's demand for an audience and also seek out his betrothed who believed he would be at the stream on the morrow.

Reconciled to it, though it was one of the hardest things he had ever had to accept, Christian stepped into his chamber ahead of Sir Abel and turned to face him. "What of Lady Gaenor?"

The knight closed the door behind him. "I would know how you intend to keep her from your brother and father who will surely turn their vengeance upon her once she resides at Broehne Castle."

Christian planted his legs apart. "Be assured, Sir Abel, my wife will be safe within my walls."

"As safe as your men who fell to the brigands on the night past?"

It was a valid concern, but it chafed, for Christian had been certain he had left the castle well defended. Of course, the absence of two men-at-arms was surely the means by which Robert and his brigands had gained entrance. Despite having dismissed men from his service months past, it seemed he had not uprooted all who stood against him. Might his father have recruited the missing men-at-arms during Christian's training at Wulfen? Might there be more? If so, how was he to route them out?

"Naught to say?"

Christian returned Sir Abel to focus. "'Tis true ill has fallen upon Abingdale, but I give my word it shall be resolved such that it will not touch your sister."

The knight took a step toward him. "Your word is all you can give?" He gave a short laugh. "The word of a Lavonne?"

This time, it was Christian who took a step forward. Bristling with anger born of the attack on Broehne, the death of his men, and the frustration of being thwarted in speaking with Gaenor one last time, he bit, "I give you the word of Christian Lavonne, and that shall suffice."

The knight, less than two inches shorter than he, drew himself taller. "It is not enough. Grant me a delay in your marriage until the matter of the attack on Abingdale is resolved, and I give you *my* word I will speak no more against this union."

It was a tempting offer, for Christian wearied of Sir Abel's opposition, but he shook his head. "Though I would have your support of my marriage, there has been too much delay already. To allow more would grant my brother another victory."

Grudgingly, the knight inclined his head. "Then it seems I shall fear for my soul."

"Your soul?"

He smiled grimly. "If anything happens to my sister, I shall surely break one of God's commandments."

Christian had no doubt which one it would be. Still, the threat against his life did not sting as sharply as it should, for it told that Sir Abel truly cared for his sister, and he could not fault him for that. "It would be deserved," he acceded.

Surprise glinted in the knight's eyes, but he blinked it away. "We should make haste, for night is upon us and we have many hours of riding ahead."

"We, Sir Abel?"

"Like it or nay, I give you my services to hunt down this miscreant brother of yours."

Argument—alongside pride—rose in Christian, but reason won out. Though he did not doubt he could bring down Robert, Sir Abel was among the worthiest warriors and would be of certain benefit.

"I do not like it," Christian said, "but I accept your offer."

"'Twas not an offer."

Christian stayed his hands from gathering into fists. "Aye, it was, Sir *Knight*." A reminder of the rank and privilege Christian enjoyed over him.

The tension between them strained, but after some moments, Sir Abel shrugged. "If 'tis as you wish to believe, so be it."

Denying himself the satisfaction of landing a blow, Christian strode to his chest.

Ten minutes later, he returned to the hall, all hope of meeting with Gaenor trampled beneath her brother's meddling. Forced to content himself with requesting a private audience with her before her sister's wedding, he, his men, and Sir Abel rode into the dark of night.

8

Stern Castle, July 1157

IT HAD ONLY been a kiss, and not her first, but she remembered it as she did not remember Sir Durand's—even though twice now in as many days she had seen that particular knight. Just as she had seen the anguish in his eyes each time they settled upon Beatrix.

Battling bitterness, Gaenor looked to her sister whose head was bent to the embroidery she worked upon the gown she would don to speak vows with Michael D'Arci on the morrow.

Gaenor did not begrudge Beatrix the happiness she deserved, but she ached to have a man look at her as Beatrix's betrothed—and Sir Durand—looked at the youngest Wulfrith daughter. More, to have a man look at her as Sir Matthew had looked at her.

He had not returned to the stream. In all the days before her departure for Stern Castle, he had not sought her out. It was as if he had left Wulfen Castle. And she told herself it was surely what had transpired, that the riders who had descended on Wulfen Castle had come for him. But try though she did to convince herself his departure was not of his choosing, she had dredged up the real reason for his absence and finally accepted it. Her talk of stealing her away had made him leave. Doubtless, the more he thought on it, the more he realized the mistake of denying the Wulfriths what they wanted. Thus, this day, sometime before the nooning hour, Gaenor would finally meet the man she would wed.

She started to clench her hands, only to realize she yet held her brother's infant son. She looked down, and all that had darkened her world seemed to lighten as she gazed into the little one's ruddy face. Sucking on the fist shoved against his mouth, he smiled at her amid drool that ringed his lips and wet his hand.

How I want this. How I want to hold my own babe near my heart. And with the arrival of Baron Lavonne this day, it was possible. Within a year, she might have a child of her own. Pity that it was not as simple as that.

"You see how s-simple 'tis?" Beatrix asked, her words and faltering speech jolting Gaenor. Though Beatrix was much recovered from the head injury sustained months past during Gaenor's attempt to escape marriage, enough of the injury remained as proof of her sacrifice.

Smiling wide, Beatrix lifted her face to Garr's wife who bent near. "I could teach you."

Annyn, who had set aside her book to watch the intricate pattern of vining leaves emerge along the sleeve's edge, exclaimed, "Ah, nay!" and sat back in her chair as if fearful Beatrix might press a needle upon her. "Truly, I am content to watch."

"Content, ha! You are restless. I know. After all, I also have ears to hear the..." Her lids fluttered as she sought the word. "...sword practice in yon bailey."

Annyn sighed. "I am restless, but I assure you, needle and thread will only make it worse."

"And I assure you, that I already knew."

They smiled at each other, and Gaenor realized this was something else she wanted—the ease of friendship. Though she had come to accept and even care for her warrior sister-in-law, her relationship with Annyn lacked the depth that Beatrix enjoyed. And it was no one's fault but Gaenor's.

Lord, why am I so difficult? Why can I not be more like Annyn? Or Beatrix? Was it You who formed me this way?

Movement drew her gaze, and she watched as her mother, Lady Isobel, turned from the window before which she had stood this past half hour watching for the arrival of Christian Lavonne. As stiffly erect as ever, despite the back pain she increasingly suffered, she crossed the solar to where Gaenor sat opposite Beatrix and Annyn.

"Our little one is awake, hmm?" She settled a hand on her eldest daughter's shoulder.

Gaenor nodded. "He is." Which was as she preferred. Sleeping children were beautiful, but those awake and in motion were truly a sight to behold.

"Let us set him in his cradle that we may make you ready," Lady Isobel said.

Ready for Christian Lavonne. As her mother bent to lift the babe, Gaenor said, "I am presentable."

Almost on level with her daughter, Lady Isobel glanced at Gaenor's bodice that bore evidence of the babe's teething. "Surely a fresh gown of finer cloth is fitting for such an occasion." She raised an eyebrow, then considered her daughter's hair, much of which her grandson had caused to escape the braid that hung over her shoulder. "Your hair would be lovely plaited and turned 'round your head."

Gaenor's first impulse was to refuse, but she knew her mother was as set against marriage to a Lavonne as was her daughter. Still, she had resolved to make the best of it. As Gaenor yet aspired to do.

"Aye, let us make ready." Gaenor rose and crossed to the cradle alongside her sister-in-law. As she lowered the little one, he made a burble of protest and snatched at her hair.

"I will take him." Annyn held out her arms.

Her son swung his head toward her and squealed. A moment later, he happily slipped into his mother's arms.

Feeling empty again, Gaenor straightened.

"Nurturing comes easily to you," Annyn said. "Certes, you shall make a fine mother one day, Gaenor."

Though her words were meant to encourage, they panged, for Gaenor knew God might also deny her this. Should she prove barren, what was left to her over the long, tedious days while breath yet filled her lungs?

"You would like me to also assist, Gaenor?" Beatrix asked, setting aside her gown.

And once more suffer her sister's talk of Christian Lavonne, her assurances and numbering of the man's qualities? "Nay, you will only fuss over me, and I am in no mood for it. 'Tis more important that your gown be ready for the morrow."

"You are c-certain?"

"I am." Gaenor turned from the concerned look Beatrix exchanged with Annyn and preceded her mother from the solar.

The preparations for the meeting with Christian Lavonne took more time than they should have, and when Gaenor finally stood from the chair on which she had perched while her mother crowned her head in braids, she felt as if released from a trap.

"Turn," Lady Isobel instructed.

Gaenor swept all the way around, then smoothed the silken material of her skirts. "Will I shame my family or not?"

Her mother winced, and Gaenor felt a slap of remorse. "You are lovely, daughter. Any man would be pleased to take you to wife."

Gaenor did not know whether to laugh or snap at so ridiculous a claim.

Neither, for either would cause pain. Thus, she bit her tongue against pointing out that those to whom she had previously been betrothed had *not* been pleased upon meeting her. Though most betrothals, once made, were kept regardless of the feelings of the two forced into a life together, *hers* had been broken.

As if aware of her daughter's thoughts, Lady Isobel looked away. "Let us go belowstairs."

Despite Gaenor's resentment at being displayed, she nodded.

As she and her mother stepped off the stairs into the hall, her brother, Garr, entered the great room. As the renowned warrior strode the rushes with long-reaching legs that reminded Gaenor of Sir Matthew, she ached anew.

Not until Garr halted before them did Gaenor notice the parchment he carried. And knew what it was. "He is not coming," she said.

With a tight, remorseful smile, Garr inclined his head. "Baron Lavonne tells that he has been delayed and sends his regrets."

"When might we expect him?" Lady Isobel's level voice did a fine job of covering her frustration.

"Mayhap on the morrow, more likely the day after."

His mother's mouth tightened. "The day after Beatrix's wedding."

Garr offered his sister the parchment. "Be assured, Gaenor, the baron's delay was unavoidable."

She unrolled the missive. The bold stroke of Christian Lavonne's quill, had he wielded it himself, told no more than what her brother had told, though he did request a private audience with her upon his arrival. "He does not say the reason for the delay, though you seem to know it."

"'Tis naught you need worry over."

And that was all he would tell. Gaenor returned her gaze to the writing, paused over the name scrawled at the bottom, and let the missive roll back on itself. "It is as it is."

Garr laid a hand on her arm. "I am sorry. I had hoped you and the baron would have more time to become acquainted ere your own wedding."

As had she, but did it matter? Indeed, she ought to consider it a reprieve, perhaps the last she would have.

She pushed a smile onto her lips. "In a lifetime, what does one day matter? Or two? They are just days."

A struggle rose on Garr's face such as she had only seen when he had been forced to decide between fealty to the man who would be king and love of Annyn. And it gave Gaenor pause. Was his struggle the evidence she had sought since her return to Stern Castle? Evidence he *did* care for her? If so, there was solace in it, for it meant he would not wed her to a man who would treat her ill—that though he wanted peace, a sacrifice he would not make of her. Dare she believe Christian Lavonne was as Garr and the others told?

Believe.

It was hard, but she determined she would, and the weight upon her lightened slightly.

She stepped forward and pressed her lips to Garr's cheek. "All is well, Brother. Think on it no more." She looked to her mother. "Shall we collect my niece and go to the garden?"

The worry in Lady Isobel's eyes waned. "It seems a good way to pass the hour."

Shortly, Gaenor, her mother, and Garr and Annyn's three-year-old daughter lay on their backs exclaiming over the pictures that God formed from the clouds.

9

"You are happy," Gaenor mused.

Beatrix smiled. "I am very happy."

"Then I rejoice with you." Gaenor looked out across the hall. "Married..." As she herself would soon be. "Michael seems a good man." She settled her gaze on him where he stood in the midst of the celebration alongside her second brother, Everard, who laughed at something Garr said. Then the entire group was laughing, including Annyn who cradled her infant son.

Beatrix sighed. "Aye, Michael is a good man."

Gaenor laid a hand over her sister's. "You are most blessed."

"As you shall be."

Gaenor laughed and hated that it sounded forced. "You have to say that to me," she said, trying to tease away the uncertainty that had attempted to gain a foothold on her since her witnessing of Beatrix and Michael D'Arci's vows.

"Aye, but it is also true." Beatrix leaned toward her. "Christian Lavonne—"

"Did not come." No sooner were the words spoken than Gaenor regretted her sharp tone.

After a long moment, Beatrix said, "Tell me of your stay at Wulfen Castle."

"As already told, our brother, Everard, mostly kept me confined to a tower room in the donjon."

"Then you saw no men other than our brother and the knights a-assigned to your needs?"

Gaenor averted her gaze. "From my window, I sometimes watched the young men train."

"Hmm. Methinks you are not telling all."

Hating how perceptive Beatrix was, Gaenor weighed the risk of revealing her meetings with Sir Matthew. In the end, she said, "'Tis true, but naught can come of what I do not tell."

"Mayhap I can help."

"You cannot. Regardless of my own wishes, I shall soon wed Baron Lavonne."

Beatrix moved nearer. "Is there someone else? Another you would wed?"

Gaenor startled and immediately tried to disguise her reaction with a shrug. "I did meet a knight at Wulfen, but I hardly know him well enough to wish marriage."

"How well *do* you know him?"

"We...talked. In the chapel. That is where I met him."

Beatrix made a sound of surprise. "Surely you were not allowed to attend mass with the men?"

"Of course not. I went only after they were done that I might have the chapel to myself."

"Then how—?"

"He was there one day when I thought myself alone."

"When he should have been training pages and squires?"

Gaenor shook her head. "He was not one of our brother's men. He was a visiting knight."

"Truly? How long did he visit?"

Beginning to wish she had not confided, Gaenor said, "More than a month, though I did not meet him until a fortnight past."

"For what purpose was he at Wulfen?"

"Abel and Everard were training him."

"A knight?" Beatrix exclaimed. "A man who has already earned his spurs?"

She should have said naught.

As if sensing Gaenor's unease, Beatrix said, "Of course, you are surely relieved to be returned to Stern Castle."

Gaenor lifted her goblet and sipped at the warm wine.

"Wulfen Castle must have been t-t-" Beatrix's search for the word caused Gaenor to wince. "It must have been tedious."

Gaenor lowered the goblet. "Do you forgive me, Beatrix?"

"For what?"

"For the ill words I spoke the day King Henry delivered his decree that a Wulfrith wed a Lavonne and it was determined that I would be the one? More, for what happened to you—what would not have happened had you not drawn the king's men away from me and Sir Durand?"

"Gaenor—"

"I thought I would die when I saw you in the ravine and realized what you had sacrificed to save me."

Beatrix recaptured her sister's hand. "There is naught to forgive. You were hurting when you said what you did and never would I fault you. As for what happened to me, had I to do it again, I would, for it gave me Michael."

Slowly, Gaenor's tension eased. "God favors you, Beatrix. You must please Him mightily. If only I knew Him as you do, perhaps I might better face what lies in wait for me."

With soft eyes, Beatrix said, "You can know God as I do. You have but to let Him in."

"It is not so simple."

"'Tis far from simple, but still a-attainable."

Gaenor looked across the hall to the group that included their mother, Garr, and Everard—and from which Abel was conspicuously absent. She had not been surprised when he had not presented at Stern for the wedding, for it had surely been determined that one of the

Wulfrith brothers remain at Wulfen Castle to oversee the training. Still, she was disappointed.

A moment later, the one Gaenor sought joined the group. As Sir Durand had done at the chapel where Beatrix and Michael had exchanged vows, he brooded. Not that it surprised, for any remaining hope he might have had for claiming Beatrix as his own was stamped out by her marriage.

Though Gaenor did not want to feel for him, she did, despite all that had happened between them. And remembrance of her sin made her wonder if it was possible to know God as Beatrix knew Him. *Was* such a relationship attainable?

She sighed. "Attainable even when one has sinned greatly?"

Beatrix considered her a long moment. "Whatever you have done, you have but to ask for forgiveness and it will be granted."

As guilt and embarrassment flushed Gaenor, the musicians once more began to play for the wedding guests. Hoping to lighten the mood, Gaenor quipped, "And if I ask Him to deliver me free of marriage to Baron Lavonne, will that also be granted?"

"If it is in His will."

"Always His will, which means I shall wed Lavonne—unless the baron determines he does not want me. Which is possible." And it was, though to seek such means of escaping marriage would bring great shame on her family. Gaenor rose, glanced at the gathering, then bent and kissed Beatrix's brow. "God willing, I shall one day see through the eyes of love as you do, little sister."

"I am certain you shall."

"Now"—Gaenor summoned a smile—"I am going to dance at my sister's wedding."

Though the knight who held out a hand to pull her amid the dancers was not as tall as she, he turned her about the floor with ease. And for some minutes, Gaenor lost herself in the music that played through her body and caused her feet to step lightly. Indeed, at one point she felt as if she were flying.

It was then Sir Durand appeared. The household knight, being of lower rank, relinquished Gaenor before she could protest.

Finding her hand and waist gripped by a man she had vowed to never again allow so near, Gaenor glared at him where he stood two inches shorter than she. "I do not wish to dance with you, Sir Durand."

His mouth was a severe line. "There is a matter of import we must needs discuss."

"Here?"

"Elsewhere if you will allow it." He turned her in time with the lively music.

"I will not."

"Then here it must be."

He turned her again, and she realized he had worked her from the middle of the dance floor to the edge where it was less likely they would be overheard.

"Do tell, that we might be done with this farce, Sir Durand."

"I would steal you away."

She stumbled, and only his hand on her waist prevented her from landing at his feet. "What?"

"I would see you free of this marriage into which you are being forced."

"Why?"

"You are being sacrificed."

As she had believed but had endeavored to disprove to herself.

"I cannot bear it," he said.

This time, she did laugh. "Nay, Sir Durand, you cannot bear that my sister is wed to another. *That* you cannot bear. And now, when you find all is lost, you come to me resolved to contenting yourself with mere leavings."

His face hardened. "'Tis more than that."

"Then now that my sister is wed to Michael D'Arci, you realize you *do* have feelings for me. You *do* love me?"

"That would be a lie, but I care—"

"Care! Methinks I shall take my chances that my betrothed will come to care for me and that I will not suffer his anguish over a lost love." At least, she prayed she would not suffer so, for it was true she knew little about the baron. All she knew of Christian Lavonne's past was that he had been a monk previous to gaining his inheritance. Meaning, she hoped, he had not set his heart elsewhere.

Sir Durand tightened his hold on her. "He is a Lavonne, Gaenor."

"That he is, but different from the others." As she had been told numerous times—and longed to believe.

"Nay, he is as deceptive and dangerous as his father and brothers whose blood runs through his veins."

"How do you know this?" she demanded as her skirts brushed against those of another lady. "You have not—"

"But I have. Do you recall, I was at Broehne Castle during your sister's trial."

"Even so—"

"Listen to me. When your brother was summoned by Christian Lavonne ere the trial, I accompanied him."

The baron had summoned Garr? "Aye?"

"Do you wish to know the bargain struck between them?"

Again, her feet faltered.

"In exchange for testimony of Beatrix's innocence from the baron's man—a knight who knew the truth of the one your sister was told to have murdered—Christian Lavonne demanded that your brother accede to the king's decree and hand you over."

Like chattel.

"Your brother agreed. For Beatrix."

Beloved Beatrix. Trying not to resent the sister she loved, Gaenor reasoned that Garr had been given little choice. Refuse and cost Beatrix her life? Or accept and cost Gaenor her happiness? Providing, of course, Sir Durand spoke true. And she prayed he did not for what it also told of Christian Lavonne. It did not fit that the man who was said to be honorable—different from his father and brothers—would bargain so. And with Beatrix's life.

Gaenor shook her head. "I do not believe you. Christian Lavonne saved my sister's life and proved himself a man of—"

"Proved himself?" Color seeped into Sir Durand's cheeks. "By throwing a dagger that wounded his illegitimate brother, a man for whom he cares nothing, who stands against him? *That* is proving himself? Nay, Gaenor, you have been betrayed." He stepped back, and only then did she realize they had ceased dancing.

From where he had guided her away from the others, she stared at him.

"Think on it," he rasped, "and if you weary of being made to play the pawn and desire a life of your own choosing, I shall be at the sally port come midnight. Otherwise, I will not see you again, for I am bound for France."

Insides crawling with uncertainty, sorrow, pain, and anger, all of which she told herself she should not feel, Gaenor watched him go—a man who had offered comfort when she had believed Beatrix had died for her. For whom she had felt deeply. Who cared enough to deliver her from the obligation her family pressed on her, thereby breaking fealty with the Wulfriths as few dared to do.

Realizing she was staring at the emptiness left by his departure and that it would draw attention, Gaenor composed her face and turned to those who stepped to the music. There was Beatrix and her Michael, faces reflecting the love they shared. Love that Gaenor desperately wanted to experience herself.

Though she knew she should not do it, she could not help but ponder whether Sir Durand might come to feel something for her like what Michael felt for Beatrix. However, almost immediately, the memory of Sir Matthew returned, and she shivered as she recalled his kiss.

He had felt for her, though to what extent she had not had the opportunity to explore. Of course, considering he had disappeared following her suggestion that he steal her away, his feelings could not have been very deep. Regardless, Sir Matthew *was* lost to her, just as Sir Durand would be lost to her on the morrow if she remained true to the family that had bargained her away.

Anger tied a knot in Gaenor's belly and, despite her attempt to loosen it, it knotted again. And again until she thought she might scream if she did not escape the joyous voices and peals of laughter.

As she grabbed up her skirts and turned toward the stairs, her gaze fell upon Annyn who stood on the far side of the hall. The frown furrowing her lovely brow told that she had witnessed Gaenor's dejection. Had she also seen the encounter with Sir Durand?

Knowing that if she did not allay her sister-in-law's concern, the woman would attempt to engage her, Gaenor forced a smile. Annyn's frown eased, though not entirely.

Longing for solitude but fearing an abrupt withdrawal would result in attention she could not bear, Gaenor forced herself to return to the dais.

As she sat there, blindly observing the merriment that knew every corner save hers, one word turned through her again and again: midnight.

10

"GAENOR IS GONE."

The anguish in his mother's voice striking Garr ahead of her words, he looked up from the journal he had been poring over while awaiting Baron Lavonne's arrival, tidings of which had been delivered a quarter hour past. "What do you mean, Mother?"

Lady Isobel, accompanied by his wife, crossed the hall and ascended the dais. "When I went to her chamber to make her ready as you asked, I found it empty."

"You have looked in the garden?"

"Aye. I even sent out servants to search the inner and outer baileys to see if she had taken herself to the falconry or stables, but she is not to be found. She is gone—has once more fled the marriage you press upon her."

How long gone? When Gaenor had not come belowstairs for the breaking of fast two hours past, he had thought little of it, for there had been many faces absent following the wedding feast that had lasted past the middling of night. At least two hours gone, then, likely more.

Gathering a deep breath to calm his fear for his sister, Garr pushed back his chair and stood. "Where might she have gone?"

His mother shook her head. "I do not know."

"Summon Sir Durand," Annyn said. "Methinks he may know something of her disappearance."

"Why Durand?"

"On the night past, I witnessed an exchange between him and your sister. Though I was too distant to hear what was said, both appeared disturbed by the encounter."

Annyn was too wise for Garr to not find merit in her observation. He motioned a man-at-arms forward who shortly hastened from the hall to search out Sir Durand, as well as Everard.

Garr was not surprised when only his brother appeared amid preparations to arrest Gaenor's flight. Though the blind might not know of Sir Durand's feelings for Beatrix or his anguish over her marriage to Michael, all others knew. Only a few, however, were aware of Gaenor's feelings for the knight who had delivered her safe to Wulfen Castle the first time she had fled Christian Lavonne.

Months past, when Garr had arrived at Wulfen and found Sir Durand had been given charge of her, he had noted the way Gaenor looked at him and how her face flushed when the knight was near. He had not thought much on it, knowing Sir Durand could not return her feelings with his heart bound elsewhere, but now...

What else was there to conclude but that Sir Durand, aware of Gaenor's feelings and openly disaffected as he was with the Wulfriths' decision to allow the marriage between her and Christian Lavonne, had forsaken his fealty and offered to aid in her escape?

"What goes?" Everard asked as he strode across the hall. "Why is your man searching out Sir Durand?"

"To confirm 'twas he who took Gaenor from Stern." Garr met his gaze over the bent head of his squire who adjusted his chain mail tunic.

Everard's stride faltered. "What?"

"Leave us," Garr ordered his squire. When the young man departed, Garr stepped before his brother. "It would appear Sir Durand has taken Gaenor."

"Abducted her?"

"Methinks she went willingly, that she accepted his aid to once more flee Lavonne."

Everard grunted and thrust a hand over his shaved pate. "What hope can Durand have of secreting our sister when the king will soon enough set men after him and all of England will know what he has done?"

"No hope, which is why he will take her to France where he has family."

Everard was silent for some moments, then said, "Mayhap we ought to let her go, Garr. She does not wish to wed Lavonne—"

"And neither does Durand wish to wed her," Garr spoke more harshly than intended. "We must bring her back, not only for *her* well-being, but our family's. Too often I have pushed the king too far, and Henry will surely see this as yet another act of defiance. He will tolerate no more, Everard. You know it to be so."

Grudgingly, Everard nodded.

"So we ride and bring her back ere more damage is done," Garr continued, "ere Baron Lavonne—"

"He has come, Garr. Even as I was summoned from the outer bailey, the baron rode upon Stern. Likely, he and Abel are now within the walls."

Though Garr allowed no words to pass his lips that would be displeasing to God, his tongue was tempted as it had not been in a long time. The plan to set after Gaenor and Sir Durand before the baron's arrival shattered, he said, "Then it seems they will be joining our search."

Everard caught his arm. "'Tis possible that when Lavonne learns what has passed," he said slowly with the turning of his thoughts, "he will defy the king's decree and forsake a union with our family. After all, twice now our sister has run from him, and this time with a man who was not given charge over her by our family."

Aye, though Sir Durand had been her escort all those months past, it was Lady Isobel who had set him the task of seeing her daughter safe to Wulfen Castle. This was different. The knight had defiantly spirited her away. Thus, what else was there for Christian Lavonne to conclude than that Sir Durand and Gaenor were lovers?

Garr ground his teeth. "The baron can certainly make a case for rejecting her. And 'tis possible King Henry will concede, as a man can only be expected to tolerate such behavior so many times before being released from his obligation. Unfortunately, if he refuses Gaenor, the king will extract some price for finding himself once more thwarted. It would not surprise me if he punishes our sister by wedding her to some wretched old man who will make misery of her days."

Frustration flickered in Everard's eyes. "Then mayhap we should allow her to escape to France."

Garr stared at his stalwart brother who others mistook to be lacking in feelings. However, behind his composed face were emotions that writhed with concern for their sister.

"Do you think better on it, Everard, you will realize this is the only course for the Wulfriths, for all will go worse for Gaenor if the king captures her. Even if she makes it to France, Henry has allies there who will do his bidding."

Everard sighed. "Then we must bring her back."

"And pray the baron will yet wed her." Garr settled his shoulders beneath the mail. "Let us go meet Lavonne."

"Garr? Everard?" their mother called from the lowermost stair. Guessing she had heard their conversation, Garr said, "Do not fear, Mother, we will find her."

"I know." She stepped down into the hall. "I just pray you will not be too angry with her. She—"

"I shall endeavor to be fair," Garr said. Then, remembering Beatrix and her new husband were yet abed, he added, "I would not have this unfortunate event mar Beatrix and Michael's first day of marriage. Speak naught of it and, if they ask, tell that Everard and I have been called to Wulfen."

She inclined her head. "Godspeed, my sons."

Only himself to blame.

Still, Christian fomented over the tidings received upon reaching Stern Castle six hours past. Though occupied this past sennight with the havoc wreaked by his brother who yet evaded capture, he had been set for his private audience with Gaenor. Now, it seemed it would be public—providing they overtook her and Sir Durand. Durand who was surely the one to whom Gaenor had entrusted her heart, with whom she had spent the night past, and who might have stolen the gift of her virtue that was to have been Christian's.

Alternately gripped with jealousy, anger, and a sense of betrayal for what they had shared at the stream, he perspired deep into the tunic beneath his chain mail as the declining sun blistered the sky. It would be dark before long, but even if the Wulfriths paused for the night, he would press on.

He gripped the reins tighter and squeezed his eyes closed. *Lord, let her not have so easily gone into the arms of another. Let the feelings between us sustain her though she surely thought never to see me again.*

He opened his eyes. Was he asking too much? Especially considering her feelings for Sir Durand?

"I hope 'tis for my sister you pray," Sir Abel raised his voice above the pounding of hooves, "and your forbearance."

Christian looked at the knight where he had drawn alongside. He resented the interruption, but it did not anger him as it might have done a sennight past. Despite the strain that was yet between him and Abel, during their pursuit of Robert and his brigands they had come to a kind of understanding and grudging respect for the other's abilities. They tolerated one another well—when they pursued a common enemy. Now they pursued Abel's sister whose flight from Stern Castle portended ill for her family.

Though Baron Wulfrith and his brothers had not appealed to Christian to wed their sister regardless of her having once more fled, Christian knew that if he petitioned the king, Henry would likely release him from the decree. But he would make no such petition, for he was determined to wed Gaenor. Of course, if she had given herself to—

"Well?" Sir Abel pressed.

Christian narrowed his gaze on the knight. "I do pray for your sister and my forbearance. You should as well."

"I shall consider it."

As obstinate as ever...

Christian urged his mount ahead.

She had made a mistake. She had known it the moment she stepped through the sally port and found Sir Durand waiting for her...when they crept to the wood...when they mounted the horse there...when she put her arms around him to hold tight and felt him stiffen. But still she had gone, and with each league she had grown heavier with regret. Once could be forgiven, but to twice flee marriage was beyond dishonorable to the Wulfrith name. Could she do it again, she would do it different, but it was too late. By now, Baron Lavonne had arrived and found his bride gone. Soon, the king would set men after her and Durand. What else was there but to press on?

Weary from hours of clinging to Sir Durand, with only two brief stops to allow them and their mount to eat and drink, she sank deeper against the knight's back and blinked at the landscape that sped past now that they had left the shelter of the wood.

Were they yet upon the barony of Abingdale? Though Sir Durand had told her it was fastest to pass through the southernmost corner, the thought of entering Baron Lavonne's lands, even for a short time, caused chill bumps to rise across her limbs. Or was the waning day responsible?

She lifted her head from the knight's back and glanced at the sky. It was streaked with oranges, reds, and purples, the rays of the setting sun all that remained of daylight.

They would ride through the night, a difficult undertaking but necessary to outdistance their pursuers. Unfortunately, their flight had not gone unobserved, for once they had met with a group of villagers and twice they had spotted riders in the distance. If it was told that a single horse bearing a knight and lady had passed near, their course would be known.

Wishing it was not too slow and dangerous to often make use of the cover of the wood, Gaenor pressed her face to Sir Durand's back again and once more felt him stiffen. How it hurt, this regret of his that she was not Beatrix!

Hours later, mantle drawn tight about her, eyes closed against the night sky, mind meandering between dream and reality, she was shaken awake when the horse lurched.

Gripping Sir Durand tighter, she jerked her head up as the man before her spat one oath after another and dragged on the reins. Without any pretense of gentleness, he unclasped Gaenor's hands from about his waist and jumped to the ground.

"Let us pray he has but taken a stone." He bent to inspect the horse's hooves.

As he did not offer to assist her down, Gaenor slid from the animal's back. In silence, she watched as Sir Durand lifted the left hoof. Since the quarter moon provided only bare light, he ran his hand over it before moving to the right hoof.

A moment later, a foul curse flew from his mouth, at the end of which he growled, "He is lamed!"

Then no longer of use to them. If not for their flight, it was possible the horse could be healed of its affliction, but now it would have to be put down. As much pained by the animal's sacrifice as the fear stealing upon her, Gaenor turned away in anticipation of the dagger Sir Durand would draw.

"We will send him opposite," he said.

She looked around and saw him remove the packs from behind the saddle. "Opposite?"

"If I put him down now and he is found, it will be known we have entered the wood here."

"You could put him down in the wood." Gaenor winced at the tremble in her voice.

"Better we send him opposite. Without the burden of carrying us, he will be able to distance himself and perhaps lead our pursuers astray."

Their pursuers who were surely drawing near and would not pause for the night. How near were they? And without the speed of a horse, was it possible that she and Sir Durand might yet escape? Not likely.

Sir Durand slapped the animal's hindquarter. With a whinny, the destrier trotted off, the severity of its laming less obvious now that it was unburdened.

"Come." Sir Durand pivoted.

She followed him to the bordering wood, stumbling often as the uneven ground that had proved the destrier's undoing attempted to undo her. Momentarily entertaining the possibility that Sir Durand might also send her opposite if she was lamed, she trailed him among the darkly-shadowed trees.

His silence made her ache, as did the distance he maintained between them as if he was relieved that she no longer clung to him. Though he did not voice his regret of stealing her from Stern, she felt it now that their chance of escape was so greatly diminished. The knight had sacrificed much to aid her, and perhaps all if her brothers captured him. Or if he fell into King Henry's hands.

Knowing what she must do, she halted and called out, "Our cause is lost, Sir Durand." If ever there were a cause.

Presenting as little more than a shadow between the trees ahead, he turned. "We do not have time for regrets, Lady Gaenor. If we are to stay ahead of your brothers, we must continue."

"You go. I will return."

He strode back. "I said I would deliver you from marriage, and I shall."

She opened her mouth to argue, but something told her to swallow the words that would only alert him to the strength of her resolve and cause him to take measures to assure she did not slip away. Feigning acquiescence, she sighed. "If you are certain."

"I am."

She followed him and, for the next half hour or so, Sir Durand often glanced around to assure himself that she was yet there. When he finally eased his watch, she seized the first opportunity to escape.

Grateful for the moist leaves underfoot, she changed course and hastened tree to tree lest he realized he was alone. She soon lost sight of him, and many minutes passed before she heard him call to her.

He was so distant that she no longer had to worry about branches snapping underfoot. Thus, as quickly as the darkness allowed, she sped among the trees.

She heard him call her name, at times more distant, other times nearer, but always she stayed far enough ahead that her escape was assured. What would come of it with the dawning of day, she did not know, but her hope was that, from the bordering wood, she would spy her brothers. If not, she would keep to the trees as much as possible and make her way back to Stern Castle.

11

GAENOR, GARR REALIZED as the figure stepped from the trees and dropped the hood of her mantle to reveal her dark blonde hair. And it appeared she was alone.

Wondering what had become of Sir Durand, he reined in and lifted a hand to halt the others. Three drew alongside—Abel, Everard, and Baron Lavonne.

"I would ask that you remain here," Garr said, looking to the latter whose gaze was fixed on the woman at the edge of the wood. "'Tis better this way."

Eyes shadowed, unshaven jaw set in a hard line, the baron considered Garr. "I will wait, but 'tis to Broehne Castle we journey next."

Though Garr would have preferred to return Gaenor to Stern, there could be no argument. Not only were they less than two hours from Lavonne's home, but it was, ultimately, his sister's destination—providing the baron did not seek release from their marriage.

"To Broehne," Garr agreed, then exchanged glances with his brothers. "I go alone." He gentled his mount forward, not wanting to rush on his sister who, after all, had come forward to be found and would surely be grateful for the extra time in which to prepare herself to receive him.

As he neared, she propped her chin high on the cool, morning air.

"Gaenor," he said, easing his destrier to a halt ten feet distant from her.

"Garr."

He looked from her hair that had snagged leaves and twigs, down her mantle that had faired just as poorly with the wood she had tramped for what must have been hours. "You are well, Sister?"

"I am."

"What of Sir Durand?"

"He is gone."

The anger rippling beneath his surface threatening to rise above it, he said between his teeth, "He left you?"

"Nay."

"Then?" he growled, frustrated by her refusal to elaborate without prompt. But perhaps it was the best she could do, he considered. Though her bearing was erect and eyes and chin did not waver, emotions surely abounded within.

"I left," she said.

"Why?"

She clasped her hands before her, and he saw they trembled. "I am responsible for this day, not Sir Durand."

She protected the knight, but was the man truly such a coward? Garr, himself, had trained him, and many times Sir Durand had proved he was above fear.

"It seems I do not know this knight as well as I thought," he said. "He breaks fealty with the Wulfriths by stealing our sister away, and when she determines to return to her family, he allows her to go on foot—alone!"

"His horse was lamed, and I left under cover of night so he would not know I had gone."

Then she had stolen away from him, doubtless to protect him from the Wulfriths. Without a mount to keep ahead of their pursuers, who had thrice been pointed in their direction by those whose paths Durand and Gaenor had crossed, they would soon have found themselves overtaken.

Garr's anger toward Sir Durand pushing through despite his attempt to suppress it, he said, "When he is found, his punishment will be dire."

She drew a deep breath. "I am ready to return home and wed the man chosen for me."

"*If* he will have you," Garr said, more sharply than intended.

"I do not doubt he is angered."

Gritting his teeth, he sent up a silent prayer for God to direct his tongue. "I will not lie to you. He *is* angry that, once again, you have fled. But this time it is a more serious matter, for you did so without your family's consent and with a Wulfrith knight who broke fealty to aid you. Surely you know that the two nights shared with Sir Durand do not speak well of you."

Gaenor stared at her brother. She was not such a fool to hope none would think the worst of her and Sir Durand. After all, what loyal knight forsook his lord and his honor merely to aid a lady discontented with an arranged marriage? It could only be assumed they were lovers. And they would be right, though only about that first time months past when Sir Durand had comforted her over what they had believed was Beatrix's death.

Pained with remembrance of what had come of the solace the handsome knight had offered, Gaenor shook her head in an attempt to cast off the sin that made her feel soiled and foul. She had repented, but it persisted like a disease no medicinal could treat.

"Gaenor?"

She saw the question in her brother's gaze that he did not ask. Even if it meant the baron rejected her, bringing further disgrace upon her family, she would give Garr his answer, but not now when it took all of her strength to remain standing.

On legs that felt as if they might melt out from under her, she crossed to her brother's side. "Take me home, Garr."

"We are destined for Broehne Castle."

Holding back surprise that she knew she should not feel since the baron's home was surely nearer than Stern, she said, "As you will."

Garr nodded toward the dozen men on the distant rise. "The baron awaits you in yon meadow."

This time, there was no suppressing her surprise. "You brought him?"

"It could not be helped." Regret grooved his mouth. "He arrived as we were preparing to depart Stern."

Heart thrusting against her ribs, she surveyed the other riders. Though she identified her brothers where they sat on their destriers at the fore, there was no way to know which of the others was her betrothed. However, she remembered that Baron Lavonne was told to be a large man, and there was no mistaking the proportions of the one whose destrier stood to the left of Everard's.

"I am sorry, Gaenor. I would not have had it be this way."

Wishing she could better conceal her emotions, she looked back at Garr.

"I will be with you," he said and, with a tight smile, reached for her.

She laid her chill fingers in his warm hand and stepped her foot atop his in the stirrup. Unlike Sir Durand, her brother took her up in front of him to provide the comfort and safety of his arms.

As he turned his horse, she glanced over her shoulder. "I am afeared, Garr."

"This I know." He slid an arm around her waist and eased her back against him.

Though all of her urged her to make ready for flight, she sank into her brother who had never allowed harm to touch her—who, though she had willfully tainted the honorable name of Wulfrith, would never raise a hand to her.

And yet, he bargained you away like chattel.

Wearily, she turned aside Sir Durand's revelation, choosing numbness over the roiling that would only pain her more.

Though tempted to close her eyes and surrender to fatigue that she might delay her acquaintance with Baron Lavonne, she knew it was the coward's way. Thus, as Garr guided his destrier toward the riders, she firmly held her gaze to the large man beside Everard.

It was his broad shoulders that first struck her as familiar, then his fair hair lifting in the cool, morning breeze, next his determined chin. And she needed to look no nearer to know it was Sir Matthew.

What was he—?

"Gaenor?" The concern in Garr's voice evidenced he felt the alarm surging through her.

She stared at the knight she had thought never to see again and warily mulled the reason for his presence.

She looked over her shoulder. "Baron Lavonne"—she nearly choked on the name—"which one is he?"

"He is mounted to the left of Everard."

She thought she might die. What had she done? In secret she had met with a man who called himself Sir Matthew, told him things she should not have, felt for him, sought him out, allowed him to kiss her, asked him to steal her away. And, thinking him lost to her, she had fled with Sir Durand without regard for what any might think of her and the two nights spent alone in a man's company.

But then, what had Baron Lavonne done? Knowing who she was, he had deceived her, likely laughed at her ignorance, disappeared without farewell, and now reappeared wearing a wrathful countenance as if ill had only been worked upon him—this man who had struck a bargain with Garr that, if not accepted, might have resulted in Beatrix being found guilty. Then her death.

Regret and anger warred in Gaenor, but it was the latter she embraced.

Christian knew the moment she recognized him. As emotions struggled across her face until all that remained was ire—ire due her, just as it was due him—he tightened his grip on the reins and silently conceded that this was not the way to begin a marriage. If a marriage at all.

He looked closer on her as she and her brother neared and wondered if her eyes might reflect the truth of what had happened between her and Sir Durand who was conspicuously absent. Had the Wulfrith knight abandoned the woman who had risked all to be with him? Regardless, the knave would not go unpunished, no matter how far he had or had not trespassed. *Had* something happened between him and Gaenor?

"Baron Lavonne," Wulfrith said as he halted his destrier before him, "there is much to discuss, but suffice it for now that I introduce my sister, Lady Gaenor Wulfrith."

Would she reveal their previous acquaintance? If not, should he? Christian searched her eyes, but if virtue yet resided there, it was obscured by anger.

"Gaenor," Wulfrith spoke across Christian's silence, "your betrothed, Baron Lavonne."

Neither did she speak. When the uncomfortable silence remained unbroken, her brother reined around. "Let us ride."

The pace he set was no less rigorous than when they had sought to overtake Gaenor and Sir Durand. Thus, it was not two hours before they passed over Broehne's drawbridge and Christian's betrothed gained her first glimpse of the towering donjon where she would serve as lady for the remainder of her life. Perhaps.

It was useless to try to sleep as Garr had encouraged her to do, for there was no rest to be found behind her lids—only deepening anger, resentment, and frustration. When the knock sounded on her chamber door two hours later, she felt as coiled as a snake.

She swung her feet to the floor and stood from the bed. "Enter!"

Garr stepped inside. "You are rested?"

She glanced past him to Everard, then Abel who eased the door closed. "As best as I was able to."

He considered her face and, from his troubled brow, did not like what he saw there. "Ere we proceed with this marriage, there are things that must needs be addressed."

"My virtue."

He blinked. "Aye, but first I would know what you want—that which is within your grasp *and* my ability to deliver."

She had not expected to be asked such. "You are saying you will give me what I want?"

"I shall try."

"Even if it bodes ill for the Wulfriths?"

"Whatever is within my power—"

"Does your power extend to promises made that would have to be broken to give me what I ask?"

He drew a deep breath. "Gaenor, 'tis possible I might yet find a way to release you from this betrothal, even though I believe it will be a good marriage and—I will not lie—of benefit to our family."

She clasped her hands hard. "But then your word would be made a lie, and that is not permissible for a Wulfrith." She looked to her other brothers. "Is it?"

Garr laid a hand on her shoulder. "Of what do you speak?"

"I speak of the bargain struck with my betrothed—that, in exchange for testimony to prove Beatrix's innocence, you would hand me over."

Garr's mouth turned grim. "Sir Durand told you."

"He did."

"And for this you fled Stern Castle."

"I did."

Another deep breath. "I can only say it was what was required at the moment, and I believed you would agree to it to save Beatrix."

Moisture collected in Gaenor's eyes. "I would have, but why did you not tell me?"

Abel stepped forward. "For fear it would reflect poorly on your betrothed."

"It does," she exclaimed, "for what kind of man forces such a bargain? Threatens the fate of another for his own gain? The fate of the sister of the woman he is to wed?"

"A man weary of the hostilities between his family and ours," Garr said. "A man who wishes peace, unlike his father or brothers. Believe me, Gaenor, had Christian Lavonne shown himself to be like those of his blood, I would risk heaven's wrath to keep you from him. I would find a way."

She searched his eyes and saw he spoke true.

"And do not forget, Gaenor, 'twas Baron Lavonne who threw the dagger that saved Beatrix from *his* brother."

"I do not forget, and I am grateful, but I know the baron cares not for his illegitimate brother who is a thorn in his side. Thus, mayhap 'twas done for his own gain, not Beatrix's."

"Had he killed him, perhaps, but he did not."

"And more the pity," Abel grumbled.

Gaenor looked to her youngest brother, but before she could question him, Garr pressed on. "Tell me what you want."

Though niggled by Abel's remark, she said, "No different from what Beatrix wants: a good husband, children, happiness. Can you give me that?"

"I believe Baron Lavonne can—that he will prove such a husband to you and father to your children."

A man of deceit. But Garr did not know what had happened between her and Christian Lavonne at Wulfen. And she would not tell him, though she longed to ask the reason she had not been told that the baron had trained with her brothers at Wulfen. Of course, one did not have to be sharp of wit to guess the reason Christian Lavonne had sought training. Having been raised for the Church, his skill at weaponry was surely neglected, and there was no better place to learn how to wield a blade well than at Wulfen.

"Though 'tis a difficult thing I must ask," Garr said, "it must be known ere we proceed further. If Baron Lavonne takes you to wife, will it be a maiden in his bed when he comes to you on your wedding night?"

"As opposed to a whore?" she asked before she could clip the wings of bitterness.

His jaw hardened. "I am not here to condemn you but to learn the truth—a truth that might free you from marriage, if that is what you truly wish."

But which would condemn Sir Durand if ever he was found. Hoping he was many leagues distant, she said, "Nay, Garr, 'twill not be a maiden in his bed."

Wrath rose in his eyes, and when she looked to Everard and Abel, their feelings were as potently visible.

Woe to Sir Durand if he ever came within sword's reach of any of them. Praying he would not, she said, "Do not mistake that what happened between us was without my consent. I am as much to blame, if not more."

Seeing little change in their countenances, especially Abel's that reflected imaginings of what he would do to Sir Durand given the chance, she crossed to the window.

"What you do not know..." She stared at the activity in the bailey below. "...is that what happened between Sir Durand and I happened months past. Not days or nights."

In the ensuing silence, she knew her brothers exchanged glances.

It was Garr who finally spoke, and in a voice so level it evidenced great control. "What say you?"

She turned. "My sin was committed following my first flight from marriage to Baron Lavonne when Sir Durand and I thought Beatrix was dead. It was not meant to happen, but Sir Durand comforted me and—"

"Comforted!" Abel spat.

Garr turned his steely gaze on his youngest brother. "Leave."

Abel looked as if he might argue, but then he swiveled around.

Though Gaenor expected Garr would also send Everard away, he did not.

As Abel slammed the door closed, her oldest brother looked back at her. "You say that during this most recent flight from Stern, you had no such relations with Sir Durand."

"That is what I say."

With an easing of his shoulders, Garr said, "Then there is no reason to fear you bear Sir Durand's child."

"None." Strange that, months past, she had hoped she might.

"You know the baron must be told."

"I would not have it be otherwise."

"And if he requires that you submit to an examination?"

As examinations were most often pressed on women who claimed to be virtuous despite evidence to the contrary, his question was unexpected. "Why would he wish an examination?"

"You have given him cause to suspect your claim to lost virtue is but another means of escaping marriage."

She drew a deep breath. "Then if the baron requires it, I shall submit."

Garr strode forward and laid his hands on her shoulders. "I will pray for you, Gaenor."

Though she knew that if she leaned in he would enfold her in his arms, the comfort he offered would likely cause her tears to spill. "I thank you," she said, "and I would have you know that I am sorry for the shame my sin casts upon our family."

He swept the hair off her brow. "All you must do is repent."

She had repented, and still she...

It struck her then—what she had known deep within. Though she had knelt at the altar and spoken words of repentance, they had not reached her heart. Now might they? Now that her sin and deception were laid bare? Now that her brother could yet lay hands on her without revulsion?

She glanced at Everard who had not moved. Though the eyes that met hers were troubled, she saw no condemnation there either. Her brothers were disappointed but would not turn from her.

"I shall repent, Garr."

His smile was slight. "If the baron determines he will not wed you, I will take you home to Stern."

Meaning she would not be hidden away in a convent to live out her life in shame?

"But if he still wishes marriage, what say you?"

What was there to say? If she asked Garr to dishonor himself by breaking his vow and delivering her free of the king's decree, it would go ill for her family. And further shame would be upon them, for she did not doubt the king would learn of her indiscretion. It was possible, however, that if the baron married her despite her lack of virtue, his pride would keep him from revealing her sin. Too, there was the kiss they had shared…

Aching for what was lost to her, though it had never truly belonged—had surely been but a test—she pushed aside remembrance of that kiss and replaced it with one of the man who, this day, had silently regarded her from astride his mount. "If that is his desire, I shall submit. And to avoid further delay, I shall wed him on the morrow if he chooses." It was bold of her, but she had already lost all there was to lose.

Garr pressed his lips to her brow and released her shoulders. "I shall ask that viands be delivered to you."

She nearly protested, but her belly ached with emptiness. "I thank you."

Everard preceded his older brother from the chamber, once more leaving her to her solitude.

Afterward, she could not say how she came to be prostrated amid the rushes scattered across the floor. Nearly as strange was the platter of viands she found on the table when she finally arose. Having heard no one enter or exit, she wondered if she had fallen asleep during her prayers, but she did not believe it.

"I am forgiven," she breathed and knew it was so—that in her desperation she had found the place that heretofore eluded, that whatever path God set her upon, He would be with her.

Still, there was one threshold she could not cross though she knew it was required of her. Beneficent God could forgive her sins of the flesh, but she could not begin to forgive Christian for his deceit. Not yet.

He had told himself he was prepared for her betrayal, but he had wanted to believe her response to his kiss had meant she felt something for him—at least enough to keep her from so soon going into another's arms. But that was what she had done despite her brother's assurance that her intimacy with Sir Durand was confined to the journey to Wulfen Castle months past.

If it *had* happened then—and he would wager the mouth he had kissed at Wulfen was untried—they had surely lain together again. Only a fool would not know the motive for her denial that she had given herself to the knight following her second flight from Stern. Any child resulting from Gaenor and Sir Durand's indiscretion could be advanced as fathered by Christian. But there was a means to ensure that did not happen.

Dragging his gaze from the tapestry that draped the eastern wall of the solar, Christian looked to Wulfrith. "You say she is willing to submit to an examination?"

"She agrees," the warrior said tightly as if the matter sat heavy upon him.

Though Christian knew Gaenor's admission was true, especially when pieced with the missive he had discovered in her psalter, he was tempted to order the examination for the shame it would bring upon her. But he said, "'Twill not be necessary."

"It will be if you intend to seek dissolution of the king's decree."

Again, the temptation to strike at the betrayer. "I have no such intention, Baron Wulfrith. For the sake of our families, I place our alliance above what your sister brings—rather, does *not* bring to the marriage. Thus, as she is prepared to wed on the morrow, it will be done."

Wulfrith strode forward and looked close upon him. "You would do well not to forget my warning of months past that whatever you do to my sister, I will do to you."

Christian held his gaze. "'Twould be a lie to say I am unaffected by the grave tidings you have delivered, but I give you my word that your sister need not fear my hand."

Wulfrith's lids narrowed. "What of your tongue?"

"You ask this of a man so recently betrayed? Who expected to wed a chaste bride? Whose years will be marked by his wife's memories and longings for another? Nay, I make no promises for the words that drop from my mouth, but this I give you—I will endeavor to control them." He unclenched his hands. "If that is sufficient, tell your sister to make ready to speak vows on the morrow and that I will hold her to them lest she thinks to cuckold me again."

As he and Wulfrith stared at one another, he caught the acrid scent of blood, as if the other man was tempted to draw his sword, but then it was gone.

The renowned warrior and trainer of knights said, "I make allowances for your anger, Baron, but my warning stands. I pray we shall not one day meet at swords."

"That is for your sister to decide."

Wulfrith said no more. With strides that well matched Christian's, he crossed the solar.

As the door seated in its frame, Christian eased his shoulders. At every turn, he was tested. Was this to be a lifelong curse for having coveted his brother's inheritance? That he would never know peace? That he would ever be at war with even his own family?

He looked to the missive he had set aside when Wulfrith had requested an audience. The ragged parchment told that a fire had been set to a distant village—doubtless, by Robert and his brigands who yet eluded capture. But he would have them. Eventually there would be peace in all of Abingdale. As for Broehne Castle, the heart of Abingdale, it might prove impossible with a wife like Gaenor Wulfrith.

12

SOLEMN.

There was no kinder word to describe the ceremony in which Gaenor stood and knelt for what seemed hours, nor the lengthy meal through which she sat for nearly as long.

Her vows the only words exchanged with Christian Lavonne since discovering he was Sir Matthew, she was grateful when the priest drew her from her husband's brooding side and led her from the great hall. Her gratitude lasted only as long as her ignorance of where she was being led—to the chamber she and the baron would share as husband and wife.

Telling herself it was inevitable, she followed the priest abovestairs. Still, she could not help but draw a sharp contrast between her wedding night and her sister's. Despite Sir Durand's revelation at Stern Castle, Gaenor had later joined the procession up the stairs and gathered with the others around her sister to prepare her for the physical union of man and wife.

At Broehne, there was only the priest who, though he was kind enough, served no purpose other than to speak blessings over the bed. Of course, they were blessings of which she was in dire need, she reminded herself as she slid beneath the covers wearing her chemise that should have been shed with her borrowed gown. Fortunately, the priest merely sighed and spoke another blessing. Then they waited. And waited.

Might her husband not come? He had not humiliated her by ordering the examination, which gave her hope he was not as foul as his father and brothers, and he had agreed to wed her despite her lost virtue, but perhaps he regretted doing so. After all, if their marriage was not consummated, he could seek an annulment.

A half hour later, the priest crossed to the door and murmured that he would return. When he did, he brought her husband with him.

Christian Lavonne met her gaze, and though she half-expected his eyes to reflect a quantity of drink, they did not.

Gaenor looked away as he shed his clothes. When he slid in beside her, the priest stepped forward to bless the marriage bed again. Afterward, he extinguished all but a single candle and withdrew.

Though Gaenor longed to look anywhere but at her husband, she reminded herself she was forgiven and turned her face to him—only to warm at the sight of his bare chest and shoulders above the sheet.

"'Tis done," he said gruffly.

She tried to relax so he would not feel her tension when he reached for her, but he turned away. She did not know if she should be thankful or offended. All she knew was that she should not be ashamed. What was done was done, and long before she had met this man.

Although it pained her to speak, she said, "There is to be no consummation?"

He rolled onto his back and met her gaze. "When your menses flow as witness to your empty womb, *wife*, I will touch you. Not a day before."

His eyes were like the coldest, rain-soaked morning, but rather than rouse fear, they pointed her toward the door behind which her own anger resided. "Then you believe I have recently laid with Sir Durand." *Bar the door, Gaenor. Do not let it out.* "You think I lie."

Candlelight upon his hard face, he said, "Only a fool would believe otherwise, and I have no intention of being deceived again, my lady."

"Deceived?" *Do not!* "Again? No deceit have I worked on you. Though I sinned, I made no attempt to conceal the truth—unlike you, *Sir Matthew*, who quite enjoyed the deceit worked upon me. Who kissed me and—"

"Aye, kissed you and believed it meant something to you."

Gaenor blinked, as did her anger. His kiss *had* meant something—more than she dared tell. She swallowed. "You are saying it meant something to you?"

He stared at her, and she almost hated herself for allowing herself to hope. She really was a fool. "Nay"—she shook her head—"it meant naught to you who arranged to meet me and never appeared."

"Much to your disappointment. Escape was all you wanted, Gaenor. You allowed me near only that I might aid in returning you to your lover."

"Not so!"

"It is so. Thus, do not speak to me of deceit when you wear it so well yourself."

She caught her breath. "What of the bargain struck with my brother?" She saw from the flash in his eyes that he was surprised she knew. "You trifled with my sister's life as if it was of no value other than to gain what you wanted."

"You are wrong. My bargain with your brother gained naught that I wanted—only what was necessary to ensure peace."

His words were meant to injure, and they did. Not that they should, for he had made the exchange with Garr before meeting her. He could not possibly have wanted her then, though at the stream it had seemed he did.

Fingers aching from the ferocity with which she gripped the sheet, Gaenor realized how far she was from where she ought to be after all the time she had spent prostrated before the Lord. She might not yet be able to forgive Christian, but she could prevent the discord between them from taking a more dire turn.

Determined to embrace the reprieve granted until her monthly flux, she said, "Good eve, Husband," and turned her back to him. To her surprise, she began to drift almost immediately, and it was not long before she slept.

In the hours before light peeled back the night, Christian brooded over what Gaenor had said and his response.

Though he had vowed he would not be drawn into an argument, he had risen to her bait and found himself dangling from her hook. Words had been spoken that should not have been, and if he did not more carefully guard his emotions, more would be said that was better left unsaid.

Hearing her breath catch, he hoped it did not mean she was about to toss again as she had done throughout the night. Not that it had disturbed his own rest. Indeed, he would have preferred that to be the extent of it. It was his senses that were disturbed each time her arm or leg touched his.

When Gaenor remained unmoving, he looked to the window. Though he usually rose in advance of the dawn, it was not acceptable to do so following his wedding night. Thus, willing the sun to more quickly light the sky, he threw back the covers, dropped his feet to the floor, and dragged on the hose and breeches he had left at the foot of the bed.

For a quarter hour, he paced the chamber as light crept within and avoided looking at the sleeping figure of his wife. He tried to stop turning over what had been spoken between them, but that left only what had not been spoken, specifically how Gaenor had learned of his bargain with her brother. He told himself it did not matter, but it did. If her brothers had not revealed it, and he was inclined to believe they would not, it was Sir Durand who had been present during the meeting with Baron Wulfrith months past.

Was it that which had made Gaenor flee Stern Castle with the man? Or would she have done so regardless?

Christian returned to the bed—and saw she was awake where she lay on her side. He looked from her eyes to the abundance of hair spread on her pillow and could not have been more grateful she had retained her chemise. "Good morn, Wife."

She raised her eyebrows. "How would you have us proceed?" she asked as if she'd had far enough time to ponder the day ahead.

"As man and wife."

He thought he saw relief in her eyes—as if she feared the new day would bring talk of an annulment. "Very well." She rose onto an elbow. "You know 'tis customary to...hang out the sheets?"

As proof of consummation, but even if he had been so foolish to join with her on the night past, there would be no blood to show for it. Only dishonor. "They shall be hung out."

As she averted her gaze to hide what was surely dismay, he motioned for her to rise. When she did, he swept the bottom sheet from the bed, opened a healing wound on his forearm, and used the sheet to stanch the blood.

"As the injury was gained from a Wulfrith," he said, "the blood will serve." He glanced at her where she hugged her arms against the chill morning air.

She frowned. "I do not understand."

He pitched the wadded sheet to the center of the bed and went to the chest that contained his clothes. "You are my wife now. Any dishonor that stains you, stains me. Thus, do you bring forth Sir Durand's child, only I will know."

Unlike on the night past when she had allowed her anger to spew, she controlled the emotions that made her hands clench on her arms.

Christian pulled on tunic and boots. "I am sure your brothers are anxious to know how you fared on our wedding night." He pushed a hand through his hair to bring it to order. "Do not delay in joining me at meal so that we might ease their concerns."

He started to turn away, but came back around. "I want your brothers gone from Broehne as soon as possible. Though they will know 'tis not virgin's blood that flies from the window of the lord's solar, I would not have them think our marriage remains unconsummated."

As she loosened her white knuckled hands from her arms, Christian wondered if her flesh would be bruised. "Of course," she said. "I do not wish them burdened any more than already they are."

He strode to the door and closed it behind him.

Gaenor considered the sheet. His blood, not hers. Yet again, he had spared her and her family humiliation—first in agreeing to go through with the marriage, now in making it appear she had come to him untouched. He professed to do so out of self-interest, but might he be influenced by something other than the peace and stability he sought for Abingdale? When her monthly flux arrived a fortnight hence, might there be healing between them?

From the bed, she had watched him pace in and out of her field of vision, had felt his struggle, had hoped not only for his forgiveness, but that she could forgive him for his deception. Hoped, not prayed.

Though Christian had told her not to delay, Gaenor knew she must seek her knees, for what was hope without prayer? Thus, her head was bowed and hands clasped when the door opened and the chatter of women fell away.

She completed her prayer, stood, and turned to the two who stood in the doorway—the young one bearing a gown, the older one an armful of linens.

"My lady," the latter said with a curtsy.

"My lady," the younger woman went through the motions with downcast eyes.

"Our lord has sent us to see to your needs." The older woman bustled forward. "And to hang the morning after sheet." She peered at it and nodded. "It bodes well." Her mouth curved with a smile that hinted at warmth. "I am called Josephine." She beckoned the younger one forward. "Aimee has been given to be your maid."

Aimee glanced up, and Gaenor glimpsed something like resentment in her eyes.

"I am grateful for your aid," Gaenor said, though she was not so certain. With the exception of those few days at Stern before Beatrix's wedding, it was months since she had played the lady and allowed another to see to her dress and ablutions.

"I have brought one of Lady Mary's gowns." Aimee unfolded a simply cut pale blue gown and held it up for Gaenor's approval.

"Lady Mary?" Gaenor asked.

"The baron's departed mother, my lady," Josephine said. "'Twas also her gown you wore to speak vows with our lord."

Gaenor fingered the silken material. Despite the gown's simplicity, it was cut of fine cloth and well made. "She was nearly as tall as I."

"Aye, my lady, though the baron's father..." A shadow crossed her face and she bit her lip.

"What of the baron's father?"

Josephine shrugged. "Though he is not as tall as his youngest son or departed wife, he is of good height."

"I have not yet met him."

"And you will not," Aimee muttered.

"Aimee!" Josephine rebuked.

Gaenor frowned. "I was told he is bed-ridden."

Aimee snorted, only to flinch when Josephine stepped toward her and drew back a hand.

"Do not!" Gaenor snapped.

Josephine slowly lowered her arm and looked around.

As both women stared at her, she realized what was required to take her place as lady of the castle. She must be as her mother, Isobel, who owned the respect and admiration of the castle folk.

She stood taller. "I know Broehne Castle has been without a lady for many years, but I am your lady now, and I will not tolerate such disrespect"—she narrowed her gaze at Aimee—"or retribution." She looked to Josephine.

The surprise on their faces soured, and Gaenor knew her reprimand would unite them where division had existed.

Certain that the days ahead would prove trying as she sought to establish her place at Broehne, she told herself it was to be expected, especially as it was many years since the castle folk had been under the direction of a lady.

"Now, Josephine, I would know the reason I am not to meet my husband's father." Not that it was a disappointment, for she knew it was Aldous Lavonne who had ordered his illegitimate son, Robert, to take revenge on Beatrix. And who would have succeeded if not for Christian.

When Josephine's only response was to press her lips inward, Gaenor looked to the younger woman. "Explain, Aimee."

She cast her gaze elsewhere.

Gaenor sighed. "As neither of you is capable of adding anything to this discussion, I will seek the old baron myself." Not that she wished to have any relation with him. Rather, she would know behind which of the closed doors he lay that she might avoid him.

"That, my lady, is not possible," Josephine finally loosened her lips. With an almost imperious lift of her chin, she said, "The old baron is no longer at Broehne."

Then Christian had honored her family's strongly-worded request that his father be removed so she would not suffer his hatred or ill intent.

"Ah!" Aimee turned accusing eyes on the older woman. "You told!"

Josephine swung her head around, and the hands she clenched at her sides revealed she was tempted to use one on Aimee. "'Twas you who first opened the door, insolent wench."

"You opened it wider!" Aimee stamped a foot. "I—"

"Where is Aldous Lavonne?" Gaenor raised her voice above their squealing.

All semblance of warmth having fled the older woman's face, Josephine said, "'Tis not our place to tell. You will have to ask our lord."

Gaenor sighed. "I shall do that. Now attend me that I might break fast with my husband." It was an order, and so intended that both women would know she would not be snickered at or tread upon. Though it seemed happiness was to be denied her, there was consolation in that it would not be a dull existence.

They were watched, and it seemed Gaenor was just as aware of the eyes that followed them.

As Christian reached for a piece of cheese, he considered his wife's brothers farther down the lord's table. Wulfrith and Everard were assured of returning to their homes in a timely manner, but from Abel's comment this morn that they ought to resume their search for Robert, the youngest brother planned to stay on for a time.

Christian preferred otherwise, and yet there was much to recommend the plan, for their efforts to overtake the brigands had been greatly aided by the knight's keen senses and ability to find tracks where there appeared to be none. True, Robert yet evaded capture, but he had only narrowly stayed ahead of his pursuers. If not that Christian had suspended the hunt to collect his bride, the miscreants might now be in irons. Yet another reason to resent the woman who silently shared his platter of cheese and bread.

He looked at her, only to wish he had not, for she was becoming in the pale blue gown that had belonged to his mother. Lovely, in fact, with two large plaits bound halfway down her hair's length to allow the curling ends to drape her bosom.

Of Aimee's doing, he guessed, for the maid was given to such extravagance with her own hair, as well as that of other castle women. Providing Aimee set aside her sister's resentment of Abingdale's new lady, she would make a good maid for Gaenor. Not that he ought to care.

"You stare, Husband." Gaenor looked sidelong at him.

Vexed at being caught, more at being attracted to her despite her perfidy, he leaned near and forced a smile. "I am thinking you present well, lady wife. Indeed, none would know the babe in your belly is not mine."

Her face flushed and, again, anger lit her eyes.

When Christian glanced at those at the lower tables, the lively expressions of several told they believed it was an intimacy their lord and new lady shared. As he wished it. Still, he regretted allowing his tongue to unwind.

Knowing his in-laws would not be as optimistic about what had been spoken between husband and wife, he met the steely gaze of Abel, the steadfast gaze of Everard, and the discerning gaze of Wulfrith. They knew it was no intimacy.

Berating himself for not guarding his tongue as the Bible told and which he had done faithfully as a monk, he broke off a piece of bread.

"I am told your father is no longer at Broehne," Gaenor surprised him.

Irked by the loose lips of the women he had sent to attend her, Christian turned to Gaenor and saw her flush had receded and anger had dimmed.

"Where has he gone?"

He ground his jaws. "We will discuss my father elsewhere."

"Where? And when?"

"That is of *my* choosing."

She smiled tightly and laid a hand on his arm. "If you truly wish my brothers gone from Broehne, it would serve you not to scowl so."

There was a limit to how much pretense Christian could swallow, and he had reached his. He pushed back his chair and motioned for an end to the meal.

As benches scraped and those at the tables took up muttering over the meal's duration that they had surely expected would be prolonged in celebration of their lord's marriage, Christian strode the length of the dais.

Heart heavy, Gaenor watched him depart the hall. As the porter closed the door behind him, she stood.

"You look lovely," said Garr when he appeared at her side.

In an attempt to better compose her face, she glanced down her skirts. "It seems my husband's mother was nearly as tall. If I but add two fingers of material to the hem, I shall be quite presentable."

"Necessary only if you cannot wait a few days for your own clothes to arrive."

She looked up. "You have sent word to mother."

"I have, and by now she knows you are well and wed."

Ashamed that she had not asked that word be sent, Gaenor averted her gaze.

Garr turned her so that her back was to the hall and her face hidden from others. "Since much weighs upon you, Sister, 'twas for me to do."

"I thank you."

He bent nearer. "Everard and I leave this day."

She gasped. "Must you?"

"Our duties await us."

"And Abel?"

"He shall remain at Abingdale for a time."

"My...husband knows?"

"He does, and though I do not think he is pleased, Abel will remain for as long as he is needed."

"You think I require protection?"

Garr gripped her elbow. "Let us speak elsewhere."

She allowed herself to be guided abovestairs to the chamber her brothers had been given.

Once the door was closed, Garr said, "The baron did not speak to you of his father?"

"The maids who attended me this morn said he has been removed from Broehne."

"You know the manner in which he was removed?"

"I assumed my husband sent him to another castle."

"I wish that were so, Gaenor, but the old man was taken from Broehne by his illegitimate son, Robert."

She nearly stumbled where she stood. "But Sir Robert is imprisoned in London."

"No longer. With the aid of those of Abingdale's knights and men-at-arms who were released from Baron Lavonne's service for breaking fealty, he escaped. And here he came to once more wreak havoc. He and his brigands stole into Broehne and, after killing some of your husband's men, took Aldous Lavonne with them."

Moved by realization, Gaenor asked, "When did this occur?"

"Ten days past."

Remembering those who had ridden on Wulfen when she and Christian—then Sir Matthew—were at the stream, she nearly groaned. It must be that which had taken Christian away without a word to her. Meaning he *would* have returned to the stream. But would he have revealed his identity to the one who had suggested Sir Matthew steal her away? Or would he have further indulged in his game?

"Why did no one tell me Baron Lavonne was in training at Wulfen while I was there?" Hopefully, Garr would think her husband had revealed his presence at the fortress and not delve her question further.

"As you were isolated from the others, there seemed no reason to notify you lest you become alarmed."

"But why there when you could as easily have trained him at Stern?"

"Not only is Wulfen situated nearer the baron's lands lest he was needed, but there are none better at training in the art of arms than Everard and Abel." His face turned more serious. "I vow 'twas done to better provide for your protection, Gaenor."

"Which you believe I still require."

"Only until Sir Robert and his brigands are brought to ground, and that is why Abel remains—to assist until the king sends the men he has promised to beat out the woods and bring the miscreants to justice."

"Why would the king send men?"

"'Twas from his prison that Sir Robert escaped, and his guards who fell to the sword like those at Broehne when Aldous Lavonne was taken. If not for what was nearly done to Beatrix, I might pity Sir Robert if he is captured by the king's men."

"And what if he is captured by his brother?"

Garr was silent a long moment. "Ultimately, Sir Robert will fall into the king's hands, for your husband will be required to give him over."

"And you think he can do so knowing the king will execute his brother?"

"He will have to, Gaenor."

Then he doubted Christian's resolve to bring Sir Robert to justice. Of course, it was a dagger to the shoulder, not the back, her husband had thrown to prevent the knight from murdering Beatrix. Was it affection that held him from taking his illegitimate brother's life or care for their father?

"What I do not understand," she said, "is how Sir Robert was able to take the old baron from Broehne. He is said to be infirm."

"He is."

"You think he went willingly?"

Garr raised his eyebrows. "'Tis likely, for Christian isolated his father following the attempt on Beatrix's life lest the old man tried to turn his vengeance on you."

Something of a comfort.

"The maid who tended him and slept on a pallet beside his bed was relieved of her duties," Garr continued, "and a guard set at his door to oversee any given permission to enter Aldous's chamber. Even the village woman who tended his ailing body was not permitted a private audience."

Gaenor's sister had mentioned the healer. Though Aldous had been tended by Michael D'Arci for years, the physician had withdrawn his services following the attempt on Beatrix's life. Thus, the responsibility had been given to a young village woman said to be skilled in the healing arts.

"Yesterday, ere we brought you out of the wood and delivered you to Broehne," Garr continued, "Baron Lavonne received word that the healer had disappeared from her village."

Surely of Sir Robert's doing that the woman might provide for his father's needs. "Do you think she went willingly?"

"As Helene left her five-year-old son behind, it seems likely she was taken against her will. And yet, 'tis told she sympathized with the old baron—that on more than one occasion she argued with Christian against isolating his father. Thus, though I do not like to believe a mother would abandon her child for the sake of Aldous Lavonne or the coin he may have pressed upon her, it is possible she went willingly."

"And the boy? He has family to care for him?"

"He does not, as Helene was widowed two years past and has no other family."

Gaenor's heart tugged. "Who cares for him?"

"Though some villagers took him in, your husband has this day sent men to deliver him to the castle."

The prospect of a child in the donjon caused a thrill to run through Gaenor. Still, it seemed odd that the boy would be brought here if Helene's neighbors were willing to keep him. Did Christian hope to use the boy to entice Helene away from the brigands—just as he had used the testimony in Beatrix's favor to bargain with Garr?

"Why bring the child here?"

"'Tis at the request of those who care for him. He is said to be difficult."

"Of course he is. He has lost his mother, perhaps even been abandoned."

"Aye, and he was likely present when Robert came for her."

Gaenor frowned. "You think he witnessed violence?"

"'Tis possible."

She drew a deep breath. "I will see that the child is well cared for."

"I am sure you will, Gaenor. I but pray he will not add to the burden you already carry."

Reminded of that burden and fearful her brother guessed there was more to it than what had been told, she peered warily at him.

"Though 'tis obvious all is not well between you and Christian," he said with a sympathetic smile, "I would wager—and you know I do not indulge in such folly—that you and the baron are not yet husband and wife beyond the vows you spoke."

Heat warmed Gaenor's neck, but she said, "Your wager would be won."

He nodded. "'Tis difficult, I am certain, but for the best so your husband may never question the legitimacy of the children you bear him."

Here was the ever-logical Garr Wulfrith who never wavered off center—excepting one season of defiance when he took Annyn Bretanne to wife though the king had promised her to Christian's depraved older brother, Geoffrey Lavonne.

Gaenor sighed. "Aye, for the best."

He squeezed her shoulder. "'Twill all come right. The baron is an honorable man and will surely prove an honorable husband once Sir Durand is firmly in the past. You have but to forgive one another."

What her brother left unspoken made Gaenor ask, "For what have I to forgive him?"

His mouth turned grim. "I do not know under what circumstances you encountered the baron at Wulfen, Gaenor, but 'twas obvious when you came out of the wood that he was not unknown to you."

She could hardly breathe for the depth of his perception.

"And from your surprise, 'tis certain you were unaware that the man you met at Wulfen was your betrothed—though there was no doubt he knew you."

"You see too much," she choked.

"I apologize for my trespass, but I would have you take comfort in it."

"How so?"

"In knowing that you are wed to Christian Lavonne only because I approve of him. Do not forget that, Gaenor."

She shuddered out a long breath. "I shall endeavor to remember it."

"Do, little sister."

She nearly laughed. Younger she might be and not quite as tall, but she could hardly be called little. Before she could reconsider the impulse, she stepped nearer and wrapped her arms around him. "I will trust in you, Garr." She lowered her cheek to his shoulder.

"And the Lord," he said into her hair.

"That is harder." She sighed. "But I shall try."

13

THE ACHE OF Garr and Everard's departure was lightened by the appearance of riders on the meadow before the castle.

If not that Gaenor had watched her brothers leave from the window of the lord's solar and yet stood there a half hour later, she would have missed the arrival of the healing woman's son. Having gained a glimpse of the small figure who sat on the fore of the saddle of one of two men-at-arms, she hastened from the donjon.

Just as the boy's escort crossed the drawbridge into the outer bailey, Gaenor arrived amid flying skirts and beneath the weighty disapproval of the castle folk who stared after her.

Though she knew she ought to behave in a manner befitting the lady of the castle, she determined she would not be ashamed and gathered herself to receive the boy. However, as if she were unseen, the men-at-arms started to guide their mounts past her.

Knowing they could not miss her tall figure, nor her garments that pronounced her a lady—*their* lady—she placed herself in their path.

"There now." She raised a staying hand.

The one at the fore, a thick unkempt man whose jowls brushed the collar of his tunic, scowled as he reined in. "My lady?"

She looked at the rider who drew alongside him. He was a gaunt, heavily-lidded man whose face bore a dozen angry scratches, evidence he had not been heedful of low-hanging branches.

Hoping his charge had not also been marked by his carelessness, she turned her gaze upon the boy. His face was soiled but appeared unblemished. Relieved, she sought his eyes that were just visible between strands of greasy blonde hair.

"I bid you welcome." She smiled. "I am Lady Gaenor Wul—" No longer. "I am Lady Gaenor Lavonne, wife of Baron Lavonne."

The boy stared.

"And you are?" Gaenor prompted.

"The urchin's name be John," the gaunt man broke the silence.

Urchin...Gaenor frowned at the man, then returned to the boy. "Greetings, John."

Still he stared.

She stepped nearer, "You may hand John down."

"Is that right?" the gaunt man-at-arms drawled.

"Huh!" grunted the other one.

Their insolence stung, especially as they laid it out for all to see—the milling castle folk, the garrison before the drawbridge, and those on the walls. However, Gaenor denied herself the satisfaction of revealing her displeasure lest it upset the child.

Putting steel in her gaze as her mother did when words did not suffice, she said, "That is right. Your lady commands you to hand down the boy."

Something like worry slid onto the gaunt one's brow. "I would, my lady, but—"

"Now."

He exchanged looks with his companion, then lifted the boy out of the saddle. "As you will, my lady."

As John came into her arms, Gaenor was assailed by an odor so potent her throat convulsed. The child did not merely smell bad. He reeked. Swallowing hard, she settled him on her hip. However, hardly a moment passed before he became arms, legs, and teeth that punched, kicked, and bit.

Despite the instinct to release the wild child, she held onto him lest her attempt to avoid injury resulted in him being harmed. And she paid the price when his flailing caused her to lose her balance and an ankle to twist beneath her.

No sooner did her backside take the brunt of the fall than nails raked her cheek and teeth chewed her shoulder through the material of her gown. More than her pained ankle, more than her ungainly meeting with the ground, more than her scored flesh, it was the boy's bite that made her cry out.

As she dropped onto her back, the murmuring all around gave rise to voices, followed by shouts. Desperate to gain control before others came to her aid—if any deigned to—she looked from the boy's snarling face above hers to the arm he drew back to deliver another blow. When she raised an arm to deflect his fist, the defense of her person caused him to hesitate long enough for her to catch hold of his left arm and reach for the other. However, as she curled her fingers around his right arm, he was wrenched from atop her.

"Filthy urchin," snarled the jowled man-at-arms as he hauled the boy off her.

Vaguely aware of those gathering around, Gaenor scrambled to her knees and saw the man raise a hand to the thrashing boy he held by the back of his tunic.

"Nay!" she cried and, ignoring her pained ankle, lunged at him.

Though color suffused the man's fleshy countenance as he looked from the hand with which Gaenor gripped his forearm to her face, his tone was all respect. "Such behavior toward a noblewoman is not to be tolerated, my lady," he spoke loud for all to hear.

Why? And what had so soon changed his opinion of her? Gaenor glanced at the other man-at-arms who had also dismounted. "'Tis reserved for disrespectful men-at-arms only, then?" she demanded.

"What is this?" a voice burst upon the gathering that had fallen silent except for the boy's spitting and grunting, and Gaenor knew the reason she had been given aid.

She looked over her shoulder at the two men who strode toward them—Christian who could not look more imposing were he twice his height, and Abel who could not look more lethal had the fire in his eyes leapt off his face.

"M'lord," the thick man-at-arms hastened as if for fear of what Gaenor might tell, "the boy attacked your lady wife, and so I pulled him off her."

As Christian took the last stride to her side, Gaenor released the man-at-arms' forearm and winced as she attempted to settle weight on her ankle.

Her husband surveyed her face that bore the scratches the boy had dealt, then her gown that evidenced the dust and dirt of her fall. He and Abel appeared to have fared little better themselves, having surely been roused from practice at arms by the shouts in the outer bailey.

Nostrils flaring, Christian shifted his attention from the man-at-arms who held the boy at arm's length to the gaunt one. "It cannot be said you were unaware of the boy's disposition." His voice was taut as he eyed the scratches on the man's face that Gaenor had attributed to low-hanging branches.

"We were not unaware, m'lord," the thick man-at-arms admitted. "The urchin made certain of that throughout the ride."

Abel stepped forward. "And yet you did naught to prevent him from doing the same to my sister!"

"Sir Abel"—Christian turned his gaze on him—"'tis for me to deal with."

Jaw convulsing, Abel looked to Gaenor. "You are well?" He was almost breathless, and she guessed it was from the control required to keep from drawing his sword.

She inclined her head. "I have but myself to blame."

"'Tis so, m'lord," entreated the gaunt man-at-arms. "We did warn the lady not to allow the little beast so near—that he bites, scratches, and kicks."

Gaenor could hardly be angered by the lie, for it was not a complete lie. He *had* protested when she had ordered him to relinquish the boy. But though it did not absolve him or the other man-at-arms of their amusement, she would spare them. If naught else, her mercy might sooner gain her acceptance as lady of Broehne, as well as ease Abel's wrath that portended retaliation.

"Your man speaks true, my lord, I was warned," she said. "But neither should the boy be faulted, for it was surely fear that made him behave so."

Christian scrutinized her, and she knew he searched for proof that all was not as told. If he found it, might he finally prove worthy of his family's name? Might he show himself to be as cruel as his father and brothers? Though she had been spared such knowledge of him thus far, now that they were wed and there was only Abel—

But what of the man who came to you in the chapel at Wulfen? Who kissed you by the stream?

That man had been Sir Matthew, a part played merely to uncover her vulnerabilities.

Christian looked to the man-at-arms who continued to hold the boy tightly though he had quieted. "Am I wrong in believing Lady Gaenor tried to prevent you from striking the child?"

The man's throat bobbed. "After what the urchin did to your lady wife, I felt he must needs be corrected, m'lord."

"Did you?" It was not a question. Thus, no answer was forthcoming and the man-at-arms lowered his eyes.

"You are John?" Christian asked the boy.

No response.

Gaenor held her breath as her husband lifted the boy's chin.

"You are John?" he asked again, and from the narrowing of her husband's eyes it was certain he had caught his scent.

Though the boy tried to blink away his awe that was surely born of the size of the man before him, his eyes grew larger. Finally, he whispered, "Aye, John."

Christian nodded for the man-at-arms to release the boy. "You shall be punished for your assault on the lady, John, though not unjustly, for you are a child and surely acted out of fear as my wife tells."

Relief fluttered through Gaenor. Still, for fear of disappointment, she did not allow it to fully spread its wings.

"However, be you five or fifty, you would do well to not further test my patience. Do you understand?"

A slight nod.

"Then let us see to that punishment."

The boy tensed.

"We shall start with a bath," Christian said.

Gaenor would not have believed it possible, but the boy's eyes grew larger. "Nay!" He lunged opposite.

Christian made no move to thwart his escape, and it was not necessary, for Abel swept up the child as if he was an errant pup—one that not only reeked, but growled, kicked, and tried to bite the hand that held him.

"Cease this moment, or I shall personally see to your bath," Abel rumbled. But John was too young to realize it was no idle threat.

Abel tossed him over his shoulder and, with a grimace that told he had also been struck by the odor, strode across the bailey as small fists beat upon his back.

Christian dismissed the castle folk and returned his attention to his men-at-arms. "In future, do you not better protect my wife who is now your lady, you shall suffer for your failing."

"Aye, m'lord," the men murmured.

Gaenor pulled her bottom lip between her teeth. Christian's warning had not been spoken lightly. If she did not know better, she might believe he was truly concerned for her well-being.

"See to your mounts," he ordered.

They caught up their horses' reins and hastened toward the stables.

"As for you, *wife*"—Christian eyed her—"henceforth you will heed my men's warnings. Are we of an understanding?"

She did not wish to argue, but neither could she agree to something to which she was not certain she could adhere. "I shall be more heedful."

He took a step toward her. "I did not ask that you be more heedful, but that you heed, Gaenor. There is a difference."

She held his stare. "Aye, and because of that difference, I do not accede to the latter."

He stared at her a long moment, then released a harsh breath and turned on his heel. "Come!"

Wondering if her ankle would bear up long enough for her to reach the donjon, she tested more weight on it. It twinged, but she would not beg Christian for assistance. Certain that if she went slowly she could make it on her own, she took a step forward. Her ankle held, but Christian's patience did not.

He swung around. "What is it?"

She took another step, but could not move without a hitch.

He strode back and closed a hand around her arm. "What have you done?"

"I turned my ankle." As his lids narrowed, she rushed to explain, "I lost my balance when the boy was handed down to me."

"Do you not mean when he assaulted you?"

She shook her head. "As told, I am to blame for what happened."

"That I do not dispute, but regardless of where the blame lies, it does not absolve others of their actions—or lack, thereof."

Not until she clasped a hand over his that gripped her arm and felt him tense did she realize what she did, but she held on. "Pray, let this matter pass, Christian."

Inwardly, she shuddered at the realization it was the first time she had called him by his name, and ached that, despite his deception and rejection, she liked it better than the name he had given her at Wulfen.

From the flicker in his gaze, he was also affected by her familiarity. But considering what he believed of her, it might be offense he took—a sharp reminder of what had first caused her to speak his name.

"Let it pass," she said again, "even if only that my injury serves as a measure of justice for the wrong you believe I have done you."

Ire flared in his eyes. "I am angered by your deceit, but once more you wrong me by thinking I would be gladdened to see you injured."

Though tempted to point out that he was more familiar with deceit than she, as evidenced by their meeting at Wulfen, Gaenor chewed down the argument. "Then I apologize. Now, do you intend to aid me or nay?"

"I do not see that I have a choice."

His words stung, but again she stamped down pride that would have her behave like a child by refusing his aid. "If you would lend me your arm—"

"That would require patience, of which I am sorely lacking at the moment." He swept her into his arms and started across the bailey.

Gaenor was breathless with surprise, for it was many years since any had lifted her off her feet, so ungainly had she become past her twelfth year. And yet Christian seemed unaffected by her long limbs, striding forth as if she was not much more than a child.

It was a peculiar thing to be carried, and she wondered at the feeling that she was safe within the arms of a man who could never love her as Michael loved his Beatrix.

Chancing a glance at her husband's face, she was relieved to see no strain there, only determination, surely born of his desire to deliver her as quickly as possible that he might once more put distance between them.

He carried her across the drawbridge into the inner bailey where, hung from an upper window, was the sheet put out this morn, the blood visible for all to see. Christian's blood. *His* blood that spared her the humiliation of it being said she had not come to him chaste.

Though she was grateful others would never know of her sin, it hurt that he knew. She did not understand it, but more than what others thought of her, she cared what this man thought. Unfortunately, even when her menses flowed and their marriage was consummated, he would not likely ever believe she had not lain with Sir Durand days before her marriage. Of course, it could be worse had he not rejected her on the night past and she too soon bore a babe, for an innocent child would ever suffer its father's pronouncement of illegitimacy.

Realizing that, despite the pain of the night past and the days to come, she had much for which to give thanks, Gaenor closed her eyes. Prayer did not come easy, even within the safety of her mind, but she praised the Lord and asked that He continue to watch over her.

When she lifted her lids, Christian had ascended the donjon steps and was passing through the door that the porter opened for him.

Though she expected her husband to unload her once they were inside, he called to Josephine and ordered her to fetch towels and a basin of cool water.

The woman scurried away, while the others who freshened the rushes and cleaned the hearth paused to watch their lord and lady pass through the hall.

When Christian's long strides delivered them to the stairway, Gaenor ventured another glance at his face. Still no sign of discomfort. In a world comprised of three classes—those who fought, those who prayed, and those who labored—none could dispute that Christian Lavonne seemed born to the first class. Even tonsured and bent over a manuscript, he must have appeared out of place in the monastery. Did he resent the obligation that had ended his life of prayer? Or had the Church been forced on him, making his ascension to the title of baron a blessing?

As much as Gaenor longed to ask that she might know him better, she knew he would not welcome her probing.

Halfway up the stairs, she caught the sound of a struggle. The boy and her brother, she realized when a squeal was answered by a sharp command. If not that it was Abel who attended John in the chamber her brother had been given, Gaenor would have insisted that Christian ensure the child was not being ill-treated. Fortunately, Abel was not of a bent to harm children. Like it or nay, the boy would be scrubbed head to toe. And learn to obey commands.

As Christian ascended to the landing, a crash resounded from behind the closed door on the left. "I fear your brother has set himself a most unpleasant task," he muttered.

"And, I wager, you are thinking the same of the task you have set yourself," Gaenor quipped before she could halt the words that sounded self-pitying.

Christian's step faltered, but he resumed his stride and entered the solar.

"I should not have said what I did," she offered a semblance of an apology as he lowered her to the edge of the postered bed.

"Why not?" He drew back. "'Tis true."

Though she knew she had as good as invited him to hurt her, she searched for a fitting rejoinder. However, the ache of knees unaccustomed to the amount of prayer to which she had subjected them made itself felt.

Grudgingly, she acknowledged that to respond in kind would only build the wall higher between them. Her parents had suffered such an unscalable marriage, and her mother had lived to regret her role in making it so. There was a difference, though. Whereas Lady Isobel had never stopped loving the man who had tried to steal her from her betrothed—and who had died for it on the edge of Drogo Wulfrith's sword—Gaenor did not feel so deeply for Sir Durand that she would love him all the days of her life. He had made sure of that by not loving her in return. It was almost laughable how grateful she now was.

"Something amuses you?" Christian asked.

She had not realized a smile had turned her lips. Humorless though it was, she liked the feel of it, so much that she would not give it up no matter how much her husband wished it. She might be an unwilling participant in the games men played in wielding power over their lessers—King Henry forcing Garr and Christian to unite their warring families, they in turn forcing her to become the means by which the families united—but the worst had to be behind her. Surely that was something to smile about.

"What are you thinking, Gaenor?"

Though her husband's gaze was narrow where he stood above her, she glimpsed wariness in his eyes. "That I am free."

The wariness became suspicion. "What do you—?"

"Milord, I brought what you asked." Standing in the doorway, towels over an arm and a basin hugged to her chest, Josephine looked between her lord and lady.

"Set them there," Christian said with an impatient swipe of a hand.

She hurried forward, lowered her burden to the bedside table, and turned to Gaenor. "You hurt your leg, my lady?"

"My ankle. I—"

"That is all, Josephine."

The woman craned her neck to meet Christian's gaze. "Milord?"

"I will tend my wife."

Gaenor knew concern for her wellbeing was not behind his pronouncement. Rather, her declaration of freedom had opened a door—one he obviously did not trust her to leave wide indefinitely. Did he think she might flee again?

When Josephine had gone, Gaenor met Christian's gaze. His gold-flecked brown eyes searched hers, then he retrieved the basin and towels and went down on a knee.

Though he had told Josephine he would tend the injury, it was a surprise to see him kneel before her, and it was all she could do to draw her next breath.

"Now you will tell me how you are free," he said as he bent his fair head.

It was not a difficult question, and yet when he lifted the hem of her skirt, there were not words enough to answer him. And they became scarcer when he eased the slipper from her foot and curled his fingers in the top of her hose. As he drew off the woolen garment, his calloused fingers brushed her calf...ankle...arch...

He dropped the hose to the rush-covered floor. "I would know, Gaenor."

She tried to retrieve her smile so he would not realize how deeply he affected her, but it was gone. And she felt—

These feelings have naught to do with the heart, Gaenor. Not with one as deceitful and cunning as Christian. They are but things felt between men and women to ensure the population of the earth.

Aye, but knowing it did not make it easier to disregard his touch—or to be so near him, their faces inches apart. Though it was a coward's way out, she lay back on the bed.

Christian did not move for some moments, but then he began to probe her heel and ankle. "The swelling is slight. Do you rest it and keep cool cloths on it today, it will likely serve you fine on the morrow."

He lowered her foot and she heard the slosh of water in the basin, then its drip as the towel was wrung out. The wet cloth with which he bound her ankle was soothing, and she closed her eyes to savor the relief.

The mattress gave beneath her. Flinging her lids open, she met Christian's gaze above hers. Arms braced on either side of her, he said, "I am done waiting."

She held his stare though it felt dangerously intimate, especially in light of the ragged turn her breath had taken and the heat that ran up her face. "'Tis a bitter reality," she said, almost wishing she had kept to herself the words that had unsettled him, "but there seems freedom in losing everything. And that I have done—lost everything."

If a word could have teeth, Christian thought, that last one did, for it was surely another name for her lover—his own bitter reality. "You are right." He hated that her breath upon his face stirred him. "Sir Durand is lost to you forever. It is good you are reconciled to it."

She shook her head. "I do not speak of Sir Durand, for he is hardly lost to me."

Those words had sharper teeth, causing Christian's hands on either side of her to fold into fists. If he had to put a guard on her night and day, confine her to the donjon, lock her away—

"How can he number among my losses when I never truly had him?" she said.

He searched her eyes and picked from their depths a glint of alarm for the emotions he had let onto his face. "Explain yourself."

She moistened her lips, and how he wished she would not! "It is my sister Sir Durand loves, and for it, he can never love me. Though I would not have thought it a month past, I find I am now grateful."

Meaning she would not allow her longing for the knight to forever stand between them? Even if it was possible, there was still something that could come—and stay—between them. "And if you bear him a child?"

Though her smile was weary, it turned her face pretty and reminded him of his time with her at Wulfen Castle. "Again, I tell you, I did not come to you a maiden, but my sin was committed long ere I met you."

He wanted to believe her, to salvage something of their union, but just as much he wanted not to be more of a fool than already she had made him. "If it was not Sir Durand of whom you spoke when you claimed to have lost everything, then what?"

Her laughter was more weary than her smile. "You must think dreadfully ill of me for that not to be obvious."

"Tell me."

"I speak of my virtue, my home, the company and good regard of my family." She lowered her gaze, and when she looked at him again, her brown eyes were moist. "And I speak of Sir Matthew who is not Sir Matthew." She lifted an arm, causing the wheat-colored plait on her shoulder to shift across her breast, and laid a hand on his sleeve. "Hence, the parchment has been scraped clean, and I am free to start anew no matter what you believe of me, no matter how ill you use me."

Christian tensed, not only because of her softly beseeching fingers on him, but from the unspoken things she thought he might do to her. "I would not have you fear me, Gaenor. Upon my word, never will I raise a hand against you."

Pulling her bottom lip between her teeth—once more drawing his regard to her mouth—she released his sleeve and cautiously set her hand upon his jaw. "I would like to believe you, but I know not whether you are nearer a Lavonne or the knight who came to me in the chapel at Wulfen."

Feeling her touch through every pore, Christian acknowledged that it had been imprudent to draw so near, but he had known it even before his unanswered question provided the excuse to do so.

Chastising himself for not leaving her in Josephine's care, for subjecting himself to desire that had gained a foothold while he tended her injury, he lowered his head and turned the surprise that parted her lips into a kiss.

She lay so still it was as if she did not breathe, but slowly she opened to him, hesitantly kissed him back, tentatively drew him down to her. It was as if she was untried in the ways of men and women, had not—

What am I doing? I said I would not, and yet I am ready to forsake the truth of her womb to satisfy the needs of my flesh.

He pulled his mouth from hers, untangled his hand from her thick hair that he had unthinkingly coaxed into giving up much of its plait, and pushed off the mattress.

Standing alongside the bed, breath labored as if he had recently met at swords with her brother, he waited for her to open her eyes.

When she did, her confusion quickly turned to guardedness.

"Aye, start anew, Wife," Christian said, "but do not include me in your plans until *after* your menses flow."

Guardedness turning to indignation, she sat up, her blushing lips and the mess of hair about her face and shoulders in agreement with the sheet hanging outside the window. "If I think to include you at all, *Husband*."

As was becoming habit where she was concerned, Christian rebuked himself. Why had he said it? Though she had been willing and consummation could prove of benefit to her nine months hence, he knew that just as the seduction had ended with him, so it had begun. And yet he struck out at her when his effort would be better spent picking up where he had left off when he had knelt in the chapel at Wulfen Castle.

"Do not leave the solar," he said. "Until your ankle can support your weight, Aimee will bring your meals abovestairs." He turned, crossed the room, and closed the door on her chill stare.

14

GAENOR HAD KNOWN it would not be easy to establish herself as lady of the castle, but the past two days had pushed her patience very near the edge. The castle folk did not like answering to a woman, and that she was a Wulfrith made it less appealing since all had surely suffered from the warring between their liege and her family.

Weary, though the afternoon had yet to wane, she left the cook to his grumbling over her changes to his menu and quit the kitchens. As Christian had predicted, her ankle had recovered sufficiently to support her weight the day following its injury. And one more day had seen it back to near normal. Still, she favored the other foot as she started across the hall.

"My lady, come see!" Aimee broke from two servants who carried a chest toward the stairs and ran forward. "Your clothes have arrived." She halted before Gaenor.

It was good to see the girl smile, for she was more inclined to scowl. Gaenor returned the favor. "See them abovestairs. I shall be up shortly." For, surely, the delivery of her clothes was accompanied by a missive from her family. As Aimee turned away, Gaenor picked out the Wulfrith knight where he stood inside the great doors.

"Sir Mark," she called as she advanced on him.

"Lady Gaenor." His gaze swept her head to toe, and she knew that, besides delivering her possessions, he was tasked with reporting on her appearance—a small thing considering Abel remained at Broehne.

Glad she no longer limped, she stopped before him. "I trust your journey was uneventful."

His gaze returned to hers, and she was grateful there seemed nothing more in his eyes than there had ever been—no judgment or condemnation for her flight from Stern Castle. "We encountered no hindrances, my lady."

She was relieved, though she knew it could not last. The search for the brigands that had caused Christian and her brother to depart Broehne the day after her wedding and seen them returned but two hours ago, had yielded little according to Abel who had come to the donjon to see how she had fared in his absence. As for Christian, he had yet to appear, and she dreaded when he did, for they had last been face-to-face when his kiss would have led to consummation had he not pulled back.

Trying not to relive his words that had fairly accused her of seducing him to legitimize a child that might be born of her and Sir Durand's union, she asked the knight, "You have seen my brother, Abel?"

"Aye, and delivered him word from Baron Wulfrith."

"Have you word for me?"

Sir Mark drew forth a rolled parchment. "Your mother asked that I deliver this."

She curled her fingers around it. "I thank you, Sir Mark. Of course, you will take supper with us and pass the night at Broehne."

He gave a curt shake of his head. "Many thanks, my lady, but my men and I are to continue on to Wulfen Castle. Sir Everard expects us this eve."

As much as she longed to discourage him from riding into the darkening of day that might see him set upon, she knew he would not heed her. "Godspeed, then."

A smile tucked up the corners of his mouth. "I have faith He shall."

Gaenor watched him go before turning her regard on the half-dozen servants who were intent on the tasks she had set them, though not so intent she would feel comfortable reading her mother's missive here—and less so in the presence of Sir Hector, the aged knight whom Christian had surely set to watch over her.

Minding her ankle, she crossed to the stairs and stepped aside to allow the men who had carried her chest abovestairs to continue their descent.

When she entered the solar, Aimee was on her knees before the chest. "Oh, my lady, such fine garments! And look, be this ivory?" She held up a comb, its spine worked with beautifully carved flowers.

Gaenor considered sending her away but decided she could read her mother's missive before the brazier while the girl familiarized herself with the garments and accoutrements that it would be her responsibility to keep in order. "Aye, 'tis ivory, a gift from my eldest brother."

"Most kind he must be, my lady."

That Gaenor could not argue. She crossed to the chair situated before the warming brazier, lowered to it, and broke the missive's wax seal. While Aimee continued to chatter about her discoveries, Gaenor unrolled the parchment and felt her heart convulse over the familiar handwriting.

Beloved Daughter,
There are not words enough to tell you how sorry I am that you felt it necessary to flee Stern. I have wanted only your happiness, and it pains me that the king demanded such a sacrifice of you. I pray you will take comfort in knowing your family is most grateful and proud of you.

Gaenor closed her eyes. Proud? Did her mother know of her sin? That she had not come to her marriage chaste? She could not, for there was no gain in Garr telling her. It would only worry her more.

"And this hand mirror!" Aimee exclaimed. "It is so clear. Why, I did not think myself so pretty."

Though Gaenor's emotions were bound to her mother's words, she could not help but smile over the girl's excitement.

Of greater comfort is the surety that, had your brothers believed Christian Lavonne to be dishonorable, nothing would have impelled them to give you into his care.

The tinkle of bells preceded a gasp. "Hear that, my lady? Certes, 'tis the language of angels."

Gaenor remembered when she had bought the bells at market with the woman who would become her sister-in-law though, at the time, there had seemed no hope for it since Annyn was to have wed the rapacious Geoffrey Lavonne. The man's death had changed everything, and now Gaenor was the one sacrificed.

"Do you not think, my lady?"

Gaenor peered around the chair. "I am glad you like the bells. Take them—they are yours."

The girl startled so violently that, if not for the mouthful of teeth she showed, one might think she had been slapped. "Truly, my lady?"

"Truly." Gaenor sat back.

I expect life must seem bleak, but I know you have the courage and fortitude to make of your marriage what I refused to make of mine. As Beatrix has found love with her Michael, I believe you will find love if you but look for it and learn to forgive where I could not. My knees and hands ache with prayers for you and your Christian.

"My Christian," Gaenor whispered. Would he ever be truly hers? Or would their marriage be ever what it had been these past days—living in the same world in name only?

"This is most fine, my lady. What will ye make of it?"

Grudgingly, Gaenor heeded Aimee and saw that the young woman cradled a bolt of material the color of dewed moss. Her mother had included it, though there was no longer a need for a gown in which to be wed. "I do not know." She returned to her missive.

I hope you will also seek God and remember all that I endeavored to teach you, above all that prayer is mighty. Have faith, beloved Gaenor, and know you are loved. ~ Isobel Wulfrith

As Gaenor closed her eyes that she might rest in her mother's words, Aimee again made her presence known. "This is a psalter, is it not? Why, 'tis more lovely than I have been told."

Doubtless, Isobel had sent it to aid with Gaenor's prayers.

"Oh, a page has fallen out!"

How had that happened? Had the binding—?

Gaenor surged to her feet, advanced on the wide-eyed maid who stumbled upright, and snatched the folded parchment from amid the rushes.

"My lady, 'twas not I who loosened the page. I was most careful."

The beat of her heart insistent, as if it sought to escape its cage, Gaenor forced a calming breath and took the psalter from her. "That is all, Aimee."

Confusion furrowed her face. "I vow I did not do it, my lady."

Gaenor nodded. "The psalter is of an age." Not true, but she could not tell her that the loose parchment had never been bound with the words of God. Indeed, it was so far removed from holiness that its presence might be called an abomination. "Now leave me."

Aimee glanced at the garments she had laid out on the bed. "What of your clothes, my lady?"

"I will see to them."

"But—"

"I will see to them, Aimee."

Resentment flashed in the girl's eyes. "As you will." With a tinkling of the bells she had secreted somewhere on her person, she hurried to the door and paused. "I may keep the bells, my lady?"

"They are my gift to you." Hopefully, they would ease the sting of being sent away so abruptly.

As the door closed, Gaenor turned her attention to Aimee's discovery. She should not have panicked, for it was not as if the maid could read a word of Sir Durand's missive. Still, it boded ill that it was in the home of Gaenor's husband.

She laid the psalter atop a woolen mantle in the chest, returned to the brazier, and reached the missive to the flames, only to pull back. Strange, but she could not clearly recall the words the knight had written though she had read them again and again. She unfolded the missive.

My lady, Gaenor,
I pray one day you will forgive me. ~ Ever your friend, Durand

So few words ought to be harder to forget than to remember, and yet they had slunk away with the advent of Christian.

Gaenor tossed the missive on the flames. The parchment darkened until it was indistinguishable from the black inked words, then collapsed and began its descent into ashes.

"Farewell, Sir Durand," she whispered. "You are forgiven." The absolution reminding her of her mother's missive that advised her to learn to forgive, she spun around.

The parchment had rolled back on itself and lay beside the chair where, in her haste to retrieve Sir Durand's missive, she had dropped it. She swept it up, read it again, and felt tears. Her mother's words were to be cherished and were worthy of being always at hand—as far from abomination as the truth was from a lie.

She smoothed the parchment on the table beside the chair, folded it, and retrieved her psalter from the chest. Where Sir Durand's missive had too long resided, she placed her mother's missive. "Better," she breathed, and though she had intended to set the psalter aside, she turned instead to the first psalm.

The maid, who surely had better things to do, was jingling.

More disrespect? Having received Sir Hector's report that his wife's attempts to claim her place as the lady of Broehne had been met with much grudging, Christian halted at the center of the hall. "Aimee!"

The young woman jumped, as did the servants around whom she had been prancing. "My lord!" She hurried forward, setting herself to jingling again.

"As it is your duty to see to my wife's needs, I would expect you to be abovestairs tending to the arrival of her clothes."

She came to stand before him, and the jingling ceased. "That I was doing, my lord, and still I would be had she not sent me away."

He narrowed his lids. "Were you impertinent?"

"Nay, my lord. Indeed, she was so grateful for my help that she rewarded me with bells." She shook a leg, causing the bells to sound again.

Christian ground his teeth. "Then you have settled her possessions?"

"I would have, but as I said, she sent me away."

"Why?"

She drew a long breath. "I vow I did not do it, my lord—I was most gentle—but when I unpacked her psalter, a page fell out and methinks she blames me for it."

Christian remembered her psalter that he had trespassed upon at Wulfen Castle and by which he had first learned the name of the one to whom she had given her heart. And her body.

"I do not think she will welcome me back, my lord, but if you wish it, I shall return to the solar."

"Nay, you have done your duty." Now if only his *wife* would do hers, but she likely clung to that accursed missive, was even now—

He strode to the stairs. When he entered the solar, he did not do so quietly, and yet Gaenor did not seem to hear him where she stood with her back to him before her opened chest. Her attention was held by whatever she bent her head to, and it would not surprise him if it was that miscreant's plea for forgiveness.

Advancing on her, he said, "No welcome for the husband returned to you?"

He heard her breath catch, then the snap of what he saw was her psalter as she turned to face him. Stopping short of her, he stared at the unbound parchment just visible between the covers of the book.

She swallowed hard enough to be heard. "I did not hear you."

Hating that his jealousy should be so strongly felt, he raised his gaze over her. "So deep at prayer were you?"

He expected a guilty flush to add to the color in her face, but it did not. Pressing her shoulders back, she said, "Indeed, I was."

It was no easy thing to let her lie slip past—to not seize the psalter and expose her yearning for another man—but he pulled himself back from that edge. Still, he had to ask, "For what do you pray?"

She narrowed her lids. "That is between God and me."

If not for the content of her prayers, he would advise her to seek the spiritual guidance of the castle priest as the Church advocated, but he did not trust her beseechings, nor her confessions, to remain private any more than he trusted his own. Though the priest seemed a good enough man, he was too prone to idle chat.

"Now..." Gaenor reached the psalter behind her and dropped it atop the remaining contents of her chest. "...what welcome were you expecting?"

He stared at the psalter, the delivery of which he should have expected. How long did she intend to hold on to it—more specifically, what it secreted? Was the missive so dear she would risk its discovery by keeping it near?

"What welcome, husband?"

It was a good, albeit difficult, question, for the last time he had crossed words with her he had warned her not to include him in her plans to start anew until after her menses. Until that event, he could hardly act the husband returning home to his wife, no matter how often he recalled the sweetness of her lips.

He stepped around her and considered the garments and accessories strewn across the bed. There lay the hooded mantle she had worn to the chapel at Wulfen, also the gown of dark-blue cloth. "You are pleased to have your belongings?"

"I am."

He looked across his shoulder. "You know your brother's men also delivered your palfrey?"

Her eyes brightened. "I did not."

"It has been stabled."

She clasped her hands at her waist. "I thank you."

Christian wearied of their stilted exchange, though he knew he had turned their talk this direction by ignoring her question.

"'Twill be good to ride again," she surprised him. "Mayhap…" She shrugged. "…you could take me around the barony."

Feeling the grit and grime of two days in the saddle upon the grounds of his demesne, he said, "Abel told you our search for the brigands yielded naught?"

"He did."

"Then you know Sir Robert is still out there."

She inclined her head. "With your father."

Providing Aldous yet lived. "Though you are just the temptation to bring them out of hiding, I will not offer you up as bait, Gaenor. Hence, until they are—" He frowned, then glowered. "How know you my father is with Robert?"

She blinked. "Garr told me ere he left for Stern."

Christian turned his hands into fists. "It was not his place to do so."

She put her head to the side. "'Twas your place, but do you recall, when I asked after your father, you denied me."

He had told her he would discuss Aldous at a time of his own choosing. And he had intended to, but after what had happened between them in this chamber, then the sighting of the brigands that he had been grateful for beyond the possibility of their capture…

"You are right," he said. "I should have told you."

Her lips parted. He had surprised her—and himself, for though he had determined through prayer these past days to seek some semblance of peace with her, that was before Sir Durand's missive stole into his home. And into their bedchamber.

Anger seeking a new level, he forced his clenched hands open. *Leave it be, Christian. Soon enough you will know whether she carries his child. Then you can determine how best to proceed with this marriage.*

Wondering what darkness cast about her husband's mind that made his struggle so palpable, Gaenor said, "I am grateful you would not use me as bait, but I beseech you not to allow your brother to make of me a prisoner. Even if you will not take me riding, I am sure Abel—"

"I will think on it," Christian said sharply, then less so, "How fares your ankle?"

She sighed. "Better."

"And John?"

He was another matter altogether. Though she had hoped the boy would be a diversion from the weightiness of her marriage, he was only tolerably less difficult than he had been that first day. "He is angry and confused by the loss of his mother, so much that only today did I see anything near a smile upon his face, and only when Abel came to the donjon."

Remembering the boy's sighting of the man who had scoured him clean and how he had scurried after him when Abel departed, she smiled. "I fear that, as long as my brother is at Broehne, he will find himself in possession of a short and unrelenting shadow."

Seeing Christian's gaze was drawn to her mouth, she remembered when, in the guise of Sir Matthew, he had said she was most becoming when she smiled. And the fool she had been had told him he gave her much to smile about. She eased her lips. For nothing would she give him further reason to accuse her of seduction.

His eyes returned to hers. "It seems I no longer give you much to smile about."

He remembered too. Before she could think better of it, her thoughts wished themselves into words. "'Twas Sir Matthew who made me smile, and you are not...he." That last came out on a breath of regret.

Again she caught the folding of his fingers into fists. Though he had vowed he would not raise a hand against her, there was comfort in having the chest between them—and it was that to which he next directed his gaze. As he stared into its depleted depths, she wondered if he gauged it as an obstacle to retaliation.

"Neither am I Sir Durand," he said, almost with resignation, and once more turned his regard on her. "I am Christian Lavonne, and the sooner you reconcile yourself to that, the better it will go for us." He came around the chest, strode past her, and out of the solar.

Gaenor released the breath she had not realized she was holding, retrieved the psalter, and hugged it to her. "Lord, help me think through my thoughts ere I let them onto my tongue." She squeezed her eyes closed. "'Tis too late for love, but surely not too late for peace between us. Aye, peace is all I ask."

He knew it would end badly for him. There was little question of it, certainly not with the king also set on his demise. Nevertheless, it would also end badly for others, and that made Robert's failures tolerable and discomforts bearable. Today, however, success. Or something near it. After all, it was not a Wulfrith his men had taken, but a Wulfrith knight—and at a high price.

Though the three men-at-arms accompanying the knight on his journey to Wulfen Castle were now well on their way to hell, the bloody skirmish had taken the lives of five of Robert's men, left two so severely wounded their injuries might prove fatal, and laid down a half dozen in need of the healer's needle and thread. Unfortunately, Wulfrith's man must first be given the benefit of the woman's ministrations, for his value—whatever it might prove—lay in keeping him alive. For now.

At the center of the camp, Robert dismounted with the others, bent to the belly of the horse tethered to his own, and applied a dagger to the rope that bound the Wulfrith knight over the saddle. With a shove to the shoulder, he sent the man off the other side.

A grunt of pain sounded from the knight when he hit the ground.

Robert knew he should not have done that, not with his prisoner so injured, but the impulse had been too satisfying. "Helene!"

As if she had been awaiting his summons, she pushed back the flap of Aldous's tent and stepped out. Pretty little thing, and if not that his accursed father objected, he would have found other uses for her.

Frowning over the bloodied knight, she advanced with short steps accompanied by the clink and clatter of metal. The next time she tried to run, she would not get as far as she had two days past.

"Tend him well so he does not die on me," Robert said, "then see to my men."

She narrowed her eyes on him before dropping to her knees beside the knight.

The temptation to strike her never far, Robert took a step toward her, but no more. The problem with Helene of Tippet was that she hit—and bit—back, which led to the greater problem that if he gave the wench what she deserved, he might find himself without a caregiver for Aldous. The thought was enough to sour his stomach and make him question, as he did more and more of late, why he had not left his demanding sire at Broehne.

Helene eased the Wulfrith knight onto his back, only to have the neck of her bodice seized by the injured man.

"Ho!" one of Robert's men crowed and was echoed by others who drew near as if to enjoy a rooster fight.

Feeling no need to aid the healer, for she had well enough proved her size was not proportionate to her strength when they had stolen her from Tippet, Robert looked between the two.

She cupped a hand over the knight's where he held her. "No ill do I mean you, Sir Knight," she said in Norman French, the language of the nobility that set her apart from most commoners. "I am a healer and, if you allow me, I will see to your injuries."

"They are not mortal," the man ground between clenched teeth.

But they were surely painful, every burn, throb, sting, and twinge well deserved for the thinning of the brigands' ranks, Robert mulled with satisfaction. As with each time he encountered a Wulfrith-trained knight, including his departed brother, Geoffrey, resentment surged anew that Aldous had not sought such training for his eldest son. This knight, now at his mercy, should have died thrice considering the number of men Robert had set on him.

"Your injuries may not be mortal," Helene said, "but if infection sets in, you will likely share the fate of those who did not survive this day. Pray, let me aid you."

The knight released her, turned his head opposite, and scanned the faces of the brigands until he found Robert. "You know you will gain naught by holding me."

"I do not know that." Robert pulled his newly acquired weapon from its sheath, stepped forward, and dropped to his haunches. "Hence, rather than slit you navel to nose with your own dagger, a coveted Wulfrith dagger, no less"—he grudgingly admired the superb workmanship that had been denied him—"I will keep you around for a while." He smiled and lowered the blade to the knight's crimson-stained chest. "The only say you have is whether or not you must needs be staked to the ground that Helene may tend you."

"'Twill not be necessary," the healer said, bending nearer Wulfrith's man. "Tell him, Sir Knight."

He held Robert's gaze. "If the illegitimate issue of Aldous Lavonne fears for his life, as well he should, his only course is to stake me."

Anger burned a jagged path through Robert. He did not fear anything, not now that he accepted his circumstances would eventually conspire to see his blood flow more freely than this knight's.

He snorted, stood, and slammed the toe of his boot into the man's ribs. As Helene gasped and the knight groaned, Robert motioned two men forward. "Secure him however the healer deems best and keep a guard over him." He pointed the Wulfrith dagger at the first man's face, then the other's. "Do not fail me."

The men nodded.

Robert stepped past them. As Aldous would want to hear of the day's success, his one worthy son would deliver the tidings. He threw back the tent flap, ducked inside, and crossed to where his father huddled amid a gathering of blankets and furs.

To his surprise, the old man was asleep, his scarred and melted face flaccid but for the slight puffing of his cheeks as he expelled breath.

The need to stay ahead of their pursuers forcing them to move camp almost daily was depleting Aldous as Helene was so fond of arguing. But that was not Robert's concern. His father had agreed to leave Broehne. Of course, had he protested, he would still be here. Regardless how ill unto death the old man fell, he was not going back, for the little monk who had usurped Robert's place as surely as Geoffrey had done was more vulnerable with his father's wellbeing to consider.

Robert laughed. "Little monk," he murmured as his words went to stand alongside the broad, towering image of Christian. "I like that."

"A Wulfrith...dagger." Aldous rumbled.

Gripping the weapon tighter at his side, Robert followed his father's heavily lidded gaze to the distinctive hilt. "Aye, taken this day from a Wulfrith knight." He waited for an exclamation of surprise...praise... anything but the words Aldous next spoke.

"My Geoffrey was awarded one—an honor that told he was the worthiest of those deemed worthy."

Anger again. More jagged. Before it could set a course for his trembling hand, Robert subdued its physical expression. "Yes, and he is dead, Father." *And your little monk is next.* "Much good the Wulfrith dagger did him, eh?"

Something like a whimper sounded from Aldous. "Oh, beloved Geoffrey, all my hopes, my dreams..."

"Will die with you," Robert snarled.

Whether the old man heard was not apparent, for he turned his face into a fold of fur and continued to besiege his eldest son's ears with moanings over Geoffrey—until Robert had to decide between availing himself of the Wulfrith dagger's keen edge or taking his leave.

15

He had been in their bed last night. Nevertheless, if not for the state of the bedclothes and the impression in his pillow, she would not have known he had been there, for she had slept through his coming and going.

Gaenor lifted her bowed head and once more peered over her shoulder. Of the scant dozen who had come to the chapel to hear morning mass, Christian had yet to appear among them.

Why? Not only had he been of the Church in that first life of his, but he was now lord to those for whom he ought to set a godly example. She had been so certain she would find him here, had hoped...

The priest's closing prayer returned her attention to him, and with silent beseeching she sought God's favor in helping her and Christian mend whatever bent and broken things could be rendered workable between them.

The priest blessed them all, but as Gaenor joined the others in exiting the chapel, he overtook her. "You grace our chapel with your attendance, my lady."

"I thank you for your instruction."

He inclined his head. "Your brothers attended mass ere they departed Broehne."

Garr and Everard. Abel as well? Or was he as absent then as he was today?

"I pray you also intend to regularly attend services, my lady."

"I do."

He smiled. "Then mayhap we will yet see the chapel filled, especially if your good husband accompanies you."

She knew the answer, but asked, "He does not come often?"

The man sighed. "Alas, I fear not, but now that he is wed and, God willing, shall soon have sons in need of holy instruction, I have hope."

Would there be sons? Daughters? Might their unquestioned paternity heal the mistakes Christian and she had made?

Make it so, Lord. Let the coming of my menses be enough to begin anew.

Gaenor thanked the priest again and stepped into the dawning of day. Since Broehne's donjon did not house the chapel, it having been erected in the inner bailey, she was met by moist air, the white breath of which crawled along the ground. Tightening her mantle about her as she moved among the stirrings of life that would soon be teeming, she veered away from the donjon's main entrance. It was easier to reach the kitchen by going around the side and through the garden. It was also more pleasant.

Hoping Cook had heeded her instructions and his resentment had diminished even the smallest bit, she unlatched the garden gate and pushed it closed behind her.

Here, the morning mist did not crawl along the ground but glided among the herbs and flowers on either side of the graveled path she walked. Though tempted to settle upon one of the benches, she promised herself she would come back later when there was not so much that needed doing.

The gate groaned, and she turned to find Christian advancing on her.

He broke his stride two feet from her. "I was surprised to see you outside the donjon."

Then he did not know she had come from morning mass, likely suspected ill of her. Further temptation beset her—to serve up sarcasm alongside his suspicion—but there had been nothing habitual about her prayers this morn. What she asked of God He surely would not do if she did not take her own prayers seriously. "I attended mass."

"Ah." He nodded, causing a lock of fair hair to fall across his brow and make her fingers curl against the impulse to set it right. "I suppose the priest tasked you with persuading me to accompany you."

She liked how he looked in the bare light of day, for it reminded her of how he had looked in twilight when he had kissed her in the wood at Wulfen. Fortunately, he was more in control of his emotions than she, for she did not think it would take much to make her forget she should not lie with him until it was proved she did not carry another man's child.

She moistened her lips. "You should attend mass, if not for yourself, then those who look to you to lead them."

He seemed to consider it.

"Why do you not? You sought the chapel at Wulfen."

He almost smiled. "I did. And you are right, I should."

Then he would?

He looked up. "It appears the sun will be out full today. Will you seek it—even at the risk of freckles?"

Obviously, he remembered when, as Sir Matthew, he had found her on the roof and she had confessed to being partial to the sun no matter the consequences to her skin. "If I have the opportunity, I shall, but there is much to busy me."

"And much opposition."

Sir Hector was not remiss in reporting her movements. "As a Wulfrith, 'tis to be expected." She started to turn away. "I must speak with Cook about the morning meal."

"I shall take you riding today."

Gaenor stilled and looked over her shoulder. "Truly?"

"After we break our fast." He raised his eyebrows. "If you wish."

Was God acting on her behalf? So soon? Tears threatening, she said, "I do," and hurried toward the kitchens that he might not see how moved she was.

She did not expect him to follow, but he did. She did not expect to find herself the topic of conversation by those on the other side of the partially opened door, but she was.

"Accursed Wulfrith woman! Thinks she knows better than I how to run my kitchen."

"Um hmm."

The whine belonged to Cook. The murmur could be any one of those who scurried amid the heat and din to do his bidding.

"Tells me the broth is too watered. So what do I say, eh? I can thicken it with a wad of spit if it please ye, m'lady."

It was what he had said. Though Gaenor had longed to leave him to his kitchens, she had reached inside herself and found her mother. Having sustained Cook's challenging gaze without waver, she had turned and spat into the enormous pot. "Nay, spit will not do it," she had said, "and now that it is fouled, you shall have to make a new batch. This time thicker."

Sensing dark tension behind her, Gaenor looked around. Christian's face was grim, nostrils flared, jaw hard.

"Ain't right our lord be made to wed somethin' like that," Cook continued. "'Tis no wonder the old man took his leave."

Christian's arm shot past Gaenor, but she grabbed it before he could throw the door wider. As the cook continued to grumble, she stepped near her husband. "Do not do this," she whispered. "Pray, do not."

"You are my *wife!*" he rasped, his harsh breath warming her face.

His defense of her was heartening, but this was not the place for it. "You can force them to show me respect"—she held to the tense muscles beneath her fingers—"but you cannot force them *to* respect me." She took a step nearer and pressed a hand to his chest. "That is what I want, Christian, and your wrath will not grant it."

He searched her eyes, then looked to the doorway. When he returned to her, it was her mouth his gaze fell to, and she sensed they were in the wood again—the moment before he had kissed her.

With a sharp breath, he stepped back and pulled his arm from her grasp. "*This* time I let it pass." He turned and, over his shoulder, said, "Be ready to ride after you have broken your fast."

In the time it took for him to stride to the gate, the talk on the other side of the door receded. Thus, when Gaenor entered the kitchens, the cook could not be certain his words had found her ears.

"I would go with you!"

"Nay, you will stay." Abel leaned down from his destrier and ruffled the boy's hair. "And you will behave."

John, who Gaenor had nearly trod upon this morn where he had made his bed outside Abel's chamber, glowered.

"You will, John." Abel straightened in the saddle. "Do you understand?"

The boy's jaw shifted, gaze wavered and, with a catch in his voice, he said, "You will come back?"

Gaenor ached for him. In the absence of his mother, he had further attached himself to Abel who, twice now, had broken the attachment in order to do his duty.

"I will return, and soon," her brother said. "Indeed, so soon that you may await me here if you like."

It was true, for he had but offered to join the men-at-arms who would serve as escort to Christian and Gaenor.

John thrust his chin forward. "I shall wait here, Sir Abel."

"Good boy." Abel looked to Christian where he was mounted beside Gaenor. "Shall we?"

It seemed to take forever to guide their horses over the drawbridge, so anxious was Gaenor to gain speed beneath her and rushing air upon her face and through her hair.

"I advise we stay in the open," Abel called as the drawbridge gave onto the beaten dirt road.

Gaenor knew he did not trust the cover of the wood. Were they watched? Nay, she would not think on that. She would enjoy this moment, this truce, even if the man beside her was still in an ill mood over Cook's words.

At last they were off the path and the horses were allowed to run. The air made free with Gaenor's hair, tugging and whipping at her braids, loosing strands and tresses. The sun sidled up the sky, breathing warmth upon her face and coaxing her freckles to show themselves. The man who was her husband stayed at her side, setting the pace and drawing her eye time and again.

She had deemed him not quite handsome, but as he relaxed into the ride, she thought she might have been wrong. His chin was defined, nothing weak about it, cheekbones broad, mouth far from thin-lipped, hair...

Whereas the air disheveled hers, it played in his, tugging at the fair strands, pushing them this way and that as if they were but fingers combing at them. Imagining the fingers were hers, she ran the thumb of her free hand over the pads of her fingers.

Christian felt Gaenor's gaze, and not for the first time. However, when he looked around, her eyes met his as they had not before. And she smiled. Her show of teeth and dimpling of cheeks gave him hope he knew he should not risk until given proof she was not with child, but he defied reason and smiled back.

To his surprise, she laughed and urged her palfrey ahead of his.

The ride was exhilarating, and Christian would have liked it to last longer, but Abel called out a warning when they were out of sight of the castle.

Resenting Robert's stranglehold on the barony, Christian overtook Gaenor. "We must needs turn back."

She slowed her palfrey to a walk. "So soon?"

"Aye. Until the brigands are routed from Abingdale, I will risk no more than this where you are concerned."

She considered him a long moment, then turned her palfrey back the way they had come. "I understand."

"Do you?" He wished he did—or, perhaps, that he did *not*.

As he regained her side, she said, "Nay, I suppose I do not understand."

Christian sought out the men-at-arms and Abel who flanked them, determined they were not near enough to hear, and once more defied reason. "At Wulfen, you said you liked that I did not look through you—that I saw *you*."

Stiffening in the saddle, she withheld her gaze.

"In spite of all, I still do, Gaenor, and now you know 'tis not because I had not laid eyes on your sister."

She said nothing, and while he waited on her, he turned his head to survey the bordering wood. He trusted the vigilance of Abel and his men-at-arms, but as had been stressed during his training at Wulfen, it was his responsibility to protect his back—more, Gaenor's back.

"I know that now," she said so low her words nearly slipped past. "Just as I know that, in exchange for testimony of Beatrix's innocence, you forced Garr to agree to hand me over. Like chattel."

It was too late to do things differently. He eased his destrier nearer, the brush of his calf against hers causing her to look around. "I wished for an end to the warring between our families—the suffering of both our peoples, Gaenor—and you were the promise of that. But I would have you know, had your brother not agreed to my terms, I would not have denied your sister her testimony. God forgive me, I am not above lying, but I am above the taking of innocent lives."

He held her gaze, letting her search his for the truth. It was there, if she would but see it.

She looked toward the castle walls that were yet distant and would be for some time at this pace.

Christian scanned the trees again. "Was it Sir Durand who told you of the bargain?"

She hesitated, but when she said, "Aye," he knew her admission was likely the result of her belief that the knight was safely out of his reach.

"That is why you fled Stern?"

"That is why."

"Though you knew it was Beatrix for whom he felt?"

"Though I knew." Her shoulders rose with a deep breath. "It was foolish, but it seemed preferable to marrying a Lavonne who had made a game of my sister's life, a man I did not know." She looked sidelong at him. "I *thought* I did not know. Do I?"

Christian laid a hand over hers that gripped the reins. "I would have you believe me, Gaenor. The bargain I made was but an ill-conceived ploy."

She lowered her gaze to their hands. When she looked back at him, her eyes were pools of sorrow. "I want to believe, just as I want you to believe that what happened between Sir Durand and me happened months ago." She put her head to the side. "But who will be the first to believe?"

She asked this when she dared to keep her lover's missive? A missive secreted in the psalter he had seen beside the bed when he had come to their chamber after the middling of night? He withdrew his hand from hers.

When there was once more space between their horses, Gaenor said, "Of course, you will come nearer to believing me when my flux is upon me." She frowned. "Though still it will not be enough, will it? All it will prove is that when I fled Stern with Sir Durand, a child was not conceived."

She was right, but more because of the missive. How was he to believe her response to him at Wulfen was genuine when that accursed piece of parchment was yet between them?

Lord, she near sleeps with the thing!

He ought to tear it apart...burn it. And he would if not that it was of use to him—as a test of sorts. It would mean nothing if he took the missive from her, everything if she disposed of it herself.

Sensing the bore of Abel's gaze, he glanced beyond her to where her brother kept pace. Doubtless, he questioned the exchange between his sister and her husband.

Gaenor put her chin up and shook her braids back. "I thank you for the ride," she said, then put her heels to her palfrey.

Christian spurred after her but allowed her to keep the lead. As long as she did not get any farther ahead, she would be safe.

Gaenor leaned over her palfrey's neck, closed her eyes, savored the cool air against her lids, and tried to think only on this. She could not, for Christian was nearly as corporeal in her thoughts as when he stood before her.

Lifting her lids, she noted the work day had begun, as evidenced by the appearance of villagers and their carts on the road before the castle.

She sighed. She had not meant to reject Christian's attempt at peace, and she had not, but neither had she taken hold of it. To do so would require trust, and trust was not like a river, flowing only in one direction. It had to flow both ways, did it not?

Mayhap not in the beginning. It could start with you.

She shook her head. To trust first would mean lowering her defenses. If she did that, she would fall in love with Christian as she had come far too close to doing already, and the thought of loving another man who did not love her was unbearable.

The castle steadily gained in size, and still Christian let her stay out ahead, for which she was grateful when a tear slid down her face. She let it go, knowing that, by ride's end, no trace would remain.

Nearing the castle, she straightened in the saddle, but before she slowed her palfrey, a cry sounded from the far end of the dirt road where it wound out of the wood. A wagon careened forward. It was too distant to be certain, but the one driving the horse appeared to be a woman, and a larger figure was slumped across her lap.

Despite the fear that shot through Gaenor, she turned her palfrey away from the castle and urged it to greater speed.

"Gaenor, nay!" It was Christian. Or was it Abel? Both? Regardless, they were not far behind, though far enough that they were unable to overtake her before she reached the wagon.

The woman dragged on the reins, stopping the wagon so abruptly the man rolled off her lap and landed at her feet. "Lord have mercy!" She dropped to her knees beside him. "Look what they done to him!"

He pressed a bloodied hand to his ear, groaned, and rocked side to side. "Cut it off, they did!"

Registering a frighteningly rank smell, Gaenor gripped the pommel to dismount.

A hand closed on her arm. "Stay astride," Christian growled.

She jerked her head around. Where there had been gold flecks in his eyes before, there were none now. Though she had seen him angry, this was not that.

"Aye," she breathed.

He released her and swung out of the saddle.

Abel had already dismounted and threw her a look nearly equal to Christian's as he strode to the wagon around which the rest of the escort had gathered.

"It was the brigands, Margery?" Christian asked as he came alongside the woman.

Plump chest rising and falling rapidly, she said, "Aye, my lord. And Sir Robert." Chin dimpling with the effort to control her emotions, she bobbed her head. "'Twas he who told them to cut off Will's ear—and it weren't as if he refused 'em or nothin' like."

"Refused them what?"

She jerked her chin over her shoulder. "That ain't grain to be milled, my lord. 'Tis a message from your brother. 'Deliver 'em to the little monk and his dirty Wulfrith bride,' he did say."

Gaenor looked to the rear of the wagon, her fear trebling when her gaze settled on the lumps beneath a stained blanket. The stains…the stench…the blood…Whose?

"Ranulf!" Christian called. "Return my wife to the donjon."

As the man-at-arms came for her, Gaenor nudged her palfrey forward and leaned down. Once more, her husband and brother objected, but she whipped off the blanket. And gagged.

The bodies were savaged in ways she could never have imagined. All that remained intact were faces that did not belong to Garr or Everard. But they were men she knew.

When Ranulf took the reins from her and turned her palfrey, Gaenor was too cold to protest—as if caught out in a snow in naught but her chemise.

Behind, her brother cursed and Christian asked, "You know them?"

Teeth beginning to chatter, Gaenor peered over her shoulder.

Abel stood at the rear of the wagon, handsome face contorted into something fearfully ugly. "They are from Stern, the same who delivered my sister's chest on the day past ere continuing on to Wulfen."

Christian stepped alongside him, and Gaenor ached that he and her brother appeared so well-matched in anger, something that might see them both dead. "You think they hold Sir Mark?"

The knight who had delivered her mother's missive…

"I wager they do, and that he is alive." Abel turned to Christian. "Accept it now if you have not, Baron Lavonne—whether it is by my sword or another's, your brother is dead."

16

"The cold will not leave me be."

Christian had expected to find her abed, not sitting before the brazier that had little to recommend it for warmth at this hour of the night.

He turned from the bed he had longed for after a day spent tracking the brigands and strode to the chair. When he came around it, the faint glow of the dying fire revealed Gaenor huddled there, legs drawn to her chest, blankets up to her ears. For all her exceptional height, she looked painfully slight.

"You should be abed."

Her gaze drifted from the brazier at his back, up his chest, to his eyes. "They are still out there."

He knew his failure to bring Robert to ground showed in his face, but he said, "They are," though twice he and his men had come maddeningly close thanks to Abel's tracking skills. Considering the number of men Christian had taken with him, one thing was certain—Robert and those who had attacked Margery and her husband had not had Aldous with them, for speed had been their ally. Unfortunately, wherever their camp was located, it was moved often.

"I knew the men they tore apart," Gaenor said so low he nearly missed her words.

Forgetting how weary he was, Christian sank to his haunches before her. "Gaenor—"

"I wanted to wed one of them when I was a girl." She stared past him. "He was handsome and kind and strong. What they did to him…" Her breath caught and eyes glittered. "A wild animal might do that, not a human." Her gaze shot to Christian's and, past chattering teeth, she said, "I do not understand."

Her brothers had shielded her well from the reasons so many vied to have their sons train at Wulfen.

Christian reached forward and slid the backs of his fingers down her moist cheek. "I have yet to understand it myself. 'Tis ungodly, but it is what some men do."

"Where is God when they do it?"

Christian knew what his abbot would have said, but he could not believe God was so wrathful to punish people for their unconfessed sins that he sent such evil into their midst, and he would not have her believe it either. "I think He must be there with the sufferers, longing to help, but with a greater purpose than we can know."

She shuddered. "Such pretty words for such an ugly thing."

"I am sorry, but they are all I have." He straightened. "And now, I want you to come to bed."

"I would stay here."

"You will not." He leaned down, slid his hands beneath her blanketed form, and lifted her into his arms.

When he laid her on the bed, he was not surprised to find the mattress bare of bedclothes. He reached to peel the layers from her, but she clutched at them and whispered, "I am so cold."

"Then I shall warm you." Though he did not trust himself and knew temptation was a touch away, he lay down beside her and gathered her to him.

So rigid was she that Christian thought holding her was probably not much different from embracing a fence post, but slowly she began to ease, her teeth ceased their chattering and her body its shuddering, and the fence post became womanly curves.

Feeling the warmth of her sigh against his neck as she tucked her head beneath his chin, he said into her hair, "Better?"

She was slow to respond, and when she did, it was simply, "Some."

Enough. Fatigue dragged at Christian, and he was grateful for its distraction that meant he would be engaging in no more battles this night. He closed his eyes, pushed past images of his brother's victims, and leaned into the rest he so badly needed.

"What have you gained in wedding me?"

He lifted his lids. "You need sleep, Gaenor, as do I."

"What have you gained?"

He was too tired for this. And too aware of her.

She tilted her head back. Though he could barely make out her features, he longed for the smile he knew was not there. "You have but traded enemies, Christian, the Wulfriths for your brother and his brigands. Your people are no safer. Thus, you have gained naught."

This was not the time, and especially not the place, to discuss it, and yet Christian felt drawn into this moment that was rife with her grieving. "I have gained you," he said gruffly.

A huff of disbelief swept his jaw. "By the king's decree."

He slid a hand up her shoulder and cupped her cheek that his body had warmed. "That day at the stream...if not for the attack on Broehne, I would have met you again. Indeed, methinks I would have stolen you away that I might reveal and explain my deception."

Her breath on his face ceased, and it was some moments before she spoke. "I fear I would have gone with you."

Surely it would have been better for them had she, but Robert's attack had stolen the opportunity and she had fled with Durand. The thought of the knight tempted Christian to distance himself from her, but she tempted him in another way by turning her mouth into his hand and pressing her lips to his palm.

"I am glad you see me," she whispered.

He squeezed his eyes closed, but the temptation was too great. "Even in the dark, Gaenor," he rasped. Sending the voices in his head into the abyss of the morrow, he swept her onto her back, lowered his head, and kissed her. And kissed her again.

She could not recall ever being so wonderfully warm, though when she realized the cause of it, worry crept in.

But he was still here. Where she lay on her side, she could feel the heat of his body, and since he had not waited on her menses, surely that meant she had gained his trust. Or had she? She bit her lip. The day would tell.

Regardless, her hope had increased ten-fold, for last eve it was *her* name on Christian's lips. Hers and no other's. And even across the dim of night she had felt his eyes upon *her*. It had been lovely, not at all like—

Hearing her husband draw a deep breath, she opened her eyes to the bare light of dawn and found he did not lie beside her but sat on the mattress edge with his back to her, his face turned up as if he consulted heaven.

She touched his back and felt his muscles tense. "Christian?"

"What happened should not have, Gaenor."

She dropped her hand from him. "You think I seduced you?"

A long moment passed before he looked over his shoulder. "I do not. But that does not make it less of a mistake. Now…"

Aye, *now*. Dragging the sheet up over her shoulders, she turned onto her back and set her gaze to the ceiling. "Now if my menses do not come, only I will know for certain that my child is also yours."

He did not deny it, but said, "I vow, 'tis not you I am angry with." He turned and leaned over her. "I should have stopped."

The only way to avoid looking upon him in his state of undress was to close her eyes, but she did not.

"The answer was an easy one," he growled. "We had but to wait."

Her resentment raised its ugly head. "Aye, 'twould have been far easier to wait than to believe me!"

His lids narrowed and jaw jutted. "How can I when you—?" He snapped his chin around and stilled.

What was he looking at? Something on the bedside table? There was only a cup and her psalter there. Her chest against the wall?

She raised herself onto her elbows. "When I what?"

He looked back at her and, despite the dim, she caught his startle at finding her face so near his. He lowered his gaze to her mouth, then her neck, lingered over her collarbone from which the sheet had slipped, and abruptly sat back. "We can but pray your menses come. And soon."

Something turned in Gaenor, something she recognized as passed to her by her mother who had held her head high through all manner of adversity, especially that which had been found in marriage. True, it would have been better had last eve not happened, for she would not have their child suffer the lie of illegitimacy, but neither could she pray for her monthly flux.

She lowered to the pillow and turned onto her side to face her husband. "I will not pray that, Christian, lest there is a child growing in me. *Our* child."

He stared at her.

"I will pray that, should our babe be born come spring, you believe me as you do not now."

He stood from the bed, and she closed her eyes at the sight of him. "We ride again today," he said, his footfalls revealing his clothes chest was his destination.

Gaenor was not surprised that he left her words unanswered, but still it made her ache.

"We may be gone many days," Christian said amid the rustle of the clothes he donned. "God willing, when I return, all this will be at an end."

Her hurt self wanting to deny him a response as he denied her, she reached for the blanket around her calves, pulled it over her to recapture the warmth she had felt in his arms, and closed her eyes.

You are stronger than this, Gaenor. You have to be.

She opened her eyes, sat up, and ventured a look at the foot of the bed. Christian was clothed, his tunic cut of a dark material that appeared to be nearer homespun than fine linen.

Holding the blanket to her chest, she said, "Garr will send men to aid you." There was no question of it now that Wulfrith men had been murdered and a knight might soon be.

He dropped the lid on the chest. "I do not doubt he will." If he resented it, his voice did not tell.

"And the king?"

"Henry has promised men, but methinks they will not appear."

"Why?"

He glanced at her. "Though I do not doubt the king is eager to see my brother's blood spilled, Robert is but a fly on Henry's backside when there are matters far more pressing." He turned a belt around his waist and bent his head to fasten it. "Then there is the issue of my defiance."

"You defied the king?" Garr had done so in wedding Annyn. How had Christian?

"When my men pulled your injured sister out of the ravine and brought her to Broehne, I did not send word to Henry as was his due."

"Why?"

He came around the side of the bed, retrieved the boots abandoned among the rushes on the night past, and dragged them on. When he straightened, he met her gaze.

"Though the proof was great that Beatrix had murdered one of my men, I knew that, as inclined as I was to believe it, others would as well. I wanted justice for the dead man, but it was certain that if I had any part in that justice, the conflict between our two families would turn to war. And if still Henry forced a union, there could be no hope for you and me."

Was there hope?

"Thus, I determined none would know Beatrix yet lived until I decided the best course."

"What course did you decide?"

"I did not, for as she recovered, I began to doubt her guilt." He turned up a hand. "Then she escaped."

She blinked. "Did you allow it?"

His eyebrows rose. "I can only say I did not prevent it." He turned away. "Take your ease another hour, then I will send my squire to pack for the ride."

Gaenor had not realized he was missing the customary attendant. He had to have one, but the young man, whoever he was, had yet to come to her notice. But then, her husband was gone from Broehne more than he was present. And he was going again.

"Christian?"

At the door, he looked over his shoulder.

Why had she called to him? To beseech him to stay, to not allow Robert to keep him from returning, to believe her? All that and more, but it was best said in the fewest words. "I shall also pray that you see me again."

His brow gathered, and his lips parted as if to naysay her, but realization was not far behind. Without further word, he opened the door and did not look back.

17

"It could be a trap."

Abel nodded. "That is why I go alone."

"What of Barone Lavonne?"

That could not be helped. Abel met the gaze of the young knight who, with a dozen men from Stern and a dozen from Wulfen, had been sent by Garr to uproot the murderers of the Wulfrith men-at-arms—welcome aid, for it had allowed Christian and Abel to divide into two contingents and cover more ground.

"Send word that our rendezvous must needs be delayed until I determine the truth of what the lad tells." Abel looked past the knight to the boy who had appeared as their camp was awakening. Squatting before the fire, the messenger who was aged perhaps a dozen years, greedily tore into the biscuits he had been given.

It could be a trap, but it might also lead to what they had sought these past four days, two of which had been spent slogging over the sodden ground of a summer rain so hard and wet it threatened the harvest.

Most unfortunate, the boy claimed he did not know who had paid him to deliver to Abel—most curious, Abel alone—the whereabouts of the brigands. He knew only that the man was bearded and carried a sword. It was likely a brigand, but whether he had been sent by Sir Robert to bait a trap or sought to undermine his leader could not be known. What Abel did know was that no more Wulfrith retainers would die for that misbegotten knave's perverse pleasure.

He pivoted toward his tent. "And now I shall require garments most foul."

Not a trap.

Whoever had sent the boy was an ally. However, if he was among the dozens whose behavior spoke poorly of their leader's ability to lead, it was impossible to say. Most of those idling about the disordered camp wore swords *and* an abundance of facial hair—including the red-headed, red-bearded Sir Robert.

As Abel watched the man emerge from the largest of the stained and tattered tents that likely lodged the old baron, he closed his hand around his dagger and calculated its range. Highly questionable. It was for the best, though, since to give in to the impulse to sever the man's life would surely see Abel surrounded and his own life forfeited.

He uncurled his fingers from the hilt and once more considered the Wulfrith knight who was bound to the base of a tree. Though bandaged from whatever injuries he had sustained, Sir Mark appeared alert and more angered than pained. Obviously, the healer knew her craft.

Sir Robert called several men to his side. It was impossible to piece together the few words that made it to Abel's ears intact, for whatever the man told, it was not for all to hear.

For the next quarter hour, Abel held his position, committing to memory the camp's layout and determining the best approach to guarantee his men and Sir Mark did not reap as Sir Robert's men would reap.

When he had seen enough and was assured there was no evidence the camp would be relocated any time soon, he surveyed the wood around him. He would steal out the way he had stolen in. As he had come on foot, it would take two hours moving fast to make it back to his men, but by noon the brigands would know the Wulfriths' wrath.

Abel considered his quarry one last time, marked well the betrayers' faces, paying special heed to those in Sir Robert's confidence, then started to turn away. As he did so, he caught movement at the tent out of which Christian's brother had come. He paused.

The shoulder that turned back the flap was followed by the figure of a woman whose hooded head revealed just enough of the hair beneath to give an impression of red. The healer? It must be, though her son's hair was most fair.

Resentment welled in Abel as, basin in the curve of an arm, she straightened and looked around the camp at those who seemed too intent on what was not being shared by Sir Robert to pay her heed. Here was the woman who, apparently, had left her needful son to tend a sadistic old man. As if at her leisure, she moved unhurriedly around the tent to the rear where, doubtless, she emptied the basin.

Abel waited for her to reappear, but she did not for some time, and when next he saw her, it was not much more than a glimpse of her distant backside as she picked her way through the thick wood.

Guessing her purpose was to fill the basin rather than empty it and the stream was her destination, he wavered between what he knew he ought to do—rarely the wrong course, as taught to him during his training at Wulfen—and what he wanted to do. Accursed woman!

He could have overtaken her sooner since he knew where the outlying sentries were posted but, lest she resisted, he determined that the farther from the camp the better.

Nearing the stream, he circled around to the side and ahead of her. Thus, when she reached the bank, he was waiting. Unwilling to risk hysterics, the sounds of which would carry to the camp, he did not come out from behind the tree until she stepped past him.

Her mouth was the first to feel the weight of his hand, her waist the next. As she cried out against his palm and began to flail, he swung her around, pushed her back against the tree, and held all five feet and few of her there with the length of his body so he would not take a knee to the groin.

"Be still!" he rasped in her language as her slender form arched and wide blue eyes flew over his face. A moment later, her teeth closed on the soft flesh of his upper palm. He was ten times a fool to react as he did, but unaccustomed as he was to those who did not wield blades or pikes or maces—excepting Garr's wife, Annyn—perhaps he could be forgiven for wrenching his hand away.

She screamed.

Perhaps not. As loud and high-pitched as her cry was, it would alert those in the camp, but if he could quiet her, the brigands would not have an easy time locating whence the cry issued. It would buy him some minutes, and he needed every one of them.

As he sought to close his bloodied hand over her mouth, she snarled, "I will not let you ravish me, cur!"

Having aggressed upon her, and clothed as he was in coarse stinking garments the better to travel without drawing attention, he was not surprised it was not Sir Robert's enemy she feared but her own.

Recapturing her mouth, cupping his hand slightly to evade her vicious teeth, he ground out, "I am not what I look, Helene of Tippet."

She startled and her seeking teeth stilled, next her body.

"I am Sir Abel of the Wulfriths. I but intend to return you to your son."

After a long moment, her warm breath huffed against his palm.

Listening for the sound of the brigands, he slowly removed his hand. It was his first real look at the woman, the hood having fallen down around her shoulders to reveal dark red hair, its uniform waves evidencing it had recently been released from plaits. She was nothing beautiful, but she could be said to be pretty—in a spotty way if one did not mind freckles. He certainly did, though—

"You speak of my John?" she breathed, this time not in her own language, but his.

Unfortunately, there was no time to delve this English-speaking commoner's facility with Norman French. "Aye, John, the same who thinks to make of me his wet nurse."

"He is well?"

"Well enough. Now we must—" He swept up a staying hand and listened. There. To the right. "They come." He grabbed her arm, but as he pulled her forward, she yanked free and stumbled back against the tree.

"I cannot go with you."

Anger stirred in Abel's gut. "You choose Aldous Lavonne over your own son?"

Her breath caught, but she put up her chin. "Go now, else I shall scream again, and they will know all the sooner where to find you."

Abel considered knocking her unconscious and carrying her away, but there were voices and the crash of undergrowth coming from the left. Even if she came willingly, the chance of escape was narrow. Fortunately for him, she was not worth saving. With such a mother, John was better off an orphan.

"God forgive you, Helene of Tippet," he growled and swung away. As the only way out was forward through the stream, he started toward it.

"Sir Abel!"

He had no intention of wasting another moment on her, and yet he looked over his shoulder.

"Tell my boy I love him."

"I am no carrier of lies," he snapped and, with the voices and pound of feet growing louder, splashed through the stream to the opposite side.

As he wove himself into the wood that he wished was more dense, he recalled the last image of John's mother and thought it strange that her eyes glistened and that where she crouched at the base of the tree she looked more like cornered prey than a woman who had abandoned her child.

"I see her!"

Abel took cover behind a tree. The four brigands approaching from the left reached her ahead of those coming from the right. Seven in all. If she pointed them in his direction, it would take a miracle for a man armed with only a dagger to escape with his life. And for this, one ought never to choose what one wanted to do over what one ought to do.

A gaunt man with wiry hair and beard dragged Helene upright. "Sir Robert is none too happy with you, girlie."

Abel frowned. She had been going for water. What was there to be unhappy about? Then he remembered the basin she had cradled when she had come out of the tent. It had not been in her possession when she reached the stream.

"What was it made you scream?" the man's grating voice once more made it to Abel's end of the wood.

She refused him answer, but though he shook her, her mouth remained closed.

"Was it man or beast, woman?"

After a long moment, she said, "I fell."

As if he did not believe her, the man turned his head and swept his gaze over the wood beyond the stream, and Abel knew his suspicions might see the camp dismantled sooner than intended.

Finally, the man returned his attention to the healer. "How'd you get out of 'em?"

Out of what?

When she merely stared at him, he whipped up the hem of her skirt. And crowed. "Well, you are the clever one. Look here, boys, she wrapped it up nice and quiet."

Abel strained to see what the man had uncovered and saw that something stretched between her ankles.

"Pity you could not run," the brigand sneered.

As understanding slid into place, Abel muttered, "God preserve me."

She was chained, and it explained much. Wrapped in cloth as the chain was, the rattle intended to alert her captors to escape was dampened such that Abel had not heard it despite how near he had been to her. It was the reason she had moved unhurriedly through the wood, her stride limited by the reach of the links. Further, because her scream had alerted the brigands, she had known there was no chance of escape. For that, she had rejected Abel's offer to return her to her son. And sent him away, allowing him to believe ill of her that he might not also be captured.

Abel clenched his hands. He had stolen her chance of escape…failed her…failed John…possibly failed Christian. And there was naught he could do about it.

As she was tossed over the shoulder of the stoutest of the men and carried opposite, over and over he heard his father's words. *Lesson four, Abel, do what you ought to do, not what you want to do.*

He would be back. God willing, the camp would still be standing.

Aimee and her bells.

As much as Gaenor longed to tell the girl to remove them, she was loath to do so. Not only had Aimee become more biddable in the days since Gaenor had gifted her with the bells, but they appeared to give her much pleasure.

Putting an elbow on the table, Gaenor pressed a hand over her left ear to muffle the sound. It helped, though not enough to allow her to fully concentrate on the numbers that Christian's steward had been less than happy to lay out for her.

"You add naught to your position by allowing her such license, my lady."

She peered over her left shoulder at where Sir Hector stood at the back of the dais in front of an enormous tapestry. She had known he was there, as he had been since she first sat down to pore over the barony's books in an attempt to acquaint herself with her husband's lands and dealings.

The aged eyes that met hers were kind. "Indeed," he added, his voice at a register that would not carry, "you weaken your position."

"I am sorry, Sir Knight?"

"She knows they annoy you." He jutted his chin toward the hearth where Gaenor had set Aimee, Josephine, and another woman to mending the linens. "I myself am oft tempted to throw up her skirts and sever those accursed bells from whatever place she has sewn them."

Gaenor smiled. She liked the man though it was rare he could be lured into conversation, and she thought he liked her too, even if it was by Christian's orders that he watched over her. "And I, Sir Hector, am tempted to give you leave to do just that."

His mouth curled, deepening the lines in the thin flesh beneath his cheeks. "If you order it, I shall do it, but methinks you would gain more by seeing to the matter yourself."

He is right. I saw to Cook and he questions my orders less often now. And when he scowls, he does so with not nearly as much resentment.

"Your advice is well met, Sir Hector. I thank you."

He inclined his head.

Gaenor turned back to the books. Unfortunately for the knight, who must wish to be anywhere but here, this would take hours. She returned her gaze to him. "Could I order it, I would release you from your obligation."

His head listed right. "Of what obligation do you speak, my lady?"

"That which my husband imposes on you—to keep watch over me."

"Ah." He nodded. "Though the baron is not displeased with the arrangement, my lady, I would have you know he did not order me to it."

She blinked. "Then who?"

"'Tis a task I undertake myself."

"I do not understand."

He looked momentarily away. "Then you do not know 'twas I who failed your sister."

Gaenor turned in her chair to fully face him.

His glance toward the hearth brought to her attention the uncommon quiet of the great hall—not a giggle or word or single bell to be heard. Those doing the mending listened.

Gaenor swept a hand to the chair beside her. "Draw near, Sir Knight."

Regret furrowed his face, but he had said too much for her not to hear it all.

As he settled into the chair, she pushed a journal toward him so it would appear she consulted him on the numbers, then she bent her head near his.

"Tell me, Sir Hector."

Gaze on the page, he said, "I was among those who gave chase last winter when you fled with your sister to avoid marriage. 'Twas I who did not heed Lady Beatrix's fear when Simon D'Arci captured her." He looked up from the journal. "Despite misgivings, I left her with him that I might aid those who continued to search for my lord's bride."

Now she understood. Simon had nearly ravaged Beatrix and, amid her struggles, had fallen into the ravine with her and died, leading to the charge of murder over which Beatrix had barely prevailed.

"I am sorry, my lady. 'Twas a grave mistake I made."

"And now you watch over me not to report my movements to my husband but to ease your guilt by ensuring no ill befalls me."

"In large part."

She ought to be angered with him for his abandonment of Beatrix, but considering his contrition and how he had sought to redeem himself, she could not. "Are you not the one who saved my sister's life when her escort was attacked en route to the trial?"

"I stepped in."

"And you spoke for her at trial."

He glanced at the women at the hearth who, though they were once more talking among themselves, did so with less volume than before. "I did." He returned his attention to the journal.

Gaenor stared at his profile as she struggled with what to say. How could she ask what she needed to? More, could she believe his answer? He *was* Christian's man.

"I should not presume, my lady"—he glanced at her as he turned the page—"but methinks you wish to know of the bargain made between my lord and your brother."

The man was not to be underestimated. "I do."

"Have you asked your husband?"

"I have."

He sat back. "Then I can be of no help, for you have your answer."

Did she? Or was this but loyalty?

"All I will add," he raised his voice slightly as those at the hearth laughed over something, "is that I am more honored to serve the son than ever I was honored to serve the father—even when Aldous Lavonne's path was more straight than crooked as it turned following the death of his eldest son. Do you believe me?"

Gaenor lowered her chin and considered her long-fingered hands. "Aye, though methinks I knew it already. 'Tis just not easy to trust myself when no one makes a better fool of me than I do." She sighed. "And how my pride rails to be so humiliated by my feelings."

"Pride," he murmured. "I wrestle with it daily and many a match I have lost to it. It is called sin for good reason."

At least she was not alone in that.

The bells sounded again, and a glance across the hall revealed Aimee was on her feet and shaking out the bed curtain she had mended.

"My lady?"

Gaenor met Sir Hector's gaze.

"I would see Christian happy," he said, "and I believe you can make him so."

She wished she had such faith.

"I also believe you can bring him back to God."

Faith again, though in this instance she would have laughed if not that it was more sad than funny that her husband's training for the Church made him more qualified than she to show the way to God. "Sir Knight, you ask much of one who is not always certain she even knows where her Heavenly Father is."

He smiled. "At least you are looking for Him in the right place."

He referred to her morning visits to the chapel, though she knew the place she ought to seek Him more often was on her knees.

I shall. I promise. Just, Lord, help me to prove worthy of what Sir Hector believes of me.

Aimee's bells rang vigorously. Now she was dancing around the other women, holding the curtain above her head and letting it fly out behind her.

"You should know that the resentment the girl bears you is her sister's," Sir Hector said, having followed Gaenor's gaze.

"How is that?"

"As the old baron was behind Sir Robert's attempt to murder Lady Beatrix at trial, your husband tried to contain his father's malfeasance by removing from him all means of communicating with those yet willing to do his bidding. That included Aimee's sister."

Gaenor leaned toward the knight. "She aided Aldous Lavonne?"

"Aye, beyond his daily needs for which she was well paid. Having allowed him to use her as a bridge between his bed and his plotting, there was no longer a place for her within these walls, especially with a Wulfrith bride soon to be in residence. Thus, she blames your family for the loss of her work here."

Gaenor shook her head. "Then why would Christian give her sister to serve me?"

"Aimee lived with the woman following their father's death, so she could not help being influenced by her sister or becoming the recipient of her wrath. A sennight after the old baron was isolated, the healer—Helene of Tippet—appealed to Baron Lavonne to intercede when Aimee was nearly thrashed to death."

Gaenor looked to Aimee. Though her slight body bore no evidence of the terrible beating her sister was told to have dealt, she imagined the bruises, cuts, and swellings that could have seen the girl laid in the cold ground. Such imaginings made it difficult to begrudge Aimee her bells.

"Thus, your husband removed her from her sister's household and brought her here."

Christian who was not like his father or brothers. But then, God was surely in her husband's every pore despite whatever had happened to make him wish He was not.

"Be assured, my lady, though Aimee's kinship makes her feel obliged to resent you, she is more inclined to like you."

"I pray you are right."

Another rash of bell ringing.

Sir Hector grunted. "But that does not mean you should not curb her behavior when it offends. As respect for God grows into love, so does respect for one's mistress."

And husband. Gaenor looked down. *Lord, I do not want to love him. It pained me to not have Sir Durand return my love, but to never have Christian feel for me?*

"My lady, are you well?"

She sat back and laid a hand on his arm. "Better now that you have honored me with your kindness and friendship. I thank you."

He did not shrink from her, though some might regard the intimacy as unseemly, but patted her hand atop his and gave a fatherly smile. "I am not only the baron's man but yours, my lady. And, if God should grant me more years, I will also serve your sons and daughters."

Might that be sooner than later? In a sennight she would know, for that was when her monthly flux came or did not.

Your will be done, Lord. I shall abide as best I can regardless of what Christian believes.

Abruptly, Sir Hector stood and said loud, "I agree, my lady. The books look to be in good order."

Hopefully, that would satisfy the curiosity of the women at the hearth. "You have been most helpful," Gaenor said.

He inclined his head and returned to the back of the dais.

She pulled the journal in front of her, but Aimee was not done with her distractions. "Respect," Gaenor muttered and stood.

As she crossed the hall, she caught the maid's eye and motioned for her to follow abovestairs. When they returned to the hall a half hour later, Aimee quietly sat down to her mending, the bells having been unstitched from her shoes and attached to the prettiest of Gaenor's ribbons that they might be worn around the girl's neck when the occasion warranted.

18

EMPTY HANDED AGAIN, and more than once it had made Christian shout to the heavens.

They had been close, and Robert had surely known it, for the camp to which Abel had led Christian had been so hastily dismantled that much had been left behind.

But that was not the worst of it. To compensate for the slower pace required to transport the infirm Aldous Lavonne, Robert had bought time by setting fire to crops as he and his men fled—crops nearly ready for harvest, the loss of which would devastate the villagers.

Abel blamed himself for it, as Christian would have blamed himself had he been the one to follow the healer. It seemed the man who had demanded that Christian want and think only of his enemy's death was not as stripped of humanity as his lessons taught. In this instance, the loss of his conviction had proved detrimental.

Now, two days since they had been near to ending the scourge, Christian pondered Castle Soaring that rose before him. It had always been impressive, but more so since he had awarded its keeping to the man at his side, Michael D'Arci, husband to Gaenor's sister.

The deterioration once so evident wherever the eye fell had been arrested. More restoration was needed, but the walls were as impregnable as one could make them. And safe behind them was a woman who would eagerly welcome home the husband who had answered Christian's call to arms.

Remembering how D'Arci had tried to suppress a smile at the acceptance of his liege's suggestion that they pass the night here before continuing on to Broehne, Christian felt his jaw tense.

I envy him. I want to have with Gaenor what he has with Beatrix. But how?

As the sun trailed its golden fingers down the sky, Christian and the men of the Lavonne and Wulfrith contingents reined in before the castle to await confirmation of their identity that would cause the drawbridge to be lowered.

If her menses come, still she might have lain with Sir Durand as if what happened between us at Wulfen meant naught. And still that knave will share my bedchamber if I do not myself burn his missive.

The drawbridge's great chains began to rumble and grind.

Unless I give her reason to burn it herself and set the man aside forever that I might be the one she longs for. Am I capable of that?

Envy gripped him again when they passed from the outer bailey into the inner bailey where Lady Beatrix did, indeed, await her husband.

Christian halted his destrier before the steps and watched as D'Arci lifted his wife off her feet and kissed her there as if he cared not what any thought.

"A good marriage," a familiar voice came at him from the left, the words stretching well beyond the three used.

Ignoring Abel, Christian swung out of the saddle, passed his destrier into his squire's care, and strode to where D'Arci and his wife awaited him before the steps.

"My lord"—Beatrix curtsied—"well come."

She was lovelier than most women, and yet Christian was no more moved by her attractions now than he had been when a head-injured Beatrix had been brought to Broehne six months past. It was Gaenor who moved him, even when a smile was not to be had from her.

"My lady." He inclined his head, then followed his hosts up the steps to the donjon.

As men had been sent ahead to alert the household of their baron's visit and his extensive entourage, the hall was set up to receive them.

"Though supper will be delayed," Beatrix said as they crossed the hall, "Cook assures me there will be v-victuals aplenty."

Christian caught the word she tripped across, though he did not think he would have had he been unaware of her injury.

"Until then, my lord, if you would like to avail yourself of the solar, it has been readied for you."

He knew it was his due as baron to be given the bedchamber of the castle's lord and lady during his visit, but he had yet to become comfortable with the arrangement. Still, he said, "I shall make good use of it, for I cannot recall being more filthy in all my life." The rain that had turned the ground to mud had seen to that.

"I...could have a bath sent up to you."

Her hesitation likely had nothing to do with her injury, for to provide a bath when the kitchen fires were better spent on cooking than heating water would cause supper to be further delayed. "A basin and towel will suffice, my lady."

At the steps that led abovestairs, Beatrix turned to her husband. "There are some matters your steward wishes to discuss with you. I will escort the baron to the solar."

D'Arci nodded and met Christian's gaze. "I shall see you at meal."

When Beatrix stepped ahead of Christian into the bedchamber a short while later, he thought he was prepared for her question, for he had sensed her restraint in not demanding word of her sister, but her candor nearly set him back a stride.

"Do you make my sister happy, Baron?"

He halted just inside the room and stared at her where she had swung around to face him. He was dirty and tired and disgusted at being thwarted time and again by Robert, but though he had good reason for venting his displeasure, he could not. "Nay, my lady, I do not make Gaenor happy."

She momentarily closed her eyes. "I am sorry to hear that—forsooth, even angered."

"It gives me no pleasure to tell it." He stepped forward. "Now I will see to my ablutions."

"'Tis the matter of her f-f-fleeing with Sir Durand, is it not?"

Halting before the chest at the foot of the postered bed, Christian considered the high color in her cheeks and allowed, "That knave yet stands between us." He bent his head to unbuckle his sword belt. "Now, Lady, I intend to unclothe."

He heard her breath catch, then she hurried from the solar and slammed the door closed.

The meal had been more satisfying than any of which Christian had previously partaken at Castle Soaring. For certain, Beatrix was as accomplished at running a household as Gaenor was proving to be.

"The good of it is that Sir Mark is of value to the brigands," Michael D'Arci said, "else they would not have kept him alive."

But for how much longer? Christian wondered as he listened to and observed the exchange between D'Arci, Beatrix, and Abel, which was nearly the extent of his participation this half hour since meal's end. If Robert did not soon find a use for the Wulfrith knight, the man's life was forfeit.

"And then, of course, there is the h-healer." Beatrix raised her eyebrows at her brother where he sat on the opposite side of the table she had ordered placed before the hearth. "Now you know she is not there of her free will and that she did not so easily leave her son."

The brooding Abel grunted and glanced at Christian. "I wager that Baron Lavonne is thinking that, for all I taught him of arms and warring, it did me no service two days past."

Christian nearly smiled. "Though I would have had the outcome be different, 'tis good to know you are as human—and fallible—as I."

This time when Abel looked to Christian, his gaze settled as if to stay. "My lessons stand, Baron, and you would do well to live by them better than I did."

As Christian considered a response, Beatrix said, "What do you say, Abel? That the baron trained with you?"

Refusing to feel ashamed at having availed himself of Wulfrith training, Christian said. "I did train with Abel, my lady, and Everard."

Her lids narrowed. "At Wulfen?"

"Aye."

A bit more narrowing, and Christian felt a stir of discomfort. "This training..." She leaned toward him. "...it was recent?"

For all of the injury she had sustained, her mind seemed to work well. Thus, with grudging and foreboding, Christian said, "It was."

Her lids rose, along with a slight smile. "I see."

She probably did. Her interest went beyond the incongruity of a baron who sought training reserved for the transformation of boys into knights. She knew her sister had also been at Wulfen recently and, from her self-satisfied smile, it was possible Gaenor had spoken of the man Christian had pretended to be. Did that not bode good, though? Had he meant nothing to Gaenor but a means of escape, surely this exchange with Beatrix would not be.

"Well, I do not see." Abel's plowed brow made him appear much older.

"Nor do I." D'Arci laid a hand on his wife's arm. "Enlighten us."

She shrugged. "I am but piecing together the man who is not only our liege but my brother-in-law." She squeezed her husband's hand. "And now I will take myself abovestairs and write a missive to my sister so that Baron Lavonne may deliver it on the morrow."

What would it tell? Christian wondered as she rose and bid him good eve.

When she was gone, her brother said, "And now we plot."

19

It was determined that they would wait, that rather than continue to pursue their quarry, they would allow it to come to them, just as it had done when the boy had brought word of the location of the brigands' camp. Since someone had tried to aid them once and proved reliable, it seemed probable he would try again. But that did not mean Christian would be complacent. There were crops that needed protection if they were to make it to harvest, and that was where he would concentrate his men for the time being, ensuring they kept their eyes and ears turned to any sightings or murmurings of the brigands.

Though the devastation wrought by his brother pressed hard on him, he lightened some when he strode into the hall and found Gaenor waiting for him—not in the inner bailey as Beatrix had done for Michael, but waiting nonetheless.

A multitude of honey-colored plaits draping her shoulders becomingly, hands clasped at her waist, she said, "Is it at an end?"

That had been the hope he had voiced before departing Broehne, but hope was not enough to bring his brother to heel. Just as it was not enough to cause Gaenor to receive him as Beatrix received her husband. He halted before her. "I would that it were."

Her gaze faltered. "I am sorry." She moistened her lips, drawing his gaze to the mouth denied him. "We received word yesterday that crops had been destroyed."

Were they alone, he thought he might chance seeking the welcome from her that he desired. "When we set the brigands to flight, such was their answer."

She drew a deep breath. "I have sent word to the afflicted villagers that they need not fear that they and their children will hunger this winter—that their liege will see them through the loss of their crops."

Considering how sharply she watched him, he guessed she was awaiting a reaction with which to measure him against those Lavonnes who had been her family's enemies.

Measure away, Gaenor. "I am pleased to have you speak for me, Wife."

Her lips parted, and though he did not hear the breath pass from them, he saw her shoulders ease. "As I am pleased to do, Husband."

He inclined his head. "I would hear more of what has gone in my absence, but I am much in need of a bath."

The corners of her mouth turned into a small smile that made him yearn to see her smile as large as the ones she had shown him when she had called him Sir Matthew. "'Tis being made ready now," she said.

He raised his eyebrows. "How is that?"

"When I was told of your arrival, I set the kitchen to boiling water and the servants to delivering the bath to the solar." She moved to step past him and, in doing so, wafted the scent of cloves in which her hair had surely been washed. "Now I shall send word to your squire to make haste so that he might tend your bath."

Christian turned a hand around her arm. "You could tend it."

Shoulder to shoulder with him, she lifted her chin. "Surely you know that idea is ill met."

It was, especially considering how she stirred him, but he liked the color that bloomed in her cheeks. "Tend me."

The disbelief in her eyes waxing larger, she leaned near. "My flux has not come and, if it should, 'twill not for more than a sennight."

He held her gaze and slowly moved his thumb up the inside of her arm. "I have determined I will be the one to first believe."

She blinked. "Why?" The word was more breath than voice.

Though his accursed pride balked at her uneasy acceptance of his gesture, he said, "Because I first deceived. Had I revealed myself at Wulfen, what happened would not have."

She stared at him. "You believe what I have told of Sir Durand?"

He did not mean to hesitate and hated that he did. "I am determined to."

Pressing her lips inward, she looked down.

"Gaenor." He removed his hand from her arm and urged her chin up. "This is not the place to speak of such things. Will you tend me or nay?"

She nodded.

Shortly after they entered the solar, the final buckets of steaming water were poured into the tub that had displaced the chair before the brazier.

When the door closed behind the servants, Christian strode to where his wife stood with her back to him before an unshuttered window, reached into his tunic, and thrust the missive in front of her. "Your sister asked me to deliver this."

She closed a hand around the rolled parchment and swung around to face him. "You were at Soaring?"

"We passed last eve there."

"My sister is well?"

"Quite."

Heart fluttering, Gaenor considered the unbroken wax seal that showed Christian had not trespassed and gave in to the smile that sought to claim her face. "I thank you."

"I am glad its receipt gives you pleasure."

Pleasure that, unfortunately, would have to be suspended until after his bath. She stepped past him and reached the missive toward the bedside table on which her psalter lay.

"You will not read it now?"

She peered over her shoulder. "You are in need of a bath."

"I am, but I would not keep you from your sister. Read, if you wish. I shall see to my ablutions until you are finished."

Though she rejoiced in his generosity, suspicion threw a long shadow. Was he now questioning the wisdom of having her attend his bath? Not quite ready to first believe as told? No matter. It truly was best that temptation be allayed until her menses were upon her. "Thank you."

He turned from her and began unfastening his belt.

Knowing he would soon be shed of his clothes, Gaenor lowered to the mattress, bent her head to the missive, and broke the seal.

Beloved Sister,

I hope my words find you in fine health and of good courage. I am well, as is my husband and those of our household. Like Broehne, Castle Soaring has long been without a lady, but with the passing of each day, I settle more comfortably into my new home. I pray you shall soon be as content as I.

As the water was noisily displaced to receive Christian, Gaenor whispered, "She knows I am not." It saddened her that Beatrix worried, and yet she was grateful her sister did not pretend to be unaware that Gaenor's circumstances were far different from her own.

Though Christian's long sigh tempted Gaenor's gaze, she dragged her attention back to the missive.

In advance, I ask for your forgiveness, for where your sister next goes you may not wish her. This day I was most bold with your husband in asking if he makes you happy. I near wish he had lied, but he did not spare me, though he told the truth in as few words as possible.

It *was* bold of Beatrix to ask. The surprise, however, was that Christian had deigned to answer, for though Beatrix was his sister through marriage, she and her husband were first his vassals and such a personal question was unseemly.

Then this eve I was privy to a conversation in which it was told that the baron had recently trained with Abel and Everard. It is a grand rarity for any but pages and squires to train at Wulfen, so grand I have heard of it only once before. During my wedding celebration, you told that you had met a knight in training during your stay at Wulfen. More, you spoke of him with longing. Now I shall be bolder yet and venture that the knight you met at Wulfen and Baron Lavonne are the same. I can make no sense of it but to conclude there was deception afoot and you did not know the knight for whom you felt was also your betrothed. Had you, I am certain you would not have fled with Sir Durand.

Gaenor momentarily closed her eyes and thanked the Lord that, despite her sister's head injury, she was as clever as ever.

And so a wall of discord is between you and your husband, but I tell you, the stones of it can be pulled down and crushed to dust as Michael and I have proved.

It was what Gaenor wanted and, it seemed, what Christian wanted, but whereas Beatrix had been shown to be innocent of the murder of Michael's brother, there was no innocence in the virtue Gaenor had given to Sir Durand. She was guilty and could not prove when her sin had been sown.

I long to see you, dear sister. Until that blessed day, take heart in knowing your name is fast on my lips when I kneel before God. Be strong, be patient, be forgiving. Above all, trust in the Lord. ~Beatrix D'Arci

Gaenor swept a thumb across her sister's name. She tried to be all those things that Beatrix advised, and yet there was no day she did not ache though surely she ought to be trusting in—and praising—the Lord. After all, her loved ones were well, no king's displeasure had they suffered for her foolishness, Christian had not cast her aside as had been his right, her belly did not ache unto death for lack of sustenance, the castle folk were beginning to accept her, no lives had been lost in the fires set by the brigands, her husband and brother had once more returned without injury, and the man who had good cause not to trust her had told he would be the first to believe.

"You are troubled by your sister's tidings?" Christian's voice carried across the solar.

Gaenor looked around, and her pulse quickened at the sight of his glistening shoulders and wet, disheveled hair that revealed far more time had passed than was felt.

With difficulty, she retrieved his question and wondered how to answer him. Truthfully, she decided. All was told, and though she knew he might doubt her, she had nothing to hide. Straightening her bowed shoulders, she said, "Beatrix has guessed we met at Wulfen."

Christian narrowed his lids. "Merely because I trained there?"

"There is that, but methinks she would not have come upon it had I not spoken of you—of Sir Matthew."

"When?"

She stood, turned to the table, and began to fold the missive on the smooth surface. "At her wedding celebration, she asked if there was someone I would rather wed than the man to whom King Henry had given me."

Silence.

She folded the missive one last time. "I told her I hardly knew the knight I had met at Wulfen, certainly not enough to wish marriage, but..." She shrugged, retrieved her psalter, and fit Beatrix's missive atop her mother's.

"And yet that eve you fled with Sir Durand."

Psalter in hand, she turned to Christian. "I have already explained that."

His gaze dropped to the psalter. "Tell me again."

How many times must she—?

Bend, Gaenor. Bend or you will both break.

"As I believed Sir Matthew was lost to me, I chose a man who did not love me over a man who was told to have ill-used my sister. And that is all there is to tell. I know you do not like it since you are determined to believe 'twas then I yielded up my virtue, but you have only to think upon my reason for fleeing to understand why I did it."

His gaze returned to hers. "I understand."

Her heart tensed as if to leap, but she knew better than to yield to joy that could so easily be mocked. "That is not enough, though, is it?"

"I said I would be the first to believe, Gaenor, but I struggle over Sir Durand who stands between us as surely as he lies between the pages of your psalter."

She glanced at the book, and it was on her tongue to question him when realization struck. Sir Durand *had* been there. But she had burned his missive the day it had come into Broehne. "I do not understand."

"Do not lie to me." He raised his bulk from the tub. "I have seen it, Gaenor."

And I see you, though I should look away, but I will not cower or act the coy maiden after all I have undertaken to claim my right as your wife and lady of the castle.

She stood taller and was grateful for the height that had been a burden much of her life. "I know you speak of Sir Durand's missive," she said as Christian advanced on her, "and I do not deny having been in receipt of it. What I do not understand is how you know of it."

He yanked his robe from the hook on the bed's corner post and, as he took the last strides to where she stood, shoved his arms into the sleeves.

"I saw it at Wulfen." He halted before her and, eyes fast upon her face, tightened the robe's belt.

Gaenor shook her head. "How? When?"

"After I met you on the roof, when I returned your slippers to your chamber."

She remembered. It had taken her breath away to find her slippers on the chest and know he had been within, but it had not occurred to her he might have trespassed further. "You had no right."

"I did not, nor was it my intent, but when I saw your psalter, I was compelled to read what you had read. Truly, I did not expect to find any but God's words within, but Sir Durand's were also there."

"And still you think his words are here." She lifted the psalter between them.

His jaw tensed. "I have seen the parchment that protrudes from between the covers."

Imagining how it must have chafed—indeed, angered—him to see the book beside their bed, she felt sympathy stir across her resentment. "You have seen wrong, Husband."

His nostrils flared. "Gaenor, pray do not—"

"Look." She pressed the psalter to his chest. When he took it, she stepped back and lowered to the mattress edge.

It did not take long for him to discover that Sir Durand's missive had been supplanted. He closed the psalter. "'Twas your mother's missive I saw."

"Aye. And now will you ask where I have hidden my lover's?" Instantly, she regretted the bitter words that would bring her no nearer her sister's prayers for her.

Why can I not be more like you, Beatrix? Forgiving and eager to trust in the Lord?

Christian set the psalter on the table, slid a hand beneath Gaenor's chin, and lifted her gaze to his. "I have been laboring under false belief, and I am sorry that you were also made to bear its weight."

His sincerity and regret, met with his gentle touch, caused a shiver to course her spine. "The day my chest was delivered," she said, "I burned his missive, for it no longer held meaning for me and I did not wish it to come between us. Will you believe me?"

"I do." His words surprised her, and she was more surprised when he knelt and cupped her face in his hands. "Forgive me?"

Joy again, knocking on her breast in the hope she would swing the door wide. Tears stinging her eyes and nose, she said, "Aye. And you? I did not come to you a maiden, Christian."

Though she sensed his struggle, he did not tarry in throwing it off. "There is naught to forgive." He slid a hand around her neck and drew her head down.

Their lips met, and the kiss was as sweet as the one they had shared at Wulfen before the riders had come to take him from her. Remembering, Gaenor opened her eyes and pulled back. "The stream at Wulfen—the missive is why you were so cool toward me when I came upon you."

His lids lifted to reveal gold-flecked brown eyes that she did not think she would ever tire of feeling move upon her. "I thought you meant to use me to get to the man you loved."

She laid a palm to his chest. "If I used you at all, 'twas to store up a moment of happiness to last me all the days I would be bound to my family's enemy."

"I am not your enemy." He urged her head down and said against her lips, "Never your enemy."

His kiss was deep, thrilling, and ripe with promises she had thought never to be kept. However, when he eased her back on the bed, she returned to the last time they had been so near. "Christian?"

"My lady?" his voice rumbled from the hollow of her neck.

"If you will regret this—wish you had waited until after my menses—pray, stop."

He raised his head. As he searched her face, she knew that though Sir Durand was no longer between the pages of her psalter, still he remained between Christian and her, even if it was only a shadow he threw. "When I kiss you...touch you...is it me you see, Gaenor?"

Though his question made her ache, she could not fault him for wondering, for the man to whom she had given her virtue had not seen her. "I see only you, Christian, just as mine is the only name upon your lips."

His frown was fleeting, but by it she knew he understood what need not be spoken. "Never will I regret this," he said, his breath warming her face, "for you are mine. And any child you bear will be ours."

It frightened her to embrace his declaration, but she did. And opened her arms to him.

"What is this?"

Wishing obligation away that she and Christian might linger abed, Gaenor turned onto her back and smiled at her husband where he stood before his chest, a garment in hand. "'Tis a tunic befitting a baron, do you not think?"

His gaze lingered on her face, then he looked back at the moss green fabric. "Made by your hand?" He fingered the neckline embroidered around with oak leaves.

"Aye, mine."

"Why?"

She raised herself onto her elbows. "I wished to believe you as you believe me, though I must tell that Sir Hector aided in confirming you are not the same as your father or brothers. Too, he assured me that whatever you told of the bargain struck with Garr for Beatrix, I ought to believe. I do, Christian. And I am sorry for thinking ill of you."

His smile was almost pained. "I gave you good cause."

"'Tis behind us."

He nodded.

"You like the tunic?"

"It is wonderfully worked, but I favor it more because it was made by you."

Her heart twinged, and she imagined the beautiful crack that had opened in it to let in love. "Pray," she beseeched, "put it on that I might know it fits proper."

He retrieved an undertunic, donned it, and pulled her gift over it. "Never have I worn such fine cloth," he said as he came around the side of the bed.

"You ought to. Are you not the baron of Abingdale?"

A frown passed over his face and, almost to himself, he said, "I was not meant to be. And should not have been."

Sensing something restless within him, Gaenor gripped his hand. "But you are, and because you are worthy, no longer are your people made to suffer the discord between our families."

His laugh was forced. "Now they suffer worse—the discord within *one* family."

As told by the raids on villages and the burning of crops. "You will bring the brigands to ground." She held his gaze. "I am sure of it."

After a long moment, he said, "God willing, I shall."

20

Abel brooded, as he had done often this past sennight since Christian's suspension of the search for the brigands. He knew the need to protect the crops until the harvest was done, for much of the survival of Abingdale's people was dependent on the grain sustaining them through winter. Still, it was obvious where his thoughts lay, and never more so than when John was underfoot.

Gaenor knew of the encounter between her brother and the boy's mother, but she sensed something deeper there that Abel was not telling—allowing glimpses of it in the acts of ruffling the boy's hair or slinging him onto his back when John's legs tired of keeping pace with the reach of Abel's. And now, perhaps, this. Not that Abel didn't bow his head during the blessing of meals or attend mass on occasion, but she did not know him to be one to seek the Lord on his own as it appeared he did where he knelt before the altar.

Clasping her hands before her, she settled in to wait for however long it took him and God to conclude their business.

It took quite some time, and when Abel finally stood, he did so with a heavy sigh. He turned and met her gaze where she stood on the chapel's threshold. "I thought it was you."

"And I thought you too deep in prayer to know you were not alone."

His mouth forming a semblance of a smile, he strode forward. "Though methinks it does not please God that I divide my attention between Him and my present surroundings, I long ago learned not to leave myself open for attack—whether in a chapel or my own chamber."

He referred to his short-lived marriage to the woman who had turned a dagger on him in their bed. "'Tis wise."

"It serves." He halted before her, leaned in, and kissed her cheek. "Especially in my case, eh?"

When he drew back and his eyes told that he had moved past her, even if only in thought, she laid a hand on his arm. "Abel?"

"Aye?"

"You are fond of John."

He frowned. "As I would be of any dog that so faithfully followed me hither and yon."

She shook her head. "I think not. Just as I think you are too preoccupied with the brigands' whereabouts."

The grooves in his handsome face deepened. "You know I will not resume my duties at Wulfen until I am certain Robert and Aldous can do you no harm."

"Aye. Still, it seems more to me."

The emotions that skimmed his face evidenced he was not inclined to indulge her, but he said, "Speak."

She set her shoulders and, recalling what Aimee had told of the healer's comeliness, said, "I cannot help but think you were affected by your meeting with John's mother."

He raised his eyebrows. "Affected in the same way you are affected by Christian Lavonne?"

Remembering the night past when she lay in her husband's arms, she felt her cheeks warm. "You were most distressed that you could not free her."

"If I feel anything for Helene of Tippet, it is remorse at being thwarted in my attempt to reunite her with her son who suffered much when she was taken from him."

Gaenor frowned. "John has spoken of that day?"

"Just enough that I better understand his behavior when he was brought to Broehne."

"Then he was present when the brigands took Helene."

Abel inclined his head. "They came in the middling of night, forced their way into her home, and struck her down when she fought them. John is angered that he was too frightened to aid her."

"But he is only five."

"Of which he does not care to be reminded." Abel drew a deep breath. "So you see, my sole concern for the healer is that she be restored to her son."

She put her head to the side, considered him, then dared as she had never dared with Abel. "Or so you tell yourself."

Color suffused his face. "That is enough!" he snapped, but rather than loose angry words that were surely fast upon his tongue, he momentarily closed his eyes. "I am pleased that you and your husband seem reconciled to one another," he finally spoke, "but you err in thinking I suffer the same hazards of the heart. I train boys into men worthy of fighting for family, country, and king. That is my life."

"It could be more." She groaned inwardly at the words that sounded more like a plea than a suggestion.

He glowered. "Lest you forget, I had more once, and it was far enough to last me 'til my end days."

The long months when he had been husband to a wife whose mind was not her own. Gaenor sighed. "I am sorry. I just—"

"Sir Knight?" a small voice called.

Abel peered past her and smiled wryly. "'Tis for him I seek to free Helene of Tippet."

As Gaenor turned, John's deceptively long shadow slipped across the threshold and ran up her skirts.

He skidded to a halt and looked between her and Abel. "My lady," he allowed, his behavior sharply contrasting with the boy who had attacked her when he had first come to Broehne. Not surprisingly, Abel's influence had been of good benefit to him, further evidence that her brother excelled at training up knights.

Gaenor smiled. "Good day, John."

"I..." He shifted from one foot to the other. "Sir Abel said he would make me a wooden sword if I rose early and washed my face and hands." He put his chin up and presented his palms. "I did. See?"

"I see," she said. "And very clean you are. I am certain my brother will make you a fine sword."

The boy drew a breath that, on its exhale, shuddered with excitement. "I am ready, Sir Knight."

Abel stepped forward. "As am I."

As the boy whooped and swung away, Abel grumbled in passing, "'Tis not as if there is much else to do while we await the harvest."

Gaenor watched him cross the threshold, then turned her back to him and John. There were prayers that needed praying, and though she knew as her mother oft told that a house of God was not required to speak with the Lord, it was easier here in the chapel where the distractions were fewer.

Shortly, she knelt where her brother had knelt, but as she clasped her hands, a mild cramp gripped her. She opened her eyes and stared at the altar until it lost focus and another cramp turned inside. Was it her belly whence it came? Or her womb? Most likely the latter.

She dropped her chin and let out a breath so long and shuddering she might have been holding it a fortnight. But then, in a way she had—ever since the consummation of her marriage. As cramping usually preceded her menses, within a day her husband would likely be assured that she bore no other man's babe.

Gaenor felt such relief that no child of hers would suffer doubt about its parentage that she thought she might cry.

"Thank you, Lord," she said with trembling lips that turned toward a smile. However, in the next instant, the expression dropped from her mouth. The blessing she had been granted was not all blessing, for it also meant she did not carry Christian's child.

"Not yet," she tried to reason away the sense of loss that hovered as if in search of a place to settle. "Truly, I am pleased."

For now. What if next month brings the same, and the month after? What if you never bear children, if your womb remains forever empty for the sin of having lain with Durand? 'Twill not be much of a blessing, will it?

"I will bear children," she breathed. "But this is for the best."

Is it?

Feeling as if caught up in a melee between reasoning and emotion, she sank back on her heels and pressed her palms to her face. "For the best," she said more forcefully, though still her voice barely ascended beyond a whisper. The next time she said it, it came out on a sob.

"Gaenor?"

She snapped her chin around and startled at the sight of the figure that filled the height and much of the breadth of the doorway. "Christian."

He stepped forward. "What is amiss?"

"Naught, I..." She pushed to her feet and, as she turned, blinked back tears destined for her cheeks.

His long legs carried him forward. "Tell me."

Moved by his concern, she had to look away to keep control of her emotions.

"Come." A hand to her elbow, he guided her to the right where concrete benches lined the side wall.

As she sank onto the nearest bench, she remembered the chapel at Wulfen Castle when the man known to her as Sir Matthew had sat with her on a bench fashioned of wood. It was not so long ago, and yet it seemed many months.

She looked up at where he had lowered beside her. "'Tis good to see you here."

He slid his gaze around the chapel. "Though I should not say it, I came seeking you, not God."

"Still, I am glad."

He inclined his head. "Tell me what has upset you."

"That is just it—I should be upset and I am, I should not be, and I am not." She sighed. "In one breath, my emotions are here, in the next, they are there."

His brow furrowed. "What say you?"

She touched her belly. "My monthly flux comes. I know it by the cramping." She held his gaze. "It would seem I am not with child, Christian."

His gaze wavered and she glimpsed kindred emotions there. "This both pleases and saddens you?" he asked.

"It pleases me because our child shall not suffer suspicion over its legitimacy—"

"I said I would be the first to believe," he reminded her.

After a hesitation, she said, "You told that you were determined to believe. That does not mean you would believe were I delivered of a child eight months hence."

"Gaenor—"

She shook her head. "Mayhap 'tis more me than you, but this guilt I carry—that I have tried to set from me though still it clings—would surely make me question the truth of your belief when our child was laid in your arms. For that, I am pleased by the coming of my menses. As for it saddening me, it is because I do wish to carry our child, and now I am fair certain I do not. And mayhap I never will if my womb remains closed as it did when…" She closed her eyes. What a fool she was to speak of her sin! Of *him*.

"When what?" Christian's voice was deeper, its edges ragged as if she had spoken what she had not. But then, he was not the fool that she was.

This, too, was probably for the best, for she longed for all of Christian, and that was not possible without honesty that hurt. From both of them.

She lifted her lids and braved his hard gaze. "When I was known that first time that I fled you, I prayed to God that a child would be sown so that Sir Durand would be impelled to take me to wife and I would not be made to wed a Lavonne."

Christian's nostrils flared, his jealousy so thick she felt she could curl her fingers around it. Instead, she reached up and curved a hand around his jaw and held it there as the muscles beneath jerked.

"God did not answer my prayer," she said softly, "and I am grateful now that His will was done and not my own, but still I fear He will punish me for my sin and never will a child be born of our marriage. It is for that I would weep."

Christian struggled to hear Gaenor past the anger roused by the reminder of who had first known her. Sir Durand was in the past, and that was where the man belonged—where he might never again darken the life that Christian wished to make with his wife.

"I am sorry," she said. "These are difficult things to speak of, but if we do not, methinks they will smolder between us until one day they turn to flame." She drew her hand from his face and clasped it with the other in her lap. "Though I long to go forward with you, it seems that first we must go back."

"We?" he said gruffly.

"You said you were not meant to be baron and that you should not have been. Will you tell me more?"

He was not prepared, if ever he would be. He had come to take her riding, not to bend an ear toward confession—especially his own.

"Please. " She laid a hand over his, and only then did he realize he had turned it into a fist. "Tell me."

The temptation to shake her off was overwhelming, for what she asked of him could make her grateful ten times over that she was not carrying their child.

"You sought God in the chapel at Wulfen," she prompted. "Why not here with your wife who would seek Him with you?"

He turned his hand up and gripped her hand, then bent his face near hers. "That is just it, Gaenor. I did not go to the chapel at Wulfen to seek God. I went because Abel goaded me into it. And I did not meet God there. I met you. You are why I returned."

She shook her head. "But you were raised a man of God. You were a monk. How could you not wish to seek God above all else?"

Though Christian feared he had said too much, the words were rising up out of his depths and there was too much relief in releasing the pressure of them to push them back down. "Because, God forgive me, never did I wish to seek Him above all else. As it is with so many pledged to the Church as children, it was not my choice. No matter how often I prayed and labored for God, a life devoted to Him was not what I wanted."

"What did you want?"

"The life my father gifted to Geoffrey. It was not the monk's robes, monastery, or Bible I longed for but mail, destrier, and sword. Though time and again I proved I was born to the life of a knight, often I suffered our father's displeasure, and he refused to relent because of the promise made to our dying mother after she birthed a third son who would have been destined for the church had he not been stillborn."

"I am sorry."

Christian wanted to resent the pity in Gaenor's eyes, and he would have if not that it meant she hurt for him. And could one hurt deeply for another if they did not also feel something akin to love?

He drew a deep breath. "You said that God did not answer your prayer that would have seen you wed to Sir Durand and now you are grateful, but I witness that God does answer prayers—sometimes by cruel means that He might punish us all the better."

She searched his face. "What say you?"

"Not that I prayed for Geoffrey's death. I did not. But I prayed to gain the inheritance of which I believed him unworthy."

"Then you knew the kind of man he was."

Christian laughed harshly. "If not that I quickly grew to a good size and was capable despite my youth and lack of formal training, I would surely have fallen victim to him—and Robert—more often than I did."

"You are saying you believe God allowed for Geoffrey's death that He might punish you for such prayers?"

"Certes, I sore tested Him. Even after taking my vows, I continued to lament that I was not first born and beseech Him to make a path for me out of the Church. Failing that…" Christian paused to watch for her reaction. "With a rebellious heart, I fornicated with a harlot."

Her lids fluttered, but she did not seek to distance herself or snatch her hand from his. "You thought the Church would let you go?"

She was not repulsed? Would not condemn him as he had condemned her for being intimate with Sir Durand? Tentative relief crawled through him.

"Aye, I thought my sin would see me set out of the monastery, that I might even be excommunicated. But my only punishment was flagellation and a sennight's solitary confinement. You see, God's representatives here on earth allow sin to be bought away—and my father paid well to keep me cloistered that God might reward him for the sacrifice of a son. And he paid well again when…" There it was, the current of guilt that turned to a flood each time he ventured to this place within himself.

"You speak of Geoffrey's death?" Gaenor said softly.

"I do. One year my father sent silver to keep me from being stripped of my monk's robes, a year later he did so again to buy me out of those same robes." He drew a deep breath. "I was shaken by news of my brother's death, and even before I read my father's missive, I knew shame."

"For what?"

"For what I had wrought." As Gaenor's brow furrowed, he continued, "My father's missive told that God had punished our family for my covetous and rebellious nature by allowing Geoffrey to fall into the hands of the Wulfriths."

Gaenor drew a sharp breath.

"Thus, because of Aldous's ill health due to his burn injuries, I was to take my brother's place."

"And you did."

"Not immediately. I sent word to my father that he should look to his misbegotten son, Robert, instead. If not that Aldous suffered a stroke after the receipt of my missive and, when he was sufficiently recovered, demanded again that I assume the title, I would have forsaken my obligation."

Gaenor leaned nearer. "Why did you wish to stay at the monastery?"

"Must I speak it, Gaenor?"

She pressed her lips inward.

"Then I will tell you. As my father believed, God punished my family for my covetous prayers and rebellious behavior by granting me the opportunity to assume my brother's life. Knowing that, I determined I would pay away as much of my sin as possible by spending the remainder of my life in duty to the Church."

Gaenor slowly shook her head. "Though, methinks, my faith is more often a weed than a flower—that sometimes it might be better were it pulled and the seed sown on more fertile ground—what I do know of God is that He would not take your brother's life to punish you. That is not my mother's or my brothers' or my God. It is you and your father punishing you for what you did not do. Aye, you longed for the knight's life denied you by a promise made by another, but it was Geoffrey's ill choices, not your prayers, that ended his life and made you baron."

He had silently argued that many times, but it would not stick. "My father would not agree, Gaenor." And, perhaps, that was why it would not stick.

She brushed the hair off his brow. "I am sorry at all he has lost and that he is so bitter, but he is wrong. And blind, for he has you and there is none worthier to lord the barony. You must believe that, Christian."

"I have tried."

She drew her hand down his face to his jaw. "Try again, this time with me at your side."

He loved her touch, ached for it even.

"And God," she added.

His jaw tightened, and he saw in her eyes that she felt it.

She smiled softly. "Because of Geoffrey's death you do not seek God?"

"Aye, in part because I have been angry with Him for His answer to my prayers. In part because I fear His answers to the prayers I might yet pray."

"My mother would say we need not fear God's answers to our prayers providing we ask that His—not our—will be done."

More and more he liked her mother. "She is wise."

"What say you?" Gaenor asked. "Can we start again, from this day forward knowing one another and knowing God, putting our sins behind us and accepting the Almighty's forgiveness?"

She made it sound simple, as if it was but a decision and then done. "I would go there with you, Gaenor, but I struggle to ask for His forgiveness."

"Why?"

"Lest my confession be used against me."

"I do not understand."

He swept his gaze around the chapel before returning to her. "I speak of the priest."

"What of him?"

"When I returned home, I sought his counsel and told him these things I have told you—things that were to have remained between God and me. They did not."

Her eyes widened. "Was it your father he told?"

"Aye, and the wall between Aldous and me grew thicker and taller. There is no getting through or over it now."

She nodded. "I understand why you would not wish to enlist the priest as your confessor, but that does not mean you cannot be forgiven by God."

"Aye, I could find another priest, but still I am not certain I could trust—"

"Nay." She gripped his hands. "I know you have been taught that by way of a priest you find absolution, but 'tis not the only way. Indeed, it may not even be the best way."

He narrowed his gaze on her. "You are saying I should myself confess to God?"

"Aye."

He knew of such talk, just as he knew it was ill-tolerated by the Church—viewed by many as heretical. "Methinks this is your mother again, Gaenor."

His mild rebuke made her smile, turning her as lovely as she had been at Wulfen. "It is," she said. "But, truly, I do not see how it could not be so. If God is everywhere, can do all things, and knows our deepest thoughts, why would we not ourselves speak to Him?"

He smiled wryly. "I asked the same when I was a boy and was severely punished."

Her face took a serious turn. "Wrongly so."

"You truly believe that?"

"Talk to God, Christian. He is listening."

It seemed too easy. And yet…"Will you pray with me, Gaenor?"

She nodded. "If you wish."

"I do."

21

"Do you pray for me again?"

The gruff voice slipped into Helene's prayers and pried open a place between her and God that she tried to close with more silent beseeching.

Lord, keep my John safe. Let him not be frightened or lonely—

"Do you?" The rebuke in Aldous's voice was softened by the chatter of his teeth.

Helene sighed, sat back on her heels where she knelt on her pallet, and looked over her shoulder at where the old man huddled among blankets and furs that, despite their great mass, could not keep the chill from him.

"Though just now I prayed for my son," she said, "I pray daily for you, my lord." She shifted her jaw that, blessedly, moved more easily today. "And do you tell me again I should not, still I shall."

"'Tis a waste of breath."

"I do not believe that."

"Because you are young and foolish and do not yet realize…" His teeth clicked again. "…God has turned His back on you. Aye, He most certainly has."

"Nor do I believe that."

"You—" His body jerked beneath his coverings and head quaked.

As quickly as she could manage, Helene unfolded her protesting joints and, with a clatter of chains, exchanged the lovely coolness near the cave entrance for the fire that flickered ten feet from Aldous.

"If your son died on the morrow as my Geoffrey died," he said as she added branches to the flames, "then you would believe it."

She did not want to think on that possibility, but it rounded on her and stared her in the face, paining her more cruelly than her swellings and bruises. With a shake of her head, she dropped the last branch and stared as its summer leaves curled in on themselves like the hands of this bitter old man who, too, had fueled a fire.

"I pray I would not believe it," she said, raising her gaze to peer through the smoke at Aldous. "I hope I would know it was not God's doing and would turn to Him to ease my loss and suffering."

His eyes shied away from hers as they had done for more than a sennight. She almost smiled, for there was comfort in knowing it disturbed him to look near upon what Robert had done to her. Aldous Lavonne was not a good man, though once he was esteemed as such, but neither did she believe he was evil.

"I turned to Him when I was ravaged by fire," he said, "clung to Him though He did little to ease my agony as I fought to stay in this world." He shook, chattered, and groaned. "For all the faith I placed in Him, still He allowed the Wulfriths to murder my Geoffrey."

Though Helene was inclined to return to her pallet rather than play the audience to another of his rants, she stepped around the fire and lowered to her haunches before him. As she molded the coverings to his shuddering frame, he tucked his chin and squeezed his eyes closed so he would not be made to look upon her.

She sighed. "Forsooth, God did not prevent what happened to your son, but—"

He cried out. "Pray, Woman, is there not some medicinal to make this cold go away?"

Woman...Always he eschewed her name, though she did not doubt he knew it well.

"Is there?" he demanded.

Wishing there were something she could slip between his lips that would warm him, she said, "I have naught, my lord."

He convulsed. "'Tis as if death is in my bones."

Though, in recent days, she had sensed the specter at his door, it had now crossed the threshold. Aldous Lavonne would not be much longer in this world.

"So cold," he muttered.

There was something that might ease his discomfort, but she hesitated. Though she was a healer and would only be exercising her skill as such, she did not know how her offer would be received. It was one thing to be rebuked by Aldous, quite another to suffer Robert's displeasure. She lifted a hand and skimmed the flesh around her eye, then drew a deep breath. "Do you allow it, my lord, I will give you the warmth of my body."

His lids lifted, and though he winced over her face, he did not look elsewhere. "I will..." His head shook on his scarred neck. "...allow it."

Helene rose, skirted him with the short steps permitted by her chains, and quickly slid beneath the covers at his back to prevent the escape of what little heat he generated.

The thin, aged body she curved around was chill, and it was some time before it took enough notice of hers to ease its shaking. Though it was much too warm for her, she did not pull back. And when Aldous's hand crept over his side, clawed its way along hers, and weakly gripped her fingers, she remained unmoving.

"I thank you," his words came out on a rattled breath.

This she had not expected. "I am glad to be of comfort, my lord."

He was silent some minutes, then said, "You know of King David?"

"Of the Bible?"

"Aye."

"I know what the priest tells of him."

"Did he tell that, in David's old age, when he suffered from cold, he had a beautiful young woman to warm him in his bed?"

Face pressed against Aldous's spine, Helene smiled and nearly pointed out that, unlike the biblical bed warmer, she was hardly beautiful, but to her mind it sounded like vanity—a plea to be assured otherwise. "Such I have not heard, my lord."

A strange sound vibrated from his chest—not a laugh, but perhaps as near one as he could manage. "Her name was Abishag. You, Woman, are my Abishag."

Helene felt the smile drop from her mouth, and though she counseled her tongue to silence, she heard herself say, "My name is not 'woman.' It is Helene. After all this time, why do you not call me by it?"

He did not answer for a long moment and, truly, she did not expect him to. Thus, she was jolted when he rasped, "Once I knew a Helene." His voice caught as if tears moved behind it. "Though it was a long time ago, the name belongs to her alone."

Helene released a breath she had not realized she held. "Why?"

Again, he was slow to answer. "I did not know it then...I still am not certain now...but methinks I must have loved her."

Helene felt a warm shiver move through her. "But was not your wife's name Mary?"

He sighed. "Aye, and methinks I loved her too—or nearly so."

This was not the bitter and wrathful Aldous Lavonne whose verbal abuses Helene had tolerated since being given care of him months ago. It was as if something good had turned inside him. If so, why? Because death drew near? Because of memories of a time when something like love had filled the places that hate had more recently filled? Because of her small kindnesses?

He gripped her hand tighter. "Aye, you are my Abishag," he muttered so low it took her a moment to piece the words together. "But I am no David."

She waited.

"No matter the evil done him, no matter his sin, always he returned to God." His body shook, but it seemed more from emotion than chill. "I cannot."

Helene returned the grip on her hand. "I believe you can, my lord."

His back stiffened. "You are wrong."

She knew she risked much but rose onto an elbow and peered over his shoulder at his terrible, puckered profile. "I am told that once you were a godly man, Aldous Lavonne, that though you struggled to reconcile with God after the fire, still you did."

His eyes were open, but he did not look around. "Aye." He grunted. "And know you how God rewarded me?"

Geoffrey again. How she wearied of him elevating his departed son to a place he had not deserved. He was not worthy of such mourning. She herself had witnessed the young baron's cruelties—and nearly suffered a terrible one herself a year after birthing John when Geoffrey happened upon her gathering herbs. Fortunately, no sooner had he tossed her to the ground than her husband appeared and, wisely, scraped and bowed and thanked the baron for aiding his clumsy wife.

"Guess my reward, Woman!" Aldous demanded, and she was almost sorry for giving him the heat that afforded him the strength to speak such.

She lowered herself and once more pressed her front to his back. "Though I am not certain 'tis how God works His wonders, I would say your reward was given to you by way of your son, Christian."

He jerked, but before he could rebuke her, she continued, "For he is nearly as loved by your people as you are, my lord." As Aldous *had* been loved. Now the old baron was feared nearly as much as Robert.

She heard him swallow—a raspy, choking sound. "'Tis true? The people love Christian?" Something like wonder was in his voice.

"Aye."

"What of respect?"

"They respect him as well. And, methinks, one day he will be as deeply respected as you."

"But Robert…"

"What?"

Though he gave a shake of his head, she guessed what he would not voice—that his illegitimate son told a different tale about his privileged legitimate brother.

"You do not tell it in words," he finally spoke again, "but methinks you are saying the people did not love Geoffrey."

She had not expected to land here, but here she was. "I regret, my lord, that they did not, for they did not see you in him."

"As they see me in Christian."

"They do. He is an honorable man."

Through his back, she heard the long, slow rattle of air as he filled his lungs. "He has wed a Wulfrith."

"That he might put an end to the warring between your families, my lord. For that, your people are grateful. Now if only..." Nay, she need not say that all that was left was to bring an end to the warring between the Lavonnes. Aldous might be terribly infirm, but he knew.

He was quiet a long time, but when she thought he must have drifted into sleep, he said, "'Tis nearly over. Soon you will return to your son and Christian will stand unopposed."

Despite being so overheated that her garments clung, she shivered over the certainty with which he spoke.

Lord, let it be so. Preserve me that I may hold my son again. Be with Christian Lavonne that he may triumph over Robert and knit this barony back together.

She exhaled her breath against Aldous's back and heard him sigh as if the heat of it gave him relief. "What of you, my lord?"

A short laugh yanked at his body, and though there was bitterness in it, it did not seem as stark as before. "I die."

She opened her mouth to deny it, closed her mouth, and nodded. "You do, my lord, but not yet. Not yet."

Robert roared, and Aldous found no comfort in it, for it likely meant his misbegotten son would soon subject his father to the rigors of another retreat.

The cart that carried him over rock and branch-strewn ground would jar his brittle bones and stir up bile such that his belly would not rest until its contents were expelled. The warm breezes of August that ought to be a balm upon his thickly scarred flesh would chill him through. And if the sun was out, it would pierce him...blind him...make his head ache as if to split open.

He turned his face out of the thick fur that failed to warm him as the healer had done earlier in the day. "What has happened?" His voice was so threadbare it struggled to reach his own ears.

The woman whose damp gown clung so close that it could not be said she was as immune to the warming fire as he, turned from the cave's opening. As she crossed to his side, the sound of her chains pained his ears.

"The Wulfrith knight has escaped, my lord." She knelt and tucked the blankets more securely around him.

Aldous winced, though not because of his own discomfort or that Robert had fallen short again. Nay, it was because of the healer's face that he preferred not to look near upon. His son had been displeased by her escape attempt all those days past, as had Aldous who would not have survived this long without her, but had he been able to stop Robert from thrashing her then—and once more since—he would have. He hoped she would be lovely again.

"How did he escape?" he asked.

"I do not know but, certes, he is gone." She sat back on her heels. "I have made you broth. You must eat."

"And have it slosh about my belly when..." He replenished his breath. "...Robert tosses me in the back of that accursed cart?"

She glanced at the cave's opening. "Night is near upon us. Surely he will not—"

"Unless Wulfrith's man is soon recaptured, the camp will be dismantled, for the miscreant will return with..."

"Christian," she said softly, sorrow reflected in her eyes, one of which had also known Robert's fist.

Aldous fought the emotion that seemed determined to leap from her to him, but its claws caught on the edge of his heart and hoisted itself over. "Christian," the name whispered from him. "My son."

She laid the back of a hand to his forehead, and he nearly whimpered. In all the years since the fire had left him a scarred shell of a man, she was the only one who touched him with gentleness and compassion, as if she truly worried over his suffering. Not that Christian had not tried.

"Aye, your son," she murmured.

He returned her to focus. "I will try to eat."

As she rose and turned away, once more rousing the links beneath her skirts, Robert threw a shadow through the cave's opening. Face shot with color, he strode forward. "The Wulfrith knight has escaped."

Aldous opened his mouth, but it was a phlegm-laden cough that broke from him, and it was some moments before he could clear his throat sufficiently to speak. "How?"

"There is a traitor amongst us." Though the healer stepped out of Robert's path, he seized her arm and dragged her to him. Gripping her chin, he forced her face up. "Was it you? Did you sever his ropes?"

Aldous glimpsed the whites of her eyes that told she feared his son would finish what he had begun. "Though I tended him early this morn, I did naught but cleanse and bandage his wounds," she said. "Ask your man, Wexley. He was there throughout."

Robert yanked her onto her toes. "Be it so, someone aided him, and who more likely than our reluctant healer, hmm?"

"I did naught!"

Robert slapped her, and she cried out.

Aldous moaned low in his throat for fear of what his son's unfolding ire might next visit upon her.

"You listened in where you should not have, eh, wench?"

She hunched her shoulders against further attack. "I do not know of what you speak."

Once more, her captor drew back a hand.

"Of what do you speak, Robert?" Aldous managed.

His son peered over the healer's head. "As I have found no advantage in keeping Sir Mark alive, I determined there would be an execution this eve. I vow, 'tis no coincidence the man escapes the very day the decision is made."

It might be coincidence, it might not. What Aldous did know was that he balked at once more being a silent accomplice to his son's brutality against the healer. "'Twas not the woman. She has not been"—he coughed—"outside the cave all day without one of your men close at her heels."

In the silence of Robert's seething, Aldous knew his misbegotten son saw the truth of it, but that did not mean the healer was safe.

Robert crudely raked his gaze over her as if tempted to carnal urgings that Aldous would be powerless to avert. At last, he shoved her aside. "Make haste in preparing my father to travel. We depart ere nightfall."

Aldous was ashamed of the whimper that slipped out the sides of his mouth and sounded as if made by a lad barely out of fouling cloths. He had been foolish and filled with ungodly vengeance to crow with satisfaction when Robert had taken him from Broehne all those weeks ago. For what? For what?! All he wanted now—*Just one thing, Lord, if you would spill your grace upon one so unworthy*—was to die in peace.

"Pray, hear me, Sir Robert," the healer said. "Your father should not be moved."

Aldous brought her back to focus where she stood three feet from Robert. As if she was not painfully intimate with the consequences of displeasing him, she raised her lovely and far too vulnerable chin. "Do you subject the baron to another retreat, death will come all the sooner for him."

Robert took a step toward her and thrust his lower jaw forward. "All the sooner?"

Her shoulders rose as if in preparation to defend her head and face. "I have told you, his condition worsens each day he is out of doors, and travel makes it worse. If your father is to be moved again…" Her eyelashes fluttered, but she held before Robert's darkening countenance. "…let his last journey be to Broehne that he might mark his final days amid the peace and comfort due him."

Aldous revised his thoughts of moments earlier. There was not one thing he wanted. There were two. Mayhap three. The second was to see the healer restored to her child. The third…

As much as he had refused to acknowledge his longing to see his youngest son and heir again, he felt the need move within him.

Robert laughed, causing the woman to startle where she stood. The sound did not surprise Aldous, though, for he knew it for the cruel and bitter thing that often presaged violence.

"Do you hear that, Father? The wench believes your battle is done and pretends she has a care for your wellbeing."

Distance was what the healer needed between herself and the angry man who would never be baron. With effort, Aldous extricated a hand from the covers and beckoned. "Come, my son." His body convulsed with the exposure to air that felt like a dip in the coldest stream. "I would speak with you."

Robert shot the healer a warning look and crossed to his father. When Aldous reached to him, his son hesitated, but then he dropped to his haunches. "What is it?"

Aldous had never been much for showing affection, especially these last years when he had felt too little to show, but he was strangely desperate to disarm his son's anger. Thus, he settled his crippled hand over Robert's and wished to God he had made room to feel more for this son than obligation. Had he, the end that came swift and sure might be different from this. "I fear the healer is right. I can venture no farther on this journey with you. Even now, death's breath fouls my nostrils."

Robert's hand bunched beneath his father's. "You wish me to return you to Broehne?"

Aldous longed for the comfort of home, but would the admission bring Robert's anger to a boil? He steeled himself. "I do wish it, my son."

A muscle in his jaw convulsing, Robert put between his teeth, "'Tis Christian that draws you. Tell me it is not so."

"I...would see him again. He is, after all, my heir and—"

Robert jerked his hand free. "*I* am your first born!"

"First born, but—"

"Misbegotten. I have heard it all my life—and worse—but still I am first." He thrust to his feet and splayed his arms. "And now look what you have made of me by setting me to do your bidding and denying me my birthright. Your *son* is a fugitive sought by King Henry himself, reduced to a man with naught left to him but revenge." His chest heaved. "Even if now you acknowledged me as heir, my end would be told such as it is."

Aldous dragged his dry tongue from the roof of his mouth and searched the lower reaches for moisture that would allow him to form words. "I am sorry, Robert, but this is the way of things. Your mother—"

"Was a peasant." Robert dropped his arms to his sides. "Do not waste breath on tidings far older than I."

Wishing too many years too late that he had not given in to sin and lain with the pretty village girl who had made him feel things a man of nobility ought not to feel for one of inferior birth, Aldous said, "Pray, see me home, Robert."

Sour laughter issued from lips that had known only to wail when this misbegotten son was born to Aldous so many years ago. "I think not. If you will not travel, you shall remain here."

As the implications licked like fire through Aldous, the healer's chains clanked. "Dare not, Sir Robert. Your father requires respite from the damp and dark of this place."

Robert snapped his head around. "You are more the fool, wench, if you think mutual affection unites my father and me. Just as he never considered me a worthy heir…" He returned his gaze to Aldous, eyes so cold there was no question he would make no further effort to muffle what could not be mistaken for anything other than hatred. "…never did I consider a better end for him than this."

His words should not have affected Aldous, but had they been capable of taking form, they would have been a blade that knew well the art of evisceration. Still, Aldous held. "If this is to be the way of it, Robert, I bid you to flee England and escape King Henry's reach."

"Why, I could almost believe you care, *Father*."

Did he? He did. Some. "Do you not leave England, the king will see you dead—and most painfully if you are handed up to him with breath yet in your body."

Robert's lids narrowed. "This I know, just as I know the revenge we set ourselves is worth the risk."

Revenge on the Wulfriths. It was what Aldous had wanted. Still did. Or did he? Aye, for what they had done to Geoffrey. But now Christian was wed to one of them, and the children he would make with his wife would mix Lavonne and Wulfrith blood—

"I will not forego it now that we are so near," Robert said.

Aldous almost laughed. They had been *so near* revenge for weeks, and all evidence to which he was privy indicated they were farther from it than they had been the night Robert had taken him from Broehne. But Aldous still had enough wit about him to not speak the truth that stared them both down.

"If I am soon to meet the Almighty, Robert," he said, "I would not also have your death to account for. Pray, let me pass from this world comforted by the knowledge you yet live."

His son stared down his long nose at him. "Mayhap I shall depart England, but not before I leave my mark upon the Wulfriths."

Aldous had known he was wasting his breath. "What do you intend?"

Robert's mouth twitched into a smile. "I have had word, and though I had not thought to act upon it, the Wulfrith knight's escape changes everything."

"What word have you received?"

Robert surveyed his father's disfigured countenance. "I dare not say lest the Wulfrith knight leads Christian here and your aged tongue lets slip my plan. All you need know is that the Wulfriths will pay in blood."

Was it Gaenor Wulfrith—Christian's bride—he spoke of, a woman whose womb might even now carry a Lavonne, a grandson he would never see? As something reeking of regret twisted inside Aldous, he watched the smile on Robert's face broaden.

"Aye," rasped the misbegotten one, his gaze on Aldous's face and yet not, as if it was the very mind of his father he peered into, "much blood." A moment later, he blinked and returned to the disfigured surface. "Oft you told that drawing and quartering would be the best death for a Wulfrith."

Aldous remembered, though the shiver that had shaken his devastated body whilst fomenting over Geoffrey's death was far different from what shook him now. Then he had delighted in such imaginings but, strangely, now he was almost repulsed by them.

Robert huffed a sigh of satisfaction. "So it shall be," he pronounced. "As for your heir, dear father, just pray he does not come between me and my prey."

Aldous did not flinch, for he was not so fool to believe that, given the chance to inflict ill on his legitimate brother, Robert would deny himself. There had never been a question of it, and Aldous had done little dwelling on it. Now, however...

Aldous swallowed hard. "Christian is not much, I grant, but still he is your brother."

Robert's upper lip peeled back. "One whose every breath displaces mine. Nay, given the chance to face him, I will not turn my sword aside."

Dear Lord, Aldous silently beseeched, *I know I am the one who set this in motion, but if You would but give me your ear, heed my beseeching that Christian not pay the price for my sins.*

"Now"—Robert peered over his shoulder—"all that is left to decide is what to do with you, Helene of Tippet."

Aldous looked to the healer who stood beyond Robert's shoulder and saw the fear he had known would be in her eyes. "If you intend to abandon me, Robert," he pushed past a dry, constricted throat, "have mercy and... leave the healer that she might comfort me during my final hours."

Robert snorted. "You think she would not also abandon you the moment my men and I ride?"

Would she? Would he die here alone? If ever he was found, would there be enough left of him to identify whom he had once been? Or would the wild things that crept into the cave ravage his remains? Carry away his bones?

A wind wound through the cave. Nay, not a wind. It was his old body whence the rushing air issued. Heart pounding fiercely, breath panted past his lips as if he ran with the devil at his heels. And perhaps he did.

He squeezed his eyes closed. He would do better to think on righting the wrong done the healer that he might have fewer marks against him when he stood before the seat of judgment.

Hoping that what he was about to suggest would not prove the woman's undoing—that the Wulfrith knight would return with Christian—he looked up. "If you chain the healer to me, she will not be able to flee."

As the sound of Helene's sharply indrawn breath traveled around the cave, Robert's lowered eyebrows rose. For a long moment, he said nothing, and then he mused, "'Twould solve the problem, especially if the Wulfrith knight is incapable of tracking his way back here."

Meaning the healer might share Aldous's tomb.

Robert straightened. "Mayhap I will grant you this mercy, though I admit much of its merit lies in knowing you will have the sweet taste of benevolence in your mouth when you are consigned to hell and, thus, miss it all the more."

Aldous stared at his son who clearly believed he no longer had anything to gain from his sire. "So you do hate me."

Robert shrugged. "Hate for Aldous Lavonne is not hard to come by. Ask anyone. Nay, the scraping and bowing and all other manner of respect where none is due... *That* is hard to come by—a hell all its own." He raised his eyebrows. "But soon enough you will know how it feels to ask and not receive, to know no hope, to accept that yours is a discarded life."

Though the backs of Aldous's eyelids beckoned, he kept his son in sight—a man so embittered he wished hell upon his sire.

Is that truly my destination, Lord? I do not argue against having earned it, but...

What, Aldous Lavonne? What excuse can you possibly offer?

No excuse, just regret for what I have thought and said and done that has delivered me and so many others to this moment.

Robert sighed. "Aye, your end is near and, like me, 'tis too late to change the outcome." He pivoted, pushed heavily against the healer in passing, and strode from the cave.

When he and his followers broke camp an hour later, a four-foot length of chain bound Aldous and the woman ankle to ankle—one bruised and abraded, the other skeletal and scarred.

22

THE DAY WAS beautiful, sprung as it was from the night that Gaenor had spent in her husband's arms, a night that had slipped into dawn and lingered into late morning. Though she had yet to speak words of love or feel them caress her own ear, she sensed the emotion in the spaces between her and this man. And yet...

Where she lay on her side, cradled against Christian's chest, head tucked beneath his chin, she sank her teeth into her bottom lip. She supposed they had not known each other long enough for love to grow across those spaces, but what if it never did? What if it did not deepen into something that would last to their end days? Worse, what if the love between them was hers alone?

She uncurled her hands and pressed them against his chest. His heart beat strong beneath her palms and, in moments, it beat faster. He desired her. He left her in no doubt of that—only of love.

"Wife," he spoke into her hair.

Breathing deep in an attempt to suffocate her misgivings, she tilted her face up to his. "Husband."

He lifted an eyebrow. "Are we to lay abed all day?"

Though her cheeks warmed at what she longed to speak, she spoke it anyway. "Could we?"

A smile curved his mouth, and he fingered the tress that fell across her brow. "As I am now most awake and refreshed, what would we do?" His eyes laughed at her, but not in a cruel way.

"Though yesterday's cramping has not yet delivered my menses, methinks I will bleed this day."

Both eyebrows rose. "Aye?"

He knew what she suggested, but did he truly mean for her to speak it? Fighting back the temptation to roll aside and grab her garments from where he had discarded them among the rushes last eve, she pushed up on an elbow, pressed him onto his back, and settled her face over his. "I would have your arms around me."

With his face in the shadow thrown by her curtaining hair, he reached up and touched the curve of her neck. "That is all?"

"Nay."

His calloused fingers traveled to the base of her throat. "Then?"

"I..." She shivered. "...like being your wife."

"Certes, you do a fine job of ordering my household."

She gasped. "You know that is not of what I speak!"

He sighed. "Just as I know the barony does not manage itself and that already I have spent too much of the day without regard to my duties."

Disappointment bristled through Gaenor, but as she started to pull away, Christian swept her onto her back with such ease she felt as near a feather as one of her height might feel.

"What is one more hour?" he rasped where he bent over her.

She smiled. "Truly?"

"Anything that is in my power to give, I shall."

Love as well? But she could not bring herself to ask it—not directly. As his head descended and their breaths became one, she provided him a way out if he chose to take it, asking instead, "Why?"

At the instant she felt the brush of his lips, he hesitated, and it was some moments before he spoke. "You are my wife, and I am pleased it is so."

Only pleased?

Stop it, Gaenor. Not so many days ago he was not pleased, believed terrible ill of you, would not touch you for the ruin of your virtue, would not stand before God. You are only at the beginning of two becoming one. Be patient.

"I hope you are as pleased to have me as your husband," he murmured, and she realized he had seen whatever emotions she had let loose on her face.

Though tempted to pride, she determined she would let him know more of her than she knew of him. "I am beyond pleased," she said and raised her head from the pillow. When she pressed her lips to his, she felt his hesitation again, but then he claimed her mouth. And breath. And perhaps even her heart. Hopefully, one day he would feel as deeply for her.

In the next instant, Christian was off the bed.

Gaenor gasped. "What is it?"

Lower jaw thrust forward, he swept his garments from the rushes. "Someone has come."

"What?" No sooner did the word exit her mouth than she heard the pound of hooves, the snap of reins, and the urgency of voices beyond the windows. "Christian?"

"They would not ride into the inner bailey," he said as he thrust his arms into the sleeves of his tunic, "nor with such urgency, if they did not bear tidings of great import."

Dread seeped into Gaenor. "You think it has to do with Robert?"

He lashed on his sword-burdened belt. "I would do well to think so."

Lord, let the tidings be good—that Robert is captured and will work no more ill upon the land.

Determined to be at her husband's side, she tossed back the covers.

"Stay there." He raised a hand to her as the pound of boots on the stairs warned there would soon be pounding on the door.

Gaenor turned and lowered her feet to the floor. "I would accompany—"

The heavy knock sounded. "My lord, riders have come!"

"Cover yourself," Christian ordered as he shoved his feet into boots.

Gaenor complied, though she determined that the moment they were alone again, she would throw on her own clothes.

Christian strode to the door, glanced over his shoulder to be sure she had covered herself, and wrenched the handle. In the corridor stood his anxious squire, but before he could tell what was to be told, his lord said, "Come," stepped forward, and pulled the door closed behind him.

Gaenor threw off the covers and stood. Whether her husband wished it or not, whatever had befallen Broehne, it was for her to know as well.

At last the king's men had come—and bearing a gift. Of sorts.

Sir Mark lay on a trestle table, the fresh blood seeping through his tunic brightly contrasting with the dried blood of injuries dealt him a fortnight past. Fortunately, Michael D'arci was present, having been called to Broehne two days ago to contain the fever that had struck several of the castle guard. Armed with his physician's bag, he entered the hall just ahead of Gaenor.

Christian ground his teeth. He had been foolish to think his wife would remain abovestairs. Leaving Abel's side, he strode around the table and into her path. When she tried to step around him, he caught her arm. "You need not be here."

She met his gaze. "I do." She glanced past him to those gathered around the table. "Who is it?"

"Sir Mark. The king's men came upon him as they rode on Broehne."

She drew a strident breath. "The brigands did to him as they did to his men-at-arms?"

Remembering how the savagery in the back of the wagon had affected her, Christian quickly reassured her, "Nay, he is whole. He lives, and not badly."

Her lids flickered. "Truly?"

"He but requires tending. You need not—"

"I will remain."

"Gaenor—"

"Do you think me faint of heart?"

She who stood so tall and proud that she could look down upon many a man? Forget that she had been shaken by the atrocities committed against Sir Mark's companions. Forget that she was womanly and near vulnerable when she lay in his arms. She was a Wulfrith. *His* Wulfrith. "I would never think that, Gaenor."

"Then I would go to my brother's knight."

Christian sighed, lightened his grip on her arm, and led her back the way he had come.

As they approached the table, D'Arci looked up from where he had cut away the knight's tunic to expose the source of bleeding. "It looks worse than it is," he said. "Considering what Helene had to work with, he was well tended. I am fair certain infection has not set in."

At the table, Christian deferred to Gaenor, allowing her to take the position he had earlier filled alongside her brother near the knight's head.

"Sir Mark." She caught up his hand.

He turned his face toward her and opened his eyes wider, though still they were not much more than slits. "I am well, Lady Gaenor. I but tore my stitches during my flight from the brigands. Soon I will be ready to return to your family's service."

"I do not doubt it, brave knight."

On an expelled breath, he relaxed deeper into the table and closed his eyes.

Abel bent near him. "I am sorry to give you no rest, Sir Mark, but since you will not recover soon enough to lead us back the way you came, we must know more about the caves that Baron Lavonne might better determine our course of pursuit."

Gaenor looked to Christian. "Caves?"

He inclined his head and said low, "The brigands' encampment ere he escaped on the day past. There are three areas on the barony known to have caves. As the king's men came upon Sir Mark but a league from Broehne, we cannot know at which caves he was held."

"The ones that lie to the west," Sir Mark said, lids remaining lowered. "Within hearing distance of a waterfall—though barely, for 'twas only when the camp was at its most quiet that I could discern it."

Abel peered past his sister.

Christian nodded. "I know the caves. Though the brigands have surely broken camp, 'tis our best chance of picking up their trail."

"Then we should ride." Abel took a step back from the table, hesitated, and leaned near the knight again. "What of the healer? How does she fare?"

Christian almost smiled for the pride it surely cost his brother-in-law to make such an inquiry. His wife had shared with him her belief that her brother's distress over his inability to return the woman to her son was more than concern for the boy.

Sir Mark opened his eyes enough to allow light to enter them. "If she were not of use in keeping the old baron alive, methinks the knave would not have stopped at beating her."

Abel jerked. "He beat her?"

"Aye, and more than once after her last escape attempt."

Christian ground his teeth. Was there no end to this disease called Robert?

Sir Mark sucked breath as D'Arci began to ply his needle. "But now that it appears Aldous Lavonne is near his end..." he said between clenched teeth.

Abel growled something that might or might not have been a word.

Though Christian felt Gaenor's gaze, he kept his eyes on the knight. "How do you know my father is dying?" Not that Aldous hadn't been dying for a long time, but this sounded nearer, like the roil of nausea moments before its violence is known.

Sir Mark grimaced beneath D'Arci ministrations. "Yesterday, when the healer tended me, she whispered that your father is not much longer for this world."

Christian nodded. "Did she aid in your escape?"

"Nay, she did not lift a finger to me without being closely watched."

"Then how did you manage to free yourself?"

Sir Mark grunted—half laugh, half discomfort. "It seems one of Robert's men is less than eager to number among his followers. Likely, I would now be dead had he not aided me, for a half hour earlier, Robert loudly declared that my capture had proved of no benefit and he would take pleasure in leisurely relieving himself of my presence."

Christian thought it safe to assume that whoever had aided Sir Mark was the same who had sent word of the camp's location ten days past. "Who helped you?"

The knight shook his head. "He was at my back when he cut my bindings, and he spoke in a whisper I did not recognize."

"What did he say?"

"That I should remain where I was until I was not watched."

"Then there is no way to know which of Robert's men it is."

Sir Mark's attempt at a humorous grunt made him wince. "'Tis possible I could identify him by his odor, for I do not think I have ever smelled a human so foul." He shrugged. "Still, I am grateful, for not a quarter hour passed ere I was able to steal away."

"How long before they gave chase?"

Sir Mark frowned. "I heard shouting and knew my absence was discovered minutes afterward, and yet no horses overtook me. Indeed, I did not even catch the distant sound of hooves." He sighed when the piercing and tugging at his flesh ceased.

"I will dress the wound," D'Arci said as he cut the thread, "then you will rest."

"I thank you," Sir Mark rasped and returned his attention to Christian. "As I was on foot and my injury kept me from traveling quickly, I do not understand why they did not come after me."

Christian shifted his gaze to Abel who was flushed with a restlessness that told he was past ready for the saddle and woe to any who did not match the pace he set. "'Tis time to put your tracking skills to use."

"Aye." Abel gripped the Wulfrith knight's shoulder. "It is good to have you back among us." Without awaiting a reply, he turned and strode across the hall.

Christian looked to the king's men whose task it was to aid in hunting his brother to ground, then back at his wife. "We will be gone a day, perhaps more."

She turned to face him, and he saw worry in her tight smile. "I will be waiting for you."

He lifted her hands in his. "'Twill be over soon." They were watched, but still he kissed her, albeit briefly. Then he released her and called to his squire.

A half hour later, as he and his armored entourage of twenty strong rode from Broehne, Christian sensed Gaenor. Maintaining Abel's pace, he looked back and saw she had left the inner bailey against his wishes and stood before the drawbridge watching him ride away. If not that there was a man-at-arms on either side of her and the castle walls were well fortified, he would have turned back and seen her bound hand and foot if that was what was required to keep her safe in his absence.

He looked forward again. "'Twill be over soon," he repeated his reassurance to the air that rushed past. Then life could truly begin for him and his Wulfrith bride.

The baron of Broehne could not know that his time and effort—and that of the king's men—would be better spent riding in a different direction. But he would know soon enough, providing the man's wife could be got alone and was of a mind to cooperate.

Of course, once Lady Gaenor learned who was at stake, she would come willingly regardless of how it might appear to the man she had been forced to wed. At least, that was the hope of Sir Mark's savior. If he was to do what desperately needed being done, he required Gaenor Wulfrith—now Lavonne—to keep him alive.

From the cover of the wood, he watched her husband and his men ride from sight. When all that was left was the haze stirred up by the multitude of hooves, he turned his attention to the woman before the drawbridge who was too tall to be any other than Gaenor. After a long moment, she swept around and hurried beneath the portcullis into the outer bailey.

The savior held his breath, praying the drawbridge remained lowered to accommodate villagers who had business within the castle walls.

It did not move, evidence the baron believed he had left the castle secure. And the one in the wood did not doubt it was secure, but he had not survived these past weeks that should have seen him dead a dozen times without furthering his capacity for stealth and diversion.

He felt the tug of a grim smile as he turned his attention to the beaten dirt road. He would have to bide his time to find the right opportunity to gain entrance to Broehne. It was unfortunate he did not have more time to bide.

23

"PARDON, M'LADY..."

Forgetting to lower her frown, Gaenor looked up from the household books that she had once more asked the grudging steward to open to her. To her surprise, the cook stood before her, his ascent of the dais—lumbering, no doubt—lost amidst her journey through column after column of freshly inked numbers.

"What is it, Cook?"

He wrinkled his long narrow nose that stood like a surprise in the middle of his fleshy face. "I would not bother ye, m'lady, but there be a problem with the cost of the vegetables you ordered from the village."

Gaenor sat taller. "The price was agreed upon."

"With Arnaut, aye, but he has taken ill and this other has come in his place. He says the quality of his vegetables requires more coin than what you promised Arnaut." Cook scowled. "Says he won't unload his cart 'til he has had an audience with the steward."

Whom she had sent away that she might better concentrate on the journal entries. She rose. "As I dealt with Arnaut, I shall myself set the man right."

Behind, she heard Sir Hector step from alongside the tapestry. Though she required no escort, she would not argue it—for his sake and Christian's.

"He is in the kitchen?" she asked as she came around the table.

With a grunt of effort, Cook descended the dais. "Nay, m'lady," he said as she drew near. "Though he asked to come into the hall to speak to the steward, he is so foul he would sour the soup were he to pass through my kitchen. I told him to wait in the garden."

The heat of the kitchen struck Gaenor before she set foot in it. Though it took seconds to cross to the door that let outside, moisture flecked her brow when she stepped out into a day that had advanced little more than an hour since her husband's departure.

Settling her gaze on the man who stood with his back to her at the gate on the far side of the garden, his shabby state of dress matching his ability to sour soup, she murmured, "A very long day."

"My lady?"

She looked over her shoulder as Sir Hector pulled the door closed behind him, leaving Cook to his domain. "I fear 'tis going to be a very long day," she said.

The aged knight inclined his head.

Gaenor looked back around. The villager, who demanded more coin for vegetables that were past due in the kitchen, had turned to her. There was not much of his face to be seen, as the upper half was curtained in stringy hair and the lower half covered in thick beard, but out of his shadowed face burned eyes, and they were staring wide at her as if her appearance was as unsettling as his own. But then, he had been expecting the steward.

"My lady," he said gruffly and bowed his head.

With Sir Hector at her heels, Gaenor traversed the path and halted before the man who was, indeed, quite foul of odor. "Your name?" she asked, fighting the temptation to raise a hand to her nose.

Slowly, his chin came up, but even before his lips parted, she had her answer.

Whatever his response, she was too shocked to make sense of the single word that landed between them. She stumbled back into Sir Hector, and her reaction proved her protector's undoing.

The man, who was not a villager at all, sprang to the side. With a flash of silver, he raised a dagger and swept it down.

The crack of bone sounding in Gaenor's ears, she spun around, though not in time to ease the aged knight to the ground.

Breath coming fast, she dropped to her knees beside Sir Hector and touched his temple that bled a thin red line. The hilt of the dagger had been used on him, but that did not mean the damage would be any less severe than a wound that drew blood. Mayhap worse considering the struggles Beatrix had faced following her head injury.

Gaenor snapped her chin around and glared at the man who stood over her. "What have you done?"

He returned his dagger—a Wulfrith dagger—to the short scabbard on his belt. "I but take advantage of a situation you have made blessedly easy for me, Lady Gaenor."

"Of what do you speak?"

"I requested an audience with the steward that I might gain entrance to the donjon and find my way to you, and here you are delivered to me as if I ordered it."

She pushed to her feet. "I do not know why you are here, but you must leave." She started for the kitchen, but he caught her arm and pulled her around. "I must needs get help for Sir Hector," she said, straining against his hold.

He lowered his face near hers, further assailing her with his odor. "Nay, you must needs come with me. Now."

She stepped nearer the man who stood shorter by several fingers. "If you force me to reveal you, Sir Durand, I shall. Now release me."

He yanked her closer still. "There is not much time, so listen well. I am not here for you or myself. I am here for Beatrix."

She drew a sharp breath, but this time hardly noticed his foul scent. "What of my sister?"

"Doubtless, the brigands are even now approaching Castle Soaring and will soon—if they have not already—breach the walls. Then Sir Robert will work his revenge on her."

Fear shot through Gaenor. This time, would Christian's brother succeed in killing Beatrix? Would—?

She shook her head in an attempt to shake loose the suffocating thoughts that had no cause to claim her. "You seek to work trickery on me."

"Upon my vow," he growled, "'tis not trickery."

"It is! Beatrix is safe."

He gripped her other arm and shook her. "The brigands know D'Arci was called to Broehne. That makes Soaring vulnerable. A Lavonne through and through, Robert knows all the castle's secrets, and he will use them to finish what he and his father began."

Gaenor searched his face that was barely familiar beneath so much hair and grime. What he told had to be a lie. After all, he had been so intent on taking her to France that she had been forced to use trickery to escape him. She jerked at her arm, but he held fast.

"I would be a fool to trust you," she hissed.

He cursed, then demanded, "Do you wish to save your sister or nay?"

"If she needs saving, aye, but you offer no proof."

"There is not time!"

She blinked amidst the saliva he spat out with his words. "Tell me, else leave, Sir Durand."

Beneath his coarse beard, his jaw convulsed, and when he spoke, his voice was so tight it seemed one more turn of it might cause it to shatter. "I claim responsibility for the word sent to your brother, Sir Abel, that revealed the location of the brigands' camp—"

Gaenor stopped breathing.

"—and the release of Sir Mark ere Sir Robert could make an end of him."

Had Durand not maintained a grip on her, she was sure she would have had to sit down to avoid losing her balance.

"'Twas you?" Even as the question passed her lips, she knew it was so, and not because Sir Mark had told of the terrible odor that clung to his savior.

"The night you slipped away from me," he said, his frustration so thick it could be felt, "I happened upon the brigands' camp. I could not depart for France knowing the man who had failed to kill Beatrix might try again. Thus, I followed him camp to camp, waiting for and being denied the opportunity to put down your husband's brother. Last eve, after I freed Sir Mark and the brigands prepared to abandon camp, one of Robert's men whom he had sent out returned with news that D'Arci had been called to Broehne. Robert determined then that they would ride on Soaring."

Gaenor let out her breath. "Then you speak true. But why come for me when you should be at Castle Soaring?"

He bared his teeth. "Think, Gaenor! I cannot take the brigands alone. If they are to be stopped, it will be with the aid of your husband and his men."

Of course.

"They must be intercepted and turned toward Soaring, but my only chance of gaining their ear before my blood is spilled and Beatrix is lost is if you stand between me and your husband and brother's wrath."

Indeed, for the man who had first known her would not be given a chance to tell his tale. Thus, she must serve as Durand's shield. Trying not to think on how her accompaniment would appear to Christian, though dread and worry spread through her, she said, "I will go with you."

The sound that blew from Durand was nearer a sob of relief than a sigh. "I thank you."

Behind, Sir Hector stirred.

Gaenor looked over her shoulder and saw his lids were yet lowered. But he would surely come to his senses soon. No sooner did she acknowledge it than Durand pushed her aside.

"If he raises the alarm ere we gain the wood, your sister is dead," he said, "and I have not time to bind him." It was all the warning he gave, then his booted foot struck the knight in the head.

Gaenor clapped a hand over her mouth to keep from crying out and raising the alarm herself.

"Fear not," Durand said as he pulled her toward the gate. "The cook will soon enough come looking for his vegetables. Just hope 'tis not too soon."

In the narrow alley outside the garden gate stood a handcart that held vegetables belonging to another.

"Arnaut?" she whispered.

Durand glanced around to be certain they were not watched. When the alley proved deserted, he released her arm and said, "He is bound and awaiting our return—a surly fellow, unfortunately for him."

Meaning the villager had likely tried to fight off Durand and would bear the marks of his attempt to evade a man trained in war.

Durand whipped the canvas off the vegetables, swiftly raised the cart's handles, and dumped the contents on the ground. "Get as tight to the front as you can." He pointed to the cart's bed.

Gaenor climbed onto it and, as much as she could considering her height, folded herself into the space.

The canvas dropped over her, draping her in loose darkness and filling her nostrils with the scent of earth that was an odd mix of pleasant and unpleasant.

Durand's jarring pace made her teeth snap and, time and again, knocked her head against the boards, but the fear of being discovered by those patrolling the baileys and walls was worse, and it wasn't until she heard the wooden wheels rumbling over the drawbridge that she drew her first conscious breath of air that was far too thin and uncomfortably warm.

"Lord, let this not be for naught," she whispered as the cart transitioned from drawbridge to dirt road. "Let Christian hear me, believe me, act upon Durand's tidings. Above all, keep Beatrix safe."

It seemed an hour, though it could not have been one-quarter that, before a measure of relief was granted by their entrance into the wood and the shade thrown by the canopy of leaves.

Gaenor pushed back a corner of the canvas and gulped the clean air.

Shortly, the cart halted and tipped backward as Durand raised the handles.

"We are here." He threw the canvas off her.

Gaenor sat up and suppressed a groan as the ache of unfolding added to the aches acquired throughout the rough passage from donjon to wood.

"Make ready to ride," he called, striding opposite.

She felt foolish. Until that moment, she had not considered how they would intercept Christian. As Durand's horse had been lamed during her flight with him, he must have acquired another in the weeks since. As she watched his progress over the undergrowth, she saw it was so. And the horse tethered to a tree was no simple plow horse. It was a much-prized destrier.

She climbed out of the cart and hurried after Durand. As she neared, she realized the destrier was not alone in being tied to the tree. Arnaut sat on the opposite side, arms splayed backward against the trunk, mouth filled with a gag, eyes widening as they lit upon her.

"You will let him go?" Gaenor asked.

Durand untied his horse. "Nay, though I will remove his gag that he might call for help and distract those who will soon be after us."

It could not be long, for Cook had to have discovered Sir Hector by now.

Gaenor veered toward the villager and bent before him. "I am sorry for this, but as soon as Broehne's guard finds you, you must tell them Castle Soaring is under attack by the brigands."

The man's brow puckered.

"That is where I am going—to aid my sister."

He shook his head.

"Tell them so."

"Gaenor!" Durand snapped as he led the destrier toward her. "Get astride now."

She straightened and, with his aid, mounted the horse.

Durand yanked off Arnaut's gag. "Now yell," he said.

Arnaut did, and Durand sprang into the saddle. "Hold on to me!"

Before Gaenor could get her arms fully around him, he put heels to the horse. Clamping her elbows hard against his sides, she managed to mesh her fingers against his abdomen.

In the next moment, realization emptied bitter laughter into her mouth, but she pressed her lips to hold it in. She had been here before, with this same man, riding wildly through the wood, but that time he had been taking her to France that she might flee marriage to Christian. Now he was taking her to Christian who would—

She did not want to think about the accusations that lay ahead. Anything but that. Trying to ignore Durand's scent, she leaned near his ear. "Where did you get the destrier?" she asked, knowing that, until they were free of the wood and making better speed, her words would not be lost to him.

"It was Robert's, and he is most vexed." There was satisfaction in the voice he sent over his shoulder. "I took it after I freed Sir Mark. Not only did it provide a fine horse of which I had need, but it prevented the brigands from pursuing their prisoner since they believed he was the one who stole it and there was little chance of overtaking him."

That was why they had not searched for the Wulfrith knight. Clever Durand.

"As I saw your husband and his men ride in the direction of the caves, I assume Sir Mark made it to Broehne without ill effect."

"He tore his stitches and was bleeding heavily, but the physician restitched his wound and says he will be fine."

"D'Arci remains at Broehne?"

"Nay, he accompanied my husband that he might tend the old baron if the brigands are found."

She more felt than heard Durand's laugh. "Though Christian Lavonne will not yet have cornered the brigands, soon enough he will find his father—dead or alive, I do not know."

Gaenor shook her head alongside his. "I do not understand."

"The only gain to which Robert can now aspire is revenge." Durand looked over his shoulder and met her gaze. "And in pursuing it, he has abandoned the old baron to the cave that he might all the sooner reach Soaring."

At her look of surprise, he raised his eyebrows in the manner of one who has proved a point, then turned forward again.

Though Gaenor knew it best to keep as much space between them as possible, she lowered her forehead to his shoulder and squeezed her eyes closed. She was acquainted with Christian's brother by the ill he had wreaked, but this last cruelty was almost too much to ponder.

Robert had left his own father to die, much like she had heard tale some left their deformed newborns to the wild, unforgiving appetites of nature. There truly was evil in the world, and it was drawing nearer Beatrix.

Gaenor drew a strengthening breath and put her head back. No matter what happened, no matter what Christian thought or said when she came before him with Durand at her side, she would not regret leaving Broehne in a handcart. There had been no other way.

There were no words to name the emotion that struck Christian when he entered the cave in answer to the woman's cries. The voice belonged to the healer as he had thought it must, but the one to whom she was linked by chain was silent and unmoving amid a mess of furs and blankets.

Wide-eyed, Helene of Tippet stared at her lord, then crumpled to the ground and began to weep.

Christian shook free of the emotion that sought to spread numbness to his every extremity and strode forward. However, it was Abel who reached her first, thrusting past Christian with such speed the scene momentarily took on the proportions of a dream.

"John?" Helene gasped as Abel hunkered down beside her. "My boy? John?"

"He is well." Abel's soothing tone rendered his voice almost unrecognizable. "He but requires his mother."

Christian nearly resented the usurpation of his duty to Helene, and not a small piece of that resentment was due to being made to all the sooner face the death of his sire and the fear of what he would—or would not—feel when he did so.

Behind, he heard the others enter the cave but did not break his stride as he crossed to the crude bed that held Aldous Lavonne. He halted and clenched his hands into fists as he stared down into the scarred and still face of the man who had fathered him and, for a time perhaps, felt something near love for his youngest son.

"Father," he breathed, and jerked when the old man's lids flickered and eyes opened to narrow slits.

After a long moment, the twisted and puckered flesh around Aldous Lavonne's mouth moved. "My…son."

The unexpected acknowledgment—not only unexpected because the words were spoken by a man he had believed was beyond this world, but that they were spoken by the father who had too many times denied him—made Christian swallow hard.

"My lord?" D'Arci said.

Christian looked to the man who had halted several feet behind him. "Hold a moment," he said and dropped to his haunches beside Aldous. "I am here, Father."

The old man drew a wheezing breath. "And prepared to gloat."

Feeling a burn against the backs of his eyes, Christian momentarily wondered how many years it was since he had last shed tears. He shook his head. "I see naught over which to gloat."

Aldous's chin tremored side to side as if it was as near as he could come to shaking his head. "Then you are a fool."

No sooner did anger pry at Christian's self-control than his father's chest gave an almost metallic rattle. "After what I did…you have earned the right to gloat."

Anger ebbing in the face of disbelief over what his words might mean, Christian leaned nearer. "You should know that is not who I am, for 'twas by your hand I was groomed and wed to the Church."

Aldous's lids slowly lowered, but just when Christian feared his father's end was upon him, the old man murmured, "And now God has righted my wrong."

They were words Christian had thought never to hear. He stared at the ruined face amid the blankets. What had happened to bring his father around, he who had struck out at his youngest son by allowing

Robert to steal him from Broehne? Why this now? Was it all these weeks of absence? The final breath of life drawing near? Or was it someone?

Christian glanced at the healer, and only then did the sounds that bounded around the cave reach him. He had not heard metal striking metal, but as he saw Abel return his sword to its scabbard, he knew the blade's keen edge was responsible for severing the chain that bound the two who had been left here to die.

Christian looked back at his sire and saw his eyes remained closed. "I thank you, Father."

Aldous made a sound low in his throat, then breathed, "What now?"

"Now you go home to Broehne."

Christian motioned D'Arci forward.

It was only minutes before the physician confirmed what his son already knew—if Aldous Lavonne survived the ride to Broehne, he would not long enjoy the comforts of his bed.

"We must maintain a gentle pace," D'Arci said.

Christian inclined his head and slid his arms beneath his father. As he lifted him against his chest, he ached for the weight that seemed more covering than man.

Pray, Lord, let our journey be swift and uneventful that he might see home again ere he passes.

24

"WHY HAVE WE stopped?"

Durand's back stiffened, then broadened with a long breath. He shifted around in the saddle and met Gaenor's gaze. "They ride."

Feeling a stab to the heart, she glanced past him but saw no evidence of Christian and his men. "How do you know?"

"The brigands' camp was in that direction." He nodded toward the wood ahead that was more dense than any they had passed. "The road to Soaring lies there." He jutted his chin to the left. "Behind us is Broehne. Regardless of your husband's destination, he must needs leave the trees to make good time. Thus, he will pass this way, and if 'tis not Soaring he seeks, we shall soon enough turn him that way."

That would be difficult, for Christian would hardly be receptive to the word of a man who, it would appear, had not only stolen his betrothed but now his wife. "What if he has already passed and we have missed him?"

"'Tis possible, but considering the number of caves in this area and that he will surely be tracking the brigands, it is more likely he and his men are still in the wood."

Gaenor nodded. "And so we wait."

"Wait and pray."

She startled, and he nearly smiled. "You do not think I pray?"

She shook her head. "Forgive me, but I did not expect it."

He sighed. "I have given you cause for that. Thus, I must ask, is all well between you and your husband?" His gaze flickered. "He surely knows that..."

Though memories of their shared intimacy had dimmed to near dark, Gaenor felt heat in her cheeks. "He knows."

"And wishes me dead."

"I fear he might."

He looked away, and it was some moments before he spoke again. "I would not have compromised you again, Gaenor, but I saw no other way to quickly gain your husband's ear that we might save Beatrix."

Always Beatrix. Strange that Durand's feelings for her sister did not make her ache as once they had. But then, Gaenor's heart was no longer engaged to this man. "Still you love her," she said softly.

After a long moment, he said, "I wish it were not so that I might be long gone from England, but 'tis true I love her and ever will."

The futility of his feelings for one wed to another not only in word but in heart, caused emotion to fill Gaenor's throat. Not so long ago, she had been as hopeless, and now...

Now she had hope, and perhaps something more—providing Christian did not condemn her for acceding to Durand's plan. "I am certain my sister would not wish to chain you so," she offered.

"And yet she does."

Unexpected tears sprang to her eyes, causing Durand to startle. "Pray, forgive me. I do not mean to pain you with my foolish confession, nor would I have you think I do not care for you. 'Tis just that..."

She curled her fingers into her palms to keep from smoothing the stricken lines from his face. "You misunderstand me, Sir Durand. There was a time when your words would have hurt deeply, but it is my husband who now possesses my heart. What I feel for you..." She shook her head. "I ache for all you have lost."

A sharp laugh pushed past his lips. "Pity, then."

She could not lie. "I do feel for your plight."

Resentment flashed in his eyes, only to be replaced by something weary that matched the sinking of his shoulders. "'Tis my due. All I can hope for now is a measure of redemption."

"How do you mean?"

"I would make my peace with the Wulfriths and your husband if they will allow it—" He snapped his head around.

And Gaenor knew, though it was yet some moments before she also heard the beat of hooves over summer earth. The steady, almost rhythmic sound was not the fierce pounding of pursuit she had expected. Still, she did not doubt it was Christian and his men. "He comes," she breathed.

The slight breeze delivered Durand's next words to her. "Do not fear."

Did she? Aye, for what her husband would believe of her. But more, she feared for Beatrix. As much as she loved Christian, she could easier face his accusation of betrayal than any ill that might befall her sister had she refused to aid Durand. She would just have to pray that, given time, her marriage could be salvaged.

"There!" Sir Durand shouted.

The glint of chain mail worn by the riders first caught Gaenor's eye. Then, despite the great distance, she picked out Christian. She knew him not only by his position at the fore, but his size and the color of his hair. And, as guessed, the riders' advance was almost leisurely. Why?

"And there!" Durand peered over his shoulder and past her.

She looked around and saw what his keen senses had landed upon—more riders, likely sent from Broehne to not only bring Gaenor's abductor and Sir Hector's attacker to ground but to alert their lord of the breach.

Dear Lord, be with us all.

The lone rider who held his mount unmoving ahead did not raise an alarm nearly as potent as the half dozen riders farther out. Brigands?

Christian threw a hand up to halt the progress of his men whose impatience he had felt this past quarter hour. Unfortunately, with his father expiring in his arms, the relatively sedate pace was necessary.

As he reined in his destrier, he looked down at the pitifully bundled figure he supported on the fore of his saddle. Aldous's eyes were closed, but his lips moved slightly in what Christian hoped was prayer.

"It may be a trap," Abel said, drawing alongside.

Christian looked around and briefly acknowledged Helene who had gained the Wulfrith knight's arms about her. She was awake, eyes large in her pale face as she stared at the riders ahead. "It may, indeed," Christian said and motioned his squire and a man-at-arms forward.

"My lord," they said in unison.

"I am giving my father and the healer into your care. Do not fail me."

Helene went onto his squire's horse easily enough, but Aldous's transfer was awkward and likely painful though the old man made no sound.

"Look!" Abel commanded.

The lone rider had put heels to his horse and was advancing on them, while behind the mass of riders steadily drew near.

"Let us go meet them." Christian gave his destrier its head.

Abel and his men followed, but it was only moments before the lone rider once more halted and a previously unseen figure dismounted from behind. The skirts showed his companion was a woman, her lofty stature that she was no stranger.

Christian slammed his gaze to the man who remained astride as the woman walked forward. Who was the bearded knave? And what was he doing with another man's wife?

"'Tis Gaenor!" Abel shouted.

Christian slammed his gaze to the riders in the distance. A moment later, he made out the colors of the barony of Abingdale. They were his men, and they surely gave chase.

A hundred yards from Gaenor, Christian once more halted his men.

Gaenor also checked her advance, and he saw her posture square and shoulders rise as if with a strengthening breath.

The scene was painfully familiar, hurtling Christian back to the day she had come out of the wood to yield to an unwanted marriage.

"It is Sir Durand," Abel growled.

Christian knew he should not be surprised, but he was. And the pain of his surprise tempted him to search out the knife wound out of which his life must surely bleed. Gaenor had betrayed him again, and after all the soft words and kisses and feelings they had shared—he *thought* they had shared.

"I will kill him if you do not," Abel said. "Indeed, I pray you will give me leave to make a quick end of him."

Once more, Christian considered the men who had come after the adulterous couple and clenched his jaws in an attempt to control the rage that might see the ground run red. "She is my wife," he strangled. "I will deal with him—and her."

Abel's hand fell to Christian's arm. "I do not condone what she has done, but lest you forget, she is my sister."

Christian pulled free. "I will raise no hand to her, but that does not mean all is well between us. Far from it."

Abel inclined his head. "I am not such a fool to believe otherwise."

Christian returned his attention to his wife who awaited him with hands clasped at her waist.

Lord, I thought You had blessed me, and now...Is there naught true for me to build my life upon? Am I ever to be betrayed? To know no peace? I have loved her—aye, loved her, even if only in thought and deed.

Christian drew his sword and met Abel's gaze. "Remain here."

Abel narrowed his eyes. "Do not forget what I have told."

Christian urged his destrier forward, and his advance had the effect of causing Sir Durand to draw his own sword—and the riders beyond him to rein in to await their lord's instructions.

Noting it was Sir Hector who led them, Christian returned his attention to Gaenor. He did not rush on her, though he was tempted to do so that he might all the sooner put distance between her and the man to whom she had given herself. Rather, he advanced at a measured pace and used the time to consider the situation and better prepare for the reunion.

For what reason had Gaenor dismounted and shown herself? Defiance, abject though it surely was now that she found herself surrounded? To beg mercy for a man who suffered no qualms at allowing her to place herself between him and her husband's wrath? What if her menses were not soon in coming as she had told? What if even now she bore—?

What if all is not as it appears? What if you wrongly condemn her? What if she does love you as you have felt she might?

The thoughts slipped in, and his pride, railing at once more being made a fool, sought to trample them. But they would not be ground into dust, strengthened as they were by the hope he feared to feel.

Lord, I have struggled to regain Your favor, sat my knees and bowed my head alongside this woman. Tell me it was not in vain—that the prayers that passed my lips were constant with those that passed hers.

Despite the silent beseeching that flowed out of hope, outraged pride continued to grip him, and he knew it showed when he halted his destrier and looked into Gaenor's upturned face. "Wife."

Her gaze did not waver. "Aye, wife—now and evermore."

He narrowed his lids.

She raised her chin higher. "You believe I have betrayed you."

"If not betrayal, what?"

After a long moment, during which her eyes moistened, she said, "Love."

Christian felt the imagined knife sink deeper. Jaw gripping so tight he thought the bones might crack, he said between his teeth, "You love Sir Durand."

"Nay, 'tis my sister I love—and you, though you refuse to see it. But you will see it if you lower your sword and allow me to explain why I am here."

"What is there to explain? Once more, you have chosen him over me." He jutted his chin at the man who hardly looked a knight, unshaven and bedraggled as Sir Durand was.

"I have not. I but agreed to accompany him that we might convince you and your men to turn toward Castle Soaring."

Christian blinked. "What fantastic tale is this?"

Knowing the minutes that ought to be carrying them toward her sister were fast slipping away, Gaenor fought back her own feelings of betrayal, stepped forward, and spread a hand upon Christian's thigh. "'Tis, indeed, fantastic, but not as you think, and there is not much time for the telling." Relieved that he did not shirk her touch, she peered over her shoulder. "Do you not recognize the horse upon which Sir Durand sits?"

His gaze shot past her and, for a moment, no recognition shined in them. Then he frowned.

"Aye, 'tis your brother's, taken from his camp on the day past after Sir Durand freed Sir Mark."

Christian looked back at her.

She nodded. "The same who sent word of the location of the brigands' camp weeks past. He has been following and keeping watch over them."

"Why?"

"He feared for Beatrix, and with good reason. Your brother seeks to scale Soaring's walls and work revenge upon my sister. For that, and not me, Sir Durand stole into Broehne and overpowered Sir Hector—that he might gain my aid in convincing you to ride on Soaring." She stepped nearer and moved her hand from his thigh to his white-knuckled fist. "Pray, believe me and delay no more."

The tension in his jaw eased slightly, and for that she was unprepared for his next words. "Does it pain you that 'twas not for you that Durand stole into Broehne?"

She pressed her lips against a gasp and, with great ache, removed her hand from him. "The only pain I feel is pain of fear for my sister and pain of love for a man who thinks so ill of me he would ask such a question, especially after all I have told."

His jaw loosened further. "You say you love me, Gaenor?"

The ugly beast of pride moved through her, urging her to declare that his disbelief had undone those feelings, but she could not. Still, there was no quieting the anger with which her pride would have to make do.

Fighting off tears she longed to spill, she said, "Will you or will you not ride to my sister's aid?"

Something—was it regret?—flashed in his eyes, and a moment later he sheathed his sword, opened his fist, and reached to her. "Come up in front of me."

The longing to give her hand into his was so great that she had to dig her nails into her palms to hold from doing so. "What of my sister?"

He glanced over his shoulder. "I will send my father on to Broehne and turn my men toward Soaring as you ask."

Gaenor had guessed that the bundle she had seen Christian hand off to a man-at-arms was the old baron. "Your father lives?"

"He does."

It took every bit of her fortitude to not retreat. She had not wished the vengeful Aldous Lavonne dead, but the reality that the one who had worked such ill upon the Wulfriths would share the roof beneath which she dwelt was almost too much to bear. As difficult as it had been to find acceptance at Broehne, it would be nothing compared to what awaited her when the old man and his fomenting hatred once more resided within the castle walls.

"Robert left him to die," Christian said.

As Durand had told.

"Gaenor," Christian said sharply, "you have naught to fear."

Only then did she realize how fast her breath came, causing her shoulders to heave as if she had run many leagues.

Christian reached his hand nearer. "Though, methinks, he knows his error, my father is not much longer for this life."

She could not help but grasp at the comfort of knowing that no matter what Aldous made her suffer, it would not be for long. She drew a trembling breath. "Still, Robert will do his bidding."

"And for that we must delay no more. Come."

She put her hand in his and he lifted her onto his destrier. As she touched back against him, she longed to sink into this man who, even if he did not return her love, felt enough for her that he did not relegate her to the rear of his saddle. Regardless of what he determined about her and Durand, she was precious to Christian to some degree, whereas…

It struck her that, even had Durand loved her in return, his feelings would never come near whatever her husband felt for her.

Looking to the knight who loved Beatrix, she was relieved that, as Christian had returned his sword to its scabbard, so had he. Sitting the saddle with a restlessness that bespoke impatience, he stared at them.

"Sir Abel!" Christian called. "D'Arci!"

Gaenor's brother and the physician broke from the others, and Christian turned his mount sideways to receive them.

The steely gaze Abel landed to Gaenor as he reined in told that Christian was not the only one who believed ill of her, but she did not look away. No matter how things might appear, she was redeemed.

"Our plans have changed." Christian looked to D'Arci. "Though I would have you escort my father and the healer to Broehne, I cannot ask it of you."

The physician glanced at Gaenor. "I do not understand."

"'Twould seem Durand enlisted my wife to bring word to us that the brigands have set a course for Castle Soaring—may even now be within its walls."

D'Arci paled and Abel cursed.

"Let us converse with Durand that we might ride on Soaring," Christian said and urged his destrier forward.

Though Gaenor tried to maintain space between herself and her husband, she was forced back against his chain mail-clad chest.

Moments later, the two men with whom she'd had relations faced one another, one wafting an odor so deep it nearly burned the eyes, the other wafting a jealousy so wide it threatened to swallow them whole. Aware that she was all that stood between them and the swing of their swords, Gaenor sent up a prayer that reason would prevail.

"Baron Lavonne," Durand said with an almost imperceptible lowering of his chin that held his eyes firm to the man at Gaenor's back.

"If all you have related to my *wife* is true," Christian said, foregoing the formality of acknowledgment, "then the sooner we ride, the sooner my vassal's *wife* may be delivered from harm."

Christian's emphasis on "wife" caused the knight's gaze to darken as he looked between Christian, Abel, and D'Arci. "I am no coward," he said, "but neither am I so fool to rashly seek out those who wish me dead. I have good reason for placing myself at your mercy, and that reason is Lady Beatrix."

"Another man's wife," D'Arci snarled.

Gaenor knew Durand would not welcome her pity, but still she felt it for this man who faced not only the husband of the woman he loved and could never have, but the husband and brother of the woman whose virtue he had claimed.

Durand inclined his head, more perceptibly this time. "God willing, still she is your wife. Unfortunately, much depends on how much time you waste discussing the matter."

He was right. At this very moment—

Gaenor whipped her chin around and landed her gaze upon her husband. "Enough posturing. We must ride."

Light flared in Christian's eyes, but as he stared at her, it dimmed. "You will return to Broehne with my father and—"

"Nay!" Something had been building in Gaenor of which she was only vaguely aware until that moment. "I did not risk all, especially your good opinion of me, that I might skulk back to the castle. Like it or nay, I will accompany you to Soaring." She looked to her brother. "And neither will you gainsay me, Abel."

Of course, neither had to gainsay her. They had but to pass her to a man-at-arms who would return her to Broehne—but not without a fight. And, it seemed, both men realized this, for the order was not forthcoming.

"Very well," Christian said, "but you will do as told."

Perhaps she would. Perhaps she would not. Much depended on what lay ahead. If they believed she would simply stand by when she could aid her sister, they did not know the woman she was becoming.

She raised her eyebrows. "And now can we ride?"

Christian's jaw tensed, and she knew he wanted to demand her submission, but it would be a waste of yet more time.

Within minutes, the party was organized, a small escort sent to Broehne to deliver Aldous and the healer to safety, and the larger number of knights and men-at-arms spurring toward Soaring.

25

GAENOR WAS ONLY as yielding in her husband's arms as the fierce ride forced her to be. And Christian knew regret time and again as the sun lowered and the leagues passed too slowly though the horses could give no more.

What have I done? What has my jealousy wrought? Will she forgive me as she did when I believed she clung to Durand's missive?

He glanced at the bedraggled knight where he rode alongside Abel. All this time, the man had been on the barony of Abingdale and, it seemed, had made himself the unlikeliest of allies. All for love of Beatrix D'Arci, not Gaenor, though it had appeared—

Aye, this day it looked to all that Gaenor betrayed, but I should have listened ere believing what ought not to be believed of her. And what if the time wasted on bringing me around proves the difference between saving her sister and not?

The terrible thoughts crowded Christian though he repeatedly turned from them to how he must make use of the skills taught him by the Wulfriths if he was to put an end to the terror his half-brother wreaked on Abingdale.

Think death, Abel had commanded. *Feel death. Breathe death. Embrace death.* And yet—

If he did not, how many more lives would be ravaged and lost to Robert's misbegotten revenge?

Christian gripped the reins tighter. He must not waver, must remember he was no longer of the class of men who prayed, must now and forever claim his place among those who fought.

When Castle Soaring came into view, it looked as it always did. But that was hardly telling, especially as night had nearly overtaken day. More telling were the four riders who came out of the wood to the right of the castle. They were expected, for D'Arci favored night patrols, especially when he was absent from the castle, but that did not mean these men were to be trusted.

As Christian and his party slowed and drew weapons, Gaenor's head snapped around. "They are Robert's?"

Sword to hand, Christian said, "I do not believe so, but we shall know soon enough."

A moment later, D'Arci shouted, "They are mine," and spurred forward.

"What does it mean?" Gaenor asked.

"It seems all is well—that the walls have not been breached." For the first time since he had taken her up in front of him, Christian felt her relax.

"Thank you, Lord," she said so softly he nearly missed the words.

As Christian and his party assembled before the castle, D'Arci gave the order to lower the drawbridge. With a labored creak and groan and clank, the chains let out. However, as the thickly bound wooden planks began their journey toward the ground, the thanks that Gaenor had offered up were dashed by shouts and cries from within the walls.

"My lord!" a man-at-arms bellowed from atop the gatehouse. "The donjon is taken!"

As D'Arci, Abel, and Durand roared and cursed, Christian ground his jaws. Somehow, the brigands had, indeed, breached the walls, meaning it could be too late for Beatrix.

"How?" Gaenor demanded.

He met the frantic gaze she cast over her shoulder. "Likely, they came through the postern gate." Though it was surely well defended, it was the best explanation for the sudden turn of events.

"And what of my sister?"

Christian set his jaw. "She is the reason we are here, Gaenor. We will bring her out."

"Alive?"

He drew a slow, deep breath. "Aye, alive." *Lord, make not a lie of my words.* Before Gaenor asked more questions that could not yet be answered, he turned to D'Arci. "Two of your night guard shall remain outside the walls with my lady wife until we know the extent of the breach."

"Nay!" Gaenor protested. "My sister is in there."

This was a battle of wills she could not be allowed to win. As his vassal motioned his men forward to receive Gaenor, Christian said, "The sooner we are assured of your safety, the sooner we may go to your sister's aid."

He felt more than saw her resentment, but she offered no further argument and turned forward again as D'Arci's men drew alongside.

"When all this is done," Christian said in her ear, "I will right what I have wronged and give you cause to smile again. This I vow. Until then, think on forgiving me."

Though Gaenor was not exactly sure what he meant, she found hope in that moment. Scraping her teeth across her bottom lip, she once more looked over her shoulder.

He reached up and brushed a thumb across her ill-treated lip. "God willing, it will be over anon."

She stared, longing to believe this would soon be in the past and all would end well for Christian and her. However, she was too painfully aware of the wounds dealt this day—more, of the wounds that might yet be dealt.

Christian lifted her and passed her to the nearest man-at-arms. Before her guard could settle her sideways before him, she threw a leg over and straddled the horse. When she returned her gaze to her husband, there was a slight curve to his mouth and she sensed there was something he wanted to say, but he did not. Just as she did not.

And so you with all your righteous anger will let him go without a word, knowing it might be the last word he never hears from you...

The drawbridge landed heavily, causing a wave of dust to rise around them.

"Christian!" she called as he and the others surged across the drawbridge. "I do love you!"

If he heard, she could not know, but she prayed he did and that her declaration would aid in returning him to her.

"Let us take cover," the man at her back said to his companion and turned his horse toward the wood.

Gaenor peered around him and watched as the portcullis was lowered against any who might try to cross the drawbridge uninvited. When it touched down, she closed her eyes and began to pray.

The donjon was, indeed, taken, though not by breach of the postern gate. The only explanation, it seemed, was that someone had let in the brigands. Still, if it was true their numbers were as great as Sir Durand told, it was incomprehensible that so many had passed through the outer and inner baileys without raising an alarm well before they reached the donjon.

"Again!" Christian shouted, and he and the others who hefted the battering ram once more charged.

The massive doors that had been barred against them groaned and bowed inward but held.

As Christian and D'Arci and his men drew back along the landing, the force of wood on wood arose from the west side of the donjon where Abel and Durand and a dozen others attempted to gain entrance through the door that let into the kitchens.

For the third time, Christian gave the command to charge and, a moment later, the doors burst inward.

Christian and his men abandoned the battering ram, drew swords, and surged into the great hall where they were met by the eerie still of death that has come and gone.

The links of their armor settling, they surveyed the room and picked out those who had fallen to the brigands—the porter, a female servant, and three men-at-arms, all of whom were so viciously bloodied that if any had breath left in them, it would soon be their last.

Robert had timed the attack well, he and his men having entered the donjon before the supper hour that would otherwise have seen the brigands outnumbered by those of the guard and household who gathered at table.

But where had the brigands taken Beatrix and the rest of the servants? As they had barricaded themselves in the donjon, the likeliest choice was abovestairs since the winding stair made it easier to secure and defend than the cellar. The kitchen was also a possibility, but unlikely. After all, there could be no doubt Abel and his men would soon take down the door that stood between the garden and the cook's domain.

Still, Christian had learned that nothing was certain when faced with an enemy, and so he turned to divide his men. It was then a crash and the clamor of booted feet sounded from the direction of the kitchen.

When those led by Abel and Durand burst upon the hall, they were met by the steel of their allies who immediately eased their battle-ready stances.

"Three dead in the kitchen," Abel growled, sweeping his gaze over the hall. "No brigands."

"Take your men and search the cellar," Christian ordered. "We will search abovestairs."

As he led his men opposite, he saw that D'Arci was already upon the stairs. It was foolhardy considering what might await him around the first turn, but it *was* his wife whose life was in peril and Christian knew that neither would he have waited if Gaenor was in danger—Gaenor who, in spite of his jealousy and suspicion, had called to him as he had ridden away from her. If anything could sustain him through the looming confrontation with Robert, it would be the words she had spoken.

And God, she would say.

And God, he would agree, even though his conviction would lack the strength of hers.

Past the first turn of the stairs and just down from the landing, Christian and his men found D'Arci bent over a knight, the fallen man's blood smearing the stone steps, his hand turned around his sword hilt.

"Canute!" D'Arci turned the man over.

It was the weathered old knight who had been the physician's companion since before Christian had become acquainted with and indebted to D'Arci.

"Lord!" D'Arci beseeched and pressed a hand over the wound that opened his man's abdomen.

Sir Canute's lids lifted beneath eyebrows so silver that the light of the torch overhead winked through them. "Sir Robert," he huffed, "has taken your lady wife."

"Abovestairs?"

"Nay."

"Where?"

The knight's eyes closed.

D'Arci shook him.

Canute swallowed loudly but did not lift his lids again. "One moment, all was quiet," he murmured, "the next, they were in the hall. But they did not come through the great doors, nor from the kitchens." He coughed. "They appeared as if…from the bowels of hell."

"The cellar," Christian snarled.

D'Arci looked around. "I know of no passageway that leads outside the walls."

"Nor do I"—Christian swung away—"but if there is one, my father would have revealed it to Robert." And Robert would have had time to explore and exploit it during the years he served at Soaring previous to the attempt on Beatrix's life that had seen him imprisoned.

As Christian pushed past his men, he heard D'Arci direct a man-at-arms to remain with Sir Canute, then his vassal and the others were at his back.

Swords going before them, chain mail ringing, they shot across the hall and down the dimly lit northern corridor. Around a corner, they nearly collided with one of the men-at-arms sent to search out the cellar with Sir Abel.

"My lord!" The man jumped back and nodded over his shoulder at the doorway that glowed with a light from within the cellar. "Sir Abel sent me to inform you that a passageway has been discovered. He and the others have gone into it."

Christian thrust past him and narrowly avoided treading upon a servant whose head lay in a pool of blood let from his throat.

Grinding his teeth against an anger so dark it threatened to eclipse reason, he crossed the cellar threshold. As he descended the steps, he recalled that the last time he had been in a cellar was at Wulfen Castle when Everard had taught him to use the senses beyond sight to defeat darkness and the enemies who lurked there.

The cellar, lit by a single torch, appeared empty save for the barrels and shelves of food and household supplies it boasted in abundance. But out of the farthest corner came the sound of struggle, a pale echo of men's cries and grunts and the meeting of steel. Abel and his men were upon the brigands, and Gaenor's sister was likely in their midst.

D'Arci wrenched the torch from its sconce and lunged across the cellar. Christian and the others followed to where a passageway that had been cut through the donjon's foundation gaped dim beyond overturned shelves that had spilled their supplies on the earthen floor once concealment was no longer necessary.

So treacherously narrow and squat was the tunnel that it was impossible for even those of lesser stature than Christian to negotiate it with ease or speed. Fortunately, it grew in width and height and, at the point where Christian guessed they were outside Soaring's outer walls, he was able to draw alongside D'Arci and run with him.

Though the sound of men engaged in battle continued to reach them, it remained distant as if Abel and Durand and their party were beating back the brigands. It was thus for several turns of the tunnel, but at last the din became the distinct clash of swords and shouts of men. And Christian knew what must be done as Everard had impressed upon him at Wulfen.

Ahead of the next turn, he gripped his vassal's arm and forced him to a halt, causing those behind to grunt and curse as they checked their own progress.

D'Arci came around so suddenly and violently, Christian thought it possible that, had he not arrested the man's sword arm, he might have been gutted.

"Put out the torch," he rasped. "Abel and Durand are expecting us, but not the brigands."

Shortly, guided by the din and vague glow of torches that had surely been carried by those who had taken Gaenor's sister, they came around the last turn into a low-ceilinged cave.

Had Christian any reason to entertain humor, he might have laughed at his half-brother's fondness for the dens of animals.

By the light of a torch that lay on the ground, its writhing flame revealing those who fought at the mouth of the cave beyond a half dozen who had fallen to the sword, Christian and his men streamed forward and joined the fray.

The weight of her, slight though she was, slowed him.

Not that he minded now that he was so far ahead of his pursuers. Indeed, were he not so eager for his first strong taste of revenge—to press it to his palate and savor it and let it slide wet and warm down his throat—he would have been tempted to walk the remainder of the wood to where he and his men had tethered their horses at a goodly distance from the cave.

It was there that Lady Beatrix would meet her end as she should have done on the day she was pronounced innocent of Simon D'Arci's death. All was in readiness and, providing the knock to her head did not too long hold her unconscious, she would be awake to see—and feel—every bloody moment.

For this, he had not struck the stammering witch harder when she had sought to unman him. Of course, if she did not awaken, he still had hope of a worthy audience, for he knew his men could not contain all of those who had somehow learned of his plan to enter Soaring Castle.

Just barely, Robert avoided a low-hanging branch, his sudden side-step causing the woman on his shoulder to slip. Resettling her as he continued up the rise, disgusted that his breath should sound so winded for one born to sword and mail, he returned to his musing.

He would be content to have Michael D'Arci witness his wife's death, but far more pleased if Abel Wulfrith presented.

"And Christian," he muttered, then laughed across the moonlight-lit darkness and once more considered slowing. After all, he would not have any enemy of the Lavonnes miss this night's reckoning.

26

CHRISTIAN HAD THOUGHT death, felt death, breathed death and, from the amount of blood spilled to get past the brigands, might even be said to have embraced death. But only when he emerged from the cave into moonlit night and saw that Sir Abel had fallen did he feel capable of wrapping his arms around the terrible specter that, given the chance, would make a meal of his soul.

"D'Arci!" he shouted as his vassal wrenched his blade from the gut of another brigand who sought to provide his leader with time and space to work evil upon Beatrix.

The physician snapped his chin around and met his liege's gaze where Christian had dropped to a knee beside Gaenor's brother. Leaving his men to hone their sword skill on the remaining brigands, D'Arci ran across the bloodied ground and knelt beside the man who was as much his brother-in-law as Christian's.

"He breathes," he pronounced, then gripped Abel's shoulder and shook him. "Abel, hear me!"

The torn and crimson-streaked knight jerked hard as if to break death's grip, jerked again, and lifted his lids. "D'Arci?" Moonlight glittered in his eyes and skittered across the blood that covered much of his face.

"'Tis I and Baron Lavonne. Where is she, Abel? Where has he taken my wife?"

"North. On foot. Sir Durand follows, but he is injured and…requires aid." Abel squeezed his eyes closed, opened them, squeezed them closed again, and swept up a hand to clear the blood from his vision. "Robert shouted that he would send Beatrix…to the four corners…of England."

Christian felt as if slammed against a wall and could not imagine what Michael D'Arci must feel knowing that his wife was to be drawn and quartered.

"Go!" Abel barked, but D'Arci and Christian were already on their feet. "Baron!"

Hating the sacrifice of moments that could shift the line between life and death for Beatrix, Christian looked back. "Abel?"

"Do not forget all I have taught you—all Everard taught you."

"I will not." Sword in hand, Christian ran after D'Arci, leaving behind the ring of steel on steel and his brother-in-law who might not live to see how well his student's training took.

Lord, let it be Your will that he live, he prayed as he had not prayed for years, *that Beatrix live, that Gaenor forgive me my unbelief, that our marriage be blessed, that the end of all things foul upon Abingdale be near.*

Over the treacherous moonlight-pierced wood he moved, holding fast to the sight of D'Arci whose slighter build gave him the advantage of speed and agility and gradually increased the distance between him and his liege.

On and on they ran, but just as Christian allowed the terrible thought that their pursuit might be in vain—that Robert could have changed course—he caught sight of the dim and distant glow toward which D'Arci moved. A moment after that, a figure ahead of the physician separated from a tree.

Alarm shot through Christian—and anger that he could not move faster. However, the inevitable meeting of blades proved not inevitable, and the only apparent exchange between the two men was words that were without form by the time they reached Christian. Indeed, D'Arci did not appear to so much as hesitate as he lunged past the other man.

A few moments later, Christian saw that it was an injured Sir Durand who hunched over the sword he had planted in the ground that he might lean upon it.

As much as Christian loathed the loss of yet more precious moments, he halted alongside the knight and gripped his upper arm.

Sir Durand straightened abruptly, and Christian did not need to see red to know the man bled profusely from the side wound he clutched.

"Make haste!" the knight growled. "He means to kill her. Upon my word, I..." He swayed and bared his teeth as if a show of ferocity might stave off death's stalking. "...I shall not be far behind."

Doubting the knight could make good his vow, Christian squeezed his arm. "Godspeed," he said and ran.

Though in the space of those moments, D'Arci had gone from sight, the glow ahead guided Christian, and more so when it glowed brighter. For certain, Robert called to him, and Christian intended to answer him well.

Gaenor did not know what it meant for her sister, only that it had to be of great import.

Beneath the darkly inked sky that, on this night, boasted more than a passing acquaintance with the moon and stars, she tried to read the face of D'Arci's man who had turned tense the moment a muffled clamor reached their ears and their seeking eyes picked out a glow that gave wavering form to a deeper place in the wood.

"It has to be the brigands," she said, peering at him over her shoulder.

"Aye, my lady." He looked to the man saddled beside them. "Leon?"

After a long moment, a harsh sigh broke the silence. "We have our orders."

Gaenor narrowed her gaze on the grizzled man who had to be a score older than the one with whom she shared a mount. "Then you will simply sit here and ignore what is out there?" She thrust a hand in the direction of the glow.

She felt more than saw Leon's resentful gaze. "If you believe that questioning my honor will move me from my orders, my lady, you will be disappointed. Our task is to ensure your safety, and that we shall do."

"But my sister may be out there!"

"She may, but from the sound of it, our lord is in pursuit."

That *was* how it sounded, for it was inconceivable the brigands would be so fool to not guard proof of their presence even though they were a goodly distance from the castle. Still...

"Surely there can be no harm in drawing near that we might better—"

"Apologies, my lady, but we must remain here."

Squeezing her hands so hard that ache shot through her fingers, Gaenor once more focused on the faintly lit fog rising from the forest floor. Shadows moved in the midst of it—desperate shadows that met and parted and fell in time with the shouts of men and the ring of steel.

"Nay," she breathed, then eased up the slack in the reins held by the man at her back and wound the leather twice around the saddle's pommel. Though she hated that what she must do could bode ill for D'Arci's men, she saw no other course.

She drew a hand up her waist to her girdle and curled her fingers around the hilt of her meat dagger. Bolstered by the air of resentment and restlessness that spanned the spaces between her and the men who would be fighting for their lord if not for their duty to guard her, she slid the dagger from its scabbard.

Holding the saddle's pommel with her free hand and clamping her legs to the horse's sides, she gripped the hilt hard, murmured, "Forgive me," then turned, swept her arm around, and drove the dagger's hilt into the temple of the man behind as Durand had done to Sir Hector.

His eyes widened and head snapped back. However, her blow lacked the strength of a seasoned knight and he did not lose the saddle as hoped. Feeling his hand grip her waist, she struck again, this time landing the hilt to his shoulder.

He grunted, fell sideways and, a moment later, lay on his back on the forest floor, the reins torn from his hands.

"My lady!"

Gaenor snapped her head around. Seeing Leon had drawn alongside and that he reached for her, she strained opposite, jabbed her heels into the horse's sides, and loosed the reins from the pommel. She did not look back, nor did she need to, certain both men would follow. And that was just as she would have it.

As the horse sped over uneven ground, Gaenor returned the dagger to its scabbard and bent low over the animal's great neck. "I do not fear," she whispered the lie she longed to believe. "I will not lose those I love." *Lord, please do not let that also be a lie.*

Nearer she drew, the battling figures amid the moon-lit fog taking shape and making her heart pound as she struggled to pick out Beatrix and prayed her sister was, indeed, among them. If not...

It did not bear thinking upon.

A movement to the far left captured Gaenor's regard. In the next instant, it was gone, taking cover in the shadows thrown by the canopy of trees. However, almost instantly it reappeared in the moonlight that wheedled a path among the leaves. The fleeing figure seemed to bear a burden, one that made him appear impossibly thick in the shoulders and back. As if—

Aye, only Robert or one of his men would flee combat, if not out of cowardice then to serve a depraved purpose. Though Gaenor hoped Beatrix was not that purpose and it was not her slight figure that accounted for the strangely burdened form, she sensed her sister did, indeed, lay in that direction.

Determinedly, she turned her mount aside.

Four tethered horses, two facing north, two facing south. And in the space separating them, Sir Robert, rightful heir to the barony of Abingdale, tossed off his burden.

"Bind her!" he ordered one of two men left behind to watch over the horses and gear. He looked to the second man. "Light more torches."

"But 'twill reveal our position—"

"Do it!" The one torch had been just enough to return Robert to this place, but it was time to light it up most bright.

"Aye, Sir Robert."

It should be baron, not sir. Aldous Lavonne's eldest son curled his hands into fists as he watched the man who had once been an esteemed knight in his father's household hurry opposite to do his bidding. Though tempted to call out that he should be titled Baron Lavonne, the mere speaking of it between Robert's ears made a pitiful sound of it, especially since his night would likely end much the same as Beatrix Wulfrith's.

"Beatrix," he hissed and hunkered down beside her as the first of his father's displaced knights knotted one of four ropes around her right ankle. "You ought to be awake for this," he said and slapped her.

Her head snapped to the side and remained there.

He frowned. Earlier, had he struck her harder than thought? Might he have killed her? He leaned near, peered down her body, and by the light of now two—then three—torches, saw breath move her chest. A temporary condition only.

"Be quick about it," he ordered the man who rose from binding her ankles—one to a spotted palfrey, the other to a brown palfrey. "We shall soon have company."

Soon arrived moments later, but Lady Beatrix's would-be savior came not on foot or from the direction expected. From the western side of the wood, the pound of hooves portended the arrival of what Robert guessed to be two riders.

He surged to his feet and ran to where his man had gone to retrieve the ropes of the two restless destriers that would soon be sent opposite the palfreys.

"Stop them!" He thrust the man toward where the riders would soon appear and snatched up the rope tied to the pommel of the nearest destrier's saddle. Quickly, he unreeled its length to where Lady Beatrix remained unmoving. As he knotted the rope around her wrist, he felt the breath of fear at the back of his neck, but then it moved down his spine where it transformed into a thrill, the likes of which he was most familiar when the blood on his blade was hard-won. As this blood would be—but worth every drop, even if some proved his own.

27

THE FLARE OF another torch, then another, turned the clearing into which the burdened form fled from dim to distinct. The lighting of it seemed purposeful, as if it was a beacon meant to lead one home—though that certainly could not be the purpose here, which was surely to lead one to one's death.

Still, for nothing would Gaenor pull back or allow herself to be overtaken by the guard she had foiled. Fortunately, D'Arci's men rode two astride, giving her the advantage of some seconds, which was what was required to reach her destination.

She urged her mount onto the clearing. However, no sooner did she pick out Beatrix's figure that lay at its center and the red-bearded man who bent over one of her outstretched arms, than something blindingly bright and searingly hot struck her left shoulder. She cried out as she lost the saddle and the reins tore into—and out of—her hand.

Landing hard, she distantly perceived the rock-strewn ground that sought to break her, the whinny of horses, and the clop of hooves. More closely, she frantically questioned where her breath had gone and the reason all was now dark when moments earlier the clearing had been lit. Had she broken something vital? Might death perch upon her shoulder? More importantly, might that terrible specter cover Beatrix?

Gaenor forced a painfully shallow breath into her lungs. As she shuddered it out, her vision returned. Despite the wavering, blurred edges, she picked out two horses tethered to a large tree to her immediate right.

"Kill her!"

She followed the shout to the red-bearded man who had moved to Beatrix's other outstretched arm. It had to be Sir Robert, and he was pointing at Gaenor, directing his man to finish what he had begun in unhorsing her.

Struggling to right her upended senses, she shifted her gaze to her sister in hopes of seeing breath move Beatrix's body, but it was the sight of pale hair darkened as if by blood that seized her attention.

As realization struck that another head injury had been dealt her sister, Sir Robert surged to standing and pivoted toward two other horses tethered farther out, their restlessly shifting backsides testament to their eagerness to be away from here.

The thunder of hooves that could be felt as much through the earth as heard across the air, brought Gaenor's chin around. Her assailant, brandishing the torch that had surely felled her, halted his advance on her and turned with another brigand to confront the arrival of those men whose duty it was to guard the wife of Baron Lavonne.

Amid the ensuing shouts, Gaenor rolled to the right and felt the bite of rocks across her back, her side, and beneath her hands and knees. As she rose, she swept her gaze over the scene that had dimmed considerably with the casting aside of torches to allow swords to be drawn.

By the light of the one upright torch and the two sputtering on the ground, she saw that both of her guard had dismounted and were circling the brigands. And Sir Robert…

He lunged toward the skittish destriers at the far end of the clearing.

It was then Gaenor saw the four ropes that bound her sister's wrists and ankles, each running to an opposing horse. She caught her breath. Christian's misbegotten brother had but to loose both sets of horses—or merely one—and Beatrix would be torn apart.

"Dear Lord, nay," Gaenor whispered and once again drew her meat dagger.

She ran to the nearest horse. Praying that the shadow thrown by the great tree would conceal her from sight, she grabbed the rope tied to the saddle's pommel. Though her blade was not sharp enough, nor her arm of sufficient strength to allow her to quickly sever the tightly woven strands, a half dozen desperation-driven slices chewed through it.

As the rope fell to the ground, she turned and, forcing herself to go slowly lest her movements draw attention, skirted the backside of the horse that she might cut the rope from its companion's saddle. However, no sooner did she draw alongside the second horse than Sir Robert bellowed across the clearing, "Halt! Else I shall loose them!"

Gaenor stopped breathing and peered across her shoulder. And saw that the eyes of the murderer where he stood between the destriers on the opposite side of the clearing with his fists full of reins, were not fixed on her. Indeed, due to the dimming of the clearing and the narrow space between the horses, she was too deep in shadow to be clearly seen if one did not know where to look. But there was no overlooking the man to the right who had come into the clearing with sword in hand and who stood still as he heeded Sir Robert's warning.

A mix of relief that Michael D'Arci had come and fear that Christian had not, bounded through Gaenor, but she forced all feeling aside and applied her dagger to the rope meant to part her sister's left leg from her body.

"What is it you want?" Michael shouted.

Sir Robert laughed with such joviality one might think he raised a tankard of ale in the midst of beloved companions. "Revenge upon the Wulfriths. Revenge upon the one who spawned and denied me. Revenge upon the little monk who stole what is mine—and who I most wish to witness the fate of his wife's sister." He paused. "Where is Christian?"

"Baron Lavonne is dead," Michael raised his voice louder.

Whatever Sir Robert's response to the tidings, Gaenor could not hear it above the cry of her heart that preceded the cry of her mouth. Blessedly, she retained enough presence of mind to press her face hard against the horse's neck lest her anguish further loosed itself above the clamor of her guard's continuing struggle against the brigands.

"The baron was cut down by your men," Michael fed Sir Robert more heinous words, "the same as they laid down Abel Wulfrith."

Fingers spasming on the dagger's hilt, Gaenor panted against the horse's coarse, musty coat. *Dear Lord, all is lost. My husband, my brother—*

Nay, not all. Think now, *Gaenor, not of what is past. Beatrix is* now.

Setting her teeth against the pain that would have her crumble, she raised her head and viciously sawed at the rope.

"Hence," Michael said, "your revenge is complete. Not only—Hold!"

Gaenor snapped her chin around, but it was not Sir Robert whom her brother-in-law addressed. Her guard, who had bested the brigands, drew up well short of the murderer who had but to open his fists to deal the Wulfriths another mortal blow.

Michael, keeping his hand raised to his men on the opposite side of the clearing, returned his gaze to Sir Robert. "Not only have you gained what you and your father sought—the life of a Wulfrith—but no longer is there anyone who stands between you and the barony."

In that moment, the last threads of the rope gave way to Gaenor's blade, ensuring Beatrix could not be quartered, though that would not prevent her from being halved or dragged to her death.

"Indeed," Michael said, "'twould seem you are now my liege, Baron Lavonne."

Staying tight to the horse's side, Gaenor looked between her sister's husband and his men and searched for a way to alert them to what she had done. Providing they acted without hesitation, there was a chance they could cut the ropes binding Beatrix's wrists before the loosing of the destriers dragged her slight figure more than a few yards.

Sir Robert's chuckle sounded terribly bitter. "Even if 'tis true my brother is dead"—

Gaenor gasped. Had Michael lied?

—"you know I will never bear the title, that I will be extinguished with the lot of the Lavonnes. Thus, I have naught to gain by leaving your wife intact." He jerked on the reins, further rousing the destriers such that they snorted and sidled. "And since my end will be all the more tolerable with *two* Wulfriths to accompany me to hell, all that remains is to send these fine beasts their separate ways."

And he would.

Holding the recently severed rope before her that her brother-in-law and his men might better understand, Gaenor lunged into the clearing. "Cut the ropes!" she cried.

Sir Robert's eyes opened wide. Next, his hands.

Gaenor. There was no time to question her presence or more than glancingly interpret the part she played. All Christian could do as he gave up the shadows through which he had furtively moved as taught him by Everard Wulfrith, was entreat God to protect his wife.

Lest D'Arci failed to reach the rope binding Beatrix's wrist before she was torn apart, Christian veered away from Robert whose back was yet turned to him and, dagger in hand, launched himself at the nearest destrier. Though he hoped Gaenor would see him and know D'Arci had not spoken true about his fate, he knew her eyes were likely all for her sister. Such was not the case for his brother who swung around to flee.

Christian felt the slash of Robert's gaze, heard his shout of anger, saw him draw his sword, but did not waver in his purpose as he had done on the battlefield previous to his training at Wulfen. First he would deal with the destrier, then the murderous man whose atrocities roused in Christian so terrible an anger that the thought of embracing death was far more palatable than it had ever been.

The horse surged past and Christian grabbed its mane, causing it to lurch sideways. In the moment it took the great animal to regain its balance, Christian pressed his chain mail-clad torso tight to the horse's side and thrust his dagger alongside the pommel. As he was dragged forward, he sliced the blade up through the rope. It was so thick and Christian's position so treacherous that the taut strands did not immediately yield, but a second slice caused the rope to fall away.

Christian released the mane, thrust backward to avoid landing beneath frenzied hooves, and rolled over the scrabbly ground that sloped away from the clearing. On the last roll, he thrust his legs beneath him and pushed upright. The links of his mail loosing deceptively pleasing music upon the night, he swung around to face the fog-skirted ridge upon which the shadows of those overhead moved. Though he expected his prey-turned-predator to appear against that backdrop, it was not Robert who came at him but the second destrier.

Christian jumped to the side and the horse galloped past, trailing a rope to which Beatrix was no longer bound. Praying D'Arci's men had cut it before further injury was done their lady, he switched the dagger to his left hand, drew his sword, and searched the wood for his brother—for a shadow among shadows, a glint of moon in eyes, silvered light running the edge of a blade.

Nothing, though Robert was surely near.

Determined to make certain D'Arci's lie remained a lie—that he would have the opportunity to return Gaenor's love—Christian slowed his breathing and strained to catch the sound of his brother's movements beyond the anxious voices of those in the clearing above.

Listen! Everard called to him from weeks past. *And listen again. The sound that will mean the death of you if you let it slip past, will have purpose, intent, the stink of stealth...*

Though tempted to close his eyes to sharpen his hearing, Christian knew better than to yield up one of his senses.

Do not let the sound elude you, he told himself. *Separate it from the din above. Pick what does not belong from what does belong in this place.*

The stir of chain mail to his right. The squelch of a boot guardedly treading damp grass, moldering leaves, needles of the pine.

Holding close his discovery, Christian maintained his stance, though the shadows in which he stood were not deep enough to shield him from seeking eyes.

Now breathe, Baron, Everard spoke again. *Smell and taste the air beyond yourself...the sweat of your enemy that wafts fear, loathing, excitement, strain.*

There it was. Not simply to the right, but ahead, the shifting air carrying the festering filth and perspiration of a long-unwashed body. And desperation. Robert had to know that what he had begun would end this night, his sole hope that his would not be the only blood to stain Soaring's soil.

Christian let him come nearer and, out of the corner of his eye, glimpsed light on steel. Knowing the time had come to embrace the death of one with whom he shared a father, he tightened one hand on his sword and the other on his dagger. However, as he started to come around, movement on the ridge drew his regard to two figures whose swords advanced before them—D'Arci's men who had surely been charged with bringing Robert to ground.

Though the Church-bred Christian might have viewed the soldiers as respite, the man he had shaped himself into these past years, and now the Wulfen-trained warrior, saw them as interlopers. Not only was it the responsibility of Abingdale's overlord to end the terror that Robert and his brigands had wreaked, but it was Christian's responsibility to stop this depraved member of his family and ensure justice was done.

"He is mine!" he shouted and set himself at the place where his brother had been—and no longer was.

As told by the flagrant fall of retreating footsteps and the ring of chain mail, the appearance of D'Arci's men had caused Robert to run. However, he would soon learn that "the little monk" was more to be feared than soldiers who but followed orders.

Christian returned his sword to its scabbard and, keeping his dagger to hand, gave chase.

Little effort was required to espy Robert between the trees and amid the undergrowth. Indeed, so large were his movements and the din of his passing that the moonlight piercing the leaves and branches served as little more than confirmation of the path he carved across the darkness. Soon, he and Christian would meet at swords and nevermore would the miscreant—

Stay alert, Everard counseled. *No greater loss can a man suffer than when he believes victory is his ere the battle is done.*

Christian reverted to senses that would guide him far better than anger or bloodlust. Thus, he was aware when the earth beneath his boots turned firm, when the rich, loamy scent of the heavily-treed wood was infused with the smell of running water inhabited by fish, algae, and human waste, when the shush of a stream met the distant rush and ripple of a river, when something beyond corporeal warned him danger was nearer than it appeared.

Keeping Robert in sight, he slowed and halted. Shortly, the shadow ahead also arrested its flight.

Robert swung around and, after some moments, called, "Christian!"

As Christian was no longer in motion nor his mind bent on death, he placed himself and knew what had been intended for him. Just as his father's eldest son had learned Castle Soaring's secrets during his years of service to D'Arci, so he had learned the secrets of the surrounding wood. Doubtless, death lay in the direction Robert ran—a sharp drop off, perhaps into a ravine, and Christian's headlong flight would have provided his brother with another victim.

"Have you tucked that tail of yours and scampered away, baby brother?" Robert demanded, taking a step forward.

Christian remained in the shadow of an immense oak.

Robert advanced another step. "Does my sword make your heart gasp? Make you tremble like the *man of God* you were bred to be?" He barked laughter. "How old Aldous rues the day you came shrieking into the world—more, the day he chose you over me. And all because my mother did not speak vows with him ere falling into his bed. *That* is all you have and will ever have that I do not—useless words spoken before a priest who, doubtless, set many a woman upon the harlot's path."

Christian seated his dagger, drew his sword, and strode into moonlight. "I am here," he called, "and here is where this night will be decided."

"Will it?" Robert taunted.

"Aye. If there is any slaying to be done, it will be by way of the blade, not the trickery of a coward."

Christian sensed that his brother longed to test him, to flee again that the chase might resume, but those last words caused a feral growl to erupt across the night. In the next instant, Robert sped over the ground, his sword raised.

As Christian assumed the stance Abel had time and again shown to be among a warrior's best allies, he caught the sound of others and glimpsed D'Arci's men who had followed though Christian had claimed this battle for his own.

"Stand down!" he roared and, a moment later, knocked aside Robert's blade that sought to part his head from his shoulders.

Robert retreated and came again, flecking Christian with spittle as he cursed and shouted with each blow he laid across his opponent's blade.

Though he did not stand nearly as tall as Christian, he was a well-seasoned warrior and thickly muscled. Add to that his hatred and that he had nothing to live for, and he was more deadly than most who made their living by shedding the blood of others. Thus, Christian embraced Abel's strategy of defense over offense that he had said could tire a deadly opponent sufficiently such that, with the least amount of effort, one's defensive stance turned offensive.

Anticipate and counter, Abel instructed. *Seek the pattern, the bunching of muscles, the placement of feet and elbows and shoulders, the shifting of eyes.*

That last was not possible given the night, and yet as they circled and lunged, met and withdrew, Christian sensed where best to place his blade. It was as if he stood not before Robert but behind him, guiding the swings and jabs and slashes, knowing where each would land before the clang and spark of steel on steel proved it so.

Blow after blow, some bloody, others a resounding shock to muscle and bone, he felt Robert's fervor until, at last, his misbegotten brother tired and all that remained was for Christian to put his weight and height and strength behind him—to move from sword play to sword lust that he might forever end Robert's treachery and depravity.

He swept his sword left and up, preventing his adversary's blade from finding his heart.

Robert drew a guttural breath, swung again, and ran his blade up off Christian's. However, as he moved to reverse his swing, Christian abandoned his defensive stance and slammed his blade into his brother's. The force staggered Robert back, allowing Christian to claim that moment in time when his brother laid himself open. With an arcing slash, he drove his blade hard into Robert's armored forearm and felt and heard the crack of bone.

Robert bellowed as the hand of his sword arm lost its grip and the weapon dropped to the trampled ground.

Here, then, the end Christian sought that required but one final thrust of the blade to ensure Robert Lavonne never again worked harm upon any.

As Christian watched his brother take another step back and clasp a hand over his slack arm, he remembered Abel rasping, *When next you face a true enemy, you must wish his death.*

And in the dark and desperate places of Christian, he did wish it. Before today, he had doubted he was capable of embracing death, but after what Robert had wrought upon Sir Mark, Aldous, Helene, D'Arci's men and retainers, Abel, Durand, Beatrix, Gaenor...

He was a scourge, an evil if ever evil dwelt in bodily form.

"'Twould appear," Robert panted, "the little monk has learned to swing a sword."

Christian stared through the moonlight into his brother's pain-contorted face. "That I have."

"Then for what do you wait?" Robert thrust his uninjured arm out to the side, opening himself wide. "Cut me down and be done with it."

Embrace death. Finish it now.

Christian shifted his grip on the hilt in anticipation of the killing blow that would be most merciful placed at the neck.

"If I stood where you stand, already I would have done it," Robert spat. "And you know not how I would rejoice in giving the ground a good, long drink of your blood!"

Christian knew it was so, that death would be fast upon him had he been the one disabled. And yet…

Yet it was so because his father's misbegotten son embraced those dark, desperate places that anger, resentment, envy, and hatred had long ago carved into him—places that had opened within Christian with the unfolding of this night.

Was that behind Robert's taunting? His final act of revenge to turn the "little monk" into one who killed a defenseless man without thought or question? To scour God from Christian's soul?

As Christian drank deeply of the cool night air that was a balm against the heat coursing his skin above and below, he struggled to cast out the pitch-black places that sought to convince him that only the spilling of blood—here and now—would ensure that never again would those Christian loved be threatened by Robert's evil devices.

Embrace death! Abel rasped.

Christian drew a deep breath and eased it out. In circumstances such as these, Abel's road seemed the easiest to travel. But it was a road Christian would not set himself upon lest it was one he could not cede—one that would take him far from Gaenor.

Though he knew Abel's—and Everard's—instruction was surely responsible for his victory, there was something over which the youngest Wulfrith brother erred. One did not have to choose between the class that prayed and the class that fought. One could be both.

Christian lowered his sword. "'Tis done. As King Henry is eager to grant you an audience, I will give you over to his men that you may be returned to London to account for your crimes."

Robert gripped his broken arm and stumbled back to support himself against a tree. "And here I thought Abingdale's liege might finally prove worthy. But still you prefer clasping one hand with the other over clasping a sword—prostrating yourself before an altar while another does the deed and duty that is yours alone."

Christian pitied his brother who would rather die here than be given into the hands of an angry king. But though it would likely be more merciful to end this now, and he would have if they had remained matched in skill and fervor, he would not put his sword through a man no longer capable of defending himself. He would not embrace death as it was not meant to be embraced.

Christian motioned D'Arci's men forward. "Bind him."

The men hastened past him and over the shadowed ground.

"Have a care," Christian warned. "Somewhere on his person is a dagger eager to spill your blood." And for this as well, Robert had surely encouraged his brother to end his life—the possibility that, in doing so, Christian might draw near, foolishly supposing a warrior whose sword arm was injured could no longer dispense death.

Amid Robert's cursing, struggle, and shouts of pain, the men relieved him of the dagger with which he attempted to fend them off, but it was the one secreted in his boot that proved the prize.

"'Tis a Wulfrith dagger, my lord," one of the men-at-arms called as the other set to binding Robert's wrists before him.

Sir Mark's dagger. The knight would be pleased to have it returned.

"Finish it!" Robert shouted. "Now!"

Christian sheathed his sword and, when D'Arci's men herded his brother before him, said, "Methinks you need not fear the king will be slow to dispense justice for those you killed in escaping his prison."

Robert bared his teeth above the rough brush of beard. "Ah, but you ought to fear, *brother,* for as I escaped Henry once, I shall do so again. I will be back."

It was largely an idle threat, especially considering his broken arm, but still Christian would take no chances where Gaenor was concerned. "'Tis possible, and for that I shall accompany you to London and not leave your side until I see for myself that never again will you darken the lives of those I love."

Robert shoved his thick body forward, straining against his captors' hold. "Love!" he spat.

Christian turned away and led the way across the wood.

As expected, Robert did not come quietly, his anger and desperation resounding through the trees. Lest his din rouse other brigands who might have eluded capture, Christian remained alert. However, their passage was uneventful and, when they reached the clearing where Beatrix was to have met her death, the only evidence of what had happened in that place was the bloodied and torn bodies of two brigands.

Though grateful D'Arci had wasted no time seeing Beatrix and Gaenor away from there, Christian could not help but wish his wife were waiting for him. Of course, the ill of this night might not yet be done, for it was possible Beatrix had not escaped dire injury, might even now—

"Make haste," Christian called above Robert's foul protests that, thankfully, had abated considerably, likely due to the pain of his injuries.

When they neared the border of the wood a short while later, a figure separated from a thicket ahead.

Instantly, Christian put his sword to hand. "Who goes?" he demanded, motioning for D'Arci's men to halt.

"Sir Durand," the knight called in a strained voice. "'Tis you, Baron Lavonne?"

"'Tis. And D'Arci's men."

The knight lurched forward, evidencing his weakened state. "Lady Beatrix?"

"I believe she is well."

Another lurch, and Christian wondered how near to death Beatrix's champion was. "You *believe?*' Sir Durand rasped.

"As her husband has surely returned her to the castle, I cannot be certain, but soon we shall know."

"Ha!" Robert crooned. "Does she live, I wager she is more dumb than before."

Sir Durand's bent figure halted its advance and straightened in the glow of moonlight between trees. "That miscreant is alive? Again you have let him live?"

Though Christian knew he owed the knight no explanation, he was moved to alleviate Durand's distress. "Death will be his end when the king is done with him, and never again will he harm any you hold dear. You have my word."

"'Tis not enough," Durand growled. "I have not given all that Robert Lavonne should outlive me. Whether it be heaven or hell that awaits me, I will not go until I am certain Lady Beatrix is safe."

Christian did not want to take offense that Durand's concern was all for Beatrix when it was Gaenor with whom this man had lain, but he was angered that Durand had so little regard for the woman Christian esteemed and loved. Though, prior to the shock of coming upon Gaenor and Durand this day, Christian had come to believe his wife's claim that her relations with the knight had happened the one time and many months before Christian had taken the name of Sir Matthew in the chapel at Wulfen Castle, here was further proof that, just as Durand's heart did not belong to her, hers no longer lay in the knight's direction.

She is mine, Christian whispered into his soul. *I am hers.*

He drew a deep breath. "Neither my wife, nor Beatrix D'Arci, will ever again suffer at my brother's hands."

Robert's laughter was loud and almost crazed. "Only my death will ensure that. And I am far from dead, *Sir Durand*."

The injured knight took another step forward. And stilled. He did not move for a long moment, then he drew his arm back and the blade that rode the cool night air whistled as it cut a path across the wood.

A thud sounded behind Christian. As he pivoted, a gurgle rose above the sharp shift of chain mail and Robert sagged between D'Arci's men who immediately eased him to the ground.

Christian strode forward and dropped to his haunches alongside his brother. It took but a moment to determine that Durand had done what Christian had not at Beatrix's trial. He had flown a dagger meant to kill, and it had found its mark in the column of throat above the chain mail tunic.

Robert convulsed, mouth opened and closed, eyes shuddered side to side, then he seemed to sink into the ground.

Christian momentarily lowered his lids. "God forgive you," he breathed, then reached forward and closed the eyes of one who had happened upon an unexpected savior eager to give him the quick and merciful death for which he had longed.

Christian straightened and turned away, but where Durand had stood, he now lay. Christian ran forward and, shortly, confirmed that Beatrix's champion lived, his breathing shallow and labored though consciousness was wiped from his face.

"My lord?" called one of D'Arci's men.

"Leave Sir Robert," Christian said. "Bring Sir Durand."

Thus, the knight was carried out of the wood to Castle Soaring where he was laid upon a trestle table in the great hall alongside those whose wounds would, for all of their lives, tell the tale of what had transpired this night on the barony of Abingdale.

28

THE SIGHT OF her where she sat with her back to him beside the postered bed clasping Beatrix's hand and speaking in hushed tones made Christian pause. Though he had been assured that she and her sister were well enough to allow D'Arci to turn his attention to Abel's tenuous hold on life, not until this moment of seeing his wife did he turn from beseeching God to praising Him.

Grateful for the hasty shedding of his chain mail, the ring of which might remind both women of what neither wished to soon revisit, he stepped over the solar's threshold.

"'Twas you who saved me, Gaenor," Beatrix said, gingerly shifting against the pillows and drawing Christian's regard to the sling that held her left arm.

He clenched his jaws. Obviously, he had not quickly enough cut the rope to prevent her from being injured. Still, though her arm had likely been pulled out of joint, at least it had not been torn from her body.

"Truly," Beatrix continued. "Michael says it is so."

Gaenor leaned forward and brushed the hair off her sister's brow. "It was not all me, but I am glad to have given back some of what you gave me when..."

"When you first fled Christian Lavonne," Beatrix said softly.

Gaenor sighed. "Would that I had known then that I had naught to run from."

"Since we cannot know what will be, we can only a-act according to what we do know, Gaenor. And after all that has transpired between the Wulfriths and Lavonnes, you had cause to flee."

"But the second time…I should have trusted Garr's judgment, should not have heeded Sir Durand."

"Which you would not have had to choose between had you known who had tried to steal your heart at Wulfen, hmm?"

Christian turned aside his resentment. Beatrix was right. Achingly so.

With a weary laugh, Gaenor said, "When I read your missive that Christian delivered to me, I was amazed by what you saw from afar."

Beatrix gave an answering laugh that bespoke greater fatigue, its slurred edges likely the result of whatever medicine her husband had given her to alleviate the pain. "My w-words might oft drag and become lost on their way to my tongue, but still I can ponder and reason. Still I can turn pieces until I find a fit. Still I can recognize suffering and the heart's ache upon another's face. Still I can see and feel where there is l-love and where it is not."

Gaenor's shoulders rose with a full breath. "Forgive me for underestimating you."

"I shall, but only after you forgive yourself."

After a long moment, Gaenor said, "I wish to, but I fear my actions have broken more things than they have mended, that never will Christian—"

"You are wrong, Wife." He stepped into the sudden quiet of the solar and, as he trod the rushes with long-reaching strides, met the wide-eyed gaze Gaenor turned upon him. An instant later, she was on her feet. Then she was in his arms.

"You are well," she gasped. "Michael said it was so, that you cut loose one of the horses, vowed that you would prevail over Sir Robert, but still I feared."

"For naught," he spoke into her hair that, strangely, smelled of smoke. "And you need fear no more." He lowered his gaze to Beatrix whose flaxen hair poured out from beneath the bandage wound around her head. "Sir Robert is dead."

He felt the shudder that passed through Gaenor and saw the same move her sister's shoulders.

Gaenor pulled back. "'Tis over?" Her hair on the left side was singed above the charred shoulder of her gown, explaining—though not really—the smell that wafted from her. However, as much as Christian longed for an accounting, he held the demand from his lips. Whatever ill had befallen her, she was whole, and there was time aplenty to learn how she had come to be in the clearing and what had befallen her there.

"Aye," he said, "'tis over, brave wife."

She reached up and gently traced the places on his face and neck that had known the blades of brigands nearly as well as the edge of Robert's sword.

"I am well," he assured her.

She began to smile, only to let the expression dissolve. "Have you word of Abel?"

It was unfortunate that she and Beatrix knew of their brother's injuries, for Christian would not have them worry, but he had been told that they had seen Abel laid out in the hall upon their return from the wood.

"Michael tends him and says that he fares well." That was not entirely true, but she and her sister need not know the extent of the damage. Not now when later would still be too soon.

"And Sir Durand?" Beatrix asked.

"'Twas he who felled Robert Lavonne."

Both women caught their breath.

Again, the tale in its entirety could wait. "I brought Sir Durand out of the wood," Christian continued. "When D'Arci has finished with Abel, he will see to the knight."

"His injuries are dire?" Beatrix asked.

"They are."

She stared at him, then gripped her right hand over her left that the sling caused to rest upon her abdomen.

It was then Christian noticed her wrists were bandaged, evidence that she had suffered rope burns in addition to a dislocated shoulder.

"Much is owed to Sir Durand," she said.

Doubtless, Gaenor had told her sister what the knight had done for love of her. "Aye, much," Christian agreed.

She tilted her chin up. "Enough to gain f-forgiveness?"

He sensed there was more behind her words than what struck the ear. Did she know about Sir Durand's indiscretion with her sister? Had Gaenor told? Or had Beatrix fathomed the truth as she had done about Christian's training at Wulfen?

"Is it enough?" she pressed.

What had gone before no longer mattered. Though he had good reason to dislike Durand for the pain visited upon Gaenor, the knight's actions these past weeks and this day, even if only for Beatrix's sake, had earned him grace aplenty.

Christian glanced at Gaenor and found her watching him. "Aye, Lady Beatrix, where I am concerned, Sir Durand has made restitution. Hence, it falls to your brother to determine his fate."

Her shoulders eased. "I believe Garr will be as fair as you have been, though methinks he will not allow Sir Durand to return to our family's service."

That Christian did not doubt.

"I fear, though," she continued, "what the king will do to him."

"I shall speak for Sir Durand if needs be," Christian heard himself say. Of course, that was dependent on whether or not D'Arci was able to salvage the knight's life.

Beatrix smiled. "I thank you, my lord."

"As do I," Gaenor said.

Jealousy tugged at Christian, but he refused to allow it to take hold, for it was not a place he wished to go again. He owed Gaenor far more than that.

"Now," Beatrix said, sinking back into the pillows upon which she was propped, "I would like to sleep."

Gaenor stepped out of Christian's embrace and drew the covers up over her sister. "Rest well."

"Pray, wake me when you have word of Abel."

"Of course." Gaenor watched her sister's lids flutter closed, then kissed her brow. Straightening, she turned to Christian who, in answer to her prayers, had come back to her.

He held out a hand and, as she reached for it, she saw the dagger he had fastened on his belt alongside his own dagger.

"All is well," he assured her. Then, enfolding her hand in his, he led her from the solar and closed the door behind them. As the thick planks settled into the frame, he looked back at Gaenor. "Tell me of your sister's injuries."

She drew a deep breath. "Her arm was pulled partially out of its socket but, fortunately, Lord D'Arci reset it ere she regained consciousness. Too, her wrists are deeply abraded."

"What of her head injury? Has she suffered further damage?"

"It appears she is the same as before. Though she aches and is tired, she otherwise seems herself. Michael believes she will fully recover." She bit her lower lip. "You will tell me what happened in the wood with your brother?"

"I will, but..." His jaw shifted. "...first I would tell you that your words found me when I rode into Soaring and gave me more hope than I am worthy of—that they sustained me through battle and bloodshed."

Then her desperate declaration flung across the night had not been in vain. "'Tis as I hoped."

The corners of his mouth jerked as if toward a smile, but that was all, as if he did not quite trust that he had anything to smile about. "I pray that, in time, you will forgive me for allowing jealousy to rule my words and deeds, for not trusting you as you deserve to be trusted, for not sustaining you as you have sustained me."

Deciding she would be the first to smile, Gaenor stepped nearer and laid a hand upon his cheek. "The time is now. All is forgiven, for I do love you, Christian."

His mouth curved. "As I love you, Gaenor."

He did. It was in his eyes, sweeping her with a warmth more full and satisfying than any she had known. Then his mouth claimed hers, and in his kiss was the promise that their marriage would be far more than one of alliance, that they would make a good, long life together, that their love would bear children—

She startled. *What if he yet doubts? What if he does not truly believe all I have told? What if he thinks…?*

Christian lifted his head. "What is it?"

There was nothing for it. And it was better told now than later. "Christian, I believed my flux was upon me, and it should be, but still it is not. It might yet come, but I fear—"

He pressed a hand to her abdomen. "If our child grows in you, I will rejoice in knowing that soon I shall be a father. If our child does not yet seek this world, then I will rejoice in being gifted with more time in which to know and cherish you."

Feeling tears, she said, "You are certain?"

"Aye. From this day onward…" He hesitated, but before she could worry over his silence, he said, "With you at my side, I shall think love, feel love, breathe love, and embrace love."

Then here, by God's grace and Christian's love, she had found her place. "So shall I."

He lightly traced her lips with his thumb, pausing at each turned up corner, then he kissed her again, and she pressed herself so near that the hilt of the weapon on his belt dug into her ribs.

When they parted, she lowered her gaze to the question that was yet unanswered. "You wear a Wulfrith dagger."

"Aye. 'Twas taken from Robert that it might be returned to Sir Mark."

"Ah, I thought mayhap you had been awarded one."

He frowned. "You would like that?"

"I would, though only because I can think of none worthier to wear one."

He chuckled. "I am well pleased with my own dagger, Gaenor. But as for one worthier to wear a Wulfrith dagger, I would say the brave woman who defied her husband and saved her sister's life is more deserving."

She laughed. "I am no warrior."

He tilted her chin up. "Are you not?"

How she loved this man! "When I must needs be."

He lingered over her face, then said, "'Twill be a long night. While we wait for word of Abel and the others, I would hear tale of how you came to be in that clearing."

She groaned. "You will not be angry with me—or Michael's men?"

"I do not doubt you will give me cause to be so moved, but I vow to remind myself often that you are hale and whole. And a Wulfrith."

"But now a Lavonne."

"Aye, my wife."

29

Abel would live. Rather, he would not die from the savage injuries dealt him by the three brigands it had taken to drive him to the ground.

Upon regaining consciousness on the day past and learning of all he had lost, his wrath had resounded around the donjon for what seemed hours, then he had fallen silent, staring as if only darkness lay before him, speaking not a word nor letting so much as a groan part his lips, ignoring all beseeching to drink and eat—as if he was, after all, dead.

"If he wills it," Michael spoke low, "he has as much chance of reaching a good old age as Sir Durand."

Durand whose life Michael—and Beatrix—had saved, Michael with his physician's skills, Beatrix with her presence. Or so Gaenor believed, for it was not until Durand received Beatrix at his side that his sickly pallor receded. And today he was out of bed, even if only briefly. Unfortunately, many more had died, including Michael's old friend, Sir Canute.

"However," Beatrix's husband continued, "as Abel was raised to be a warrior, he surely believes his injuries make him less than whole and, thus, no longer capable or worthy. And that belief will serve him ill. Not only will he be broken in body but in soul."

Gaenor looked past her brother-in-law to Abel who lay unmoving upon the bed despite Beatrix's hand grasping his and her soothing words that were answered by not so much as a flicker of the eye—the same as when Gaenor had sat beside him hours earlier.

"He cannot die," she said.

Christian squeezed her hand. "Surely Baron Wulfrith can bring his brother around."

Gaenor met her husband's gaze where he stood alongside her at the chamber's door. With the passing of two days since the attack on Soaring, more and more hope was placed in Garr's ability to reach their youngest brother. Providing Garr was present at Stern Castle when the messenger delivered the missive, he should arrive at Soaring by this eve.

But Gaenor would not be here, for she was departing with Christian in answer to the summons from Broehne that told his father was near his end and wished to speak to him. She could only pray that the two men would reconcile sufficiently to find some measure of peace before their parting.

"Garr will not let Abel go," she said, shifting her gaze between Christian and Michael. "He will make him stay and fight."

"Worry not, Lady Gaenor," Michael said, "Your brother will be well-tended in your absence."

She forced a smile, then crossed the chamber to stand alongside her sister.

Beatrix glanced up. "Gaenor is here, Abel."

Gaenor was prepared as she had not been the first time she had seen him. Worse than his ravaged face, much of which was covered by bandages, including one eye, was what the blankets tucked up around him hid from sight.

"Abel." Gaenor laid her hand over his and Beatrix's. "Pray, hear me."

His gaze stayed upon the ceiling.

"Christian and I must needs return to Broehne, but we will not be gone long."

No response.

"If you would like, we shall bring John with us when we return."

He blinked.

"And his mother, Helene."

His uncovered eye shuddered, stilled, then swung to her. "Nay."

Beatrix gasped. "Abel?"

"Nay," he repeated with more force, though still there was not much voice behind the word.

Gaenor leaned nearer. "I am told she is a fine healer."

"Do not!" His anger was unsettling, and yet it was also heartening, for out of it shone life.

She sighed. "As you wish."

Beatrix reached for the goblet on the side table. "You need to drink." She carried the vessel to Abel's mouth, but he had once more ascended to the ceiling.

"Pray, brother," Beatrix rasped, "do not go there. Stay with us."

He remained unmoving.

Setting her jaw, she dipped her fingers in the wine and dripped droplets between his lips.

Still nothing.

She looked to her husband. "What can we do?"

"Keep trying," he said.

"And praying," Gaenor murmured.

And so Beatrix did, softly beseeching God as she slid drops of wine between Abel's lips until he reflexively swallowed, then plying him with more.

Christian touched Gaenor's arm. "I am sorry, but I must needs depart. If you prefer—"

"Nay." She looked around. "I shall go with you."

He inclined his head, and she knew he did so grudgingly—that he did not wish her exposed to his father, but even if she did come face to face with Christian's sire and he cursed her, she would stand by her husband's side.

Gaenor bent and gripped her hand over Abel's where it lay upon the coverlet. "You fought bravely and well. You must do so again."

"He shall," Beatrix said and once more dipped her fingers.

"He comes?" Aldous winced at the sound of his graveled voice and the pain that accompanied it.

"Be assured, my lord, your son will be here anon."The healer's voice was as soothing as her hands that gently drew a cool cloth across his brow.

"Ere I pass? This you vow?"

"Ere you pass. This I vow."

He closed his eyes only to spring them open and search her face above his. "Do not make vows you cannot keep, Woman."

"Woman?" A sad smile curved her mouth. "Surely after all you and I have endured—and yet endure—I warrant being called by the name given to me by my father?"

His dry mouth going drier, he stared at her. When enough saliva collected that he might use his tongue again, he said, "You are happy now that you are reunited with your son?"

Something like disappointment flitted across her face only to be displaced by a smile, one that knew no sorrow. "I am most happy, my lord, as is John to have his mother returned to him."

"John," Aldous breathed as she shifted in her chair to dip the cloth in the basin of water perched on a table beside the bed. He liked her in profile. Pretty as she was with that dark red hair, there was strength in the straight edge of her nose, the smooth line of her brow, and her sure chin.

Gathering words, he opened his mouth, but it was drier yet. "Wine," he croaked.

She retrieved the goblet, slid a hand beneath his head, and raised him just enough that he would not choke on the moisture she trickled into his mouth. "More, my lord?"

He jerked his head side to side.

She eased him back onto the pillow, returned the goblet to the table, and retrieved the cloth from the basin.

He watched her, also liking the hands with which she healed—small but with long, slender fingers and fine-boned wrists. He sighed. "I have not told you, but I had a daughter once."

Her startle was so slight that, had he not been watching for it, he would not have known her to react in any way.

Unhurriedly, she wrung out the cloth and folded it. "This I know," she murmured and reached to once more apply the cloth to his brow.

Aldous felt something cinch in the vicinity of his heart. "A misbegotten daughter the same as Robert, but unlike him, her hair was not the orange-red of a sunset. 'Twas much darker."

"Aye."

He momentarily closed his eyes and savored the tenderness with which she drew the cloth across his scarred flesh. "She was gotten when I lay with her mother after my wife..." Eyes that had been nearly as dry as his mouth were suddenly moist. "...after she died birthing our third son."

The healer met his gaze. "This I did not know." She pressed the cloth to the inside of his left wrist.

"Some years later, when my daughter was two...or was she three?"

The woman alongside him lowered her head, but not before he caught the bunching of her brow.

"Near three, I think," he said. "'Twas then her mother died, and so I sent the child to be raised at a convent."

"This I know."

Aldous stared at the crown of her head, wishing her gaze and yet not. "I asked after her from time to time but then I began to forget her."

"Aye." She pulled the blanket over his left arm, reached across him, lifted his right arm onto his abdomen, and cooled that wrist as well.

He swallowed hard to unblock his throat. "After the fire stole all from me, after I had given the barony into Geoffrey's keeping and there was none who had a care for me, I remembered my daughter and sent for her."

"This I did not know."

"Word came that she had left the convent when she was ten and seven. None knew where she had gone, and I was too infirm to look for her and too fearful to entreat Geoffrey or Robert to find her, so I forgot her again."

"Aye."

Aldous sought a deep breath, but it came so shallow it struck him that his breaths were numbered and he might not have enough with which to speak to Christian if ever he came. But he pressed on. "I wonder, do you think you could find my daughter for me?"

The healer turned aside, dropped the cloth in the basin, and filled her lungs enviably full. "Aye, my lord." When she looked back, her smile was sad again. "I believe I can."

Aldous turned his hand in hers and gave a squeeze so pitifully lacking in strength it was yet one more reminder that his end was nearly written. "I know I am not worthy of such...beneficence, but I would be grateful."

She inclined her head. "'Tis as the Lord wills it."

The Lord...Aldous used one of his precious breaths to clear his throat. "I have no right to ask another boon, but—"

She pulled her hand free, stood, and turned toward the door. "Methinks your son is come."

When the sound of boots in the corridor reached Aldous, he silently thanked God as he had not done in...He did not know how long.

Sliding his gaze to the door, he waited for the one upon whom he would spend his next breath—Christian who had come as the healer had promised, who would return honor to the name of Lavonne, whose sons would surely better follow the example set by their father than Geoffrey and Robert had followed the example set by Aldous. All would be restored through Christian, even if it was a Wulfrith who birthed his sons.

The boots halted on the other side of the door and Aldous's straining ears picked out lowered voices. Did one of them belong to a woman? *That* woman?

Without a knock, the door opened and the big man whom Aldous thought must have looked odd garbed in monk's robes strode inside without his Wulfrith bride, for which Aldous was grateful. He knew his sins and those of his sons—had let them all in when Christian had come for him in the cave—but still he could not fully release the Wulfriths from their responsibility for Geoffrey's death.

His youngest son halted at the foot of the bed and swung his gaze from Aldous who could but stare to the healer who clasped her hands at her waist. "How is my father?"

"Though he makes ready to depart, my lord, he has remained that he might speak with you."

Christian gave her a tight smile strung with what looked like apology. "I thank you for tending him, Helene. You may leave us."

"Aye, my lord."

Aldous was so gripped by the sight of Christian that he was only vaguely aware of the healer traversing the chamber, but when she neared the door, he was drawn to her again—and remembered the second boon he had wanted to ask. "Woman!"

She peered over her shoulder. "My lord?"

"When next you tend me, mayhap you would bring your son. I..." He glanced at Christian. "...long to hear a child's voice."

She was slow to respond but, finally, she dipped her chin. "Aye, my lord."

Would she bring the boy? Or was she appeasing him, either because she knew he would not live long enough for her to tend him again or she feared exposing her child to so frightful a being as he? Not that it mattered. What mattered was that she was kind—and forgiving—enough to agree, even if only for the moment.

He tried to smile though he knew the expression would render his disfigurement more hideous. "I am sorry for what you have suffered because of me...Helene," he said in a voice that shook as if it rolled around in a pouch of stones, shaming him for its desecration of so lovely a name.

He thought he heard her breath catch, but then the smile reserved for talk of her son appeared. A smile more lovely than her mother's. "This I know," she said and stepped into the corridor and pulled the door closed.

Wondering at their exchange, Christian looked to the man who had sired him and hoped that the Aldous Lavonne who had addressed the healer with civility never before extended in Christian's presence, would indeed depart this world shed of the murderous anger and hatred that had marked his final years.

"Sit by me." Aldous rasped.

Christian moved around the bed and lowered into the chair vacated by the healer.

Aldous swallowed. "Robert...?"

Christian had known it would not be easy to deliver tidings, but he had not expected to feel so deep an ache for his sire's loss. "'Tis over. Your eldest son was mortally wounded and has been laid to earth."

Aldous stiffened. "Was it you?"

He would have been the one to put down Robert had he been able to embrace death as Abel had said he must in order to preserve his own life, but he had not. Still, he had played a role, but it was one of which his father need not be told. "Nay," Christian said, "it was not me."

Shoulders quivering with the release of a breath that caused his sunken chest to sink further, Aldous lowered his lids. "It could not have ended any other way." His misshapen mouth twisted as if he struggled to suppress emotion. "He was always difficult. Always angry, and more so after his mother passed. He blamed me, and he was right to, for 'twas I who sentenced her to a hard a life." His next breath rattled more loudly. "I who did not make things right when I was given another chance to do so."

Christian frowned. "Another chance? You speak of the time following my mother's passing?"

Aldous was slow to answer. "Aye. I should have wed Robert's mother. Instead..." He shook his head upon the pillow. "...I made life yet harder for her."

"How?"

Aldous averted his gaze. "Helene knows."

Feeling his jaw cramp, Christian leaned forward. "You share with her things you will not share with me, blood of your blood?"

To his surprise, moisture glazed his father's eyes. "She has come to mean much to me. When 'tis time, I trust she will speak to you of it."

Christian nearly succumbed to resentment, but he reminded himself of all Helene had done and suffered for Aldous—that she was surely the only light come into his dark world, that it was likely her influence that allowed Aldous and Christian to speak as they had not spoken in all the years since Christian's return to Broehne.

Easing the clench from his jaw, he returned to the matter of his misbegotten brother. "You did not wed Robert's mother because she was not of noble birth?"

"That. More, though, because I knew Robert well by then. I knew that if I legitimized relations with his mother it would put him more in a mind to..." Something like a whimper slipped from Aldous. "Geoffrey was my heir, noble both sides of him, and I had to protect his position. And yours."

Then he had feared Robert would have tried to do away with the legitimate heirs and claim the barony for himself—a warranted fear.

"I think sometimes of what I could have done differently," Aldous said. "I wonder if I should not have acknowledged Robert as being born of my loins. Had it not been made known to him and had I not raised him above others of common birth, mayhap he would have been content with his lot. Mayhap the earth would not now know him so well." He grunted. "Mayhap this, mayhap that."

Christian laid a hand over the feeble hand that had held his with such strength, certainty, sometimes even affection, when he was a very young boy. "You did what you believed was right. Robert was as much your son as Geoffrey and I."

Aldous labored over crackling laughter. "And I made good use of him. And well he did my bidding, did he not?"

That Christian could not argue or excuse, not after all that had happened, all who had died, all who might yet die.

Aldous slid his gaze to the nearby goblet. "Wine."

Christian raised him up, held the rim to his lips, and slowly poured the liquid onto his tongue. Minutes and many labored swallows later, Aldous held up a trembling hand.

Christian eased him down and returned the goblet to the table.

"Ah, my son," Aldous bemoaned.

Unsettled by the edge of affection in his father's voice that he had not heard in many years, Christian looked near upon his sire.

"There can be no redemption for me," Aldous said, "but still I would make right what I can while I can."

Christian nodded. "The priest awaits your confession—"

"I do not require a priest. I require you."

"I am no longer of the Church."

Aldous snorted. "Were you ever truly of the Church? Ha! Know you how much it cost me to keep you at the monastery after you allowed yourself to be found beneath a harlot's skirts?"

"I am sorry."

Aldous expelled a shaky sigh. "I am the one who is sorry. Sorry for all I have wrought, for all I wrought through Robert. And Geoffrey, whom I indulged too often and whose behavior I excused many too many times."

Christian stared at him, regretting that only now, with the end so near, his father should speak of such things.

"I knew he could be cruel, sometimes more cruel than Robert, but I believed it was because he grieved for your mother, and so I told myself he would grow out of it. And he might have had I not allowed him to keep company with his older brother while I myself grieved, but..." Another rattling breath. "...it eased my burden to place the responsibility for Geoffrey elsewhere—for only a time, I vowed, and yet I never truly came back to him. Or you." He swallowed loudly. "I know you remember the day I came upon Robert pinning you whilst he encouraged Geoffrey to bloody your face."

Christian did remember, though it was only one of the many times his brothers had cornered and beaten him before his body had lengthened and broadened and thickened such that he was able to defend himself and give back much of what was given him.

"When they told me they but meant to teach you a lesson for running from your tutor that you might practice with your dagger as I had forbidden you to do, I did not punish them."

Instead, he had yanked his bloodied and begrimed youngest son to his feet, marched him to the chapel, and made him prostrate himself before the altar through dusk until dawn. But for all the force-fed faith, it had only made Christian yearn more for a knight's life.

"I am sorry," Aldous said, "and yet I am not, for in giving you to the Church, my influence and Robert's was deflected that you might become the man you are now, a worthy lord as I have not been for many years. As Geoffrey never was."

The words Christian had longed to hear, but had never expected to be spoken—or even felt—nearly knocked him backward. And as he stared at his father, wondering if this shell of a man was, indeed, his sire, he felt the resentment he had tried so hard to keep buried uncoil and rise up and out of him.

"In spite of all I have denied you," Aldous continued, "you are most worthy, my son."

Worthy...But even as he wrapped his heart around the word, he wondered if, had he been reared the same as Geoffrey, weapons placed early and often in his hands and guided by a resentful, misbegotten brother, he might have turned the way Geoffrey had gone. Might Gaenor have had real reason to flee their marriage?

"And I am sorry for blaming you for Geoffrey's death near as much as I blamed the Wulfriths—for my anger at your envy of all he had been given that you were not." When Aldous next he spoke, his voice trembled. "Pray, forgive me?"

Christian gripped his hand. "Do you also forgive my trespasses, all will be well between us."

Aldous jerked his chin.

"Then be troubled no more."

His father sank deeper into his pillows and regarded Christian through half-hooded eyes. "What of your Wulfrith bride? Tell me I have not ruined your marriage."

It was a far better place to venture than turning over and over a past that could not be changed. "'Tis a good marriage. I love Gaenor, and she loves me."

"Love," Aldous murmured. "I believe I knew it once—perhaps twice."

Christian almost questioned that second instance, but Aldous surely referred to Robert's mother.

"Is this Wulfrith woman sturdy enough to bear you many sons?"

Christian guessed he was thinking of the petite Beatrix whose trial he had been ejected from. Though it was not certain Gaenor was with child, he did not think there could be harm in telling his father she was when it seemed the tidings would be welcome and might ease his passing.

"Aye, my lovely wife is sturdy. In less than a nine-month, she will deliver our first child."

A whimper sounded from Aldous. "A son," he breathed, the corners of his misshapen mouth lifting. "I..." His eyes widened. "If you would allow it, I would meet the mother of my grandsons."

Christian hesitated. Gaenor had accompanied him not only to stand by his side but, given the opportunity, to make her own peace with Aldous. Still, he would have preferred to keep her from this chamber lest his father's bent mind did more harm than good.

"I beseech you," Aldous rasped, "bring your Gaenor to me. Upon my word, I will do naught that you will regret."

Grudgingly, Christian nodded.

When he opened the door, it was to the sight of Gaenor and Helene standing solemnly side by side against the opposite wall. He held out his hand to his wife.

She took it and he drew her inside, leaving the door open behind them.

Though Gaenor was not ignorant of the ravages suffered by Aldous in that long ago fire, Christian expected her to be unsettled by the sight of him when she halted beside the bed. If she was, she hid it well. Without falter, she looked upon Aldous Lavonne who would live in the children she birthed long after Christian's sire turned to dust.

"You are she?" Aldous asked.

"I am Lady Gaenor of the Wulfriths, now of the Lavonnes, my lord."

He slid his gaze down her, and when he returned to her face, it might have been wonder that shone from him. "You are most...sturdy, Christian's wife."

She did not appear to take offense. "That I am, my lord."

A long moment passed, then Aldous rattled out a sigh. "You know that I have hated you and yours."

Christian stiffened.

"I do," Gaenor said. "Forsooth, neither have I liked you or yours."

Aldous's mouth twitched as if toward a smile.

"But now I love." She glanced at Christian.

"You will give my son a son?" Aldous asked on a wheezing breath.

Gaenor laid a hand upon her abdomen. "Mayhap, my lord."

"Or a daughter," Christian said, "though it seems the Lavonnes and Wulfriths are more apt to bear sons."

Aldous's brow puckered further amid the scarred flesh. Then, with what seemed desperation, he rasped, "Come near, Christian."

He leaned down. "Aye?"

"Nearer."

He turned his ear to his father's mouth, and the words breathed into it made him jerk, pull back, and glance to where the healer stood outside the door.

Aldous nodded. "All is told that must needs be told except..." His next breath was hard won. "...I have felt great affection for you, even when I did not know it."

His words jolted, for they were not only unexpected, they were parting words that begged a reply. Momentarily putting aside Aldous's cryptic words, he pressed his lips to his sire's cheek. "I have felt great affection for you, Father."

A long sigh broke the ragged seam of Aldous's lips and, when Christian straightened, his father's eyes were fixed and unseeing.

Christian looked to Gaenor.

Sorrow in her gaze, she said, "His pain is past," and stepped nearer and slid her arms around her husband.

He drew her against him and breathed in the woman with whom he had been blessed. "Aye," he spoke into her hair. "'Twas a good parting."

Epilogue

Broehne Castle, England
April 1158

"'Tis a good beginning," Annyn said as she gently swept the damp strands off Gaenor's brow.

"A good beginning?" Beatrix protested from the opposite side of the bed where she cradled the infant who had not made his entrance into the world easy on his mother. But then, he was of good size. Indeed, Gaenor thought her son might weigh nearly twice what Annyn and Garr's first child had weighed at birth. It was good he had not been born a girl.

Annyn smiled. "I have seen our Gaenor and her husband when they think no one watches, and there will surely be many more little Lavonnes crawling and running about the donjon, just as I believe you and Michael will be so blessed."

Gaenor swept her gaze from her sister-in-law to Beatrix, but her sister's brow remained untroubled. She and Michael also wished children, but both seemed at peace that, thus far, none were forthcoming.

"In God's time," Beatrix said and looked to Gaenor. "You would hold your son again?"

Though she ached to once more put him to her breast, she yearned for the man who had too long paced the corridor outside the solar, waiting to meet his son.

"Soon," she said and considered the healer who had come to stand alongside Annyn following her after-birth ministrations that had included directing the beaming Josephine and the bell-tinkling Aimee in the removal of the birthing chair and all other evidence of the hard labor. "I am ready for my husband, Helene."

The woman inclined her head, traversed the solar, and pulled open the door. "Your wife and son await you, my lord."

Christian was inside the chamber before half her words were spoken. As he strode across the rushes with fewer strides than most men required, his gaze shifted between Gaenor and the infant in Beatrix's arms, but it was Gaenor's side he gained first, accommodated by Annyn who jumped aside.

Bending near, he laid a hand to his wife's cheek. "You are well?"

"More well than I can say." She turned her mouth into his palm and kissed it. "Now meet our son."

He lowered his head, briefly touched his lips to hers, then straightened and rounded the bed.

As he peered into the cloths that bundled their child, he said with urgency, "May I hold him, Beatrix?"

She laughed. "You need not ask permission to hold your own son, my lord."

"Indeed." He reached, only to hesitate and splay his hands as if uncertain as to how to handle an infant.

Beatrix stepped close, settled the babe in his arms, and guided his hands to where they would best support the little one.

Christian stared. "He is so small."

This time it was Annyn who laughed. "That is no small babe, Baron Lavonne, and no small task was it for your wife to deliver him unto you."

Once again, Christian sought Gaenor's gaze. "Truly, you are well?"

She smiled at the man who seemed younger than ever she had seen him. "Quite."

"Two days, my lord," Helene spoke up, "and your lady wife will be out of bed. Two days after that, she will be about the castle again."

Christian turned to where the woman stood at the foot of the bed. "Thank you, Helene. Again, my family is in your debt."

She averted her gaze, and an uneasy silence fell as often happened when the two exchanged words.

Inwardly, Gaenor sighed. It had been no great feat to unravel the meaning of the words Aldous Lavonne had whispered in his son's ear so many months past.

"I have a daughter," he had said and, for a moment, Christian had believed he meant Gaenor, but the old baron had added, "And you have a sister." Not Gaenor, but she who had come to mean much to him, she who knew the reason that the life of Robert's mother had been made more difficult, she who would tell it herself when she deemed the time was right, she of red hair of a much different shade from her departed brother's. Helene.

But still the healer turned aside Christian's questioning and made no attempt to claim kinship with the Lavonnes. Of course, considering what had happened between her and Abel when he had become her unwilling patient months and months past, the woman's silence likely had more to do with Gaenor's brother than Christian.

"I will leave you now," Helene said, "though I shall pass the night in your hall should Lady Gaenor have need of me."

Gaenor was glad to have her near and grateful she had brought John with her so she would not be pressed to soon return to her village. The boy had long ago recovered from the trauma of his mother's abduction—indeed, even in the absence of Abel's influence, he was more often pleasant than not. Of course, he did challenge any man he perceived as a threat to his mother with the wooden sword Abel had fashioned for him before the attack on Castle Soaring had so altered her brother—

Gaenor did not want to think on Abel's struggle to regain what he had lost, not now when there was so much joy after so much pain.

"Methinks 'tis time for us to depart," her sister-in-law said, motioning for Beatrix to follow. "Send for us if there is anything you need."

"Thank you, Annyn...Beatrix," Gaenor called after them.

As the door closed softly behind them, Gaenor shifted in the bed to watch Christian where he stood regarding their son, a smile of wonder upon his face. *Their* son, a little Lavonne who was surely destined to quickly outgrow his swaddling and, one day, stand as tall and broad as his father.

When Christian finally met her gaze, his had turned troubled. "Still I do not know by what name he shall be called."

There were some, especially those who had long served upon the barony of Abingdale, who expected a firstborn son to be named after Christian's father. However, despite having made peace with Aldous, neither Christian nor Gaenor believed it would serve any good purpose to pass the name on to their child when it could prove a burden considering the havoc—and death—birthed by Aldous's bitterness.

"Then we must needs think more on it," Gaenor said.

"Aye." Christian considered the mattress, and she guessed he was measuring the space between her and the edge.

"Come." She smoothed a hand over the coverlet. "There is room for us all."

"You are certain? I would not wish to cause you discomfort."

"Quite the opposite, Husband."

Still, he hesitated, and when he glanced at the bundle in his arms, she knew he also worried as to how he would gain the bed without unsettling their son.

"Here." Gaenor reached. "Hand him to me."

Relief smoothing his brow, he leaned down and placed their son in her arms with such gentleness that Gaenor thought she might cry.

"He is so quiet," Christian said as he stretched out alongside her and settled his head on a pillow. "When Helene told that I was a father, the wailing could be heard throughout the donjon, but now he looks about him as if he is quite content with this new world."

"Of course he is." She considered the bright eyes that regarded her. "But methinks that has more to do with a full belly than all he beholds."

Christian grinned, slid an arm beneath her, and carefully drew her against his side.

As she shifted the babe to the seam where their bodies met, their son popped a fist free of his swaddling, jerked it side to side, and gurgled when his fingers introduced themselves to his mouth.

"Methinks those cloths will not long hold him," Christian mused.

She looked up into her husband's face. "As I am sure yours did not long hold you."

"I am certain you are right. So, what shall we name him?"

She started to think on it some more, then shrugged. "It matters, but not so much that we must name him now."

"You are right, and I do prefer the sound of 'my son.' It says more than any name could."

She raised an eyebrow. "*Our* son says more than any name could."

"Aye, ours." He kissed her brow. "Just as I am yours and you are mine, Gaenor Lavonne. Unto death."

Excerpt

THE KINDLING

Age Of Faith: Book Four

Castle Soaring upon the Barony of Abingdale, England
September 1157

SHE CAME TO him in the still of a night whose dark edges were beginning to fray.

As she opened the door wider the better to see him where he lay upon the bed with arms and legs thrown wide as if to test the reach of the mattress, the hinges gave a betraying creak.

She winced. She knew she should not be here, for if he awakened he would likely think she had come to offer comfort between the sheets, but despite the long journey that had delivered her to Castle Soaring after the setting of the sun, she was unable to sleep. And all because of this man.

Drawing a slow breath, more for courage than fear she might rouse him, she stepped forward and frowned over the dust and stale scent that rose from the rushes. The floor covering ought to have been replaced days ago. However, from the bits of 'this and that' picked up from the castle folk who had regarded her with suspicion upon her arrival, the state of the chamber was the fault of its angry occupant rather than neglect of his care.

But she was prepared—or would soon be—for what she would face in a few short hours when she stood before this possibly dangerous man.

She halted an arm's reach from the bed and, by the glow of a brazier that would not much longer warm away the chill, considered the figure atop the rumpled bed coverings.

If not for a tunic splayed open at the neck and twisted around his upper thighs, he would be bared. Still, she was not alarmed by his state of undress. Not only did her profession as a healer require that she be well acquainted with the human body, but it was told that he had been given a sleeping draught. Of course, lest he was near the end of its influence, she would do well to proceed with caution.

She took a last, heedful step forward and looked closer upon the leg nearest her. Not even the brazier's dim, forgiving light could disguise the severity of his injury—nor that he had begun to waste away during all the weeks spent abed. She reached forward, only to draw back. She was here to look, not touch. Touching would come later.

There were other healing cuts on the left leg, as well as the right, but those he had not likely noticed. *This* one he certainly had, for it was far more than a wound to his warrior's pride.

Moving toward the head of the bed, she caught her breath when the rushes crackled, then stilled when something between a grunt and a growl sounded from him. However, when she peered into his thin, coarsely bearded face, she saw no reflection of light to indicate he had arisen from the depths of the sleeping draught.

Noting the tension in his jaw and neck, she guessed he dreamed dreams he did not wish to have unfold within the darkness of his mind, but though she was tempted to try to awaken him, it would be a mistake. Blessedly, it was not long before he relaxed.

Though she would have liked to familiarize herself with the injuries to his torso, she was fairly certain he was not wearing braies, and for naught would she risk having him awaken to find her raising his tunic. Since his right hand was too deep in shadow on the opposite side to verify its injury without moving it, she also let it be. Fortunately, there was enough light on his face that, when she bent close, the injury inflicted by a cruel blade was well enough told.

"Dear Lord," she whispered and, too late, sealed her lips. However, her softly spoken words seemed not to penetrate the fog that provided him the rest required to heal.

Forcing her fingers into her palms to keep from tracing the stitched flesh that cut a path from his left eyebrow to the outer corner of his eye to the lower edge of his jaw, she lingered over his face though she had done what she had come to do.

She pitied him for the unsightly scar but reminded herself that, were it allowed to heal properly, its appearance would greatly improve. Too, once he began to eat regularly and resumed exercise, the hollow and angular planes of his face would fill in. But even then, would he ever again resemble the man she had known, if "known" could even be used to describe their two brief encounters? Of course, she also knew him by way of a boy who missed him more than was good for so young a soul...

She squeezed her eyes closed. This warrior who believed he would never again wield a sword ought to have stayed in her past. Had his brother, Baron Wulfrith, and her liege, Baron Christian Lavonne, not asked this of her, she would not have had reason to see him again. And she wished she had not, though not because it made her ache to gaze upon his disfigurement. Her longing to remain as firmly in his past as she wished him to remain in hers had more to do with who she was and who, even if not by his own hand, had done this to him.

He made another sound low in his throat, and distress once more hardened his face. This time it was accompanied by a marked increase in the rhythm and strength of his breathing. This time it did not soon resolve.

Go, she told herself. *They are his demons to undo, not yours.* At least, not directly...

His uninjured leg kicked out, head snapped toward her, and lips drew back to reveal clenched teeth. But still his lids remained lowered, eyes moving rapidly beneath them. As she continued to ignore the good sense that urged her to leave, perspiration broke upon his brow.

She bit her lip. Though she could abide the suffering of others as was required of one who made her living as she did, still it caused the soft places in her to ache.

"Nay," he rasped, his voice so tight and deep she did not recognize it as the one she had known when his life had been other than what now made his heart beat.

His breathing took the next turn with greater speed. "Do not!"

They are not your demons, she reminded herself, and yet she laid a palm to the uninjured side of his face, bent nearer, and whispered in his ear, "They are slain, Sir Abel. Pray, leave them there."

His breath that moved the tendrils of hair escaping her braid stopped and, before she could berate herself for being so foolish, his right hand shot up and captured her wrist. Though she felt his fingers convulse, they did not turn tight around her. And she understood the reason just ahead of the impulse to wrench free that might have undone the healing of his hand.

"Not again!" he spat.

Dreading what she would see, she raised her head. The light reflected in his eyes causing her heart to jerk violently as if to free itself from her chest, she braved a face so contorted that the anger with which he had regarded her all those weeks past seemed hardly anger at all.

"I..." What? Was there any way to excuse her presence that would not further enrage him? Surely he would—

The pressure of his hand on hers eased and, though his eyes remained open, he seemed to stare through her. Was he yet dreaming?

She forced herself to remain still, hoping he did, indeed, see something beyond her, praying he would sink into a restful sleep.

At last, his lids lowered, as did his hand, drawing hers downward until her palm lay against his chest and, beneath it, she felt the work of his heart that, beat by beat, moved from a rushing river toward a calm stream.

Back aching, legs beginning to cramp from holding her bent and awkward position, she tried to pull her hand from beneath his, but he pressed it tighter against him.

Patience, he will soon move to the next realm of sleep and relax his hold.

But it was not soon enough for her straining muscles, and she sought relief by pressing her free hand to the mattress and lowering to her knees in the dry rushes alongside the bed. Minutes passed and more, and throughout he retained his hold on her.

When sleep began to tempt her to rest her head upon the mattress, she pushed her drooping chin high and studied his face. He looked almost peaceful—more approachable than ever she had seen him. And she wanted—

Nay, that would be more foolish. She knew her purpose here and that, even if she was not perceived as far beneath his rank, still he would want naught to do with her when—if ever—he knew all of her, especially considering how much he had lost and suffered in his quest to end the terror that had stalked these lands.

Testing the weight of his much larger hand and finding it had slackened, she slowly drew her arm back. When her fingers slid free, he did not stir, nor when her knees creaked with their unfolding.

"God speed your rest," she whispered and, with as light a step as possible, crossed the chamber to the door that stood open as she had left it.

She slipped into the passageway and eased the door closed. The worst was over. Now to claim what would likely be fewer than two hours of sleep before the castle began stirring toward a new day.

Hooking her fingers in her skirts, she hitched them clear of her slippers and took a step forward—only to take it back when a large shadow parted from a deep pool of darkness upon which the light of the expiring torches did not waste their efforts.

She would have cried out if not that she knew who it was even before he stepped into the dim light. How could one not know such a man who was rivaled in size only by her liege?

Guessing that from behind whichever door he slept he had heard the creak of the hinges or his brother's protestations, she straightened to her full height, every hair of which was needed to come as close to appearing as adult as he.

When he halted before her, her search for words to explain her presence yielded only the truth, and she put her shoulders back. "My lord, Wulfrith, I apologize if I did wrong, but I could not sleep for thinking on seeing your brother again as he would not want me—or anyone—to see him. Pray, believe me, I but meant to prepare myself."

"And did you?" he asked low.

He did not sound angry. "As best I could without rousing him from sleep."

"A troubled sleep."

Did he know it was troubled only by the anguished words the open doorway had spilled into the passageway? Or had he peered within and seen her standing over his brother? Worse, on her knees with her hand pressed to his chest?

As much as she longed to explain away what he might have seen, she determined it was best to simply answer his question. "Aye, most troubled, my lord, though Sir Abel does appear to have settled now and, God willing, will pass the remainder of the night in peace."

Baron Wulfrith inclined his head, and though it was too dim to read whatever his eyes might tell, she sensed something in his gaze that would likely fluster her in the light of day.

"God willing," he agreed, then said, "Come. The day will be long, and you shall require all the rest that remains to be had." He turned away.

When her feet did not follow, he looked around. "You need not fear me, Helene of Tippet."

Strangely, she knew that. And yet the years had taught her to be cautious even where she might not sense danger.

"Come," he said again.

She did as told and, when he had seen her back to the hall and settled upon her pallet between two softly snoring women servants, he slipped so silently away that she had to wonder how a man of such size could make it seem as if he had never been.

Would he sleep now that he was assured she meant his brother no harm? Of course, had he truly believed ill of her? It was *he* who had sought her in her village, coming as near to pleading as a man as powerful as he might come. Too, it was not as if he knew her secret. Or did he?

Of late, when she visited Broehne Castle, often she caught her liege's stare and saw questions form upon his brow. Thus, she would be a fool to not know he was suspicious of her past which the death of his father had caused to bleed into her present. Might Baron Lavonne have shared those suspicions with this man, his ally and brother-in-law?

Nay, had Baron Wulfrith been told, he surely would not have brought her here to try to undo what had been done to his brother. He would revile her and think her a weed best torn from the earth before its roots went deep and fouled the good soil. And her John, who had fixed himself to Sir Abel's side during the long weeks of her absence, would be hated as well. *That* she could not bear. It had not been easy, but she had made a good life for herself and her son here on the barony of Abingdale, and to be forced to leave and begin anew...

Baron Wulfrith was wrong. She would do well to fear him. And, perhaps more, Sir Abel. But also, she would do well to pray.

Pulling her hands from between her knees where she had pressed them for warmth, she put her palms together and turned to prayer as the sisters at the convent had taught her to do all those years ago.

First, she prayed for John whom she had not wanted to leave behind though he had been enthusiastic about the offer made by Baron Lavonne and his wife for him to stay at Broehne Castle. Then she prayed for those of the household whom her son would surely test. Next, she asked that Abel Wulfrith would respond well to her ministrations. And, as sleep drew over her, she prayed that when she left Castle Soaring she would be no worse in heart and soul than when she had come to it.

2

EMBRACE DEATH. IT was as Abel had aspired to do, but they had refused to let him go, plying him with medicinals and drink and words they believed would raise him from a body so broken that it could never again serve as it had once done.

He clenched one hand into a fist and raised the other that no longer did his bidding. And never again would, according to the physician. As he stared at the flushed, newly formed scar that divided the upper half of his palm from the lower, he heard again the words he longed to put a blade through, most loudly those spoken by his brother, the least welcome of all who had denied him the respite of leaving this life for what lay beyond.

Garr Wulfrith's words had not reeked of pleading or encouragement or prayer like those of the others who had come around his bed, sat hours beside him, gripped his hand, and touched his brow. Rather, the head of the Wulfrith family had been resolute and demanding and might even be said to be cruel if Abel did not know him as he did.

Unfortunately, it did little good to be so well acquainted with Garr, for some instinct—some unanswered part of Abel—had listened. But for what? That a once-esteemed warrior might face the thousands upon thousands of days before him as a pitiable shadow of a man?

"Embrace death," he muttered the creed he had often extolled, though never in regard to his own life or the lives of the young men he trained into knights. Always it had been directed outward—a reminder that if one did not seek an opponent's death in battle, if one wavered and cast mercy where it was not due, such a fool would yield up his own life.

But on days like this, like every day since Garr had dragged Abel from the bed that should have been the last place he drew breath, resentment welled that he had not turned his creed inward. That he *did* want the next breath and the next and the one after that, even if they added up to endless days and nights, even if every step in and through and out of them was not without hitch or burn.

Thinking it would not take much more force to break the teeth he ground so hard his jaws ached, he stared at the dawn-drenched wood beyond the window and pushed his one functioning, accursedly awkward hand down his tunic-covered thigh. Its journey was soon arrested, not only by the transition from smooth muscle to thickly ridged scar, but the pain his probing fingers sent deep to the bone.

"God Almighty," he groaned and dropped his chin to his chest and squeezed his eyes closed. He drew a deep breath and another before continuing his exploration of the length and width and weakness of his pieced together flesh, following its path mid-thigh to just below the knee.

"Look at it," he growled. "Know it well, for 'tis your lifelong companion." And this companion, unlike the one he had buried in his past, would never set him free.

He released his breath in a rush, but it did not blow away memories that played against the backs of his lids as they had done often since his life had nearly been sundered beyond the walls of Castle Soaring.

Opening his eyes, he dragged up the hem of his tunic and, still loath to gaze upon his leg, sought the old scar that curved up from his hip to his lower rib, and which had proved nearly as dire as those that now ridged his body as if his flesh were a newly furrowed field.

When it required no shift of the eyes to move from the pale scar that had formed years ago to fix on the more recent injury dealt not by the wife who had wielded a meat dagger against him but a brigand with a sword, he thought he might laugh. And were he a bit angrier, a bit more bitter, quite a bit full of wine, he would have.

Unbeknownst to him until this day when finally he had determined that he would witness the work of the three brigands who had taken him to ground, the line of stitched flesh cut through the lowermost portion of the old scar, forming the crossbar of what appeared to be an upended crucifix.

Did not the priests tell of one of Jesus' disciples who, facing crucifixion, asked that he be suspended upside down, believing he was unworthy to die as his Lord had done?

Abel grunted. In his own case, it was the crucifix that was set wrong side up. And he lived, though how it was possible, even with the strongest of wills to give death one's back, he did not know. Michael D'Arci, his brother-in-law and keeper of Castle Soaring, was said to be a fine physician, but surely his patient had lost too much blood and the blades had cut too near vital organs for him to be this side of life, let alone able to rise from bed without aid as he had done this day.

For which you have much to be grateful, he heard his mother's voice, she whose prayers at his bedside had not consoled but, rather, made him wish her away.

He lowered his tunic and once more reached to his thigh, only to arrest his hand and turn his gaze out the window to the wood where sunlight now streamed through branches and glided over tree tops. It had happened out there, though then the moon had been full up, its light running the blade he had swung time and again.

Remembering the black and gray of night that had known only the color of blood, he curled his fingers around an imagined hilt. Or tried to, for his hilt hand trembled as the fingers strained to meet the thumb.

Lifting his hand before his face, he clenched his teeth and strained harder despite the tearing pain that warned he would likely cause further damage, but the fingers would draw no nearer. Though that night he had cut down men far less versed in sword skill, personally delivering them over death's threshold, that battle—that life—was in his past. *This* was his present.

"Curse all!" he spat.

"I would myself be tempted."

Abel stilled and, in the silence, heard panting—his own, coming so hard and fast that it had masked the sound of the door opening and the heavy tread of the man whose boots ground the dry rushes that should have been freshened on the day past.

Recalling the frightened maids who had fled in response to the shouts of the man who, heretofore, had ignored their comings and goings, Abel felt a pang of remorse. And wondered why he should feel anything other than anger.

Keeping his back to his brother, he said, "As you can see, 'tis not a good time for me to grant you an audience."

"Then it is good I do not wish an audience."

What, then? For what did he—?

"Worry not," Garr said. "I vow I will not allow my brother to bite you."

Only then did Abel become aware of the other footfalls among the rushes. Forgetting the injury to his leg, he turned so quickly he lurched and had to catch hold of the sill to avoid further humiliation.

"What is this?" he demanded, causing the maid who approached the brazier with burdened arms to falter and the other to nearly lose her grip on the broom poised to sweep away the rushes.

"'Tis chill in here," Garr said where he had positioned himself just over the threshold, his arms crossed over his chest.

"Is it?" Abel snapped, though now he did feel the cold, standing as he did before the window which he had stripped of its oilcloth upon reaching his destination a quarter hour past.

"Worse, it stinks." Garr hitched an eyebrow. "I was not told your sense of smell was also afflicted."

Abel narrowed his eyes. When his displeasure but caused his brother to raise the other eyebrow, he gritted his teeth and glanced at the maid who attempted to kindle the fire in the brazier that had burned so hot on the night past, next the woman whose efficiency with the broom was no match for Abel's impatience.

"This can be done later, Garr." He knew it was disrespectful to address his brother by his Christian name rather than "Wulfrith" in the presence of non-family members, but he did not care.

"Nay, it cannot." Garr lowered his gaze to Abel's bare legs. "'Tis good to see you willingly out of bed, but it would be better to see you fully clothed."

Though Abel knew the lower portion of the injury to his leg was visible beneath the tunic's hem, he did not flinch or turn away.

Garr jerked his chin toward the chest against the wall. "If 'tis too much for you, I could ask one of these young women to raise the lid and search out clean braies and hose." This time it was Abel's torso he scrutinized. "And tunic. That one might best be burned."

Feeling his upper lip peel back, Abel rejoined it with the lower and pressed them tight. He knew he was being baited, that Garr believed anger was better than brooding.

When finally he could speak again without presenting as outraged or, worse, petulant, he said, "I thank you, Brother, but I can attend to my own needs." Unfortunately, he could make no move to do so without casting more light upon his infirmity and rousing pity, the scent of which might ignite the smoldering within and far surpass the speed with which the maid coaxed the brazier to life.

Thus, Abel stared at Garr and Garr stared back, and all the while Abel tried not to envy—or resent—his brother whose own battle wounds, once healed, had no ill effect upon his ability to take up sword and defend family and home, and whose face bore no disfigurement. Beneath his garments, Garr Wulfrith might be abundantly scarred, but he was as able as ever. Abel Wulfrith was not, and the self pity that ran through him burned like bile full up in his throat.

He swallowed hard and, with much consideration of the leg that would betray him again given the chance, turned back to the window.

The rousing of day had caused the inner bailey below to stir with life, and he found this unremarkable scene that he had not witnessed in many weeks strangely interesting. Unlike his life, the lives of those whose legs quickly traversed the beaten dirt ground had not come to a halt, and he wondered how many times others had looked upon him as he now looked upon the castle folk, oblivious to the suffering of the unseen observer. Oblivious to a life lost.

He did not know how much time passed in the space between his brother's entrance and the hand that gripped his shoulder, but some part of him had been aware of the broom's shush and scrape, the brazier's warmth that radiated upon his back even as the risen sun breathed upon his face, the scent of fresh rushes and the herbs scattered over them, the slosh of water, the creak of the bed, and the rustle of sheets. More, though, he was aware of his legs, the uninjured one that cramped from so long supporting most of his weight, the lame one that throbbed and ached at being forced to remain upright.

"'Tis done," Garr said. "Now you must only decide whether to bathe yourself or allow the healer to assist you."

Abel snorted. "As already told, I can attend—"

Despite having warmed, a chill spread across Abel's every pore. Garr could not possibly mean *her*. He would not have brought her here—unless their sister, Gaenor, who had recently wed Baron Christian Lavonne and believed she saw more than there was to see, had told their older brother of the healer and her son, neither of whom Abel cared for beyond concern for their well being.

Holding his feet tight to the floor lest his leg further shamed him, Abel looked around. "Of what do you speak?"

Garr squeezed Abel's shoulder, then stepped to the side. "Helene from the village of Tippet has come."

She stood inside the chamber to the right of the open doorway, hands clasped at her waist, chin up, dark red hair woven into a fat plait draped across one shoulder.

The chill left Abel, and though he knew the color that rose up his neck was mostly born of anger at having his wishes ignored, he knew it also bore shades of shame.

The last time he had seen—and held—this woman, he had been a man in full. One whose hands knew well the ridges and furrows of a sword hilt. One with two legs solid beneath him. One who had thought it a worthy challenge to face not one but two opponents at once. One whose countenance many a woman had found pleasing.

He was none of these, and yet the woman who stood a half dozen strides from him did not wince or look away, as if accustomed to what her eyes beheld—so accustomed that no pity shone from her. And it was the lack of that detestable emotion that permitted Abel to contain the anger that might otherwise have exploded from him.

"I shall leave you to decide," Garr said and strode from the chamber.

Helene, all five feet and few of her, was the first to speak, though she did so only after his brother's footsteps receded. "How shall I best assist you, Sir Abel?"

Her effortless Norman-French surprised him, though not as much as it had that first time when she had eschewed the language of the commoner in favor of his own. More, he was unsettled by how familiar her voice sounded though it was some time since last he had heard it.

Keenly—painfully—aware of his every move, he turned to fully face her. "You are not needed."

She glanced at his injured hand that, until that moment, he had not realized was attempting to shape itself into a fist. "Would it not be better said that I am not wanted?"

Though tempted to shout down the implication that he was incapable of caring for himself, he controlled his emotions and, feeling the strain upon his hand, eased his fingers. "Regardless, you may go."

"That I may, for it was my decision to grant your brother's request."

"Why did you?" He did not mean to ask, and yet the question rose so swiftly he could not check it.

"I am indebted to you."

She surely referred to her son, John, whom she had been forced to leave behind weeks—or was it months?—past, although Abel had initially believed she had abandoned him. "Your boy but followed me around like a puppy," he said, "and I did little more than toss him scraps. For that, you owe me naught."

He heard her breath catch and knew it was cruel to equate her child with a dog, but if it offended her sufficiently that she would all the sooner be gone, it would serve.

She stared at him and, when no response was forthcoming, he gave what he hoped was the final push. "However, if you insist upon being indebted, I vow your absence will be payment enough, for I am most eager to see your back."

Drawing a breath that raised her shoulders, she stepped forward. "Ah, but then Lord D'Arci would have to continue tending you when it is the business of Castle Soaring to which he ought to turn his attention."

Abel narrowed his gaze on her. "Just as I do not require your services, I no longer require his. Now leave."

Still she came, the coarse, heavy material of her homespun gown rustling almost obscenely upon one so slight and comely. As she neared, she slowly raised her chin to hold her gaze to his and, when she halted before him, he could pick out the many shades of blue that colored her eyes—and the dark shadows beneath that told she had either not slept well or been ill.

When she reached forward and lifted his crippled hand, he was so stunned by her boldness that, before he could think to wrench free, she had turned his palm up and bent her head to it. Worse, his traitorous fingers curled toward hers as if they remembered them though never had he held her hand. For that—and only that—he was glad his range of motion was so limited.

She probed the flesh on either side of the scar and looked up. "It heals well."

Though her smile was one of approval, he was unsettled by his body's response to her brief bowing of lips and show of teeth. He pulled his hand free and, unable to put space between them without limp or loss of balance, said, "The physician did all he could."

She lowered her arms to her sides. "Then Lord D'Arci has told you that hand will not hold a sword again? That you will only impede its healing by forcing it to do what can no longer be done?"

As if her smile had never been, Abel's left hand made the fist his right could not, his knuckles aching for want of something hard to drive against. "I need none to tell me that."

Her gaze flicked to his clenched hand, but when she once more lifted her eyes to his, the wariness there was so fleeting as to have been imagined. "Know this, Abel Wulfrith," she said with a surprisingly hard edge to her voice, "do you raise a hand to me, I shall defend my person with all that I have. And, I vow, I will not be the only one bruised and bloodied."

He stiffened. Did she truly believe him capable of beating a woman? Ever he had defended the weak and vulnerable, using his blade and fists only against those who preyed upon others—or nearly so, for he had done his wife no harm when he had wrested from her the dagger with which she had sought his death. And yet this woman believed—

In that instant, he recalled the ill that had befallen Helene when he had failed—and misjudged—her the day they had met. Though he had not witnessed the beating given her by Sir Robert, the leader of the brigands who had stolen her from her home, he had seen the remnants of that violence upon her face, neck, and wrists on the day of the last night that he had wielded a sword against those same miscreants. Of course Helene of Tippet did not trust him. Likely, she did not trust any man.

He forced his hands at his sides to relax. "I have never hit a woman, and I never shall."

She delved his face and slowly inclined her head. "Then, it seems, we shall be at peace with one another."

He frowned and, in so doing, was made all the more aware of his scarred face that he had yet to look upon though the ridge of its sweeping path evidenced it was unsightly. "Were you to remain at Castle Soaring, that would be most desirable," he said, "but you shall be gone from here this day."

She settled into her heels. "Only if you yourself deliver me beyond these walls." She ran her gaze down him and up again. "Most unfortunate for you, Sir Abel, in your current state of apathy and self pity, that is something of which you are incapable."

Only remembrance of that glimpse of wariness in her eyes held him from once more manifesting his anger in the form of a fist. "Go," he rumbled.

"I shall—*after* I have cleaned and examined your injuries that I might determine how best to tend you." She pointed her chin toward the bed. "Can you reach it unaided?"

In that moment, Abel wanted nothing more than to lift her off her feet, carry her across the chamber, and deposit her in the passageway. But as well she knew—and boasted—that simple act was beyond him. And it made him feel more abhorrently helpless than before.

"You think I will meekly lie down at your command, *Helene of Tippet?*" The laughter that barked from him was so coarse it felt torn from his throat. "That I shall willingly bare myself to you?"

She parted her lips as if to answer, hesitated, then said, "Like it or nay that I am a woman, healing is my gift and profession. However, if you fear I will be horrified by what is beneath your tunic, know that already I have seen it."

Abel was certain her meaning was different from how it sounded—that she referred to similar wounds upon others she had tended. And yet, that was not what he saw in her eyes.

Containing the impulse to step nearer her, he asked low, "What say you?"

"Whilst you slept ere the dawn, I did come to you and look upon your leg, as well as your face."

All of him tightened. She had been here? In the dark of his alone? When the sleeping draught had held him down? When it had fed him dreams across which he had bled?

He felt something then, heard something, saw something—pieces of a heretofore forgotten dream. Rather, what he thought was a dream.

She *had* been here. His hand *had* known her hand, his ears her voice, his eyes her eyes.

Abel could not remember the last time he had thrown something against a wall, but surely he had not been beyond five years of age, for his father would not have tolerated such loss of control. Though he was now well beyond his twentieth year, in that moment, the longing to break something upon the stone walls of his chamber was almost overwhelming. And the woman before him must have felt it, for wariness once again made a fleeting appearance in her eyes. Still, she did not retreat, though he wished her to. Not that he feared he would do her harm, for he had spoken true that he would never hit a woman, but he wanted her gone—no matter the cost to his pride, especially since she had already ground it underfoot.

Hardly able to hear above the sound of blood rushing in his ears, he wrenched up his tunic. "Did you look upon this as well?"

Rather than turn away as expected, and as he had intended she should do, she cautiously lowered her eyes down his bared chest and fixed on the old and new scar that intersected. Head tilting, smooth brow furrowing as if his injuries, rather than his behavior, was of great interest, she said, "Nay, I did not trespass that far."

Struggling to keep his breath from sounding loud between them, he dropped the hem of his tunic. "But still you trespassed."

"I did."

His protesting legs protested with greater urgency, and he knew it was because his every muscle had tensed—and that if he did not soon rid himself of this woman, he might collapse at her feet. Regardless, he demanded, "Why?"

Movement at her sides drew his gaze and he saw her clench handfuls of her skirts. However, she surely noticed what had captured his attention, for she immediately splayed her fingers. "I did it that I might prepare myself."

"Do you always prepare yourself by stealing upon your patients? Invading their privacy?"

"Nay, 'tis just that…you are unlike most who require my services."

He nearly asked in what way he was different, but he knew. "I am disfigured."

She blinked. "I do not speak of that. You know I have tended far worse—"

"Aye. How could I forget the heinous Aldous Lavonne whom the devil so admired he allowed his spawn to survive a fire that nearly melted the flesh off his bones?"

Helene stared at the gaunt, unshaven Abel Wulfrith. That was, of course, how he would remember the old baron. And she could not blame him. Lacking the cooperation of his legitimate son, Christian, Aldous had enlisted his misbegotten son, Sir Robert, to do whatever was necessary—including murder—to thwart the king's attempt to unite the warring Wulfriths and Lavonnes through marriage. But, unbeknownst to Sir Abel, Aldous had come as near to repentance as he could before death had seen him out of this world. Even if the scarred, suffering old man had not made it to heaven, he surely could not be as deep in hell as those he had harmed would wish.

Hating the convulsive bob of her throat that she feared sounded as loud to Sir Abel as it did to her, Helene determined she would bend to her patient's will—this once. "As there are others who await my services, I will leave you to see to those needs for which you believe you require no assistance."

"What others?" he snapped as she turned away.

She paused. "You sound displeased."

His nostrils flared. "I am but curious."

She did not believe him, though neither did she know what to make of his reaction. "Since you are not in such a terrible state as to need my full attention," she said, "I am to tend any others who have yet to fully recover from the injuries gained in defending Castle Soaring."

"Sir Durand as well, then."

She frowned. "I do not know who that is, but if he needs me, certainly."

"'Twas he who took the prize I was after—the death of Sir Robert."

The leader of the brigands who had beaten her following her near escape that had also been her first meeting with Sir Abel.

As she stared at the man before her, a caustic smile rose amidst his beard, putting a face on the hatred he exuded. "You might want to thank him," he said.

Though she tried to keep her expression impassive, she could not. Thus, she pivoted and, subduing the impulse to hasten away, measuredly crossed the chamber.

"If 'tis not my disfigurement of which you spoke," he called as she reached the door, "then how am I unlike most who require your services?"

She paused and, wishing she had more carefully guarded her weakness, looked over her shoulder. "'Twould be best for your pride, Sir Abel, if you have seen your way into clean clothing when I return. Thus, I can determine how to speed your healing that you may all the sooner see my back."

She inclined her head, stepped into the corridor, and closed the door.

About The Author

Tamara Leigh holds a Master's Degree in Speech and Language Pathology. In 1993, she signed a 4-book contract with Bantam Books. Her first medieval romance, *Warrior Bride*, was released in 1994. Continuing to write for the general market, three more novels were published with HarperCollins and Dorchester and earned awards and spots on national bestseller lists.

In 2006, Tamara's first inspirational contemporary romance, *Stealing Adda*, was released. In 2008, *Perfecting Kate* was optioned for a movie and *Splitting Harriet* won an ACFW "Book of the Year" award. The following year, *Faking Grace* was nominated for a RITA award. In 2011, Tamara wrapped up her "Southern Discomfort" series with the release of *Restless in Carolina*.

When not in the middle of being a wife, mother, and cookbook fiend, Tamara buries her nose in a good book—and her writer's pen in ink. In 2012, she returned to the historical romance genre with *Dreamspell,* a medieval time travel romance. Shortly thereafter, she once more invited readers to join her in the middle ages with the *Age of Faith* series: *The Unveiling, The Yielding, The Redeeming, The Kindling,* and *The Longing*. Tamara's #1 Bestsellers—*Lady at Arms, Lady Of Eve, Lady Of Fire*, and *Lady Of Conquest*—are the first of her medieval romances to be rewritten as "clean reads." Look for *Baron Of Blackwood,* the third book in *The Feud* series, in 2016.

Tamara lives near Nashville with her husband, sons, a Doberman that bares its teeth not only to threaten the UPS man but to smile, and a feisty Morkie that keeps her company during long writing stints.

Connect with Tamara at her website www.tamaraleigh.com, her blog The Kitchen Novelist, her email tamaraleightenn@gmail.com, Facebook, and Twitter.

For new releases and special promotions, subscribe to Tamara Leigh's mailing list: www.tamaraleigh.com